The "Genius"
Book III The Revolt

by

Theodore Dreiser

The "Genius"
Book III The Revolt
by Theodore Dreiser

Copyright © 2024

All Rights reserved.

ISBN: 978-93-68097-96-9

Published by

DOUBLE 9 BOOKS

2/13-B, Ansari Road
Daryaganj, New Delhi – 110002
info@double9books.com
www.double9books.com
Tel. 011-40042856

ABOUT THE AUTHOR

Theodore Dreiser (1871–1945) was a prominent American journalist and novelist who made important contributions to the literary naturalism movement. Dreiser was born in Terre Haute, Indiana, on August 27, 1871, and was raised in a working-class household. His early life and difficulties with poverty had a big impact on the writing he produced later. Because of his novels' candid depictions of sexuality and social issues, Dreiser faced criticism and restriction, but his writings were vital in forming American literature. His naturalistic approach deviated from popular literary traditions by highlighting the impact of environment and genetics on human behavior. In addition, Dreiser was a journalist who wrote for magazines including Harper's Magazine and The New York Times. Throughout his career, he participated in literary and political circles and was an advocate for social justice. On December 28, 1945, Theodore Dreiser passed away. He is remembered for being a significant figure in American literature and a forerunner of literary naturalism.

CONTENTS

As a matter of fact, favored as she was by nature and fortune, her very presence was dangerous—provocative, without thought of being so. If a true artist had painted her, synthesizing her spirit with her body, he might have done so showing her standing erect on a mountain top, her limbs outlined amidst fluttering draperies against the wind, her eyes fixed on distant heights, or a falling star. Out of mystery into mystery again, so she came and went. Her mind was not unlike a cloud of mist through which the morning sun is endeavoring to break, irradiating all with its flushes of pink and gold. Again it was like those impearled shells of the South Sea, without design yet suggestive of all perfections and all beauties. Dreams! dreams!—of clouds, sunsets, colors, sounds which a too articulate world would do its best later to corrupt. What Dante saw in Beatrice, what Abélard saw in Héloïse, Romeo in Juliet, so some wondering swain could have seen in her—and suffered a like fate.

Eugene encountered Mrs. Dale at a house party on Long Island one Saturday afternoon, and their friendship began at once. She was introduced to him by Colfax, and because of the latter's brusque, jesting spirit was under no illusions as to his social state.

"You needn't look at him closely," he observed gaily, "he's married."

"That simply makes him all the more interesting," she rippled, and extended her hand.

Eugene took it. "I'm glad a poor married man can find shelter somewhere," he said, smartly.

"You should rejoice," she replied. "It's at once your liberty and your protection. Think how safe you are!"

"I know, I know," he said. "All the slings and arrows of Miss Fortune hurtling by."

"And you in no danger of being hurt."

He offered her his arm, and they strolled through a window onto a veranda.

The day was just the least bit dull for Mrs. Dale. Bridge was in progress in the card room, a company of women and girls gambling feverishly. Eugene was not good at bridge, not quick enough mentally, and Mrs. Dale did not care much for it.

"I have been trying to stir up enough interest to bring to pass a motor ride, but it doesn't work," she said. "They all have the gambling fever today. Are you as greedy as the others?"

"I'm greedy I assure you, but I can't play. The greediest thing I can do is to stay away from the tables. I save most. That sharp Faraday has cleaned me and two others out of four hundred dollars. It's astonishing the way some people can play. They just look at the cards or make mystic signs and the wretched things range themselves in serried ranks to suit them. It's a crime. It ought to be a penitentiary offense, particularly to beat me. I'm such an inoffensive specimen of the non-bridge playing family."

"A burnt child, you know. Stay away. Let's sit here. They can't come out here and rob you."

They sat down in green willow chairs, and after a time a servant offered them coffee. Mrs. Dale accepted. They drifted conversationally from bridge to characters in society—a certain climber by the name of Bristow, a man who had made a fortune in trunks—and from him to travel and from travel to Mrs. Dale's experiences with fortune hunters. The automobile materialized through the intervention of others, but Eugene found great satisfaction in this woman's company and sat beside her. They talked books, art, magazines, the making of fortunes and reputations. Because he was or seemed to be in a position to assist her in a literary way she was particularly nice to him. When he was leaving she asked, "Where are you in New York?"

"Riverside Drive is our present abode," he said.

"Why don't you bring Mrs. Witla and come down to see us some weekend? I usually have a few people there, and the house is roomy. I'll name you a special day if you wish."

"Do. We'll be delighted. Mrs. Witla will enjoy it, I'm sure."

Mrs. Dale wrote to Angela ten days later as to a particular date, and in this way the social intimacy began.

It was never of a very definite character, though. When Mrs. Dale met Angela she liked her quite well as an individual, whatever she may have thought of her as a social figure. Neither Eugene nor Angela saw Suzanne nor any of the other children on this occasion, all of them being away. Eugene admired the view tremendously and hinted at being invited again. Mrs. Dale was delighted. She liked him as a man entirely apart from his position but particularly because of his publishing station. She was ambitious to write. Others had told her that he was the most conspicuous of the rising figures in the publishing world. Being friendly with him would give her exceptional standing with all his editors. She was only too pleased to be gracious to him. He was invited again and a third time, with Angela, and it seemed as though they were reaching, or might at least reach, something much more definite than a mere social acquaintance.

It was about six months after Eugene had first met Mrs. Dale that Angela gave a tea, and Eugene, in assisting her to prepare the list of invitations, had suggested that those who were to serve the tea and cakes should be two exceptionally pretty girls who were accustomed to come to the Witla apartment, Florence Reel, the daughter of a well-known author of that name and Marjorie Mac Tennan, the daughter of a well-known editor, both beautiful and talented, one with singing and the other with art ambitions. Angela had seen a picture of Suzanne Dale in her mother's room at Daleview on Grimes Hill, and had been particularly taken with her girlish charm and beauty.

"I wonder," she said, "if Mrs. Dale would object to having Suzanne come and help serve that day. She would like it, I'm sure, there are going to be so many clever people here. We haven't seen her, but that doesn't matter. It would be a nice way to introduce herself."

"That's a good idea, I should say," observed Eugene judicially. He had seen the photo of Suzanne and liked it, though he was not over-impressed. Photos to him were usually gross deceivers. He accepted them always with reservations. Angela forthwith wrote to Mrs. Dale, who agreed. She would be glad to come herself. She had seen the Witla apartment, and had been very much pleased with it. The reception day came and Angela begged Eugene to come home early.

"I know you don't like to be alone with a whole roomful of people, but Mr. Goodrich is coming, and Frederick Allen (one of their friends who had taken a fancy to Eugene), Arturo Scalchero is going to sing and Bonavita to play." Scalchero was none other than Arthur Skalger, of Port Jervis, New Jersey, but he assumed this corruption of his name in Italy to help him to success. Bonavita was truly a Spanish pianist of some repute who was flattered to be invited to Eugene's home.

"Well, I don't care much about it," replied Eugene. "But I will come."

He frequently felt that afternoon teas and receptions were ridiculous affairs, and that he had far better be in his office attending to his multitudinous duties. Still he did leave early, and at five-thirty was ushered into a great roomful of chattering, gesticulating, laughing people. A song by Florence Reel had just been concluded. Like all girls of ambition, vivacity and imagination, she took an interest in Eugene, for in his smiling face she found a responsive gleam.

"Oh, Mr. Witla!" she exclaimed. "Now here you are and you just missed my song. And I wanted you to hear it, too."

"Don't grieve, Florrie," he said familiarly, holding her hand and looking momentarily in her eyes. "You're going to sing it again for me. I heard part of it as I came up on the elevator." He relinquished her hand. "Why, Mrs. Dale! Delighted, I'm sure. So nice of you. And Arturo Scalchero—hullo, Skalger, you old frost! Where'd you get the Italian name? Bonavita! Fine! Am I going to hear you play? All over? Alas! Marjorie Mac Tennan! Gee, but you look sweet! If Mrs. Witla weren't watching me, I'd kiss you. Oh, the pretty bonnet! And Frederick Allen! My word! What are you trying to grab off, Allen? I'm on to you. No bluffs! Nix! Nix! Why, Mrs. Schenck— delighted! Angela, why didn't you tell me Mrs. Schenck was coming? I'd have been home at three."

By this time he had reached the east end of the great studio room, farthest from the river. Here a tea table was spread with a silver tea service, and behind it a girl, oval-faced, radiantly healthy, her full lips parted in a ripe smile, her blue-gray eyes talking pleasure and satisfaction, her forehead laid about by a silver filigree band, beneath which her brown chestnut curls protruded. Her hands, Eugene noted, were plump and fair. She stood erect, assured, with the least touch of quizzical light in her eye. A white, pink-bordered dress draped her girlish figure.

"I don't know," he said easily, "but I wager a guess that this is—that this is—this is Suzanne Dale—what?"

"Yes, this is," she replied laughingly. "Can I give you a cup of tea, Mr. Witla? I know you are Mr. Witla from ma-ma''s description and the way in which you talk to everybody."

"And how do I talk to everybody, may I ask, pleasum?"

"Oh, I can't tell you so easily. I mean, I can't find the words, you know. I know how it is, though. Familiarly, I suppose I mean. Will you have one lump or two?"

"Three an thou pleasest. Didn't your mother tell me you sang or played?"

"Oh, you mustn't believe anything ma-ma' says about me! She's apt to say anything. Tee! Hee! It makes me laugh"—she pronounced it laaf—"to think of my playing. My teacher says he would like to strike my knuckles. Oh, dear!" (She went into a gale of giggles.) "And sing! Oh, dear, dear! That is too good!"

Eugene watched her pretty face intently. Her mouth and nose and eyes fascinated him. She was so sweet! He noted the configuration of her lips and cheeks and chin. The nose was delicate, beautifully formed, fat, not sensitive. The ears were small, the eyes large and wide set, the forehead naturally high, but so concealed by curls that it seemed low. She had a few freckles and a very small dimple in her chin.

"Now you mustn't laugh like that," he said mock solemnly. "It's very serious business, this laughing. In the first place, it's against the rules of this apartment. No one is ever, ever, ever supposed to laugh here, particularly young ladies who pour tea. Tea, Epictetus well says, involves the most serious conceptions of one's privileges and duties. It is the high-born prerogative of tea servers to grin occasionally, but never, never, never under any circumstances whatsoever— —" Suzanne's lips were beginning to part ravishingly in anticipation of a burst of laughter.

"What's all the excitement about, Witla?" asked Skalger, who had drifted to his side. "Why this sudden cessation of progress?"

"Tea, my son, tea!" said Eugene. "Have a cup with me?"

"I will."

"He's trying to tell me, Mr. Skalger, that I should never laaf. I must only grin." Her lips parted and she laughed joyously. Eugene laughed with her. He could not help it. "Ma-ma' says I giggle all the time. I wouldn't do very well here, would I?"

She always pronounced it "ma-ma'."

She turned to Eugene again with big smiling eyes.

"Exceptions, exceptions. I might make exceptions—one exception—but not more."

"Why one?" she asked archly.

"Oh, just to hear a natural laugh," he said a little plaintively. "Just to hear a real joyous laugh. Can you laugh joyously?"

She giggled again at this, and he was about to tell her how joyously she did laugh when Angela called him away to hear Florence Reel, who was going to sing again for his especial benefit. He parted from Miss Dale reluctantly, for she seemed some delicious figure as delicately colorful as Royal Dresden, as perfect in her moods as a spring evening, as soft, soulful, enticing as a strain of music heard through the night at a distance or over the water. He went over to where Florence Reel was standing, listening in a sympathetic melancholy vein to a delightful rendering of "The Summer Winds Are Blowing, Blowing." All the while he could not help thinking of Suzanne—letting his eyes stray in that direction. He talked to Mrs. Dale, to Henrietta Tenmon, to Luke Severas, Mr. and Mrs. Dula, Payalei Stone, now a writer of special articles, and others, but he couldn't help longing to go back to her. How sweet she was! How very delightful! If he could only, once more in his life, have the love of a girl like that!

The guests began to depart. Angela and Eugene bustled about the farewells. Because of the duties of her daughter, which continued to the end, Mrs. Dale stayed, talking to Arthur Skalger. Eugene was in and out between the studio and cloak room off the entry way. Now and then he caught glimpses of Suzanne demurely standing by her tea cups and samovar. For years he had seen nothing so fresh and young as her body. She was like a new grown wet white lily pod in the dawn of the year. She seemed to have the texture of the water chestnut and the lush, fat vegetables of the spring. Her eyes were as clear as water; her skin as radiant new ivory. There was no sign of weariness about her, nor any care, nor any thought of evil, nor anything except health and happiness. "Such a face!" he thought casually in passing. "She is as sweet as any girl could be. As radiant as light itself."

Incidentally the personality of Frieda Roth came back, and — long before her — Stella Appleton.

"Youth! Youth! What in this world could be finer — more acceptable! Where would you find its equal? After all the dust of the streets and the spectacle of age and weariness — the crow's feet about people's eyes, the wrinkles in their necks, the make-believe of rouge and massage, and powder and cosmetics, to see real youth, not of the body but of the soul also — the eyes, the smile, the voice, the movements — all young. Why try to imitate that miracle? Who could? Who ever had?"

He went on shaking hands, bowing, smiling, laughing, jesting, making believe himself, but all the while the miracle of the youth and beauty of Suzanne Dale was running in his mind.

"What are you thinking about, Eugene?" asked Angela, coming to the window where he had drawn a rocking-chair and was sitting gazing out on the silver and lavender and gray of the river surface in the fading light. Some belated gulls were still flying about. Across the river the great manufactory was sending off a spiral of black smoke from one of its tall chimneys. Lamps were beginning to twinkle in its hundred-windowed wall. A great siren cry broke from its whistle as six o'clock tolled from a neighboring clock tower. It was still late February and cold.

"Oh, I was thinking of the beauty of this scene," he said wearily.

Angela did not believe it. She was conscious of something, but they never quarreled about what he was thinking nowadays. They had come too far along in comfort and solidity. What was it, though, she wondered, that he was thinking about?

Suzanne Dale had no particular thought of him. He was nice—pleasant, good-looking. Mrs. Witla was quite nice and young.

"Ma-ma," she said, "did you look out of the window at Mr. Witla's?"

"Yes, my dear!"

"Wasn't that a beautiful view?"

"Charming."

"I should think you might like to live on the Drive sometime, ma-ma."

"We may sometime."

Mrs. Dale fell to musing. Certainly Eugene was an attractive man— young, brilliant, able. What a mistake all the young men made, marrying so early. Here he was successful, introduced to society, attractive, the world really before him, and he was married to someone who, though a charming little woman, was not up to his possibilities.

"Oh, well," she thought, "so goes the world. Why worry? Everyone must do the best they can."

Then she thought of a story she might write along this line and get Eugene to publish it in one of his magazines.

CHAPTER II

While these various events were occurring the work of the United Magazines Corporation had proceeded apace. By the end of the first year after Eugene's arrival it had cleared up so many of its editorial and advertising troubles that he was no longer greatly worried about them, and by the end of the second year it was well on the way toward real success. Eugene had become so much of a figure about the place that everyone in the great building, in which there were over a thousand employed, knew him at sight. The attendants were most courteous and obsequious, as much so almost as they were to Colfax and White, though the latter with the improvement of the general condition of the company had become more dominating and imposing than ever. White with his large salary of twenty-five thousand a year and his title of vice-president was most anxious that Eugene should not become more powerful than he had already. It irritated him greatly to see the airs Eugene gave himself, for the latter had little real tact, and instead of dissembling his importance before his superiors was inclined to flaunt it. He was forever retailing to Colfax some new achievement in the advertising, circulation, and editorial fields, and that in White's presence, for he did not take the latter very seriously, telling of a new author of importance captured for the book department; a new manuscript feature secured for one or another of the magazines, a new circulation scheme or connection devised, or a new advertising contract of great money value manipulated. His presence in Colfax's office was almost invariably a signal for congratulation or interest, for he was driving things hard and Colfax knew it. White came to hate the sight of him.

"Well, what's the latest great thing you've done?" Colfax said once to Eugene jovially in White's presence, for he knew that Eugene was as fond of praise as a child and so could be bantered with impunity. White concealed a desire to sneer behind a deceptive smile.

"No latest great thing, only Hayes has turned that Hammond Packing Company trick. That means eighteen thousand dollars' worth more of new business for next year. That'll help a little, won't it?"

"Hayes! Hayes! I'll be switched if I don't think he comes pretty near being a better advertising man than you are, Witla. You picked him, I'll

ocean a magnificent seaside city where the lots should sell at so expensive a rate that only the well-to-do could afford to live there. His thought was of something so fine that it would attract all the prominent pleasure-lovers he had recently met. If they could be made to understand that such a place existed; that it was beautiful, showy, exclusive in a money sense, they would come there by the thousands.

"Nothing is so profitable as a luxury, if the luxury-loving public want it," Colfax had once said to him; and he believed it. He judged this truth by the things he had recently seen. People literally spent millions to make themselves comfortable. He had seen gardens, lawns, walks, pavilions, pergolas, laid out at an expense of thousands and hundreds of thousands of dollars, where few would ever see them. In St. Louis he had seen a mausoleum built upon the lines of the Taj Mahal, the lawn about which was undermined by a steam-heating plant in order that the flowers and shrubs displayed there might bloom all winter long. It had never occurred to him that the day would come when he would have anything to do with such a dream as this or its ultimate fruition, but his was the kind of mind that loved to dwell on things of the sort.

The proposition which Winfield now genially laid before him one day was simple enough. Winfield had heard that Eugene was making a good deal of money, that his salary was twenty-five thousand a year, if not more, that he had houses and lots and some nice stock investments, and it occurred to him, as it would have to anyone, that Eugene might be able to shoulder a comfortable investment in some kind of land speculation, particularly if he could see his way to make much more money in the long run. The idea Winfield had was as follows: He was going to organize a corporation to be known as The Sea Island Development Company, to be capitalized at ten million dollars, some two or three hundred thousand dollars of which was to be laid down or paid into the treasury at the start. Against this latter sum stock to the value of one million dollars, or five shares of one hundred dollars par value each, was to be issued. That is, whoever laid down one hundred dollars in cash was to receive in return three shares of common stock and two of preferred, valued at one hundred dollars each, bearing eight per cent. interest. This ratio was to be continued until $200,000 in cash was in the treasury. Then those who came afterward and were willing to buy were only to receive two shares of common and one of preferred, until one million in cash was in the treasury. After that the stock was to be sold at its face value, or more, as the situation might dictate.

The original sum of two hundred thousands dollars was to go to purchase for the corporation an undeveloped tract of land, half swamp, half island, and facing the Atlantic Ocean beyond Gravesend Bay, now owned by Winfield himself, where a beautiful rolling beach of white sand stretched some three miles in length and without flaw or interruption. This would clear Winfield of a piece of property which was worth, say $60,000, but at present unsaleable, and give him magnificent holdings in the new company besides. He proposed to take a mortgage on this and all improvements the company might make in order to protect himself. At the west end of this tract—inland from the sea—was a beautiful bay, which, though shallow, gave access to a series of inlets and a network of waterways, embracing nine small islands. These waterways, when dredged, would be amply deep enough for yachts and small craft of all descriptions, and the first important thought which occurred to Winfield was that the mud and sand so dredged could be used to fill in the low, marshy levels of soil between them and the sea and so make it all into high, dry, and valuable land. The next thing was to devise a beautiful scheme of improvement, and it was for this that he wished to talk to Eugene.

CHAPTER III

The matter was not difficult to arrange. Before Winfield had gone ten sentences, Eugene began to take the ideas out of his mind.

"I know something of that property," he said, studying a little outline map which Winfield had prepared. "I've been out there duck shooting with Colfax and some others. It's fine property, there's no doubt of it. How much do they want for it?"

"Well, as a matter of fact, I already own it," said Winfield. "It cost me sixty thousand dollars five years ago when it was a vast, inaccessible swamp. Nothing has been done to it since, but I will turn it over to the company for what it is worth now—two hundred thousand dollars—and take a mortgage for my protection. Then the company can do what it pleases with it; but as president, of course, I should direct the line of development. If you want to make a fortune and have fifty thousand dollars to spare, here is your chance. This land has increased in value from sixty to two hundred thousand dollars in five years. What do you fancy it will be worth in ten years from now the way New York is growing? It has pretty near four million people now. In twenty-five years it is safe to say that there will be fourteen or fifteen millions scattered over this territory which lies within twenty-five miles. Of course, this is thirty-two miles away on a direct line, but what of it? The Long Island Railroad will be glad to put a spur in there which would bring this territory within one hour of the city. Think of it— one of the finest beaches on the Atlantic Ocean within one hour of New York! I expect to interest Mr. Wiltsie, the President of the Long Island, very heavily in this property. I come to you now because I think your advertising and artistic advice are worth something. You can take it or leave it, but before you do anything, I want you to come out and look over the property with me."

All told, in stocks, land, free money in the banks, and what he might save in a year or two, Eugene had about fifty thousand dollars of good hard cash which he could lay his hands on at a pinch. He was well satisfied that Winfield was putting before him one of those golden opportunities which, prudently managed, would make him a rich man. Nevertheless, his fifty thousand was fifty thousand, and he had it. Never again, however, once this other thing was under way, if it were true, would he have to worry about a position, or whether he would be able to maintain his present place in society. One could not possibly say what an investment like this might not lead to. Winfield, so he told Eugene, expected eventually to clear six or eight million dollars himself. He was going to take stock in some of the hotels, casinos, and various other enterprises, which would be organized. He could clearly see how, later, once this land was properly drained and laid out, it would be worth from three to fifteen thousand dollars per lot of one hundred by one hundred feet—the smallest portions to be sold. There were islands which for clubs or estates should bring splendid returns. Think of the leases to yacht and boat clubs alone! The company would own all the land.

"I would develop this myself if I had the capital," said Winfield, "but I want to see it done on a gigantic scale, and I haven't the means. I want something here which will be a monument to me and to all connected with it. I am willing to take my chances pro rata with those who now enter, and to prove my good faith I am going to buy as many shares as I possibly can on the five-for-one basis. You or anyone else can do the same thing. What do you think?"

"It's a great idea," said Eugene. "It seems as though a dream which had been floating about in the back of my head for years had suddenly come to life. I can scarcely believe that it is true, and yet I know that it is, and that you will get away with it just as you are outlining it here. You want to be very careful how you lay out this property, though. You have the chance of a lifetime. For goodness' sake, don't make any mistakes! Let's have one resort that will be truly, beautifully right."

"That's precisely the way I feel about it," answered Winfield, "and that's why I am talking to you. I want you to come in on this, for I think your imagination will be worth something. You can help me lay this thing out right and advertise it right."

They talked on about one detail and another until finally Eugene, in spite of all his caution, saw his dreams maturing in this particular proposition. Fifty thousand dollars invested here would give him two thousand five hundred shares—one thousand preferred, and fifteen hundred common—whose face value, guaranteed by this magnificent piece of property, would be $250,000. Think of it, $250,000—a quarter of a million and that subject to a natural increase which might readily carry him into the millionaire class! His own brains would be of some value here, for Winfield was anxious to have him lay this out, and this would bring him in touch with not only one of the best real estate men in the city, but would bring him into contact with a whole host of financiers in business, people who would certainly become interested in this venture. Winfield talked easily of architects, contractors, railroad men, presidents of construction companies, all of whom would take stock for the business opportunities it would bring to them later and also of the many strings to be pulled which later would bring great gains to the company and save it from expenditures which would otherwise mean millions in outlay. Thus this proposed extension by the Long Island which would cost that railroad two hundred thousand dollars would cost the Sea Island Company nothing and would bring thousands of lovers of beauty there the moment conveniences were established to receive them. This was true of hotels to be built. Each would bring business for everything else. The company would lease the ground. The great hotel men would do their own building according to restrictions and plans laid down by the Sea Island Company. The only real expenditure would be for streets, sewers, lights, water, walks, trees, and the great one hundred foot wide boardwalk with concrete ornaments which would be the finest sea stroll in the world. But these could be undertaken by degrees.

Eugene saw it all. It was a vision of empire. "I don't know about this," he said cautiously. "It's a great thing, but I may not have the means to dip into it. I want to think it over. Meanwhile, I'll be glad to go out there and look over the ground with you."

Winfield could see that he had Eugene fascinated. It would be an easy matter to land him once he had his plans perfected. Eugene would be the type of man who would build a house and come and live there in the summer. He would interest many people whom he knew. He went away feeling that he had made a good start, and he was not mistaken.

Eugene talked the matter over with Angela—his one recourse in these matters—and as usual she was doubtful, but not entirely opposed. Angela had considerable caution, but no great business vision. She could not really tell him what he ought to do. Thus far his judgment, or rather his moves, had been obviously successful. He had been going up apparently because he was valuable as an assistant, not because he was a born leader.

"You'll have to judge for yourself, Eugene," Angela finally said. "I don't know. It looks fine. You certainly don't want to work for Mr. Colfax all your life, and if, as you say, they are beginning to plot against you, you had better prepare to get out sometime. We have enough now, really, to live on, if you want to return to your art."

Eugene smiled. "My art. My poor old art! A lot I've done to develop my art."

"I don't think it needs developing. You have it. I'm sorry sometimes I ever let you leave it. We have lived better, but your work hasn't counted for as much. What good has it done you outside the money to be a successful publisher? You were as famous as you are now before you ever started in on this line, and more so. More people know you even now as Eugene Witla, the artist, than as Eugene Witla, the magazine man."

Eugene knew this to be so. His art achievements had never forsaken him. They had grown in fame always. Pictures that he had sold for two hundred and four hundred had gone up to as high as three and four thousand in value, and they were still rising. He was occasionally approached by an art dealer to know if he never intended to paint any more. In social circles it was a constant cry among the elect, "Why don't you paint any longer?" "What a shame you ever left the art world!" "Those pictures of yours, I can never forget them."

"My dear lady," Eugene once said solemnly, "I can't live by painting pictures as I am living by directing magazines. Art is very lovely. I am satisfied to believe that I am a great painter. Nevertheless, I made little out of it, and since then I have learned to live. It's sad, but it's true. If I could see my way to live in half the comfort I am living in now and not run the risk of plodding the streets with a picture under my arm, I would gladly return to art. The trouble is the world is always so delightfully ready to see the other fellow make the sacrifice for art or literature's sake. Selah! I won't do it. So there!"

"It's a pity! It's a pity!" said this observer, but Eugene was not vastly distressed. Similarly Mrs. Dale had reproached him, for she had seen and heard of his work.

"Some time. Some time," he said grandly; "wait."

Now at length this land proposition seemed to clear the way for everything. If Eugene embarked upon it, he might gradually come to the point at which he could take some official position in connection with it. Anyhow, think of a rising income from $250,000! Think of the independence, the freedom! Surely then he could paint or travel, or do as he pleased.

As a matter of fact, after two automobile rides to the nearest available position on the site of the future resort and a careful study of the islands and the beach, Eugene devised a scheme which included four hotels of varying sizes, one dining and dancing casino, one gambling resort after the pattern of Monte Carlo, a summer theatre, a music pavilion, three lovely piers, motor and yacht club houses, a park with radiating streets, and other streets arranged in concentric rings to cross them. There was a grand plaza about which the four hotels were ranged, a noble promenade, three miles in length, to begin with, a handsome railway station, plots for five thousand summer homes, ranging from five to fifteen thousand in price. There were islands for residences, islands for clubs, islands for parks. One of the hotels sat close to an inlet over which a dining veranda was to be built—stairs were to be laid down to the water so that one could step into gondolas or launches and be carried quickly to one of the music pavilions on one of the islands. Everything that money wanted was to be eventually available here, and all was to be gone about slowly but beautifully, so that each step would only make more sure each additional step.

Eugene did not enter on this grand scheme until ten men, himself included, had pledged themselves to take stock up to $50,000 each. Included in these were Mr. Wiltsie, President of the Long Island; Mr. Kenyon C. Winfield, and Milton Willebrand, the very wealthy society man at whose home he had originally met Winfield. The Sea Island Company was then incorporated, and on a series of dates agreed upon between them and which were dependent upon a certain amount of work being accomplished by each date, the stock was issued to them in ten-thousand-dollar lots and then cash taken and deposited in the treasury. By the end of two years after Eugene had first been approached by Winfield he had a choice collection of gold-colored certificates in the Sea Island Realty and Construction Company, which was building the now widely heralded seaside resort—"Blue Sea"—which, according to those interested, was to be the most perfect resort of its kind in the world. His certificates stated that they were worth $250,000, and potentially they were. Eugene and Angela looking at them, thinking of the initiative and foresight of Mr. Kenyon C. Winfield and the men he was associated with, felt sure that some day, and that not so very far distant, they would yield their face value and much more.

CHAPTER IV

It had been while he was first perfecting his undertaking with Winfield as to what his relationship to the new Sea Island Construction Company was to be that Eugene had been dwelling more and more fondly upon the impression which Suzanne Dale had originally made upon him. It was six weeks before they met again, and then it was on the occasion of a dance that Mrs. Dale was giving in honor of Suzanne that Eugene and Angela were invited. Mrs. Dale admired Angela's sterling qualities as a wife, and while there might be temperamental and social differences, she did not think they were sufficient to warrant any discrimination between them, at least not on her part. Angela was a good woman—not a social figure at all—but interesting in her way. Mrs. Dale was much more interested in Eugene, because in the first place they were very much alike temperamentally, and in the next place because Eugene was a successful and brilliant person. She liked to see the easy manner in which he took life, the air with which he assumed that talent should naturally open all doors to him. He was not conscious apparently of any inferiority in anything but rather of a splendid superiority. She heard it from so many that he was rapidly rising in his publishing world and that he was interested in many things, the latest this project to create a magnificent summer resort. Winfield was a personal friend of hers. He had never attempted to sell her any property, but he had once said that he might some day take her Staten Island holdings and divide them up into town lots. This was one possibility which tended to make her pleasant to him.

The evening in question Eugene and Angela went down to Daleview in their automobile. Eugene always admired this district, for it gave him a sense of height and scope which was not easily attainable elsewhere about New York. It was still late winter and the night was cold but clear. The great house with its verandas encased in glass was brightly lit. There were a number of people—men and women, whom Eugene had met at various places, and quite a number of young people whom he did not know. Angela had to be introduced to a great many, and Eugene felt that peculiar sensation which he so often experienced of a certain incongruity in his matrimonial state. Angela was nice, but to him she was not like these other women who carried themselves with such an air. There was a statuesqueness and a sufficiency about many of them, to say nothing of their superb beauty and sophistication which made him feel, when the contrast was forced upon him closely, that he had made a terrible mistake. Why had he been so silly as to marry? He could have told Angela frankly that he would not at the time, and all would have been well. He forgot how badly, emotionally, he had entangled himself. But scenes like these made him dreadfully unhappy. Why, his life if he were single would now be but beginning!

As he walked round tonight he was glad to be free socially even for a few minutes. He was glad that first this person and that took the trouble to talk to Angela. It relieved him of the necessity of staying near her, for if he neglected her or she felt neglected by others she was apt to reproach him. If he did not show her attention, she would complain that he was conspicuous in his indifference. If others refused to talk to her, it was his place. He should. Eugene objected to this necessity with all his soul, but he did not see what he was to do about it. As she often said, even if he had made a mistake in marrying her, it was his place to stick by her now that he had. A real man would.

One of the things that interested him was the number of beautiful young women. He was interested to see how full and complete mentally and physically so many girls appeared to be at eighteen. Why, in their taste, shrewdness, completeness, they were fit mates for a man of almost any age up to forty! Some of them looked so wonderful to him—so fresh and ruddy with the fires of ambition and desire burning briskly in their veins. Beautiful girls—real flowers, like roses, light and dark. And to think the love period was all over for him—completely over!

Suzanne came down with others after a while from some room upstairs, and once more Eugene was impressed with her simple, natural, frank, good-natured attitude. Her light chestnut-colored hair was tied with a wide band of light blue ribbon which matched her eyes and contrasted well with her complexion. Again, her dress was some light flimsy thing, the color of peach blossoms, girdled with ribbon and edged with flowers like a wreath. Soft white sandals held her feet.

"Oh, Mr. Witla!" she said gaily, holding out her smooth white arm on a level with her eyes and dropping her hand gracefully. Her red lips were parted, showing even white teeth, arching into a radiant smile. Her eyes were quite wide as he remembered, with an innocent, surprised look in them, which was wholly unconscious with her. If wet roses could outrival a maiden in all her freshness, he thought he would like to see it. Nothing could equal the beauty of a young woman in her eighteenth or nineteenth year.

"Yes, quite, Mr. Witla," he said, beaming. "I thought you had forgotten. My, we look charming this evening! We look like roses and cut flowers and stained-glass windows and boxes of jewels, and, and, and— —"

He pretended to be lost for more words and looked quizzically up at the ceiling.

Suzanne began to laugh. Like Eugene, she had a marked sense of the comic and the ridiculous. She was not in the least vain, and the idea of being like roses and boxes of jewels and stained-glass windows tickled her fancy.

"Why, that's quite a collection of things to be, isn't it?" she laughed, her lips parted. "I wouldn't mind being all those things if I could, particularly the jewels. Mama won't give me any. I can't even get a brooch for my throat."

"Mama is real mean, apparently," said Eugene vigorously. "We'll have to talk to mama, but she knows, you know, that you don't need any jewels, see? She knows that you have something which is just as good, or better. But we won't talk about that, will we?"

Suzanne had been afraid that he was going to begin complimenting her, but seeing how easily he avoided this course she liked him for it. She was a little overawed by his dignity and mental capacity, but attracted by his gaiety and lightness of manner.

"Do you know, Mr. Witla," she said, "I believe you like to tease people."

"Oh, no!" said Eugene. "Oh, never, never! Nothing like that. How could I? Tease people! Far be it from me! That's the very last thing I ever think of doing. I always approach people in a very solemn manner and tell them the dark sad truth. It's the only way. They need it. The more truth I tell the better I feel. And then they like me so much better for it."

At the first rush of his quizzical tirade Suzanne's eyes opened quaintly, inquiringly. Then she began to smile, and in a moment after he ceased she exclaimed: "Oh, ha! ha! Oh, dear! Oh, dear, how you talk!" A ripple of laughter spread outward, and Eugene frowned darkly.

"How dare you laugh?" he said. "Don't laugh at me. It's against the rules to laugh, anyhow. Don't you remember growing girls should never laugh? Solemnity is the first rule of beauty. Never smile. Keep perfectly solemn. Look wise. Hence. Therefore. If. And— —"

He lifted a finger solemnly, and Suzanne stared. He had fixed her eye with his and was admiring her pretty chin and nose and lips, while she gazed not knowing what to make of him. He was very different; very much like a boy, and yet very much like a solemn, dark master of some kind.

"You almost frighten me," she said.

"Now, now, listen! It's all over. Come to. I'm just a silly-billy. Are you going to dance with me this evening?"

"Why, certainly, if you want me to! Oh, that reminds me! We have cards. Did you get one?"

"No."

"Well, they're over here, I think."

She led the way toward the reception hall, and Eugene took from the footman who was stationed there two of the little books.

"Let's see," he said, writing, "how greedy dare I be?"

Suzanne made no reply.

"If I take the third and the sixth and the tenth would that be too many?"

"No-o," said Suzanne doubtfully.

He wrote in hers and his and then they went back to the drawing-room where so many were now moving. "Will you be sure and save me these?"

"Why, certainly," she replied. "To be sure, I will!"

"That's nice of you. And now here comes your mother. Remember, you mustn't ever, ever, ever laugh. It's against the rules."

Suzanne went away, thinking. She was pleased at the gaiety of this man who seemed so light-hearted and self-sufficient. He seemed like someone who took her as a little girl, so different from the boys she knew who were solemn in her presence and rather love sick. He was the kind of man one could have lots of fun with without subjecting one's self to undue attention and having to explain to her mother. Her mother liked him. But she soon forgot him in the chatter of other people.

Eugene was thinking again, though, of the indefinable something in the spirit of this girl which was attracting him so vigorously. What was it? He had seen hundreds of girls in the last few years, all charming, but somehow this one— — She seemed so strong, albeit so new and young. There was a poise there—a substantial quality in her soul which could laugh at life and think no ill of it. That was it or something of it, for of course her beauty was impressive, but a courageous optimism was shining out through her eyes. It was in her laugh, her mood. She would never be afraid.

The dance began after ten, and Eugene danced with first one and then another—Angela, Mrs. Dale, Mrs. Stevens, Miss Willy. When the third set came he went looking for Suzanne and found her talking to another young girl and two society men.

"Mine, you know," he said smilingly.

She came out to him laughing, stretching her arm in a sinuous way, quite unconscious of the charming figure she made. She had a way of throwing back her head which revealed her neck in beautiful lines. She looked into Eugene's eyes simply and unaffectedly, returning his smile with one of her own. And when they began to dance he felt as though he had never really danced before.

What was it the poet said of the poetry of motion? This was it. This was it. This girl could dance wonderfully, sweetly, as a fine voice sings. She seemed to move like the air with the sound of the two-step coming from an ambush of flowers, and Eugene yielded himself instinctively to the charm—the hypnotism of it. He danced and in dancing forgot everything except this vision leaning upon his arm and the sweetness of it all. Nothing could equal this emotion, he said to himself. It was finer than anything he had ever experienced. There was joy in it, pure delight, an exquisite sense of harmony; and even while he was congratulating himself the music seemed to hurry to a finish. Suzanne had looked up curiously into his eyes.

"You like dancing, don't you?" she said.

"I do, but I don't dance well."

"Oh, I think so!" she replied. "You dance so easily."

"It is because of you," he said simply. "You have the soul of the dance in you. Most people dance poorly, like myself."

"I don't think so," she said, hanging on to his arm as they walked toward a seat. "Oh, there's Kinroy! He has the next with me."

Eugene looked at her brother almost angrily. Why should circumstances rob him of her company in this way? Kinroy looked like her—he was very handsome for a boy.

"Well, then, I have to give you up. I wish there were more."

He left her only to wait impatiently for the sixth and the tenth. He knew it was silly to be interested in her in this way, for nothing could come of it. She was a young girl hedged about by all the conventions and safeguards which go to make for the perfect upbringing of girlhood. He was a man past the period of her interest, watched over by conventions and interests also. There could be absolutely nothing between them, and yet he longed for her just the same, for just this little sip of the nectar of make-believe. For a few minutes in her company, married or not, so many years older or not, he could be happy in her company, teasing her. That sense of dancing—that sense of perfect harmony with beauty—when had he ever experienced that before?

The night went by, and at one he and Angela went home. She had been entertained by some young officer in the army stationed at Fort Wadsworth who had known her brother David. That had made the evening pleasant for her. She commented on Mrs. Dale and Suzanne, what a charming hostess the former was and how pretty and gay Suzanne looked, but Eugene manifested little interest. He did not want it to appear that he had been interested in Suzanne above any of the others.

"Yes, she's very nice," he said. "Rather pretty; but she's like all girls at that age. I like to tease them."

Angela wondered whether Eugene had really changed for good. He seemed saner in all his talk concerning women. Perhaps large affairs had cured him completely, though she could not help feeling that he must be charmed and delighted by the beauty of some of the women whom he saw.

Five weeks more went by and then he saw Suzanne one day with her mother on Fifth Avenue, coming out of an antique shop. Mrs. Dale explained that she was looking after the repair of a rare piece of furniture. Eugene and Suzanne were enabled to exchange but a few gay words. Four weeks later he met them at the Brentwood Hadleys, in Westchester. Suzanne and her mother were enjoying a season of spring riding. Eugene was there for only a Saturday afternoon and Sunday. On this occasion he saw her coming in at half-past four wearing a divided riding skirt and looking flushed and buoyant. Her lovely hair was flowing lightly about her temples.

"Oh, how are you?" she asked, with that same inconsequent air, her hand held out to him at a high angle. "I saw you last in Fifth Avenue, didn't I? Mama was having her chair fixed. Ha, ha! She's such a slow rider! I've left her miles behind. Are you going to be here long?"

"Just today and tomorrow."

He looked at her, pretending gaiety and indifference.

"Is Mrs. Witla here?"

"No, she couldn't come. A relative of hers is in the city."

"I need a bath terribly," said the desire of his eyes, and passed on, calling back: "I'll see you again before dinner, very likely."

Eugene sighed.

She came down after an hour, dressed in a flowered organdie, a black silk band about her throat, a low collar showing her pretty neck. She picked up a magazine, passing a wicker table, and came down the veranda where Eugene was sitting alone. Her easy manner interested him, and her friendliness. She liked him well enough to be perfectly natural with him and to seek him out where he was sitting once she saw he was there.

"Oh, here you are!" she said, and sat down, taking a chair which was near him.

"Yes, here I am," he said, and began teasing her as usual, for it was the only way in which he knew how to approach her. Suzanne responded vivaciously, for Eugene's teasing delighted her. It was the one kind of humor she really enjoyed.

"You know, Mr. Witla," she said to him once, "I'm not going to laugh at any of your jokes any more. They're all at my expense."

"That makes it all the nicer," he said. "You wouldn't want me to make jokes at my expense, would you? That would be a terrible joke."

She laughed and he smiled. They looked at a golden sunset filtering through a grove of tender maples. The spring was young and the leaves just budding.

"Isn't it lovely tonight?" he asked.

"Oh, yes!" she exclaimed, in a mellow, meditative voice, the first ring of deep sincerity in it that he ever noticed there.

"Do you like nature?" he asked.

"Do I?" she returned. "I can't get enough of the woods these days. I feel so queer sometimes, Mr. Witla. As though I were not really alive at all, you know. Just a sound, or a color in the woods."

He stopped and looked at her. The simile caught him quite as any notable characteristic in anyone would have caught him. What was the color and complexity of this girl's mind? Was she so wise, so artistic and so emotional that nature appealed to her in a deep way? Was this wonderful charm that he felt the shadow or radiance of something finer still?

"So that's the way it is, is it?" he asked.

"Yes," she said quietly.

He sat and looked at her, and she eyed him as solemnly.

"Why do you look at me so?" she asked.

"Why do you say such curious things?" he answered.

"What did I say?"

"I don't believe you really know. Well, never mind. Let us walk, will you? Do you mind? It's still an hour to dinner. I'd like to go over and see what's beyond those trees."

They went down a little path bordered with grass and under green budding twigs. It came to a stile finally and looked out upon a stony green field where some cows were pasturing.

"Oh, the spring! The spring!" exclaimed Eugene, and Suzanne answered: "You know, Mr. Witla, I think we must be something alike in some ways. That's just the way I feel."

"How do you know how I feel?"

"I can tell by your voice," she said.

"Can you, really?"

"Why, yes. Why shouldn't I?"

"What a strange girl you are!" he said thoughtfully. "I don't think I understand you quite."

"Why, why, am I so different from everyone else?"

"Quite, quite," he said; "at least to me. I have never seen anyone quite like you before."

CHAPTER V

It was after this meeting that vague consciousness came to Suzanne that Mr. Witla, as she always thought of him to herself, was just a little more than very nice to her. He was so gentle, so meditative, and withal so gay when he was near her! He seemed fairly to bubble whenever he came into her presence, never to have any cause for depression or gloom such as sometimes seized on her when she was alone. He was always immaculately dressed, and had great affairs, so her mother said. They discussed him once at table at Daleview, and Mrs. Dale said she thought he was charming.

"He's one of the nicest fellows that comes here, I think," said Kinroy. "I don't like that stick, Woodward."

He was referring to another man of about Eugene's age who admired his mother.

"Mrs. Witla is such a queer little woman," said Suzanne. "She's so different from Mr. Witla. He's so gay and good-natured, and she's so reserved. Is she as old as he is, mama?"

"I don't think so," said Mrs. Dale, who was deceived by Angela's apparent youth. "What makes you ask?"

"Oh, I just wondered!" said Suzanne, who was vaguely curious concerning things in connection with Eugene.

There were several other meetings, one of which Eugene engineered, once when he persuaded Angela to invite Suzanne and her mother to a spring night revel they were having at the studio, and the other when he and Angela were invited to the Willebrands, where the Dales were also.

Angela was always with him. Mrs. Dale almost always with Suzanne. There were a few conversations, but they were merely gay, inconsequent make-believe talks, in which Suzanne saw Eugene as one who was forever happy. She little discerned the brooding depths of longing that lay beneath his gay exterior.

The climax was brought about, however, when one July day after a short visit to one of the summer resorts, Angela was taken ill. She had always been subject to colds and sore throats, and these peculiar signs, which are associated by medical men with latent rheumatism, finally culminated in this complaint. Angela had also been pronounced to have a weak heart, and this combined with a sudden, severe rheumatic attack completely prostrated her. A trained nurse had to be called, and Angela's sister Marietta was sent for. Eugene's sister Myrtle, who now lived in New York, was asked by him to come over and take charge, and under her supervision, pending Marietta's arrival, his household went forward smoothly enough. The former, being a full-fledged Christian Scientist, having been instantly cured, as she asserted, of a long-standing nervous complaint, was for calling a Christian Science practitioner, but Eugene would have none of it. He could not believe that there was anything in this new religious theory, and thought Angela needed a doctor. He sent for a specialist in her complaint. He pronounced that six weeks at the least, perhaps two months, must elapse before Angela would be able to sit up again.

"Her system is full of rheumatism," said her physician. "She is in a very bad way. Rest and quiet, and constant medication will bring her round."

Eugene was sorry. He did not want to see her suffer, but her sickness did not for one minute alter his mental attitude. In fact, he did not see how it could. It did not change their relative mental outlook in any way. Their peculiar relationship of guardian and restless ward was quite unaffected.

All social functions of every kind were now abandoned and Eugene stayed at home every evening, curious to see what the outcome would be. He wanted to see how the trained nurse did her work and what the doctor thought would be the next step. He had a great deal to do at all times, reading, consulting, and many of those who wished to confer with him came to the apartment of an evening. All those who knew them socially at all intimately called or sent messages of condolence, and among those who came were Mrs. Dale and Suzanne. The former because Eugene had been so nice to her in a publishing way and was shortly going to bring out her first attempt at a novel was most assiduous. She sent flowers and came often, proffering the services of Suzanne for any day that the nurse might wish to be off duty or Myrtle could not be present. She thought Angela might like to have Suzanne read to her. At least the offer sounded courteous and was made in good faith.

Suzanne did not come alone at first, but after a time, when Angela had been ill four weeks and Eugene had stood the heat of the town apartment nightly for the chance of seeing her, she did. Mrs. Dale suggested that he should run down to her place over Saturday and Sunday. It was not far. They were in close telephone communication. It would rest him.

Eugene, though Angela had suggested it a number of times before, had refused to go to any seaside resort or hotel, even for Saturday and Sunday, his statement being that he did not care to go alone at this time. The truth was he was becoming so interested in Suzanne that he did not care to go anywhere save somewhere that he might see her again.

Mrs. Dale's offer was welcome enough, but having dissembled so much he had to dissemble more. Mrs. Dale insisted. Angela added her plea. Myrtle thought he ought to go. He finally ordered the car to take him down one Friday afternoon and leave him. Suzanne was out somewhere, but he sat on the veranda and basked in the magnificent view it gave of the lower bay. Kinroy and some young friend, together with two girls, were playing tennis on one of the courts. Eugene went out to watch them, and presently Suzanne returned, ruddy from a walk she had taken to a neighbor's house. At the sight of her every nerve in Eugene's body tingled—he felt a great exaltation, and it seemed as though she responded in kind, for she was particularly gay and laughing.

"They have a four," she called to him, her white duck skirt blowing. "Let's you and I get rackets and play single."

"I'm not very good, you know," he said.

"You couldn't be worse than I am," she replied. "I'm so bad Kinroy won't let me play in any game with him. Ha, ha!"

"Such being the case——" Eugene said lightly, and followed her to get the rackets.

They went to the second court, where they played practically unheeded. Every hit was a signal for congratulation on the part of one or the other, every miss for a burst of laughter or a jest. Eugene devoured Suzanne with his eyes, and she looked at him continually, in wide-eyed sweetness, scarcely knowing what she was doing. Her own hilarity on this occasion was almost inexplicable to her. It seemed as though she was possessed of some spirit of joy which she couldn't control. She confessed to him afterward that she had been wildly glad, exalted, and played with freedom and abandon, though at the same time she was frightened and nervous. To Eugene she was of course ravishing to behold. She could not play, as she truly said, but it made no difference. Her motions were beautiful.

Mrs. Dale had long admired Eugene's youthful spirit. She watched him now from one of the windows, and thought of him much as one might of a boy. He and Suzanne looked charming playing together. It occurred to her that if he were single he would not make a bad match for her daughter. Fortunately he was sane, prudent, charming, more like a guardian to

Suzanne than anything else. Her friendship for him was rather a healthy sign.

After dinner it was proposed by Kinroy that he and his friends and Suzanne go to a dance which was being given at a club house, near the government fortifications at The Narrows, where they spread out into the lower bay. Mrs. Dale, not wishing to exclude Eugene, who was depressed at the thought of Suzanne's going and leaving him behind, suggested that they all go. She did not care so much for dancing herself, but Suzanne had no partner and Kinroy and his friend were very much interested in the girls they were taking. A car was called, and they sped to the club to find it dimly lighted with Chinese lanterns, and an orchestra playing softly in the gloom.

"Now you go ahead and dance," said her mother to Suzanne. "I want to sit out here and look at the water a while. I'll watch you through the door."

Eugene held out his hand to Suzanne, who took it, and in a moment they were whirling round. A kind of madness seized them both, for without a word or look they drew close to each other and danced furiously, in a clinging ecstasy of joy.

"Oh, how lovely!" Suzanne exclaimed at one turn of the room, where, passing an open door, they looked out and saw a full lighted ship passing silently by in the distant dark. A sail boat; its one great sail enveloped in a shadowy quiet, floated wraith-like, nearer still.

"Do scenes like that appeal to you so?" asked Eugene.

"Oh, do they!" she pulsated. "They take my breath away. This does, too, it's so lovely!"

Eugene sighed. He understood now. Never, he said to himself, was the soul of an artist so akin to his own and so enveloped in beauty. This same thirst for beauty that was in him was in her, and it was pulling her to him. Only her soul was so exquisitely set in youth and beauty and maidenhood that it overawed and frightened him. It seemed impossible that she should ever love him. These eyes, this face of hers—how they enchanted him! He was drawn as by a strong cord, and so was she—by an immense, terrible magnetism. He had felt it all the afternoon. Keenly. He was feeling it intensely now. He pressed her to his bosom, and she yielded, yearningly, suiting her motions to his subtlest moods. He wanted to exclaim: "Oh, Suzanne! Oh, Suzanne!" but he was afraid. If he said anything to her it would frighten her. She did not really dream as yet what it all meant.

"You know," he said, when the music stopped, "I'm quite beside myself. It's narcotic. I feel like a boy."

"Oh, if they would only go on!" was all she said. And together they went out on the veranda, where there were no lights but only chairs and the countless stars.

"Well?" said Mrs. Dale.

"I'm afraid you don't love to dance as well as I do?" observed Eugene calmly, sitting down beside her.

"I'm afraid I don't, seeing how joyously you do it. I've been watching you. You two dance well together. Kinroy, won't you have them bring us ices?"

Suzanne had slipped away to the side of her brother's friends. She talked to them cheerily the while Eugene watched her, but she was intensely conscious of his presence and charm. She tried to think what she was doing, but somehow she could not—she could only feel. The music struck up again, and for looks' sake he let her dance with her brother's friend. The next was his, and the next, for Kinroy preferred to sit out one, and his friend also. Suzanne and Eugene danced the major portions of the dances together, growing into a wild exaltation, which, however, was wordless except for a certain eagerness which might have been read into what they said. Their hands spoke when they touched and their eyes when they met. Suzanne was intensely shy and fearsome. She was really half terrified by what she was doing—afraid lest some word or thought would escape Eugene, and she wanted to dwell in the joy of this. He went once between two dances, when she was hanging over the rail looking at the dark, gurgling water below, and leaned over beside her.

"How wonderful this night is!" he said.

"Yes, yes!" she exclaimed, and looked away.

"Do you wonder at all at the mystery of life?"

"Oh, yes; oh, yes! All the time."

"And you are so young!" he said passionately, intensely.

"Sometimes, you know, Mr. Witla," she sighed, "I do not like to think."

"Why?"

"Oh, I don't know; I just can't tell you! I can't find words. I don't know."

There was an intense pathos in her phrasing which meant everything to his understanding. He understood how voiceless a great soul really might be, new born without an earth-manufactured vocabulary. It gave him a clearer insight into a thought he had had for a long while and that was that we came, as Wordsworth expressed it, "trailing clouds of glory." But from where? Her soul must be intensely wise—else why his yearning to her? But, oh, the pathos of her voicelessness!

They went home in the car, and late that night, while he was sitting on the veranda smoking to soothe his fevered brain, there was one other scene. The night was intensely warm everywhere except on this hill, where a cool breeze was blowing. The ships on the sea and bay were many—twinkling little lights—and the stars in the sky were as a great army. "See how the floor of heaven is thick inlaid with patines of bright gold," he quoted to himself. A door opened and Suzanne came out of the library, which opened on to the veranda. He had not expected to see her again, nor she him. The beauty of the night had drawn her.

"Suzanne!" he said, when the door opened.

She looked at him, poised in uncertainty, her lovely white face glowing like a pale phosphorescent light in the dark.

"Isn't it beautiful out here? Come, sit down."

"No," she said. "I mustn't stay. It is so beautiful!" She looked about her vaguely, nervously, and then at him. "Oh, that breeze!" She turned up her nose and sniffed eagerly.

"The music is still whirling in my head," he said, coming to her. "I cannot get over tonight." He spoke softly—almost in a whisper—and threw his cigar away. Suzanne's voice was low.

She looked at him and filled her deep broad chest with air. "Oh!" she sighed, throwing back her head, her neck curving divinely.

"One more dance," he said, taking her right hand and putting his left upon her waist.

She did not retreat from him, but looked half distrait, half entranced in his eyes.

"Without music?" she asked. She was almost trembling.

"You are music," he replied, her intense sense of suffocation seizing him.

They moved a few paces to the left where there were no windows and where no one could see. He drew her close to him and looked into her face, but still he did not dare say what he thought. They moved about softly, and then she gurgled that soft laugh that had entranced him from the first. "What would people think?" she asked.

They walked to the railing, he still holding her hand, and then she withdrew it. He was conscious of great danger—of jeopardizing a wonderfully blissful relationship, and finally said: "Perhaps we had better go."

"Yes," she said. "Ma-ma would be greatly disturbed if she knew this."

She walked ahead of him to the door.

"Good night," she whispered.

"Good night," he sighed.

He went back to his chair and meditated on the course he was pursuing. This was a terrible risk. Should he go on? The flower-like face of Suzanne came back to him—her supple body, her wondrous grace and beauty. "Oh, perhaps not, but what a loss, what a lure to have flaunted in front of his eyes! Were there ever thoughts and feelings like these in so young a body? Never, never, never, had he seen her like. Never in all his experiences had he seen anything so exquisite. She was like the budding woods in spring, like little white and blue flowers growing. If life now for once would only be kind and give him her!

"Oh, Suzanne, Suzanne!" he breathed to himself, lingering over the name.

For a fourth or a fifth time Eugene was imagining himself to be terribly, eagerly, fearsomely in love.

CHAPTER VI

This burst of emotion with its tentative understanding so subtly reached, changed radically and completely the whole complexion of life for Eugene. Once more now the spirit of youth had returned to him. He had been resenting all this while, in spite of his success, the passage of time, for he was daily and hourly growing older, and what had he really achieved? The more Eugene had looked at life through the medium of his experiences, the more it had dawned on him that somehow all effort was pointless. To where and what did one attain when one attained success? Was it for houses and lands and fine furnishings and friends that one was really striving? Was there any such thing as real friendship in life, and what were its fruits—intense satisfaction? In some few instances, perhaps, but in the main what a sorry jest most so-called friendships veiled! How often they were coupled with self-interest, self-seeking, self-everything! We associated in friendship mostly only with those who were of our own social station. A good friend. Did he possess one? An inefficient friend? Would one such long be his friend? Life moved in schools of those who could run a certain pace, maintain a certain standard of appearances, compel a certain grade of respect and efficiency in others. Colfax was his friend—for the present. So was Winfield. About him were scores and hundreds who were apparently delighted to grasp his hand, but for what? His fame? Certainly. His efficiency? Yes. Only by the measure of his personal power and strength could he measure his friends—no more.

And as for love—what had he ever had of love before? When he went back in his mind, it seemed now that all, each, and every one, had been combined in some way with lust and evil thinking. Could he say that he had ever been in love truly? Certainly not with Margaret Duff or Ruby Kenny or Angela—though that was the nearest he had come to true love—or Christina Channing. He had liked all these women very much, as he had Carlotta Wilson, but had he ever loved one? Never. Angela had won him through his sympathy for her, he told himself now. He had been induced to marry out of remorse. And here he was now having lived all these years and come all this way without having truly loved. Now, behold Suzanne Dale with her perfection of soul and body, and he was wild about her—not for lust, but for love. He wanted to be with her, to hold her hands, to kiss her lips, to watch her smile; but nothing more. It was true her body had its charm. In extremes it would draw him, but the beauty of her mind and appearance—there lay the fascination. He was heartsick at being compelled to be absent from her, and yet he did not know that he would ever be able to attain her at all.

As he thought of his condition, it rather terrified and nauseated him. To think, after having known this one hour of wonder and superlative bliss, of being compelled to come back into the work-a-day world! Nor were things improving at the office of the United Magazines Corporation. Instead of growing better, they were growing worse. With the diversity of his interests, particularly the interest he held in the Sea Island Realty and Construction Company, he was growing rather lackadaisical in his attitude toward all magazine interests with which he was connected. He had put in strong men wherever he could find them, but these had come to be very secure in their places, working without very much regard to him since he could not give them very much attention. White and Colfax had become intimate with many of them personally. Some of them, such as Hayes, the advertising man, the circulation manager, the editor of the *International Review*, the editor in charge of books, were so very able that, although it was true that Eugene had hired them it was practically settled that they could not be removed. Colfax and White had come to understand by degrees that Eugene was a person who, however brilliant he might be in selecting men, was really not capable of attention to detail. He could not bring his mind down to small practical points. If he had been an owner, like Colfax, or a practical henchman like White, he would have been perfectly safe, but being a natural-born leader, or rather organizer, he was, unless he secured control in the beginning, rather hopeless and helpless when organization was completed. Others could attend to details better than he could. Colfax came to know his men and like them. In absences which had become more frequent, as Eugene became more secure, and as he took up with Winfield, they had first gone to Colfax for advice, and later, in Colfax's absence, to White. The latter received them with open arms. Indeed, among themselves, his lieutenants frequently discussed Eugene and agreed that in organizing, or rather reorganizing the place, he had done his great work. He might have been worth twenty-five thousand a year doing that, but hardly as a man to sit about and cool his heels after the work was done. White had persistently whispered suggestions of Eugene's commercial inefficiency for the task he was essaying to Colfax. "He is really trying to do up there what you ought to be doing," he told him, "and what you can do better. You want to remember that you've learned a lot since you came in here, and so has he, only he has become a little less practical and you have become more so. These men of his look more to you now than they do to him."

Colfax rejoiced in the thought. He liked Eugene, but he liked the idea better that his business interests were perfectly safe. He did not like to think that any one man was becoming so strong that his going would injure him, and this thought for a long time during Eugene's early ascendancy had troubled him. The latter had carried himself with such an air. Eugene had fancied that Colfax needed to be impressed with his importance, and this, in addition to his very thorough work, was one way to do it. His manner had grated on Colfax after a time, for he was the soul of vainglory himself, and he wanted no other gods in the place beside himself. White, on the contrary, was constantly subservient and advisory in his manner. It made a great difference.

By degrees, through one process and another, Eugene had lost ground, but it was only in a nebulous way as yet, and not in anything tangible. If he had never turned his attention to anything else, had never wearied of any detail, and kept close to Colfax and to his own staff, he would have been safe. As it was, he began now to neglect them more than ever, and this could not fail to tell rather disastrously in the long run.

In the first place the prospects in connection with the Sea Island Construction Company were apparently growing brighter and brighter. It was one of those schemes which would take years and years to develop, but it did not look that way at first. Rather it seemed to be showing tangible evidences of accomplishment. The first year, after a good deal of money had been invested, considerable dredging operations were carried out, and dry land appeared in many places—a long stretch of good earth to the rear of the main beach whereon hotels and resorts of all sorts could be constructed. The boardwalk was started after a model prepared by Eugene, and approved—after modification—by the architect engaged, and a portion of the future great dining and dancing casinos was begun and completed, a beautiful building modeled on a combination of the Moorish, Spanish and Old Mission styles. A notable improvement in design had been effected in this scheme, for the color of Blue Sea, according to Eugene's theory, was to be red, white, yellow, blue, and green, done in spirited yet simple outlines. The walls of all buildings were to be white and yellow, latticed with green. The roofs, porticos, lintels, piers, and steps were to be red, yellow, green, and blue. There were to be round, shallow Italian pools of concrete in many of the courts and interiors of the houses. The hotels were to be western modifications of the Giralda in Spain, each one a size smaller, or larger, than the other. Green spear pines and tall cone-shaped poplars were to be the prevailing tree decorations. The railroad, as Mr. Winfield promised, had already completed its spur and Spanish depot, which was beautiful. It looked truly as though Blue Sea would become what Winfield said it would become; the seaside resort of America.

The actuality of this progress fascinated Eugene so much that he gave, until Suzanne appeared, much more time than he really should have to the development of the scheme. As in the days when he first went with Summerfield, he worked of nights on exterior and interior layouts, as he called them—façades, ground arrangements, island improvements, and so on. He went frequently with Winfield and his architect in his auto to see how Blue Sea was getting on and to visit monied men, who might be interested. He drew up plans for ads and booklets, making romantic sketches and originating catch lines.

In the next place, after Suzanne appeared, he began to pay attention almost exclusively in his thoughts to her. He could not get her out of his head night or day. She haunted his thoughts in the office, at home, and in his dreams. He began actually to burn with a strange fever, which gave him no rest. When would he see her again? When would he see her again? When would he see her again? He could see her only as he danced with her at the boat club, as he sat with her in the swing at Daleview. It was a wild, aching desire which gave him no peace any more than any other fever of the brain ever does.

Once, not long after he and she had danced at the boat club together, she came with her mother to see how Angela was, and Eugene had a chance to say a few words to her in the studio, for they came after five in the afternoon when he was at home. Suzanne gazed at him wide-eyed, scarcely knowing what to think, though she was fascinated. He asked her eagerly where she had been, where she was going to be.

"Why," she said gracefully, her pretty lips parted, "we're going to Bentwood Hadley's tomorrow. We'll be there for a week, I fancy. Maybe longer."

"Have you thought of me much, Suzanne?"

"Yes, yes! But you mustn't, Mr. Witla. No, no. I don't know what to think."

"If I came to Bentwood Hadleys, would you be glad?"

"Oh, yes," she said hesitatingly, "but you mustn't come."

Eugene was there that week-end. It wasn't difficult to manage.

"I'm awfully tired," he wrote to Mrs. Hadley. "Why don't you invite me out?"

"Come!" came a telegram, and he went.

On this occasion, he was more fortunate than ever. Suzanne was there, out riding when he came, but, as he learned from Mrs. Hadley, there was a dance on at a neighboring country club. Suzanne with a number of others was going. Mrs. Dale decided to go, and invited Eugene. He seized the offer, for he knew he would get a chance to dance with his ideal. When they were going in to dinner, he met Suzanne in the hall.

"I am going with you," he said eagerly. "Save a few dances for me."

"Yes," she said, inhaling her breath in a gasp.

They went, and he initialled her card in five places.

"We must be careful," she pleaded. "Ma-ma won't like it."

He saw by this that she was beginning to understand, and would plot with him. Why was he luring her on? Why did she let him?

When he slipped his arm about her in the first dance he said, "At last!" And then: "I have waited for this so long."

Suzanne made no reply.

"Look at me, Suzanne," he pleaded.

"I can't," she said.

"Oh, look at me," he urged, "once, please. Look in my eyes."

"No, no," she begged, "I can't."

"Oh, Suzanne," he exclaimed, "I am crazy about you. I am mad. I have lost all reason. Your face is like a flower to me. Your eyes—I can't tell you about your eyes. Look at me!"

"No," she pleaded.

"It seems as though the days will never end in which I do not see you. I wait and wait. Suzanne, do I seem like a silly fool to you?"

"No."

"I am counted sharp and able. They tell me I am brilliant. You are the most perfect thing that I have ever known. I think of you awake and asleep. I could paint a thousand pictures of you. My art seems to come back to me through you. If I live I will paint you in a hundred ways. Have you ever seen the Rossetti woman?"

"No."

"He painted a hundred portraits of her. I shall paint a thousand of you."

She lifted her eyes to look at him shyly, wonderingly, drawn by this terrific passion. His own blazed into hers. "Oh, look at me again," he whispered, when she dropped them under the fire of his glance.

"I can't," she pleaded.

"Oh, yes, once more."

She lifted her eyes and it seemed as though their souls would blend. He felt dizzy, and Suzanne reeled.

"Do you love me, Suzanne?" he asked.

"I don't know," she trembled.

"Do you love me?"

"Don't ask me now."

The music ceased and Suzanne was gone.

He did not see her until much later, for she slipped away to think. Her soul was stirred as with a raging storm. It seemed as though her very soul was being torn up. She was tremulous, tumultuous, unsettled, yearning, eager. She came back after a time and they danced again, but she was calmer apparently. They went out on a balcony, and he contrived to say a few words there.

"You mustn't," she pleaded. "I think we are being watched."

He left her, and on the way home in the auto he whispered: "I shall be on the west veranda tonight. Will you come?"

"I don't know, I'll try."

He walked leisurely to that place later when all was still, and sat down to wait. Gradually the great house quieted. It was one and one-thirty, and then nearly two before the door opened. A figure slipped out, the lovely form of Suzanne, dressed as she had been at the ball, a veil of lace over her hair.

"I'm so afraid," she said, "I scarcely know what I am doing. Are you sure no one will see us?"

"Let us walk down the path to the field." It was the same way they had taken in the early spring when he had met her here before. In the west hung low a waning moon, yellow, sickle shaped, very large because of the hour.

"Do you remember when we were here before?"

"Yes."

"I loved you then. Did you care for me?"

"No."

They walked on under the trees, he holding her hand.

"Oh, this night, this night," he said, the strain of his intense emotion wearying him.

They came out from under the trees at the end of the path. There was a sense of August dryness in the air. It was warm, sensuous. About were the sounds of insects, faint bumblings, cracklings. A tree toad chirped, or a bird cried.

"Come to me, Suzanne," he said at last when they emerged into the full light of the moon at the end of the path and paused. "Come to me." He slipped his arm about her.

"No," she said. "No."

"Look at me, Suzanne," he pleaded; "I want to tell you how much I love you. Oh, I have no words. It seems ridiculous to try to tell you. Tell me that you love me, Suzanne. Tell me now. I am crazy with love of you. Tell me."

"No," she said, "I can't."

"Kiss me!"

"No!"

He drew her to him and turned her face up by her chin in spite of her. "Open your eyes," he pleaded. "Oh, God! That this should come to me! Now I could die. Life can hold no more. Oh, Flower Face! Oh, Silver Feet! Oh, Myrtle Bloom! Divine Fire! How perfect you are. How perfect! And to think you love me!"

He kissed her eagerly.

"Kiss me, Suzanne. Tell me that you love me. Tell me. Oh, how I love that name, Suzanne. Whisper to me you love me."

"No."

"But you do."

"No."

"Look at me, Suzanne. Flower face. Myrtle Bloom. For God's sake, look at me! You love me."

"Oh, yes, yes, yes," she sobbed of a sudden, throwing her arm around his neck. "Oh, yes, yes."

"Don't cry," he pleaded. "Oh, sweet, don't cry. I am mad for love of you, mad. Kiss me now, one kiss. I am staking my soul on your love. Kiss me!"

He pressed his lips to hers, but she burst away, terror-stricken.

"Oh, I am so frightened," she exclaimed all at once. "Oh, what shall I do? I am so afraid. Oh, please, please. Something terrifies me. Something scares me. Oh, what am I going to do? Let me go back."

She was white and trembling. Her hands were nervously clasping and unclasping.

Eugene smoothed her arm soothingly. "Be still, Suzanne," he said. "Be still. I shall say no more. You are all right. I have frightened you. We will go back. Be calm. You are all right."

He recovered his own poise with an effort because of her obvious terror, and led her back under the trees. To reassure her he drew his cigar case from his pocket and pretended to select a cigar. When he saw her calming, he put it back.

"Are you quieter now, sweet?" he asked, tenderly.

"Yes, but let us go back."

"Listen. I will only go as far as the edge. You go alone. I will watch you safely to the door."

"Yes," she said peacefully.

"And you really love me, Suzanne?"

"Oh, yes, but don't speak of it. Not tonight. You will frighten me again. Let us go back."

They strolled on. Then he said: "One kiss, sweet, in parting. One. Life has opened anew for me. You are the solvent of my whole being. You are making me over into something different. I feel as though I had never lived until now. Oh, this experience! It is such a wonderful thing to have done—to have lived through, to have changed as I have changed. You have changed me so completely, made me over into the artist again. From now on I can paint again. I can paint you." He scarcely knew what he was saying. He felt as though he were revealing himself to himself as in an apocalyptic vision.

She let him kiss her, but she was too frightened and wrought to even breathe right. She was intense, emotional, strange. She did not really understand what it was that he was talking about.

"Tomorrow," he said, "at the wood's edge. Tomorrow. Sweet dreams. I shall never know peace any more without your love."

And he watched her eagerly, sadly, bitterly, ecstatically, as she walked lightly from him, disappearing like a shadow through the dark and silent door.

CHAPTER VII

It would be impossible to describe even in so detailed an account as this the subtleties, vagaries, beauties and terrors of the emotions which seized upon him, and which by degrees began also to possess Suzanne, once he became wholly infatuated with her. Mrs. Dale, was, after a social fashion, one of Eugene's best friends. She had since she had first come to know him spread his fame far and wide as an immensely clever publisher and editor, an artist of the greatest power, and a man of lovely and delightful ideas and personal worth. He knew from various conversations with her that Suzanne was the apple of her eye. He had heard her talk, had, in fact, discussed with her the difficulties of rearing a simple mannered, innocent-minded girl in present day society. She had confided to him that it had been her policy to give Suzanne the widest liberty consistent with good-breeding and current social theories. She did not want to make her bold or unduly self-reliant, and yet she wanted her to be free and natural. Suzanne, she was convinced, from long observation and many frank conversations, was innately honest, truthful and clean-minded. She did not understand her exactly, for what mother can clearly understand any child; but she thought she read her well enough to know that she was in some indeterminate way forceful and able, like her father, and that she would naturally gravitate to what was worth while in life.

Had she any talent? Mrs. Dale really did not know. The girl had vague yearnings toward something which was anything but social in its quality. She did not care anything at all for most of the young men and women she met. She went about a great deal, but it was to ride and drive. Games of chance did not interest her. Drawing-room conversations were amusing to her, but not gripping. She liked interesting characters, able books, striking pictures. She had been particularly impressed with those of Eugene's; she had seen and had told her mother that they were wonderful. She loved poetry of high order, and was possessed of a boundless appetite for the ridiculous and the comic. An unexpected faux pas was apt to throw her into uncontrollable fits of laughter and the funny page selections of the current newspaper artists, when she could obtain them, amused her intensely. She was a student of character, and of her own mother, and was beginning to see clearly what were the motives that were prompting her mother in her attitude toward herself, quite as clearly as that person did herself and better. At bottom she was more talented than her mother, but in a different way. She was not, as yet, as self-controlled, or as understanding of current theories and beliefs as her mother, but she was artistic, emotional, excitable, in an intellectual way, and capable of high flights of fancy and of intense and fine appreciations. Her really sensuous beauty was nothing to her. She did not value it highly. She knew she was beautiful, and that men and boys were apt to go wild about her, but she did not care. They must not be so silly, she thought. She did not attempt to attract them in any way. On the contrary, she avoided every occasion of possible provocation. Her mother had told her plainly how susceptible men were, how little their promises meant, how careful she must be of her looks and actions. In consequence, she went her way as gaily and yet as inoffensively as she could, trying to avoid the sadness of entrancing anyone hopelessly and wondering what her career was to be. Then Eugene appeared.

With his arrival, Suzanne had almost unconsciously entered upon a new phase of her existence. She had seen all sorts of men in society, but those who were exclusively social were exceedingly wearisome to her. She had heard her mother say that it was an important thing to marry money and some man of high social standing, but who this man was to be and what he was to be like she did not know. She did not look upon the typical society men she had encountered as answering suitably to the term high. She had seen some celebrated wealthy men of influential families, but they did not appear to her really human enough to be considered. Most of them were cold, self-opinionated, ultra-artificial to her easy, poetic spirit. In the realms of real distinction were many men whom the papers constantly talked about, financiers, politicians, authors, editors, scientists, some of whom were in society, she understood, but most of whom were not. She had met a few of them as a girl might. Most of those she met, or saw, were old and cold and paid no attention to her whatever. Eugene had appeared trailing an atmosphere of distinction and acknowledged ability and he was young. He was good looking, too—laughing and gay. It seemed almost impossible at first to her that one so young and smiling should be so able, as her mother said. Afterwards, when she came to know him, she began to feel that he was more than able; that he could do anything he pleased. She had visited him once in his office, accompanied by her mother, and she had been vastly impressed by the great building, its artistic finish, Eugene's palatial surroundings. Surely he was the most remarkable young man she had ever known. Then came his incandescent attentions to her, his glowing, radiant presence and then— —

Eugene speculated deeply on how he should proceed. All at once, after this night, the whole problem of his life came before him. He was married; he was highly placed socially, better than he had ever been before. He was connected closely with Colfax, so closely that he feared him, for Colfax, in spite of certain emotional vagaries of which Eugene knew, was intensely conventional. Whatever he did was managed in the most offhand way and with no intention of allowing his home life to be affected or disrupted. Winfield, whom also Mrs. Dale knew, was also conventional to outward appearances. He had a mistress, but she was held tightly in check, he understood. Eugene had seen her at the new casino, or a portion of it, the East Wing, recently erected at Blue Sea, and he had been greatly impressed with her beauty. She was smart, daring, dashing. Eugene looked at her then, wondering if the time would ever come when he could dare an intimacy of that character. So many married men did. Would he ever attempt it and succeed?

Now that he had met Suzanne, however, he had a different notion of all this, and it had come over him all at once. Heretofore in his dreams, he had fancied he might strike up an emotional relationship somewhere which would be something like Winfield's towards Miss De Kalb, as she was known, and so satisfy the weary longing that was in him for something new and delightful in the way of a sympathetic relationship with beauty. Since seeing Suzanne, he wanted nothing of this, but only some readjustment or rearrangement of his life whereby he could have Suzanne and Suzanne only. Suzanne! Suzanne! Oh, that dream of beauty. How was he to obtain her, how free his life of all save a beautiful relationship with her? He could live with her forever and ever. He could, he could! Oh, this vision, this dream!

It was the Sunday following the dance that Suzanne and Eugene managed to devise another day together, which, though, it was one of those semi-accidental, semi-voiceless, but nevertheless not wholly thoughtless coincidences which sometimes come about without being wholly agreed upon or understood in the beginning, was nevertheless seized upon by them, accepted silently and semi-consciously, semi-unconsciously worked out together. Had they not been very strongly drawn to each other by now, this would not have happened at all. But they enjoyed it none the less. To begin with, Mrs. Dale was suffering from a sick headache the morning after. In the next place, Kinroy suggested to his friends to go for a lark to South Beach, which was one of the poorest and scrubbiest of all the beaches on Staten Island. In the next place, Mrs. Dale suggested that Suzanne be allowed to go and that perhaps Eugene would be amused. She rather trusted him as a guide and mentor.

Eugene said calmly that he did not object. He was eager to be anywhere alone with Suzanne, and he fancied that some opportunity would present itself whereby once they were there, they could be together, but he did not want to show it. Once more the car was called and they departed, being let off at one end of a silly panorama which stretched its shabby length for a mile along the shore. The chauffeur took the car back to the house, it being agreed that they could reach him by phone. The party started down the plank walk, but almost immediately, because of different interests, divided. Eugene and Suzanne stopped to shoot at a shooting gallery. Next they stopped at a cane rack to ring canes. Anything was delightful to Eugene which gave him an opportunity to observe his inamorata, to see her pretty face, her smile, and to hear her heavenly voice. She rung a cane for him. Every gesture of hers was perfection; every look a thrill of delight. He was walking in some elysian realm which had nothing to do with the tawdry evidence of life about him.

They followed the boardwalk southward, after a ride in the Devil's Whirlpool, for by now Suzanne was caught in the persuasive subtlety of his emotion and could no more do as her honest judgment would have dictated than she could have flown. It needed some shock, some discovery to show her whither she was drifting and this was absent. They came to a new dance hall, where a few servant girls and their sweethearts were dancing, and for a lark Eugene proposed that they should enter. They danced together again, and though the surroundings were so poor and the music wretched, Eugene was in heaven.

"Let's run away and go to the Terra-Marine," he suggested, thinking of a hotel farther south along the shore. "It is so pleasant there. This is all so cheap."

"Where is it?" asked Suzanne.

"Oh, about three miles south of here. We could almost walk there."

He looked down the long hot beach, but changed his mind.

"I don't mind this," said Suzanne. "It's so very bad that it's good, you know. I like to see how these people enjoy themselves."

"But it is *so* bad," argued Eugene. "I wish I had your live, healthy attitude toward things. Still we won't go if you don't want to."

Suzanne paused, thinking. Should she run away with him? The others would be looking for them. No doubt they were already wondering where they had gone. Still it didn't make so much difference. Her mother trusted her with Eugene. They could go.

"Well," she said finally, "I don't care. Let's."

"What will the others think?" he said doubtfully.

"Oh, they won't mind," she said. "When they're ready, they'll call the car. They know that I am with you. They know that I can get the car when I want it. Mama won't mind."

Eugene led the way back to a train which ran to Hugenot, their destination. He was beside himself with the idea of a day all alone with Suzanne. He did not stay to consider or give ear to a thought concerning Angela at home or how Mrs. Dale would view it. Nothing would come of it. It was not an outrageous adventure. They took the train south, and in a little while were in another world, on the veranda of a hotel that overlooked the sea. There were numerous autos of idlers like themselves in a court before the hotel. There was a great grassy lawn with swings covered by striped awnings of red and blue and green, and beyond that a pier with many little white launches anchored near. The sea was as smooth as glass and great steamers rode in the distance trailing lovely plumes of smoke. The sun was blazing hot, brilliant, but here on the cool porch waiters were serving pleasure lovers with food and drink. A quartette of negroes were singing. Suzanne and Eugene seated themselves in rockers at first to view the perfect day and later went down and sat in a swing. Unthinkingly, without words, these two were gradually gravitating toward each other under some spell which had no relationship to everyday life. Suzanne looked at him in the double seated swing where they sat facing each other and they smiled or jested aimlessly, voicing nothing of all the upward welling deep that was stirring within.

"Was there ever such a day?" said Eugene finally, and in a voice that was filled with extreme yearning. "See that steamer out there. It looks like a little toy."

"Yes," said Suzanne with a little gasp. She inhaled her breath as she pronounced this word which gave it an airy breathlessness which had a touch of demure pathos in it. "Oh, it is perfect."

"Your hair," he said. "You don't know how nice you look. You fit this scene exactly."

"Don't speak of me," she pleaded. "I look so tousled. The wind in the train blew my hair so I ought to go the ladies' dressing room and hunt up a maid."

"Stay here," said Eugene. "Don't go. It is all so lovely."

"I won't now. I wish we might always sit here. You, just as you are there, and I here."

"Did you ever read the 'Ode on a Grecian Urn'?"

"Yes."

"Do you remember the lines 'Fair youth, beneath the trees, thou canst not leave'?"

"Yes, yes," she answered ecstatically.

> "'Bold lover, never, never canst thou kiss
> Though winning near the goal—yet, do not grieve;
> She cannot fade, though thou hast not thy bliss,
> For ever wilt thou love and she be fair.'"

"Don't, don't," she pleaded.

He understood. The pathos of that great thought was too much for her. It hurt her as it did him. What a mind!

They rocked and swung idly, he pushing with his feet at times in which labor she joined him. They strolled up the beach and sat down on a green clump of grass overlooking the sea. Idlers approached and passed. He laid his arm to her waist and held her hand, but something in her mood stayed him from any expression. Through dinner at the hotel it was the same and on the way to the train, for she wanted to walk through the dark. Under some tall trees, though, in the rich moonlight prevailing, he pressed her hand.

"Oh, Suzanne," he said.

"No, no," she breathed, drawing back.

"Oh, Suzanne," he repeated, "may I tell you?"

"No, no," she answered. "Don't speak to me. Please don't. Let's just walk. You and I."

He hushed, for her voice, though sad and fearsome, was imperious. He could not do less than obey this mood.

They went to a little country farmhouse which ranged along the track in lieu of a depot, and sang a quaint air from some old-time comic opera.

"Do you remember the first time when you came to play tennis with me?" he asked.

"Yes."

"Do you know I felt a strange vibration before your coming and all during your playing. Did you?"

"Yes."

"What is that, Suzanne?"

"I don't know."

"Don't you want to know?"

"No, no, Mr. Witla, not now."

"Mr. Witla?"

"It must be so."

"Oh, Suzanne!"

"Let's just think," she pleaded, "it is so beautiful."

They came to a station near Daleview, and walked over. On the way he slipped his arm about her waist, but, oh, so lightly.

"Suzanne," he asked, with a terrible yearning ache in his heart, "do you blame me? Can you?"

"Don't ask me," she pleaded, "not now. No, no."

He tried to press her a little more closely.

"Not now. I don't blame you."

He stopped as they neared the lawn and entered the house with a jesting air. Explanations about mixing in the crowd and getting lost were easy. Mrs. Dale smiled good naturedly. Suzanne went to her room.

CHAPTER VIII

Having involved himself thus far, seized upon and made his own this perfect flower of life, Eugene had but one thought, and that was to retain it. Now, of a sudden, had fallen from him all the weariness of years. To be in love again. To be involved in such a love, so wonderful, so perfect, so exquisite, it did not seem that life could really be so gracious as to have yielded him so much. What did it all mean, his upward rise during all these years? There had been seemingly but one triumph after another since the bitter days in Riverwood and after. The *World*, Summerfield's, The Kalvin Company, The United Magazine Corporation, Winfield, his beautiful apartment on the drive. Surely the gods were good. What did they mean? To give him fame, fortune and Suzanne into the bargain? Could such a thing really be? How could it be worked out? Would fate conspire and assist him so that he could be free of Angela—or— —

The thought of Angela to him in these days was a great pain. At bottom Eugene really did not dislike her, he never had. Years of living with her had produced an understanding and a relationship as strong and as keen as it might well be in some respects. Angela had always fancied since the Riverwood days that she really did not love Eugene truly any more—could not, that he was too self-centered and selfish; but this on her part was more of an illusion than a reality. She did care for him in an unselfish way from one point of view, in that she would sacrifice everything to his interests. From another point of view it was wholly selfish, for she wanted him to sacrifice everything for her in return. This he was not willing to do and had never been. He considered that his life was a larger thing than could be encompassed by any single matrimonial relationship. He wanted freedom of action and companionship, but he was afraid of Angela, afraid of society, in a way afraid of himself and what positive liberty might do to him. He felt sorry for Angela—for the intense suffering she would endure if he forced her in some way to release him—and at the same time he felt sorry for himself. The lure of beauty had never for one moment during all these years of upward mounting effort been stilled.

It is curious how things seem to conspire at times to produce a climax. One would think that tragedies like plants and flowers are planted as seeds and grow by various means and aids to a terrible maturity. Roses of hell are some lives, and they shine with all the lustre of infernal fires.

In the first place Eugene now began to neglect his office work thoroughly, for he could not fix his mind upon it any more than he could upon the affairs of the Sea Island Company, or upon his own home and Angela's illness. The morning after his South Beach experience with Suzanne and her curious reticence, he saw her for a little while upon the veranda of Daleview. She was not seemingly depressed, or at least, not noticeably so, and yet there was a gravity about her which indicated that a marked impression of some kind had been made upon her soul. She looked at him with wide frank eyes as she came out to him purposely to tell him that she was going with her mother and some friends to Tarrytown for the day.

"I have to go," she said. "Mamma has arranged it by phone."

"Then I won't see you any more here?"

"No."

"Do you love me, Suzanne?"

"Oh, yes, yes," she declared, and walked wearily to an angle of the wall where they could not be seen.

He followed her quickly, cautiously.

"Kiss me," he said, and she put her lips to his in a distraught frightened way. Then she turned and walked briskly off and he admired the robust swinging of her body. She was not tall, like himself, or small like Angela, but middle sized, full bodied, vigorous. He imagined now that she had a powerful soul in her, capable of great things, full of courage and strength. Once she was a little older, she would be very forceful and full of strong, direct thought.

He did not see her again for nearly ten days, and by that time he was nearly desperate. He was wondering all the time how he was to arrange this. He could not go on in this haphazard way, seeing her occasionally. Why she might leave town for the fall a little later and then what would he do? If her mother heard she would take her off to Europe and then would Suzanne forget? What a tragedy that would be! No, before that should happen, he would run away with her. He would realize all his investments and get away. He could not live without her. He must have her at any cost. What did the United Magazine Corporation amount to, anyway? He was tired of that work. Angela might have the Sea Island Realty Company's stock, if he could not dispose of it advantageously, or if he could, he would make provision for her out of what he should receive. He had some ready money—a few thousand dollars. This and his art—he could still paint—would sustain them. He would go to England with Suzanne, or to France. They would be happy if she really loved him and he thought she did. All this old life could go its way. It was a dreary thing, anyhow, without love. These were his first thoughts.

Later, he came to have different ones, but this was after he had talked to Suzanne again. It was a difficult matter to arrange. In a fit of desperation he called up Daleview one day, and asked if Miss Suzanne Dale was there. A servant answered, and in answer to the "who shall I say" he gave the name of a young man that he knew Suzanne knew. When she answered he said: "Listen, Suzanne! Can you hear very well?"

"Yes."

"Do you recognize my voice?"

"Yes."

"Please don't pronounce my name, will you?"

"No."

"Suzanne, I am crazy to see you. It has been ten days now. Are you going to be in town long?"

"I don't know. I think so."

"If anyone comes near you, Suzanne, simply hang up the receiver, and I will understand."

"Yes."

"If I came anywhere near your house in a car, could you come out and see me?"

"I don't know."

"Oh, Suzanne!"

"I'm not sure. I'll try. What time?"

"Do you know where the old fort road is, at Crystal Lake, just below you?"

"Yes."

"Do you know where the ice house is near the road there?"

"Yes."

"Could you come there?"

"What time?"

"At eleven tomorrow morning or two this afternoon or three."

"I might at two today."

"Oh, thank you for that. I'll wait for you, anyhow."

"All right. Good-bye."

And she hung up the receiver.

Eugene rejoiced at the fortunate outcome of this effort without thinking at first of the capable manner in which she had handled the situation. Truly he said afterwards she must be very courageous to think so directly and act so quickly, for it must have been very trying to her. This love of his was so new. Her position was so very difficult. And yet, on this first call when she had been suddenly put in touch with him, she had shown no signs of trepidation. Her voice had been firm and even, much more so than his, for he was nervously excited. She had taken in the situation at once and fallen into the ruse quite readily. Was she as simple as she seemed? Yes and no. She was simply capable, he thought and her capability had acted through her simplicity instantly.

At two the same day Eugene was there. He gave as an excuse to his secretary that he was going out for a business conference with a well-known author whose book he wished to obtain, and, calling a closed auto, but one not his own, journeyed to the rendezvous. He asked the man to drive down the road, making runs of half a mile to and fro while he sat in the shade of a clump of trees out of view of the road. Presently Suzanne came, bright and fresh as the morning, beautiful in a light purple walking costume of masterly design. She had on a large soft brimmed hat with long feathers of the same shade which became her exquisitely. She walked with an air of grace and freedom, and yet when he looked into her eyes, he saw a touch of trouble there.

"At last?" he said signaling her and smiling. "Come in here. My car is just up the road. Don't you think we had better get in? It's closed. We might be seen. How long can you stay?"

He took her in his arms and kissed her eagerly while she explained that she could not stay long. She had said she was going to the library, which her mother had endowed, for a book. She must be there by half past three or four at the least.

"Oh, we can talk a great deal by then," he said gaily. "Here comes the car. Let's get in."

He looked cautiously about, hailed it, and they stepped in quickly as it drew up.

"Perth Amboy," said Eugene, and they were off at high speed.

Once in the car all was perfect, for they could not be seen. He drew the shades partially and took her in his arms.

"Oh, Suzanne," he said, "how long it has seemed. How very long. Do you love me?"

"Yes, you know I do."

"Suzanne, how shall we arrange this? Are you going away soon? I must see you oftener."

"I don't know," she said. "I don't know what mama is thinking of doing. I know she wants to go up to Lenox in the fall."

"Oh, Pshaw!" commented Eugene wearily.

"Listen, Mr. Witla," said Suzanne thoughtfully. "You know we are running a terrible risk. What if Mrs. Witla should find out, or mama? It would be terrible."

"I know it," said Eugene. "I suppose I ought not to be acting in this way. But, oh, Suzanne, I am wild about you. I am not myself any longer. I don't know what I am. I only know that I love you, love you, love you!"

He gathered her in his arms and kissed her ecstatically. "How sweet you look. How beautiful you are. Oh, flower face! Myrtle Bloom! Angel Eyes! Divine Fire!" He hugged her in a long silent embrace, the while the car sped on.

"But what about us?" she asked, wide-eyed. "You know we are running a terrible risk. I was just thinking this morning when you called me up. It's dangerous, you know."

"Are you becoming sorry, Suzanne?"

"No."

"Do you love me?"

"You know I do."

"Then you will help me figure this out?"

"I want to. But listen, Mr. Witla, now listen to me. I want to tell you something." She was very solemn and quaint and sweet in this mood.

"I will listen to anything, baby mine, but don't call me Mr. Witla. Call me Eugene, will you?"

"Well, now, listen to me, Mr.—Mr.—Eugene."

"Not Mr. Eugene, just Eugene. Now say it. Eugene," he quoted his own name to her.

"Now listen to me, Mr.—now, listen to me, Eugene," she at last forced herself to say, and Eugene stopped her lips with his mouth.

"There," he said.

"Now listen to me," she went on urgently, "you know I am afraid mama will be terribly angry if she finds this out."

"Oh, will she?" interrupted Eugene jocosely.

Suzanne paid no attention to him.

"We have to be very careful. She likes you so much now that if she doesn't come across anything direct, she will never think of anything. She was talking about you only this morning."

"What was she saying?"

"Oh, what a nice man you are, and how able you are."

"Oh, nothing like that," replied Eugene jestingly.

"Yes, she did. And I think Mrs. Witla likes me. I can meet you sometimes when I'm there, but we must be so careful. I mustn't stay out long today. I want to think things out, too. You know I'm having a real hard time thinking about this."

Eugene smiled. Her innocence was so delightful to him, so naïve.

"What do you mean by thinking things out, Suzanne?" asked Eugene curiously. He was interested in the workings of her young mind, which seemed so fresh and wonderful to him. It was so delightful to find this paragon of beauty so responsive, so affectionate and helpful and withal so thoughtful. She was somewhat like a delightful toy to him, and he held her as reverently in awe as though she were a priceless vase.

"You know I want to think what I'm doing. I have to. It seems so terrible to me at times and yet you know, you know——"

"I know what?" he asked, when she paused.

"I don't know why I shouldn't if I want to—if I love you."

Eugene looked at her curiously. This attempt at analysis of life, particularly in relation to so trying and daring a situation as this, astonished him. He had fancied Suzanne more or less thoughtless and harmless as yet, big potentially, but uncertain and vague. Here she was thinking about this most difficult problem almost more directly than he was and apparently with more courage. He was astounded, but more than that, intensely interested. What had become of her terrific fright of ten days before? What was it she was thinking about exactly?

"What a curious girl you are," he said.

"Why am I?" she asked.

"Because you are. I didn't think you could think so keenly yet. I thought you would some day. But, how have you reasoned this out?"

"Did you ever read 'Anna Karénina'?" she asked him meditatively.

"Yes," he said, wondering that she should have read it at her age.

"What did you think of that?"

"Oh, it shows what happens, as a rule, when you fly in the face of convention," he said easily, wondering at the ability of her brain.

"Do you think things must happen that way?"

"No, I don't think they must happen that way. There are lots of cases where people do go against the conventions and succeed. I don't know. It appears to be all a matter of time and chance. Some do and some don't. If you are strong enough or clever enough to 'get away with it,' as they say, you will. If you aren't, you won't. What makes you ask?"

"Well," she said, pausing, her lips parted, her eyes fixed on the floor, "I was thinking that it needn't necessarily be like that, do you think? It could be different?"

"Yes, it could be," he said thoughtfully, wondering if it really could.

"Because if it couldn't," she went on, "the price would be too high. It isn't worth while."

"You mean, you mean," he said, looking at her, "that you would." He was thinking that she was deliberately contemplating making a sacrifice of herself for him. Something in her thoughtful, self-debating, meditative manner made him think so.

Suzanne looked out of the window and slowly nodded her head. "Yes," she said, solemnly, "if it could be arranged. Why not? I don't see why."

Her face was a perfect blossom of beauty, as she spoke. Eugene wondered whether he was waking or sleeping. Suzanne reasoning so! Suzanne reading "Anna Karénina" and philosophizing so! Basing a course of action on theorizing in connection with books and life, and in the face of such terrible evidence as "Anna Karénina" presented to the contrary of this proposition. Would wonders ever cease?

"You know," she said after a time, "I think mama wouldn't mind, Eugene. She likes you. I've heard her say so lots of times. Besides I've heard her talk this way about other people. She thinks people oughtn't to marry unless they love each other very much. I don't think she thinks it's necessary for people to marry at all unless they want to. We might live together if we wished, you know."

Eugene himself had heard Mrs. Dale question the marriage system, but only in a philosophic way. He did not take much stock in her social maunderings. He did not know what she might be privately saying to Suzanne, but he did not believe it could be very radical, or at least seriously so.

"Don't you take any stock in what your mother says, Suzanne," he observed, studying her pretty face. "She doesn't mean it, at least, she doesn't mean it as far as you are concerned. She's merely talking. If she thought anything were going to happen to you, she'd change her mind pretty quick."

"No, I don't think so," replied Suzanne thoughtfully. "You know, I think I know mama better than she knows herself. She always talks of me as a little girl, but I can rule her in lots of things. I've done it."

Eugene stared at Suzanne in amazement. He could scarcely believe his ears. She was beginning so early to think so deeply on the social and executive sides of life. Why should her mind be trying to dominate her mother's?

"Suzanne," he observed, "you must be careful what you do or say. Don't rush into talking of this pellmell. It's dangerous. I love you, but we shall have to go slow. If Mrs. Witla should learn of this, she would be crazy. If your mother should suspect, she would take you away to Europe somewhere, very likely. Then I wouldn't get to see you at all."

"Oh, no, she wouldn't," replied Suzanne determinedly. "You know, I know mama better than you think I do. I can rule her, I tell you. I know I can. I've done it."

She tossed her head in an exquisitely pretty way which upset Eugene's reasoning faculties. He could not think and look at her.

"Suzanne," he said, drawing her to him. "You are exquisite, extreme, the last word in womanhood for me. To think of your reasoning so—you, Suzanne."

"Why, why," she asked, with pretty parted lips and uplifted eyebrows, "why shouldn't I think?"

"Oh, yes, certainly, we all do, but not so deeply, necessarily, Flower Face."

"Well, we must think now," she said simply.

"Yes, we must think now," he replied; "would you really share a studio with me if I were to take one? I don't know of any other way quite at present."

"I would, if I knew how to manage it," she replied. "Mama is queer. She's so watchful. She thinks I'm a child and you know I am not at all. I don't understand mama. She talks one thing and does another. I would rather do and not talk. Don't you think so?" He stared. "Still, I think I can fix it. Leave it to me."

"And if you can you'll come to me?"

"Oh, yes, yes," exclaimed Suzanne ecstatically, turning to him all at once and catching his face between her hands. "Oh!"—she looked into his eyes and dreamed.

"But we must be careful," he cautioned. "We musn't do anything rash."

"I won't," said Suzanne.

"And I won't, of course," he replied.

They paused again while he watched her.

"I might make friends with Mrs. Witla," she observed, after a time. "She likes me, doesn't she?"

"Yes," said Eugene.

"Mama doesn't object to my going up there, and I could let you know."

"That's all right. Do that," said Eugene. "Oh, please do, if you can. Did you notice whose name I used today?"

"Yes," she said. "You know Mr. Witla, Eugene, I thought you might call me up?"

"Did you?" he asked, smiling.

"Yes."

"You give me courage, Suzanne," he said, drawing close to her. "You're so confident, so apparently carefree. The world hasn't touched your spirit."

"When I'm away from you, though, I'm not so courageous," she replied. "I've been thinking terrible things. I get frightened sometimes."

"But you mustn't, sweet, I need you so. Oh, how I need you."

The "Genius" Book III The Revolt | 67

She looked at him, and for the first time smoothed his hair with her hand.

"You know, Eugene, you're just like a boy to me."

"Do I seem so?" he asked, comforted greatly.

"I couldn't love you as I do if you weren't."

He drew her to him again and kissed her anew.

"Can't we repeat these rides every few days?" he asked.

"Yes, if I'm here, maybe."

"It's all right to call you up if I use another name?"

"Yes, I think so."

"Let's choose new names for each, so that we'll know who's calling. You shall be Jenny Lind and I Allan Poe." Then they fell to ardent love-making until the time came when they had to return. For him, so far as work was concerned, the afternoon was gone.

CHAPTER IX

There followed now a series of meetings contrived with difficulty, fraught with danger, destructive of his peace of mind, of his recently acquired sense of moral and commercial responsibility, of the sense of singleness of purpose and interest in his editorial and publishing world, which had helped him so much recently. The meetings nevertheless were full of such intense bliss for him that it seemed as though he were a thousand times repaid for all the subtlety and folly he was practicing. There were times when he came to the ice house in a hired car, others when she notified him by phone or note to his office of times when she was coming in to town to stay. He took her in his car one afternoon to Blue Sea when he was sure no one would encounter him. He persuaded Suzanne to carry a heavy veil, which could be adjusted at odd moments. Another time—several, in fact she came to the apartment in Riverside Drive, ostensibly to see how Mrs. Witla was getting along, but really, of course, to see Eugene. Suzanne did not really care so much for Angela, although she did not dislike her. She thought she was an interesting woman, though perhaps not a happy mate for Eugene. The latter had told her not so much that he was unhappy as that he was out of love. He loved her now, Suzanne, and only her.

The problem as to where this relationship was to lead to was complicated by another problem, which Eugene knew nothing of, but which was exceedingly important. For Angela, following the career of Eugene with extreme pleasure and satisfaction on the commercial side, and fear and distrust on the social and emotional sides, had finally decided to risk the uncertain outcome of a child in connection with Eugene and herself, and to give him something which would steady his life and make him realize his responsibilities and offer him something gladdening besides social entertainment and the lure of beauty in youth. She had never forgotten the advice which Mrs. Sanifore and her physician had given her in Philadelphia, nor had she ever ceased her cogitations as to what the probable effect of a child would be. Eugene needed something of this sort to balance him. His position in the world was too tenuous, his temperament too variable. A child—a little girl, she hoped, for he always liked little girls and made much of them—would quiet him. If she could only have a little girl now!

Some two months before her illness, while Eugene was becoming, all unsuspected by her, so frenzied about Suzanne, she had relaxed, or rather abandoned, her old-time precautions entirely, and had recently begun to suspect that her fears, or hopes, or both, were about to be realized. Owing to her subsequent illness and its effect on her heart, she was not very happy now. She was naturally very uncertain as to the outcome as well as to how Eugene would take it. He had never expressed a desire for a child, but she had no thought of telling him as yet, for she wanted to be absolutely sure. If she were not correct in her suspicions, and got well, he would attempt to dissuade her for the future. If she were, he could not help himself. Like all women in that condition, she was beginning to long for sympathy and consideration and to note more keenly the drift of Eugene's mind toward a world which did not very much concern her. His interest in Suzanne had puzzled her a little, though she was not greatly troubled about her because Mrs. Dale appeared to be so thoughtful about her daughter. Times were changing. Eugene had been going out much alone. A child would help. It was high time it came.

When Suzanne had started coming with her mother, Angela thought nothing of it; but on the several occasions when Suzanne called during her illness, and Eugene had been present, she felt as though there might easily spring up something between them. Suzanne was so charming. Once as she lay thinking after Suzanne had left the room to go into the studio for a few moments, she heard Eugene jesting with her and laughing keenly. Suzanne's laugh, or gurgling giggle, was most infectious. It was so easy, too, for Eugene to make her laugh, for his type of jesting was to her the essence of fun. It seemed to her that there was something almost overgay in the way they carried on. On each occasion when she was present, Eugene proposed that he take Suzanne home in his car, and this set her thinking.

There came a time when, Angela being well enough from her rheumatic attack, Eugene invited a famous singer, a tenor, who had a charming repertoire of songs, to come to his apartment and sing. He had met him at a social affair in Brooklyn with which Winfield had something to do. A number of people were invited—Mrs. Dale, Suzanne, and Kinroy, among others; but Mrs. Dale could not come, and as Suzanne had an appointment for the next morning, Sunday, in the city, she decided to stay at the Witlas. This pleased Eugene immensely. He had bought a sketching book which he had begun to fill with sketches of Suzanne from memory and these he wanted to show her. Besides, he wanted her to hear this singer's beautiful voice.

The company was interesting. Kinroy brought Suzanne early and left. Eugene and Suzanne, after she had exchanged greetings with Angela, sat out on the little stone balcony overlooking the river and exchanged loving thoughts. He was constantly holding her hand when no one was looking and stealing kisses. After a time the company began to arrive, and finally the singer himself. The trained nurse, with Eugene's assistance, helped Angela forward, who listened enraptured to the songs. Suzanne and Eugene, swept by the charm of some of them, looked at each other with that burning gaze which love alone understands. To Eugene Suzanne's face was a perfect flower of hypnotic influence. He could scarcely keep his eyes off her for a moment at a time. The singer ceased, the company departed. Angela was left crying over the beauty of "The Erlking," the last song rendered. She went back to her room, and Suzanne ostensibly departed for hers. She came out to say a few final words to Mrs. Witla, then came through the studio to go to her own room again. Eugene was there waiting. He caught her in his arms, kissing her silently. They pretended to strike up a conventional conversation, and he invited her to sit out on the stone balcony for a few last moments. The moon was so beautiful over the river.

"Don't!" she said, when he gathered her in his arms, in the shadow of the night outside. "She might come."

"No," he said eagerly.

They listened, but there was no sound. He began an easy pretence to talk, the while stroking her pretty arm, which was bare. Insanity over her beauty, the loveliness of the night, the charm of the music, had put him beside himself. He drew her into his arms in spite of her protest, only to have Angela suddenly appear at the other end of the room where the door was. There was no concealing anything she saw. She came rapidly forward, even as Suzanne jumped up, a sickening rage in her heart, a sense of her personal condition strong in her mind, a sense of something terrible and climacteric in the very air, but she was still too ill to risk a great demonstration or to declare herself fully. It seemed now once more the whole world had fallen about her ears, for because of her plans and in spite of all her suspicions, she had not been ready to believe that Eugene would really trespass again. She had come to surprise him, if possible, but she had not actually expected to, had hoped not to. Here was this beautiful girl, the victim of his wiles, and here was she involved by her own planning, while Eugene, shame-faced, she supposed, stood by ready to have this ridiculous liaison nipped in the bud. She did not propose to expose herself to Suzanne if she could help it, but sorrow for herself, shame for him, pity for Suzanne in a way, the desire to preserve the shell of appearances, which was now, after this, so utterly empty for her though so important for the child, caused her to swell with her old-time rage, and yet to hold it in check. Six years before she would have raged to his face, but time had softened her in this respect. She did not see the value of brutal words.

"Suzanne," she said, standing erect in the filtered gloom of the room which was still irradiated by the light of the moon in the west, "how could you! I thought so much better of you."

Her face, thinned by her long illness and her brooding over her present condition, was still beautiful in a spiritual way. She wore a pale yellow and white flowered dressing gown of filmy, lacy texture, and her long hair, done in braids by the nurse, was hanging down her back like the Gretchen she was to him years before. Her hands were thin and pale, but artistic, and her face drawn in all the wearisome agony of a mater dolorosa.

"Why, why," exclaimed Suzanne, terribly shaken out of her natural fine poise for the moment but not forgetful of the dominating thought in her mind, "I love him; that's why, Mrs. Witla."

"Oh, no, you don't! you only think you love him, as so many women have before you, Suzanne," said Angela frozenly, the thought of the coming child always with her. If she had only told him before! "Oh, shame, in my house, and you a young, supposedly innocent girl! What do you suppose your mother would think if I should call her up and tell her now? Or your brother? You knew he was a married man. I might excuse you if it weren't for that if you hadn't known me and hadn't accepted my hospitality. As for him, there is no need of my talking to him. This is an old story with him, Suzanne. He has done this with other women before you, and he will do it with other women after you. It is one of the things I have to bear for having married a man of so-called talent. Don't think, Suzanne, when you tell me you love him, that you tell me anything new. I have heard that story before from other women. You are not the first, and you will not be the last."

Suzanne looked at Eugene inquiringly, vaguely, helplessly, wondering if all this were so.

Eugene hardened under Angela's cutting accusation, but he was not at all sure at first what he ought to do. He wondered for the moment whether he ought not to abandon Suzanne and fall back into his old state, dreary as it might seem to him; but the sight of her pretty face, the sound of Angela's cutting voice, determined him quickly. "Angela," he began, recovering his composure the while Suzanne contemplated him, "why do you talk that way? You know that what you say isn't true. There was one other woman. I will tell Suzanne about her. There were several before I married you. I will tell her about them. But my life is a shell, and you know it. This apartment is a shell. Absolutely it means nothing at all to me. There has been no love between us, certainly not on my part, for years, and you know that. You have practically confessed to me from time to time that you do not care for me. I haven't deceived this girl. I am glad to tell her now how things stand."

"How things stand! How things stand!" exclaimed Angela, blazing and forgetting herself for the moment. "Will you tell her what an excellent, faithful husband you have made me? Will you tell her how honestly you have kept your word pledged to me at the altar? Will you tell her how I have worked and sacrificed for you through all these years? How I have been repaid by just such things as this? I'm sorry for you, Suzanne, more than anything else," went on Angela, wondering whether she should tell Eugene here and now of her condition but fearing he would not believe it. It seemed so much like melodrama. "You are just a silly little girl duped by an expert man, who thinks he loves you for a little while, but who really doesn't. He will get over it. Tell me frankly what do you expect to get out of it all? You can't marry him. I won't give him a divorce. I can't, as he will know later, and he has no grounds for obtaining one. Do you expect to be his mistress? You have no hope of ever being anything else. Isn't that a nice ambition for a girl of your standing? And you are supposed to be virtuous! Oh, I am ashamed of you, if you are not! I am sorry for your mother. I am astonished to think that you would so belittle yourself."

Suzanne had heard the "I can't," but she really did not know how to interpret it. It had never occurred to her that there could ever be a child here to complicate matters. Eugene told her that he was unhappy, that there was nothing between him and Angela and never could be.

"But I love him, Mrs. Witla," said Suzanne simply and rather dramatically. She was tense, erect, pale and decidedly beautiful. It was a great problem to have so quickly laid upon her shoulders.

"Don't talk nonsense, Suzanne!" said Angela angrily and desperately. "Don't deceive yourself and stick to a silly pose. You are acting now. You're talking as you think you ought to talk, as you have seen people talk in plays. This is my husband. You are in my home. Come, get your things. I will call up your mother and tell her how things stand, and she will send her auto for you."

"Oh, no," said Suzanne, "you can't do that! I can't go back there, if you tell her. I must go out in the world and get something to do until I can straighten out my own affairs. I won't be able to go home any more. Oh, what shall I do?"

"Be calm, Suzanne," said Eugene determinedly, taking her hand and looking at Angela defiantly. "She isn't going to call up your mother, and she isn't going to tell your mother. You are going to stay here, as you intended, and tomorrow you are going where you thought you were going."

"Oh, no, she isn't!" said Angela angrily, starting for the phone. "She is going home. I'm going to call her mother."

Suzanne stirred nervously. Eugene put his hand in hers to reassure her.

"Oh, no, you aren't," he said determinedly. "She isn't going home, and you are not going to touch that phone. If you do, a number of things are going to happen, and they are going to happen quick."

He moved between her and the telephone receiver, which hung in the hall outside the studio and toward which she was edging.

Angela paused at the ominous note in his voice, the determined quality of his attitude. She was surprised and amazed at the almost rough manner in which he put her aside. He had taken Suzanne's hand, he, her husband, and was begging her to be calm.

"Oh, Eugene," said Angela desperately, frightened and horrified, her anger half melted in her fears, "you don't know what you are doing! Suzanne doesn't. She won't want anything to do with you when she does. Young as she is, she will have too much womanhood."

"What are you talking about?" asked Eugene desperately. He had no idea of what Angela was driving at, not the faintest suspicion. "What are you talking about?" he repeated grimly.

"Let me say just one word to you alone, not here before Suzanne, just one, and then perhaps you will be willing to let her go home tonight."

Angela was subtle in this, a little bit wicked. She was not using her advantage in exactly the right spirit.

"What is it?" demanded Eugene sourly, expecting some trick. He had so long gnawed at the chains which bound him that the thought of any additional lengths which might be forged irritated him greatly. "Why can't you tell it here? What difference can it make?"

"It ought to make all the difference in the world. Let me say it to you alone."

Suzanne, who wondered what it could be, walked away. She was wondering what it was that Angela had to tell. The latter's manner was not exactly suggestive of the weighty secret she bore. When Suzanne was gone, Angela whispered to him.

"It's a lie!" said Eugene vigorously, desperately, hopelessly. "It's something you've trumped up for the occasion. It's just like you to say that, to do it! Pah! I don't believe it. It's a lie! It's a lie! You know it's a lie!"

"It's the truth!" said Angela angrily, pathetically, outraged in her every nerve and thought by the reception which this fact had received, and desperate to think that the announcement of a coming child by him should be received in this manner under such circumstances that it should be forced from her as a last resort, only to be received with derision and scorn. "It's the truth, and you ought to be ashamed to say that to me. What can I expect from a man, though, who would introduce another woman into his own home as you have tonight?" To think that she should be reduced to such a situation as this so suddenly! It was impossible to argue it with him here. She was ashamed now that she had introduced it at this time. He would not believe her, anyhow now, she saw that. It only enraged him and her. He was too wild. This seemed to infuriate him—to condemn her in his mind as a trickster and a sharper, someone who was using unfair means to hold him. He almost jumped away from her in disgust, and she realized that she had struck an awful blow which apparently, to him, had some elements of unfairness in it.

"Won't you have the decency after this to send her away?" she pleaded aloud, angrily, eagerly, bitterly.

Eugene was absolutely in a fury of feeling. If ever he thoroughly hated and despised Angela, he did so at that moment. To think that she should have done anything like this! To think that she should have complicated this problem of weariness of her with a thing like this! How cheap it was, how shabby! It showed the measure of the woman, to bring a child into the world, regardless of the interests of the child, in order to hold him against his will. Damn! Hell! God damn such a complicated, rotten world! No, she was lying. She could not hold him that way. It was a horrible, low, vile trick. He would have nothing to do with her. He would show her. He would leave her. He would show her that this sort of thing would not work with him. It was like every other petty thing she had ever done. Never, never, never, would he let this stand in the way. Oh, what a mean, cruel, wretched thing to do!

Suzanne came back while they were arguing. She half suspected what it was all about, but she did not dare to act or think clearly. The events of this night were too numerous, too complicated. Eugene had said so forcibly it was a lie whatever it was, that she half believed him. That was a sign surely of the little affection that existed between him and Angela. Angela was not crying. Her face was hard, white, drawn.

"I can't stay here," said Suzanne dramatically to Eugene. "I will go somewhere. I had better go to a hotel for the night. Will you call a car?"

"Listen to me, Suzanne," said Eugene vigorously and determinedly. "You love me, don't you?"

"You know I do," she replied.

Angela stirred sneeringly.

"Then you will stay here. I want you to pay no attention to anything she may say or declare. She has told me a lie tonight. I know why. Don't let her deceive you. Go to your room and your bed. I want to talk to you tomorrow. There is no need of your leaving tonight. There is plenty of room here. It's silly. You're here now—stay."

"But I don't think I'd better stay," said Suzanne nervously.

Eugene took her hand reassuringly.

"Listen to me," he began.

"But she won't stay," said Angela.

"But she will," said Eugene; "and if she don't stay, she goes with me. I will take her home."

"Oh, no, you won't!" replied Angela.

"Listen," said Eugene angrily. "This isn't six years ago, but now. I'm master of this situation, and she stays here. She stays here, or she goes with me and you look to the future as best you may. I love her. I'm not going to give her up, and if you want to make trouble, begin now. The house comes down on your head, not mine."

"Oh!" said Angela, half terrified, "what do I hear?"

"Just that. Now you go to your room. Suzanne will go to hers. I will go to mine. We will not have any more fighting here tonight. The jig is up. The die is cast. I'm through. Suzanne comes to me, if she will."

Angela walked to her room through the studio, stricken by the turn things had taken, horrified by the thoughts in her mind, unable to convince Eugene, unable to depose Suzanne, her throat dry and hot, her hands shaking, her heart beating fitfully; she felt as if her brain would burst, her heart break actually, not emotionally. She thought Eugene had gone crazy, and yet now, for the first time in her married life, she realized what a terrible mistake she had made in always trying to drive him. It hadn't worked tonight, her rage, her domineering, critical attitude. It had failed her completely, and also this scheme, this beautiful plan, this trump card on which she had placed so much reliance for a happy life, this child which she had hoped to play so effectively. He didn't believe her. He wouldn't even admit its possibility. He didn't admire her for it. He despised her! He looked on it as a trick. Oh, what an unfortunate thing it had been to mention it! And yet Suzanne must understand, she must know, she would never countenance anything like this. But what would he do? He was positively livid with rage. What fine auspices these were under which to usher a child into the world! She stared feverishly before her, and finally began to cry hopelessly.

Eugene stood in the hall beside Suzanne after she had gone. His face was drawn, his eyes hunted, his hair tousled. He looked grim and determined in his way, stronger than he had ever looked before.

"Suzanne," he said, taking the latter by her two arms and staring into her eyes, "she has told me a lie, a lie, a cold, mean, cruel lie. She'll tell it you shortly. She says she is with child by me. It isn't so. She couldn't have one. If she did, it would kill her. She would have had one long ago if she could have. I know her. She thinks this will frighten me. She thinks it will drive you away. Will it? It's a lie, do you hear me, whatever she says. It's a lie, and she knows it. Ough!" He dropped her left arm and pulled at his neck. "I can't stand this. You won't leave me. You won't believe her, will you?"

Suzanne stared into his distraught face, his handsome, desperate, significant eyes. She saw the woe there, the agony, and was sympathetic. He seemed wonderfully worthy of love, unhappy, unfortunately pursued; and yet she was frightened. Still she had promised to love him.

"No," she said fixedly, her eyes speaking a dramatic confidence.

"You won't leave here tonight?"

"No."

She smoothed his cheek with her hand.

"You will come and walk with me in the morning? I have to talk with you."

"Yes."

"Don't be afraid. Just lock your door if you are. She won't bother you. She won't do anything. She is afraid of me. She may want to talk with you, but I am close by. Do you still love me?"

"Yes."

"Will you come to me if I can arrange it?"

"Yes."

"Even in the face of what she says?"

"Yes; I don't believe her. I believe you. What difference could it make, anyhow? You don't love her."

"No," he said; "no, no, no! I never have." He drew her into his arms wearily, relievedly. "Oh, Flower Face," he said, "don't give me up! Don't grieve. Try not to, anyhow. I have been bad, as she says, but I love you. I love you, and I will stake all on that. If all this must fall about our heads, then let it fall. I love you."

Suzanne stroked his cheek with her hands nervously. She was deathly pale, frightened, but somehow courageous through it all. She caught strength from his love.

"I love you," she said.

"Yes," he replied. "You won't give me up?"

"No, I won't," she said, not really understanding the depth of her own mood. "I will be true."

"Things will be better tomorrow," he said, somewhat more quietly. "We will be calmer. We will walk and talk. You won't leave without me?"

"No."

"Please don't; for I love you, and we must talk and plan."

CHAPTER X

The introduction of this astonishing fact in connection with Angela was so unexpected, so morally diverting and peculiar that though Eugene denied it, half believed she was lying, he was harassed by the thought that she might be telling the truth. It was so unfair, though, was all he could think, so unkind! It never occurred to him that it was accidental, as indeed it was not, but only that it was a trick, sharp, cunning, ill-timed for him, just the thing calculated to blast his career and tie him down to the old régime when he wanted most to be free. A new life was dawning for him now. For the first time in his life he was to have a woman after his own heart, so young, so beautiful, so intellectual, so artistic! With Suzanne by his side, he was about to plumb the depths of all the joys of living. Without her, life was to be dark and dreary, and here was Angela coming forward at the critical moment disrupting this dream as best she could by the introduction of a child that she did not want, and all to hold him against his will. If ever he hated her for trickery and sharp dealing, he did so now. What would the effect on Suzanne be? How would he convince her that it was a trick? She must understand; she would. She would not let this miserable piece of chicanery stand between him and her. He turned in his bed wearily after he had gone to it, but he could not sleep. He had to say something, do something. So he arose, slipped on a dressing gown, and went to Angela's room.

That distraught soul, for all her determination and fighting capacity, was enduring for the second time in her life the fires of hell. To think that in spite of all her work, her dreams, this recent effort to bring about peace and happiness, perhaps at the expense of her own life, she was compelled to witness a scene like this. Eugene was trying to get free. He was obviously determined to do so. This scandalous relationship, when had it begun? Would her effort to hold him fail? It looked that way, and yet surely Suzanne, when she knew, when she understood, would leave him. Any woman would.

Her head ached, her hands were hot, she fancied she might be suffering a terrible nightmare, she was so sick and weak; but, no, this was her room. A little while ago she was sitting in her husband's studio, surrounded by friends, the object of much solicitude, Eugene apparently considerate and thoughtful of her, a beautiful programme being rendered for their special benefit. Now she was lying here in her room, a despised wife, an outcast from affection and happiness, the victim of some horrible sorcery of fate whereby another woman stood in her place in Eugene's affection. To see Suzanne, proud in her young beauty, confronting her with bold eyes, holding her husband's hand, saying in what seemed to her to be brutal, or insane, or silly melodramatic make-believe, "But I love him, Mrs. Witla," was maddening. Oh, God! Oh, God! Would her tortures never cease? Must all her beautiful dreams come to nothing? Would Eugene leave her, as he so violently said a little while ago? She had never seen him like this. It was terrible to see him so determined, so cold and brutal. His voice had actually been harsh and guttural, something she had never known before in him.

She trembled as she thought, and then great flashes of rage swept her only to be replaced by rushes of fear. She was in such a terrific position. The woman was with him, young, defiant, beautiful. She had heard him call to her, had heard them talking. Once she thought that now would be the time to murder him, Suzanne, herself, the coming life and end it all; but at this critical moment, having been sick and having grown so much older, with this problem of the coming life before her, she had no chart to go by. She tried to console herself with the thought that he must abandon his course, that he would when the true force of what she had revealed had had time to sink home; but it had not had time yet. Would it before he did anything rash? Would it before he had completely compromised himself and Suzanne? Judging from her talk and his, he had not as yet, or she thought not. What was he going to do? What was he going to do?

Angela feared as she lay there that in spite of her revelation he might really leave her immediately. There might readily spring a terrible public scandal out of all this. The mockery of their lives laid bare; the fate of the child jeopardized; Eugene, Suzanne, and herself disgraced, though she had little thought for Suzanne. Suzanne might get him, after all. She might accidentally be just hard and cold enough. The world might possibly forgive him. She herself might die! What an end, after all her dreams of something bigger, better, surer! Oh, the pity, the agony of this! The terror and horror of a wrecked life!

And then Eugene came into the room.

He was haggard, stormy-eyed, thoughtful, melancholy, as he entered. He stood in the doorway first, intent, then clicked a little night-lamp button which threw on a very small incandescent light near the head of Angela's bed, and then sat down in a rocking-chair which the nurse had placed near the medicine table. Angela had so much improved that no night nurse was needed—only a twelve-hour one.

"Well," he said solemnly but coldly, when he saw her pale, distraught, much of her old, youthful beauty still with her, "you think you have scored a splendid trick, don't you? You think you have sprung a trap? I simply came in here to tell you that you haven't—that you have only seen the beginning of the end. You say you are going to have a child. I don't believe it. It's a lie, and you know it's a lie. You saw that there was an end coming to all this state of weariness some time, and this is your answer. Well, you've played one trick too many, and you've played it in vain. You lose. I win this time. I'm going to be free now, I want to say to you, and I am going to be free if I have to turn everything upside down. I don't care if there were seventeen prospective children instead of one. It's a lie, in the first place; but if it isn't, it's a trick, and I'm not going to be tricked any longer. I've had all I want of domination and trickery and cheap ideas. I'm through now, do you hear me? I'm through."

He felt his forehead with a nervous hand. His head ached, he was half sick. This was such a dreary pit to find himself in, this pit of matrimony, chained by a domineering wife and a trickily manœuvred child. His child! What a mockery at this stage of his life! How he hated the thought of that sort of thing, how cheap it all seemed!

Angela, who was wide-eyed, flushed, exhausted, lying staring on her pillow, asked in a weary, indifferent voice: "What do you want me to do, Eugene, leave you?"

"I'll tell you, Angela," he said sepulchrally, "I don't know what I want you to do just at this moment. The old life is all over. It's as dead as dead can be. For eleven or twelve years now I have lived with you, knowing all the while that I was living a lie. I have never really loved you since we were married. You know that. I may have loved you in the beginning, yes, I did, and at Blackwood, but that was a long, long while ago. I never should have married you. It was a mistake, but I did, and I've paid for it, inch by inch. You have, too. You have insisted all along that I ought to love you. You have browbeaten and abused me for something I could no more do than I could fly. Now, at this last minute, you introduce a child to hold me. I know why you have done it. You imagine that in some way you have been appointed by God to be my mentor and guardian. Well, I tell you now that you haven't. It's all over. If there were fifty children, it's all over. Suzanne isn't going to believe any such cheap story as that, and if she did she wouldn't leave me. She knows why you do it. All the days of weariness are over for me, all the days of being afraid. I'm not an ordinary man, and I'm not going to live an ordinary life. You have always insisted on holding me down to the little, cheap conventions as you have understood them. Out in Wisconsin, out in Blackwood. Nothing doing. It's all over from now on. Everything's over. This house, my job, my real estate deal—everything. I don't care what your condition is. I love this girl in there, and I'm going to have her. Do you hear me? I love her, and I'm going to have her. She's mine. She suits me. I love her, and no power under God is going to stay me. Now you think this child proposition you have fixed up is going to stay me, but you are going to find out that it can't, that it won't. It's a trick, and I know it, and you know it. It's too late. It might have last year, or two years ago, or three, but it won't work now. You have played your last card. That girl in there belongs to me, and I'm going to have her."

Again he smoothed his face in a weary way, pausing to sway the least bit in his chair. His teeth were set, his eyes hard. Consciously he realized that it was a terrible situation that confronted him, hard to wrestle with.

Angela gazed at him with the eyes of one who is not quite sure that she even sees aright. She knew that Eugene had developed. He had become stronger, more urgent, more defiant, during all these years in which he had been going upward. He was no more like the Eugene who had clung to her for companionship in the dark days at Biloxi and elsewhere than a child is like a grown man. He was harder, easier in his manner, more indifferent, and yet, until now, there had never been a want of traces of the old Eugene. What had become of them so suddenly? Why was he so raging, so bitter? This girl, this foolish, silly, selfish girl, with her Circe gift of beauty, by tolerance of his suit, by yielding, perhaps by throwing herself at Eugene's head, had done this thing. She had drawn him away from her in spite of the fact that they had appeared to be happily mated. Suzanne did not know that they were not. In this mood he might actually leave her, even as she was, with child. It depended on the girl. Unless she could influence her, unless she could bring pressure to bear in some way, Eugene might readily be lost to her, and then what a tragedy! She could not afford to have him go now. Why, in six months— —! She shivered at the thought of all the misery a separation would entail. His position, their child, society, this apartment. Dear God, it would drive her crazy if he were to desert her now!

"Oh, Eugene," she said quite sadly and without any wrath in her voice at this moment, for she was too torn, terrified and disheveled in spirit to feel anything save a haunting sense of fear, "you don't know what a terrible mistake you are making. I did do this thing on purpose, Eugene. It is true. Long ago in Philadelphia with Mrs. Sanifore I went to a physician to see if it were possible that I might have a child. You know that I always thought that I couldn't. Well, he told me that I could. I went because I thought that you needed something like that, Eugene, to balance you. I knew you didn't want one. I thought you would be angry when I told you. I didn't act on it for a long while. I didn't want one myself. I hoped that it might be a little girl if ever there was one, because I know that you like little girls. It seems silly now in the face of what has happened tonight. I see what a mistake I have made. I see what the mistake is, but I didn't mean it evilly, Eugene. I didn't. I wanted to hold you, to bind you to me in some way, to help you. Do you utterly blame me, Eugene? I'm your wife, you know."

He stirred irritably, and she paused, scarcely knowing how to go on. She could see how terribly irritated he was, how sick at heart, and yet she resented this attitude on his part. It was so hard to endure when all along she had fancied that she had so many just claims on him, moral, social, other claims, which he dare not ignore. Here she was now, sick, weary, pleading with him for something that ought justly be hers—and this coming child's!

"Oh, Eugene," she said quite sadly, and still without any wrath in her voice, "please think before you make a mistake. You don't really love this girl, you only think you do. You think she is beautiful and good and sweet and you are going to tear everything up and leave me, but you don't love her, and you are going to find it out. You don't love anyone, Eugene. You can't. You are too selfish. If you had any real love in you, some of it would have come out to me, for I have tried to be all that a good wife should be, but it has been all in vain. I've known you haven't liked me all these years. I've seen it in your eyes, Eugene. You have never come very close to me as a lover should unless you had to or you couldn't avoid me. You have been cold and indifferent, and now that I look back I see that it has made me so. I have been cold and hard. I've tried to steel myself to match what I thought was your steeliness, and now I see what it has done for me. I'm sorry. But as for her, you don't love her and you won't. She's too young. She hasn't any ideas that agree with yours. You think she's soft and gentle, and yet big and wise, but do you think if she had been that she could have stood up there as she did tonight and looked me in the eyes—me, your wife—and told me that she loved you—you, my husband? Do you think if she had any shame she would be in there now knowing what she does, for I suppose you have told her? What kind of a girl is that, anyway? You call her good? Good! Would a good girl do anything like that?"

"What is the use of arguing by appearances?" asked Eugene, who had interrupted her with exclamations of opposition and bitter comments all through the previous address. "The situation is one which makes anything look bad. She didn't intend to be put in a position where she would have to tell you that she loved me. She didn't come here to let me make love to her in this apartment. I made love to her. She's in love with me, and I made her love me. I didn't know of this other thing. If I had, it wouldn't have made any difference. However, let that be as it will. So it is. I'm in love with her, and that's all there is to it."

Angela stared at the wall. She was half propped up on a pillow, and had no courage now to speak of and no fighting strength.

"I know what it is with you, Eugene," she said, after a time; "it's the yoke that galls. It isn't me only; it's anyone. It's marriage. You don't want to be married. It would be the same with any woman who might ever have loved and married you, or with any number of children. You would want to get rid of her and them. It's the yoke that galls you, Eugene. You want your freedom, and you won't be satisfied until you have it. A child wouldn't make any difference. I can see that now."

"I want my freedom," he exclaimed bitterly and inconsiderately, "and, what's more, I'm going to have it! I don't care. I'm sick of lying and pretending, sick of common little piffling notions of what you consider right and wrong. For eleven or twelve years now I have stood it. I have sat with you every morning at breakfast and every evening at dinner, most of the time when I didn't want to. I have listened to your theories of life when I didn't believe a word of what you said, and didn't care anything about what you thought. I've done it because I thought I ought to do it so as not to hurt your feelings, but I'm through with all that. What have I had? Spying on me, opposition, searching my pockets for letters, complaining if I dared to stay out a single evening and did not give an account of myself.

"Why didn't you leave me after that affair at Riverdale? Why do you hang on to me when I don't love you? One'd think I was prisoner and you my keeper. Good Christ! When I think of it, it makes me sick! Well, there's no use worrying over that any more. It's all over. It's all beautifully over, and I'm done with it. I'm going to live a life of my own hereafter. I'm going to carve out some sort of a career that suits me. I'm going to live with someone that I can really love, and that's the end of it. Now you run and do anything you want to."

He was like a young horse that had broken rein and that thinks that by rearing and plunging he shall become forever free. He was thinking of green fields and delightful pastures. He was free now, in spite of what she had told him. This night had made him so, and he was going to remain free. Suzanne would stand by him, he felt it. He was going to make it perfectly plain to Angela that never again, come what may, would things be as they were.

"Yes, Eugene," she replied sadly, after listening to his protestations on this score, "I think that you do want your freedom, now that I see you.

I'm beginning to see what it means to you. But I have made such a terrible mistake. Are you thinking about me at all? What shall I do? It is true that there will be a child unless I die. I may die. I'm afraid of that, or I was. I am not now. The only reason I would care to live would be to take care of it. I didn't think I was going to be ill with rheumatism. I didn't think my heart was going to be affected in this way. I didn't think that you were going to do as you have done, but now that you have, nothing matters. Oh," she said sadly, hot tears welling to her eyes, "it is all such a mistake! If I only hadn't done this!"

Eugene stared at the floor. He wasn't softened one bit. He did not think she was going to die—no such luck! He was thinking that this merely complicated things, or that she might be acting, but that it could not stand in his way. Why had she tried to trick him in this way? It was her fault. Now she was crying, but that was the old hypocrisy of emotion that she had used so often. He did not intend to desert her absolutely. She would have plenty to live on. Merely he did not propose to live with her, if he could help it, or only nominally, anyhow. The major portion of his time should be given to Suzanne.

"I don't care what it costs," he said finally. "I don't propose to live with you. I didn't ask you to have a child. It was none of my doing. You're not going to be deserted financially, but I'm not going to live with you."

He stirred again, and Angela stared hot-cheeked. The hardness of the man enraged her for the moment. She did not believe that she would starve, but their improving surroundings, their home, their social position, would be broken up completely.

"Yes, yes. I understand," she pleaded, with an effort at controlling herself, "but I am not the only one to be considered. Are you thinking of Mrs. Dale, and what she may do and say? She isn't going to let you take Suzanne if she knows it, without doing something about it. She is an able woman. She loves Suzanne, however self-willed she may be. She likes you now, but how long do you think she is going to like you when she learns what you want to do with her daughter? What are you going to do with her? You can't marry her under a year even if I were willing to give you a divorce. You could scarcely get a divorce in that time."

"I'm going to live with her, that's what I'm going to do," declared Eugene. "She loves me, she's willing to take me just as I am. She doesn't need marriage ceremonies and rings and vows and chains. She doesn't believe in them. As long as I love her, all right. When I cease to love her, she doesn't want me any more. Some difference in that, isn't there?" he added bitterly. "It doesn't sound exactly like Blackwood, does it?"

Angela bridled. His taunts were cruel.

"She says that, Eugene," she replied quietly, "but she hasn't had time to think. You've hypnotized her for the moment. She's fascinated. When she stops to think later, if she has any sense, any pride— — But, oh, why should I talk, you won't listen. You won't think." Then she added: "But what do you propose to do about Mrs. Dale? Don't you suppose she will fight you, even if I do not? I wish you would stop and think, Eugene. This is a terrible thing you are doing."

"Think! Think!" he exclaimed savagely and bitterly. "As though I had not been thinking all these years. Think! Hell! I haven't done anything but think. I've thought until the soul within me is sick. I've thought until I wish to God I could stop. I've thought about Mrs. Dale. Don't you worry about her. I'll settle this matter with her later. Just now I want to convince you of what I am going to do. I'm going to have Suzanne, and you're not going to stop me."

"Oh, Eugene," sighed Angela, "if something would only make you see! It is partially my fault. I have been hard and suspicious and jealous, but you have given me some cause to be, don't you think? I see now that I have made a mistake. I have been too hard and too jealous, but I could reform if you would let me try." (She was thinking now of living, not dying.) "I know I could. You have so much to lose. Is this change worth it? You know so well how the world looks at these things. Why, even if you should obtain your freedom from me under the circumstances, what do you suppose the world would think? You couldn't desert your child. Why not wait and see what happens? I might die. There have been such cases. Then you would be free to do as you pleased. That is only a little way off."

It was a specious plea, calculated to hold him; but he saw through it.

"Nothing doing!" he exclaimed, in the slang of the day. "I know all about that. I know what you're thinking. In the first place, I don't believe you are in the condition you say you are. In the next place, you're not going to die. I don't propose to wait to be free. I know you, and I've no faith in you. What I do needn't affect your condition. You're not going to starve. No one need know, unless you start a row about it. Suzanne and I can arrange this between ourselves. I know what you're thinking, but you're not going to interfere. If you do, I'll smash everything in sight—you, this apartment, my job— —" He clenched his hands desperately, determinedly.

Angela's hands were tingling with nervous pains while Eugene talked. Her eyes ached and her heart fluttered. She could not understand this dark, determined man, so savage and so resolute in his manner. Was this Eugene who was always moving about quietly when he was near her, getting angry at times, but always feeling sorry and apologizing? She had boasted to some of her friends, and particularly to Marietta, in a friendly, jesting way that she could wind Eugene around her little finger. He was so easy-going in the main, so quiet. Here he was a raging demon almost, possessed of an evil spirit of desire and tearing up his and hers and Suzanne's life for that matter, by the roots. She did not care for Suzanne, though, now, or Mrs. Dale. Her own blighted life, and Eugene's, looming so straight ahead of her terrified her.

"What do you suppose Mr. Colfax will do when he hears of this?" she asked desperately, hoping to frighten him.

"I don't care a damn what Mr. Colfax will or can do!" he replied sententiously. "I don't care a damn what anybody does or says or thinks. I love Suzanne Dale. She loves me. She wants me. There's an end of that. I'm going to her now. You stay me if you can."

Suzanne Dale! Suzanne Dale! How that name enraged and frightened Angela! Never before had she witnessed quite so clearly the power of beauty. Suzanne Dale was young and beautiful. She was looking at her only tonight thinking how fascinating she was—how fair her face—and here was Eugene bewitched by it, completely undone. Oh, the terror of beauty! The terror of social life generally! Why had she entertained? Why become friendly with the Dales? But then there were other personalities, almost as lovely and quite as young—Marjorie McLennan, Florence Reel, Henrietta Tenman, Annette Kean. It might have been any one of these. She couldn't have been expected to shut out all young women from Eugene's life. No; it was Eugene. It was his attitude toward life. His craze about the beautiful, particularly in women. She could see it now. He really was not strong enough. Beauty would always upset him at critical moments. She had seen it in relation to herself—the beauty of her form, which he admired so, or had admired. "God," she prayed silently, "give me wisdom now. Give me strength. I don't deserve it, but help me. Help me to save him. Help me to save myself."

"Oh, Eugene," she said aloud, hopelessly, "I wish you would stop and think. I wish you would let Suzanne go her way in the morning, and you stay sane and calm. I won't care about myself. I can forgive and forget. I'll promise you I'll never mention it. If a child comes, I'll do my best not to let it annoy you. I'll try yet not to have one. It may not be too late. I'll change from this day forth. Oh!" She began to cry.

"No! By God!" he said, getting up. "No! No! No! I'm through now. I'm through! I've had enough of fake hysterics and tears. Tears one minute, and wrath and hate the next. Subtlety! Subtlety! Subtlety! Nothing doing. You've been master and jailer long enough. It's my turn now. I'll do a little jailing and task-setting for a change. I'm in the saddle, and I'm going to stay there. You can cry if you want to, you can do what you please about the child. I'm through. I'm tired, and I'm going to bed, but this thing is going to stand just as it does. I'm through, and that's all there is to it."

He strode out of the room angrily and fiercely, but nevertheless, when he reached it, he sat in his own room, which was on the other side of the studio from Angelas, and did not sleep. His mind was on fire with the thought of Suzanne; he thought of the old order which had been so quickly and so terribly broken. Now, if he could remain master, and he could, he proposed to take Suzanne. She would come to him, secretly no doubt, if necessary. They would open a studio, a second establishment. Angela might not give him a divorce. If what she said was true, she couldn't. He wouldn't want her to, but he fancied from this conversation that she was so afraid of him that she would not stir up any trouble. There was nothing she could really do. He was in the saddle truly, and would stay there. He would take Suzanne, would provide amply for Angela, would visit all those lovely public resorts he had so frequently seen, and he and Suzanne would be happy together.

Suzanne! Suzanne! Oh, how beautiful she was! And to think how nobly and courageously she had stood by him tonight. How she had slipped her hand into his so sweetly and had said, "But I love him, Mrs. Witla." Yes, she loved him. No doubt of that. She was young, exquisite, beautifully rounded in her budding emotion and feeling. She was going to develop into a wonderful woman, a real one. And she was so young. What a pity it was he was not free now! Well, wait, this would right all things, and, meanwhile, he would have her. He must talk to Suzanne. He must tell her how things stood. Poor little Suzanne! There she was in her room wondering what was to become of her, and here was he. Well, he couldn't go to her tonight. It did not look right, and, besides, Angela might fight still. But tomorrow! Tomorrow! Oh, tomorrow he would walk and talk with her, and they would plan. Tomorrow he would show her just what he wanted to do and find out what she could do.

CHAPTER XI

This night passed without additional scenes, though as it stood it was the most astonishing and tremendous in all Eugene's experience. He had, not up to the time Angela walked into the room, really expected anything so dramatic and climacteric to happen, though what he did expect was never really very clear to him. At times as he lay and thought now he fancied that he might eventually have to give Suzanne up, though how, or when, or why, he could not say. He was literally crazed by her, and could not think that such a thing could really be. At other moments he fancied that powers outside of this visible life, the life attested by the five senses, had arranged this beautiful finish to his career for him so that he might be perfectly happy. All his life he had fancied that he was leading a more or less fated life, principally more. He thought that his art was a gift, that he had in a way been sent to revolutionize art in America, or carry it one step farther forward and that nature was thus constantly sending its apostles or special representatives over whom it kept watch and in whom it was well pleased. At other times he fancied he might be the sport or toy of untoward and malicious powers, such as those which surrounded and accomplished Macbeth's tragic end, and which might be intending to make an illustration of him. As he looked at life at times, it seemed to do this with certain people. The fates lied. Lovely, blandishing lures were held out only to lead men to destruction. He had seen other men who seemed to have been undone in this way. Was he to be so treated?

Angela's unexpected and peculiar announcement made it look that way. Still he did not believe it. Life had sent Suzanne across his path for a purpose. The fates or powers had seen he was miserable and unhappy. Being a favorite child of Heaven, he was to be rewarded for his sufferings by having her. She was here now—quickly, forcefully thrust into his arms, so to speak, so that perhaps he might have her all the more quickly. How silly it seemed to him now to have brought her into his own apartment to make love to her and get caught, and yet how fortunate, too, the hand of fate! No doubt it was intended. Anyhow, the shame to him, the shame to Angela and Suzanne, the terrific moments and hours that each was enduring now—these were things which were unfortunately involved in any necessarily great readjustment. It was probable that it had to come about this way. It was better so than to go on living an unhappy life. He was really fitted for something better, he thought—a great career. He would have to adjust this thing with Angela in some way now, either leave her, or make some arrangement whereby he could enjoy the company of Suzanne uninterrupted. There must be no interference. He did not propose to give her up. The child might come. Well and good. He would provide for it, that would be all. He recalled now the conversation he had had with Suzanne in which she had said that she would live with him if she could. The time had come. Their plan for a studio should now be put into effect. It must be secret. Angela would not care. She could not help herself. If only the events of this night did not terrorize Suzanne into retracing her steps! He had not explained to her how he was to get rid of Angela apart from what she had heard this night. She was thinking, he knew, that they could go on loving each other in this tentative fashion, occupying a studio together, perhaps, not caring what the world thought, not caring what her mother thought, ignoring her brother and sister and Angela, and being happy with Eugene only. He had never tried to disillusion her. He was not thinking clearly himself. He was rushing forward in an aimless way, desiring the companionship of her beautiful mind and body. Now he saw he must act or lose her. He must convince her in the face of what Angela had said, or let her go. She would probably be willing to come to him rather than leave him entirely. He must talk, explain, make her understand just what a trick this all was.

Angela had not slept, but lay staring at the ceiling in the dark, her eyes a study in despair. When morning came they were none of them further along in their conclusions than they were the night before, save to know, each separately and distinctly, that a great tragedy or change was at hand. Suzanne had thought and thought, or tried to, but the impulse of blood and passion in her were Eugeneward and she could only see the situation from their own point of view. She loved him, she thought—must love him, since he was so ready to sacrifice so much for her; yet at the same time there was a strange, disconcerting nebulosity about her which, had Eugene fully realized it at this moment, would have terrified him. In her state, which was one of wondering delight at the beauty of life and love—a fatalistic security in the thought that joy was to come to her throughout life—much joy. She could not see the grimness of Eugene's position. She could not understand the agony of a soul that had never really tasted supreme bliss in love, and had wanted, however foolishly, the accessories of wealth, and had never had them. Terrorized lest after the first sip of so wonderful a joy it should be removed forever, Eugene was tingling in the dark of his own room— tingling and yet reaching, almost with outstretched hands, to the splendor of the life that was seemingly before him. Suzanne, however, to whom life had given so much, was resting in a kind of still ease, like that which might fill a drowsy poppyland of joy where all the pleasures had been attained and were being tasted at leisure. Life at its worst to her was not so bad. Witness this storm which had been quelled in part by Eugene and was like to blow over as nothing at all. Things came round of their own accord in time, if one let them. She had always felt so sure that whatever happened no ill would befall her, and here she was courted and protected by Eugene even in his own home!

In this situation, therefore, she was not grieving either for Eugene, for Angela, or for herself. She could not. Some dispositions are so. Eugene was able to take care of himself and her and Angela financially, she thought. She was really looking forward to that better day when this misalliance should be broken up, and Eugene and presumably Angela would be really happier. She wanted Eugene to be much happier, and Angela, for that matter—and through her, if possible, since Eugene's happiness seemed to depend on her. But unlike Eugene, she was already thinking that she could live well enough without him, if it must be. She did not want to. She felt that her greatest happiness would be in repaying him for past ills and pains; but if they must part for a time, for instance, it would not make so much difference. Time would bring them together. But if it didn't— — But it would. Why think otherwise? But how wonderful it was that her beauty, her mere physical beauty, which seemed unimportant to her, made him so wild. She could not know of the actual physical pain gnawing at his vitals, but it was so plain that he was madly stricken with her. His whole face and his burning black eyes riveted on her in intense delight and almost agony proved it. Was she so beautiful? Surely not! Yet he yearned over her so. And it was so delightful.

She arose at dawn and began silently to dress, thinking that she might take a walk, leaving a note for Eugene as to where to come and find her if he could. She had one appointment for the day. Later she would have to go home, but things would come out all right. Since Eugene had compelled Angela to relinquish her determination to inform her mother, all must be well. They would meet, she and Eugene. She would leave her home and be his and they would go anywhere, anywhere Eugene desired, only she would prefer to persuade her mother to see things from her point of view and later countenance some understanding between them here. Because of Angela's and Eugene's position here, she preferred this. Because of her youth and her poetic, erratic conception of life, she assumed that she could overcome her mother and that she and Eugene could live together somewhere in peace. Her friends might either be unaware of the situation, or they could be told, some of them, and they might countenance it because it was so beautiful and natural!

Eugene heard her stirring after a time, and rose and went to her room and knocked. When she opened the door almost fully dressed a thrill of pain passed over his heart, for he thought that she had been intending to slip away without seeing him any more—so little they really knew each other. But as she stood there, a little cool or still or sober from much thought and the peculiar nature of her position, she seemed more beautiful than ever.

"You're not going, are you?" he asked, as she looked up at him with inquiring eyes.

"I thought I'd go for a walk."

"Without me?"

"I intended to see you, if I could, or leave a note for you to come to me. I thought you would."

"Will you wait for me?" he asked, feeling as though he must hold her close forever in order to live. "Just a little bit. I want to change my clothes." He took her in his arms.

"Yes," she said softly.

"You won't go without me?"

"No. Why do you ask?"

"Oh, I love you so!" he replied, and pushed her head back and looked yearningly into her eyes.

She took his tired face between her hands and studied his eyes. She was so enrapt by him now in this first burst of affection that she could see nothing but him. He seemed so beautiful, so hungry! It did not matter to her now that she was in the home of his wife or that his love was complicated with so much that was apparently evil. She loved him. She had thought all night about him, not sleeping. Being so young, it was hard for her to reason clearly as yet, but somehow it seemed to her that he was very unhappily placed, terribly ill-mated, and that he needed her. He was so fine, so clean, so capable! If he did not want Angela, why should she want him? She would not be suffering for anything save his company, and why should she want to hold him? She, Suzanne, would not, if she were in Angela's place. If there were a child, would that make any real difference? He did not love her.

"Don't worry about me," she said reassuringly. "I love you. Don't you know I do? I have to talk to you. We have to talk. How is Mrs. Witla?"

She was thinking about what Mrs. Witla would do, whether she would call up her mother, whether her struggle to have Eugene would begin at once.

"Oh, she's about the same!" he said wearily. "We've had a long argument. I've told her just what I propose to do, but I'll tell you about that later."

He went away to change his clothes, and then stepped into Angela's room.

"I'm going to walk with Suzanne," he said dominantly, when he was ready.

"All right," said Angela, who was so tired she could have fainted. "Will you be back for dinner?"

"I don't know," he replied. "What difference does it make?"

"Only this: that the maid and cook need not stay unless you are coming. I want nothing."

"When will the nurse be here?"

"At seven."

"Well, you can prepare dinner, if you wish," he said. "I will try and be back by four."

He walked toward the studio where Suzanne was, and found her waiting, white-faced, slightly hollow-eyed, but strong and confident. Now, as so often before, he noticed that spirit of self-sufficiency and reliance about her young body which had impressed him so forcibly and delightfully in the past. She was a wonderful girl, this Suzanne, full of grit and ability, although raised under what might have been deemed enervating circumstances. Her statement, made under pressure the night before, that she must go to a hotel and not go home until she could straighten out her affairs, had impressed him greatly. Why had she thought of going out in the world to work for herself unless there were something really fine about her? She was heir to a fortune under her father's will, he had heard her mother say once. This morning her glance was so assured. He did not use the phone to call a car, but strolled out into the drive with her walking along the stone wall which commanded the river northward toward Grant's Tomb. It occurred to him that they might go to Claremont Inn for breakfast, and afterwards take a car somewhere—he did not know quite where. Suzanne might be recognized. So might he.

"What shall we do, sweet?" he asked, as the cool morning air brushed their faces. It was a glorious day.

"I don't care," replied Suzanne. "I promised to be at the Almerdings some time today, but I didn't say when. They won't think anything of it if I don't get there till after dinner. Will Mrs. Witla call up mama?"

"I don't think so. In fact, I'm sure she won't." He was thinking of his last conversation with Angela, when she said she would do nothing. "Is your mother likely to call you up?"

"I think not. Mama doesn't usually bother when she knows where I am going. If she does, they'll simply say I haven't come yet. Will Mrs. Witla tell her, if she calls up there?"

"I think not," he said. "No, I'm sure she won't. Angela wants time to think. She isn't going to do anything. She told me that this morning. She's going to wait until she sees what I am going to do. It all depends now on how we play our cards."

He strolled on, looking at the river and holding Suzanne's hand. It was only a quarter to seven and the drive was comparatively empty.

"If she tells mama, it will make things very bad," said Suzanne thoughtfully. "Do you really think she won't?"

"I'm sure she won't. I'm positive. She doesn't want to do anything yet. It's too dangerous. I think she thinks that maybe I will come round. Oh, what a life I've led! It seems like a dream, now that I have your love. You are so different, so generous! Your attitude is so unselfish! To have been ruled all these years in every little thing. This last trick of hers!"

He shook his head woefully. Suzanne looked at his weary face, her own as fresh as the morning.

"Oh, if I might only have had you to begin with!" he added.

"Listen, Eugene," said Suzanne. "You know I feel sorry for Mrs. Witla. We shouldn't have done what we did last night, but you made me. You know you will never listen to me, until it's too late. You're so headstrong! I don't want you to leave Mrs. Witla unless you want to. You needn't for me. I don't want to marry you; not now, anyhow. I'd rather just give myself to you, if you want me to. I want time though, to think and plan. If mama should hear today, there would be a terrible time. If we have time to think, we may bring her round. I don't care anything about what Mrs. Witla told you last night. I don't want you to leave her. If we could just arrange some way. It's mama, you know."

She swung his hand softly in hers, pressing his fingers. She was deep in thought, for her mother presented a real problem.

"You know," she went on, "mama isn't narrow. She doesn't believe much in marriage unless it's ideal. Mrs. Witla's condition wouldn't make so much difference if only the child were here. I've been thinking about that. Mama might sanction some arrangement if she thought it would make me happy and there was no scandal. But I'll have to have time to talk to her. It can't be done right away."

Eugene listened to this with considerable surprise, as he did to everything Suzanne volunteered. She seemed to have been thinking about these questions a long time. She was not free with her opinions. She hesitated and halted between words and in her cogitations, but when they were out this was what they came to. He wondered how sound they were.

"Suzanne," he said, "you take my breath away! How you think! Do you know what you're talking about? Do you know your mother at all well?"

"Mama? Oh, yes, I think I understand mama. You know she's very peculiar. Mama is literary and romantic. She talks a great deal about liberty, but I don't take in everything she says. I think mama is different from most women—she's exceptional. She likes me, not so much as a daughter as a person. She's anxious about me. You know, I think I'm stronger than mama. I think I could dominate her if I tried. She leans on me now a lot, and she can't make me do anything unless I want to. I can make her come to my way of thinking, I believe. I have, lots of times. That's what makes me think I might now, if I have time. It will take time to get her to do what I want."

"How much time?" asked Eugene thoughtfully.

"Oh, I don't know. Three months. Six months. I can't tell. I would like to try, though."

"And if you can't, then what?"

"Why, then—why, then I'll defy her, that's all. I'm not sure, you know. But I think I can."

"And if you can't?"

"But I can. I'm sure I can." She tossed her head gaily.

"And come to me?"

"And come to you."

They were near One Hundredth Street, under the trees. There was a lone man some distance away, walking from them. Eugene caught Suzanne in his arms and implanted a kiss upon her mouth. "Oh, you divinity!" he exclaimed. "Helen! Circe!"

"No," she replied, with smiling eyes. "No, not here. Wait till we get a car."

"Shall we go to Claremont?"

"I'm not hungry."

"Then we might as well call a car and ride."

They hunted a garage and sped northward, the wonderful wind of the morning cooling and refreshing their fevered senses. Both he and Suzanne were naturally depressed at moments, at other moments preternaturally gay, for he was varying between joy and fear, and she was buoying him up. Her attitude was calmer, surer, braver, than his. She was like a strong mother to him.

"You know," he said, "I don't know what to think at times. I haven't any particular charge against Mrs. Witla except that I don't love her. I have been so unhappy. What do you think of cases of this kind, Suzanne? You heard what she said about me."

"Yes, I heard."

"It all comes from that. I don't love her. I never have really from the beginning. What do you think where there is no love? It is true, part of what she said. I have been in love with other women, but it has always been because I have been longing for some sort of temperament that was congenial to me. I have, Suzanne, too, since I have been married. I can't say that I was really in love with Carlotta Wilson, but I did like her. She was very much like myself. The other was a girl somewhat like you. Not so wise. That was years ago. Oh, I could tell you why! I love youth. I love beauty. I want someone who is my companion mentally. You are that, Suzanne, and yet see what a hell it is creating. Do you think it is so bad where I am so very unhappy? Tell me, what do you think?"

"Why, why," said Suzanne, "I don't think anyone ought to stick by a bad bargain, Eugene."

"Just what do you mean by that, Suzanne?"

"Well, you say you don't love her. You're not happy with her. I shouldn't think it would be good for her or you to have you stay with her. She can live. I wouldn't want you to stay with me if you didn't love me. I wouldn't want you at all if you didn't. I wouldn't want to stay with you if I didn't love you, and I wouldn't. I think marriage ought to be a happy bargain, and if it isn't you oughtn't to try to stay together just because you thought you could stay together once."

"What if there were children?"

"Well, that might be different. Even then, one or the other could take them, wouldn't you think? The children needn't be made very unhappy in such a case."

Eugene looked at Suzanne's lovely face. It seemed so strange to hear her reasoning so solemnly—this girl!

"But you heard what she said about me, Suzanne, and about her condition?"

"I know," she said. "I've thought about it. I don't see that it makes so very much difference. You can take care of her."

"You love me just as much?"

"Yes."

"Even if all she says is true?"

"Yes."

"Why, Suzanne?"

"Well, all her charges concerned years gone by, and that isn't now. And I know you love me now. I don't care about the past. You know, Eugene, I don't care anything about the future, either. I want you to love me only so long as you want to love me. When you are tired of me, I want you to leave me. I wouldn't want you to live with me if you didn't love me. I wouldn't want to live with you if I didn't love you."

Eugene looked into her face, astonished, pleased, invigorated, and heartened by this philosophy. It was so like Suzanne, he thought. She seemed to have reached definite and effective conclusions so early. Her young mind seemed a solvent for all life's difficulties.

"Oh, you wonderful girl!" he said. "You know you are wiser than I am, stronger. I draw to you, Suzanne, like a cold man to a fire. You are so kindly, so temperate, so understanding!"

They rode on toward Tarrytown and Scarborough, and on the way Eugene told Suzanne some of his plans. He was willing not to leave Angela, if that was agreeable to her. He was willing to maintain this outward show, if that was satisfactory. The only point was, could he stay and have her, too? He did not understand quite how she could want to share him with anybody, but he could not fathom her from any point of view, and he was fascinated. She seemed the dearest, the subtlest, the strangest and most lovable girl. He tried to find out by what process she proposed to overcome the objections of her mother, but Suzanne seemed to have no plans save that of her ability to gradually get the upper hand mentally and dominate her. "You know," she said at one point, "I have money coming to me. Papa set aside two hundred thousand dollars for each of us children when we should come of age, and I am of age now. It is to be held in trust, but I shall have twelve thousand or maybe more from that. We can use that. I am of age now, and I have never said anything about it. Mama has managed all these things."

Here was another thought which heartened Eugene. With Suzanne he would have this additional income, which might be used whatever else might betide. If only Angela could be made to accept his conditions and Suzanne could win in her contest with her mother all would be well. His position need not be jeopardized. Mrs. Dale need hear nothing of it at present. He and Suzanne could go on associating in this way until an understanding had been reached. It was all like a delightful courtship which was to bloom into a still more delightful marriage.

The day passed in assurances of affection. Suzanne told Eugene of a book she had read in French, "The Blue Bird." The allegory touched Eugene to the quick—its quest for happiness, and he named Suzanne then and there "The Blue Bird." She made him stop the car and go back to get her an exquisite lavender-hued blossom growing wild on a tall stalk which she saw in a field as they sped by. Eugene objected genially, because it was beyond a wire fence and set among thorns, but she said, "Yes, now, you must. You know you must obey me now. I am going to begin to train you now. You've been spoiled. You're a bad boy. Mama says that. I am going to reform you."

"A sweet time you'll have, Flower Face! I'm a bad lot. Have you noticed that?"

"A little."

"And you still like me?"

"I don't mind. I think I can change you by loving you."

Eugene went gladly. He plucked the magnificent bloom and handed it to her "as a sceptre," he said. "It looks like you, you know," he added. "It's regal."

Suzanne accepted the compliment without thought of its flattering import. She loved Eugene, and words had scarcely any meaning to her. She was as happy as a child and as wise in many things as a woman twice her years. She was as foolish as Eugene over the beauty of nature, dwelling in an ecstasy upon morning and evening skies, the feel of winds and the sigh of leaves. The beauties of nature at every turn caught her eye, and she spoke to him of things she felt in such a simple way that he was entranced.

Once when they had left the car and were walking about the grounds of an inn, she found that one of her silk stockings had worn through at the heel. She lifted up her foot and looked at it meditatively. "Now, if I had some ink I could fix that up so quickly," she said, laughing.

"What would you do?" he asked.

"I would black it," she replied, referring to her pink heel, "or you could paint it."

He laughed and she giggled. It was these little, idle simplicities which amused and fascinated him.

"Suzanne," he said dramatically at this time, "you are taking me back into fairyland."

"I want to make you happy," she said, "as happy as I am."

"If I could be! If I only could be!"

"Wait," she said; "be cheerful. Don't worry. Everything will come out all right. I know it will. Things always come right for me. I want you and you will come to me. You will have me just as I will have you. Oh, it is all so beautiful!"

She squeezed his hand in an ecstasy of delight and then gave him her lips.

"What if someone should see?" he asked.

"I don't care! I don't care!" she cried. "I love you!"

CHAPTER XII

After dining joyously, these two returned to the city. Suzanne, as she neared New York proper, was nervous as to what Angela might have done, for she wanted, in case Angela told her mother, to be present, in order to defend herself. She had reached a rather logical conclusion for her, and that was, in case her mother objected too vigorously, to elope with Eugene. She wanted to see just how her mother would take the intelligence in order that she might see clearly what to do. Previously she had the feeling that she could persuade her mother not to interfere, even in the face of all that had been revealed. Nevertheless, she was nervous, and her fears were bred to a certain extent by Eugene's attitude.

In spite of all his bravado, he really did not feel at all secure. He was not afraid of what he might lose materially so much as he was of losing Suzanne. The thought of the coming child had not affected them at all as yet. He could see clearly that conditions might come about whereby he could not have her, but they were not in evidence as yet. Besides, Angela might be lying. Still at odd moments his conscience troubled him, for in the midst of his intense satisfaction, his keenest thrills of joy, he could see Angela lying in bed, the thought of her wretched future before her, the thought of the coming life troubling her, or he could hear the echo of some of the pleas she had made. It was useless to attempt to shut them out. This was a terrible ordeal he was undergoing, a ruthless thing he was doing. All the laws of life and public sentiment were against him. If the world knew, it would accuse him bitterly. He could not forget that. He despaired at moments of ever being able to solve the tangle in which he had involved himself, and yet he was determined to go on. He proposed accompanying Suzanne to her friends, the Almerdings, but she changed her mind and decided to go home. "I want to see whether mama has heard anything," she insisted.

Eugene had to escort her to Staten Island and then order the chauffeur to put on speed so as to reach Riverside by four. He was somewhat remorseful, but he argued that his love-life was so long over, in so far as Angela was concerned, that it could not really make so very much difference. Since Suzanne wanted to wait a little time and proceed slowly, it was not going to be as bad for Angela as he had anticipated. He was going to give her a choice of going her way and leaving him entirely, either now, or after the child was born, giving her the half of his property, stocks, ready money, and anything else that might be divisible, and all the furniture, or staying and tacitly ignoring the whole thing. She would know what he was going to do, to maintain a separate ménage, or secret rendezvous for Suzanne. He proposed since Suzanne was so generous not to debate this point, but to insist. He must have her, and Angela must yield, choosing only her conditions.

When he came to the house, a great change had come over Angela. In the morning when he left she was hard and bitter in her mood. This afternoon she was, albeit extremely sad, more soft and melting than he had ever seen her. Her hard spirit was temporarily broken, but in addition she had tried to resign herself to the inevitable and to look upon it as the will of God. Perhaps she had been, as Eugene had often accused her of being, hard and cold. Perhaps she had held him in too tight leading strings. She had meant it for the best. She had tried to pray for lig' nd guidance, and after a while something softly sad, like a benediction, settled upon her. She must not fight any more, she thought. She must yield. God would guide her. Her smile, kindly and wan, when Eugene entered the room, took him unawares.

Her explanation of her mood, her prayers, her willingness to give him up if need be, even in the face of what was coming to her, moved him more than anything that had ever passed between them. He sat opposite her at dinner, looking at her thin hands and face, and her sad eyes, trying to be cheerful and considerate, and then, going back into her room and hearing her say she would do whatever he deemed best, burst into tears. He cried from an excess of involuntary and uncontrolled emotion. He hardly knew why he cried, but the sadness of everything—life, the tangle of human emotions, the proximity of death to all, old age, Suzanne, Angela, all—touched him, and he shook as though he would rend his sides. Angela, in turn, was astonished and grieved for him. She could scarcely believe her eyes. Was he repenting? "Come to me, Eugene!" she pleaded. "Oh, I'm so sorry! *Are you as much in love as that?* Oh, dear, dear, if I could only do something! Don't cry like that, Eugene. If it means so much to you, I will give you up. It tears my heart to hear you. Oh, dear, please don't cry."

He laid his head on his knees and shook, then seeing her getting up, came over to the bed to prevent her.

"No, no," he said, "it will pass. I can't help it. I'm sorry for you. I'm sorry for myself. I'm sorry for life. God will punish me for this. I can't help it, but you are a good woman."

He laid his head down beside her and sobbed, great, aching sobs. After a time he recovered himself, only to find that he had given Angela courage anew. She would think now that his love might be recovered since he had seemed so sympathetic; that Suzanne might be displaced. He knew that could not be, and so he was sorry that he had cried.

They went on from that to discussion, to argument, to ill-feeling, to sympathetic agreement again by degrees, only to fall out anew. Angela could not resign herself to the thought of giving him up. Eugene could not see that he was called upon to do anything, save divide their joint possessions. He was most anxious to have nothing to do with Angela anymore in any way. He might live in the same house, but that would be all. He was going to have Suzanne. He was going to live for her only. He threatened Angela with dire consequences if she tried to interfere in any way. If she communicated with Mrs. Dale, or said anything to Suzanne, or attempted to injure him commercially, he would leave her.

"Here is the situation," he would insist. "You can maintain it as I say, or break it. If you break it, you lose me and everything that I represent. If you maintain it, I will stay here. I think I will. I am perfectly willing to keep up appearances, but I want my freedom."

Angela thought and thought of this. She thought once of sending for Mrs. Dale and communicating with her secretly, urging her to get Suzanne out of the way without forewarning either the girl or Eugene, but she did not do this. It was the one thing she should have done and a thing Mrs. Dale would have agreed to, but fear and confusion deterred her. The next thing was to write or talk to Suzanne, and because she mistrusted her mood in Suzanne's presence she decided to write. She lay in bed on Monday when Eugene was away at the office and composed a long letter in which she practically gave the history of Eugene's life reiterating her own condition and stating what she thought Eugene ought to do.

"How can you think, Suzanne," she asked in one place, "that he will be true to you when he can ignore me, in this condition? He has not been true to anyone else. Are you going to throw your life away? Your station is assured now. What can he add to you that you have not already? If you take him, it is sure to become known. You are the one who will be injured, not he. Men recover from these things, particularly from an infatuation of this character, and the world thinks nothing of it; but the world will not forgive you. You will be 'a bad woman' after this, irretrievably so if a child is born. You think you love him. Do you really love him this much? Read this and stop and think. Think of his character. I am used to him. I made my mistakes in the beginning, and it is too late for me to change. The world can give me

102 | The "Genius" Book III The Revolt

nothing. I may have sorrow and disgust, but at least I shall not be an outcast and our friends and the world will not be scandalized. But you—you have everything before you. Some man will come to you whom you will love and who will not ask and willingly make a sacrifice of you. Oh, I beg you to think! You do not need him. After all, sorry as I am to confess it, I do. It is as I tell you. Can you really afford to ignore this appeal?"

Suzanne read this and was greatly shocked. Angela painted him in a wretched light, as fickle, deceitful, dishonest in his relations with women. She debated this matter in her own room, for it could not help but give her pause. After a time, Eugene's face came back to her, however, his beautiful mind, the atmosphere of delight and perfection that seemed to envelop all that surrounded him. It was as though Eugene were a mirage of beauty, so soft, so sweet, so delightful! Oh, to be with him; to hear his beautiful voice; to feel his intense caresses! What could life offer her equal to that? And, besides, he needed her. She decided to talk it out with him, show him the letter, and then decide.

Eugene came in a day or two, having phoned Monday and Tuesday mornings. He made a rendezvous of the ice house, and then appeared as eager and smiling as ever. Since returning to the office and seeing no immediate sign of a destructive attitude on Angela's part, he had recovered his courage. He was hopeful of a perfect dénouement to all this—of a studio and his lovely Suzanne. When they were seated in the auto, she immediately produced Angela's letter and handed it to him without comment. Eugene read it quietly.

He was greatly shocked at what he read, for he thought that Angela was more kindly disposed toward him. Still he knew it to be true, all of it, though he was not sure that Suzanne would suffer from his attentions. The fates might be kind. They might be happy together. Anyhow, he wanted her now.

"Well," he said, giving it back, "what of it? Do you believe all she says?"

"It may be so, but somehow when I am with you I don't seem to care. When I am away from you, it's different. I'm not so sure."

"You can't tell whether I am as good as you think I am?"

"I don't know what to think. I suppose all she says about you is true. I'm not sure. When you're away, it's different. When you are here, I feel as though everything must come out right. I love you so. Oh, I know it will!" She threw her arms around him.

"Then the letter doesn't really make any difference?"

"No."

She looked at him with big round eyes, and it was the old story, bliss in affection without thought. They rode miles, stopped at an inn for something to eat—Mrs. Dale was away for the day—looked at the sea where the return road skirted it, and kissed and kissed each other. Suzanne grew so ecstatic that she could see exactly how it was all coming out.

"Now you leave it to me," she said. "I will sound mama. If she is at all logical, I think I can convince her. I would so much rather do it that way. I hate deception. I would rather just tell her, and then, if I have to, defy her. I don't think I shall have to, though. She can't do anything."

"I don't know about that," said Eugene cautiously. He had come to have great respect for Suzanne's courage, and he was rather relying on Mrs. Dale's regard for him to stay her from any desperate course, but he did not see how their end was to be achieved.

He was for entering on an illicit relationship after a time without saying anything at all. He was in no hurry, for his feeling for Suzanne was not purely physical, though he wanted her. Because of her strange reading and philosophy, she was defying the world. She insisted that she did not see how it would hurt her.

"But, my dear, you don't know life," said Eugene. "It will hurt you. It will grind you to pieces in all places outside of New York. This is the Metropolis. It is a world city. Things are not quite the same here, but you will have to pretend, anyhow. It is so much easier."

"Can you protect me?" she asked significantly, referring to the condition Angela pleaded. "I wouldn't want—I couldn't, you know, not yet, not yet."

"I understand," he said. "Yes, I can, absolutely."

"Well, I want to think about it," she said again. "I prefer so much to be honest about it. I would so much rather just tell mama, and then go and do it. It would be so much nicer. My life is my own to do with as I please. It doesn't concern anybody, not even mama. You know, if I want to waste it, I may, only I don't think that I am doing so. I want to live as I choose. I don't want to get married yet."

Eugene listened to her with the feeling that this was the most curious experience of his life. He had never heard, never seen, never experienced anything like it. The case of Christina Channing was different. She had her art to consider. Suzanne had nothing of the sort. She had a lovely home, a social future, money, the chance of a happy, stable, normal life. This was love surely, and yet he was quite at sea. Still so many favorable things had happened, consciously favorable, that he was ready to believe that all this was intended for his benefit by a kind, governing providence.

Angela had practically given in already. Why not Suzanne's mother? Angela would not tell her anything. Mrs. Dale was not any stronger than Angela apparently. Suzanne might be able to control her as she said. If she was so determined to try, could he really stop her? She was headstrong in a way and wilful, but developing rapidly and reasoning tremendously. Perhaps she could do this thing. Who could tell? They came flying back along lovely lanes where the trees almost swept their faces, past green stretches of marsh where the wind stirred in ripples the tall green cat grass, past pretty farm yards, with children and ducks in the foreground, beautiful mansions, playing children, sauntering laborers. All the while they were reassuring each other, vowing perfect affection, holding each other close. Suzanne, as Angela had, loved to take Eugene's face between her hands and look into his eyes.

"Look at me," she said once when he had dolefully commented upon the possibility of change. "Look straight into my eyes. What do you see?"

"Courage and determination," he said.

"What else?"

"Love."

"Do you think I will change?"

"No."

"Surely?"

"No."

"Well, look at me straight, Eugene. I won't. I won't, do you hear? I'm yours until you don't want me anymore. Now will you be happy?"

"Yes," he said.

"And when we get our studio," she went on.

"When we get our studio," he said, "we'll furnish it perfectly, and entertain a little after a while, maybe. You'll be my lovely Suzanne, my Flower Face, my Myrtle Blossom. Helen, Circe, Dianeme."

"I'll be your week-end bride," she laughed, "your odd or even girl, whichever way the days fall."

"If it only comes true," he exclaimed when they parted. "If it only does."

"Wait and see," she said. "Now you wait and see."

The days passed and Suzanne began what she called her campaign. Her first move was to begin to talk about the marriage question at the dinner table, or whenever she and her mother were alone, and to sound her on this important question, putting her pronouncements on record. Mrs. Dale was one of those empirical thinkers who love to philosophize generally, but who make no specific application of anything to their own affairs. On this marriage question she held most liberal and philosophic views for all outside her own immediate family. It was her idea, outside her own family, of course, that if a girl having reached maturity, and what she considered a sound intellectual majority, and who was not by then satisfied with the condition which matrimony offered, if she loved no man desperately enough to want to marry him and could arrange some way whereby she could satisfy her craving for love without jeopardizing her reputation, that was her lookout. So far as Mrs. Dale was concerned, she had no particular objection. She knew women in society, who, having made unfortunate marriages, or marriages of convenience, sustained some such relationship to men whom they admired. There was a subtle, under the surface understanding outside the society circles of the most rigid morality in regard to this, and there was the fast set, of which she was at times a welcome member, which laughed at the severe conventions of the older school. One must be careful—very. One must not be caught. But, otherwise, well, every person's life was a law unto him or herself.

Suzanne never figured in any of these theories, for Suzanne was a beautiful girl, capable of an exalted alliance, and her daughter. She did not care to marry her off to any wretched possessor of great wealth or title, solely for wealth's or title's sake, but she was hoping that some eligible young man of excellent social standing or wealth, or real personal ability, such, for instance, as Eugene possessed, would come along and marry Suzanne. There would be a grand wedding at a church of some prominence,—St. Bartholomew's, very likely; a splendid wedding dinner, oceans of presents, a beautiful honeymoon. She used to look at Suzanne and think what a delightful mother she would make. She was so young, robust, vigorous, able, and in a quiet way, passionate. She could tell when she danced how eagerly she took life. The young man would come. It would not be long. These lovely springtimes would do their work one of these days. As it was, there were a score of men already who would have given an eye to attract Suzanne's attention, but Suzanne would none of them. She seemed shy, coy, elusive, but above all, shy. Her mother had no idea of the iron will all this concealed any more than she had of the hard anarchic, unsocial thoughts that were surging in her daughter's brain.

"Do you think a girl ought to marry at all, mama?" Suzanne asked her one evening when they were alone together, "if she doesn't regard marriage as a condition she could endure all her days?"

"No-o," replied her mother. "What makes you ask?"

"Well, you see so much trouble among married people that we know. They're not very happy together. Wouldn't it be better if a person just stayed single, and if they found someone that they could really love, well, they needn't necessarily marry to be happy, need they?"

"What have you been reading lately, Suzanne?" asked her mother, looking up with a touch of surprise in her eyes.

"Nothing lately. What makes you ask?" said Suzanne wisely, noting the change in her mother's voice.

"With whom have you been talking?"

"Why, what difference does that make, mama? I've heard you express precisely the same views?"

"Quite so. I may have. But don't you think you're rather young to be thinking of things like that? I don't say all that I think when I'm arguing things philosophically. There are conditions which govern everything. If it were impossible for a girl to marry well, or if looks or lack of money interfered,—there are plenty of reasons—a thing like that might possibly be excusable, but why should you be thinking of that?"

"Why, it doesn't necessarily follow, mama, that because I am good looking, or have a little money, or am socially eligible, that I should want to get married. I may not want to get married at all. I see just as well as you do how things are with most people. Why shouldn't I? Do I have to keep away from every man, then?"

"Why, Suzanne! I never heard you argue like this before. You must have been talking with someone or reading some outré book of late. I wish you wouldn't. You are too young and too good looking to entertain any such ideas. Why, you can have nearly any young man you wish. Surely you can find someone with whom you can live happily or with whom you would be willing to try. It's time enough to think about the other things when you've tried and failed. At least you can give yourself ample time to learn something about life before you begin to talk such nonsense. You're too young. Why it's ridiculous."

"Mama," said Suzanne, with the least touch of temper, "I wish you wouldn't talk to me like that. I'm not a child any more. I'm a woman. I think like a woman—not like a girl. You forget that I have a mind of my own and some thoughts. I may not want to get married. I don't think I do. Certainly not to any of the silly creatures that are running after me now. Why shouldn't I take some man in an independent way, if I wish? Other women have before me. Even if they hadn't, it would be no reason why I shouldn't. My life is my own."

"Suzanne Dale!" exclaimed her mother, rising, a thrill of terror passing along her heartstrings. "What are you talking about? Are you basing these ideas on anything I have said in the past? Then certainly my chickens are coming home to roost early. You are in no position to consider whether you want to get married or not. You have seen practically nothing of men. Why should you reach any such conclusions now? For goodness' sake, Suzanne, don't begin so early to meditate on these terrible things. Give yourself a few years in which to see the world. I don't ask you to marry, but you may meet some man whom you could love very much, and who would love you. If you were to go and throw yourself away under some such silly theory as you entertain now, without stopping to see, or waiting for life to show you what it has in store, what will you have to offer him. Suzanne, Suzanne"—Suzanne was turning impatiently to a window—"you frighten me! There isn't, there couldn't be. Oh, Suzanne, I beg of you, be careful what you think, what you say, what you do! I can't know all your thoughts, no mother can, but, oh, if you will stop and think, and wait a while!"

She looked at Suzanne who walked to a mirror and began to fix a bow in her hair.

"Mama," she said calmly. "Really, you amuse me. When you are out with people at dinner, you talk one way, and when you are here with me, you talk another. I haven't done anything desperate yet. I don't know what I may want to do. I'm not a child any more, mama. Please remember that. I'm a woman grown, and I certainly can lay out my life for myself. I'm sure I don't want to do what you are doing—talk one thing and do another."

Mrs. Dale recoiled intensely from this stab. Suzanne had suddenly developed in the line of her argument a note of determination, frank force and serenity of logic which appalled her. Where had the girl got all this? With whom had she been associating? She went over in her mind the girls and men she had met and known. Who were her intimate companions?—Vera Almerding; Lizette Woodworth; Cora TenEyck—a half dozen girls who were smart and clever and socially experienced. Were they talking such things among themselves? Was there some man or men unduly close to them? There was one remedy for all this. It must be acted on quickly if Suzanne were going to fall in with and imbibe any such ideas as these. Travel—two or three years of incessant travel with her, which would cover this dangerous period in which girls were so susceptible to undue influence was the necessary thing. Oh, her own miserable tongue! Her silly ideas! No doubt all she said was true. Generally it was so. But Suzanne! Her Suzanne, never! She would take her away while she had time, to grow older and wiser through experience. Never would she be permitted to stay here where girls and men were talking and advocating any such things. She would scan Suzanne's literature more closely from now on. She would viser her friendships. What a pity that so lovely a girl must be corrupted by such wretched, unsocial, anarchistic notions. Why, what would become of her girl? Where would she be? Dear Heaven!

She looked down in the social abyss yawning at her feet and recoiled with horror.

Never, never, never! Suzanne should be saved from herself, from all such ideas now and at once.

And she began to think how she could introduce the idea of travel easily and nicely. She must lure Suzanne to go without alarming her—without making her think that she was bringing pressure to bear. But from now on there must be a new order established. She must talk differently; she must act differently. Suzanne and all her children must be protected against themselves and others also. That was the lesson which this conversation taught her.

CHAPTER XIII

Eugene and Angela had been quarreling between themselves most bitterly; at other times Angela was attempting to appeal to his sense of justice and fair play, if not his old-time affection, in the subtlest of ways. She was completely thrown out of her old methods of calculation, and having lost those had really no traditions on which to proceed. Eugene had always heretofore apparently feared her wrath; now he cared nothing for that. He had been subject, in times past, to a certain extent to those alluring blandishments which the married will understand well enough, but these were as ashes. Her charms meant nothing to him. She had hoped that the thought of a coming child would move him, but no, it was apparently without avail. Suzanne seemed a monster to her now since she did not desert him, and Eugene a raving maniac almost, and yet she could see how human and natural it all was. He was hypnotized, possessed. He had one thought, Suzanne, Suzanne, and he would fight her at every turn for that. He told her so. He told her of her letter to Suzanne, and the fact that he had read and destroyed it. It did not help her cause at all. She knew that she had decried him. He stood his ground solidly, awaiting the will of Suzanne, and he saw Suzanne frequently, telling her that he had won completely, and that the fulfilment of their desires now depended upon her.

As has been said, Suzanne was not without passion. The longer she associated with Eugene, the more eager she became for that joyous fulfilment which his words, his looks, his emotions indicated. In her foolish, girlish way, she had built up a fancy which was capable of realization only by the most ruthless and desperate conduct. Her theory of telling her mother and overcoming her by argument or defiance was really vain, for it could not be settled so easily, or so quickly. Because of her mother's appeal to her in this first conversation, she fancied she had won a substantial victory. Her mother was subject to her control and could not defeat her in argument. By the latter token she felt she was certain to win. Besides, she was counting heavily on her mother's regard for Eugene and her deep affection for herself. Hitherto, her mother had really refused her nothing.

The fact that Eugene did not take her outright at this time, — postponing until a more imperative occasion an adjustment of the difficulties which must necessarily flow from their attempted union without marriage—was due to the fact that he was not as desperate or as courageous as he appeared to be. He wanted her, but he was a little afraid of Suzanne herself. She was doubtful, anxious to wait, anxious to plan things her own way. He was not truly ruthless ever, but good natured and easy going. He was no subtle schemer and planner, but rather an easy natured soul, who drifted here and there with all the tides and favorable or unfavorable winds of circumstance. He might have been ruthless if he had been eager enough for any one particular thing on this earth, money, fame, affection, but at bottom, he really did not care as much as he thought he did. Anything was really worth fighting for if you had to have it, but it was not worth fighting for to the bitter end, if you could possibly get along without it. Besides, there was nothing really one could not do without, if one were obliged. He might long intensely, but he could survive. He was more absorbed in this desire than in anything else in his history, but he was not willing to be hard and grasping.

On the other hand, Suzanne was willing to be taken, but needed to be pressed or compelled. She imagined in a vague way that she wanted to wait and adjust things in her own way, but she was merely dreaming, procrastinating because he was procrastinating. If he had but compelled her at once she would have been happy, but he was sadly in need of that desperate energy that acts first and thinks afterward. Like Hamlet, he was too fond of cogitating, too anxious to seek the less desperate way, and in doing this was jeopardizing that ideal bliss for which he was willing to toss away all the material advantages which he had thus far gained.

When Mrs. Dale quite casually within a few days began to suggest that they leave New York for the fall and winter, she, Suzanne and Kinroy, and visit first England, then Southern France and then Egypt, Suzanne immediately detected something intentional about it, or at best a very malicious plan on the part of fate to destroy her happiness. She had been conjecturing how, temporarily, she could avoid distant and long drawn out engagements which her mother not infrequently accepted for herself and Suzanne outside New York, but she had not formulated a plan. Mrs. Dale was very popular and much liked. This easy suggestion, made with considerable assurance by her mother, and as though it would be just the thing, frightened and then irritated Suzanne. Why should her mother think of it just at this time?

"I don't want to go to Europe," she said warily. "We were over there only three years ago. I'd rather stay over here this winter and see what's going on in New York."

"But this trip will be so delightful, Suzanne," her mother insisted. "The Camerons are to be at Callendar in Scotland for the fall. They have taken a cottage there. I had a note from Louise, Tuesday. I thought we might run up there and see them and then go to the Isle of Wight."

"I don't care to go, mama," replied Suzanne determinedly. "We're settled here comfortably. Why do you always want to be running off somewhere?"

"Why, I'm not running—how you talk, Suzanne! I never heard you object very much to going anywhere before. I should think Egypt and the Riviera would interest you very much. You haven't been to either of these places."

"I know they're delightful, but I don't care to go this fall. I'd rather stay here. Why should you suddenly decide that you want to go away for a year?"

"I haven't suddenly decided," insisted her mother. "I've been thinking of it for some time, as you know. Haven't I said that we would spend a winter in Europe soon? The last time I mentioned it, you were very keen for it."

"Oh, I know, mama, but that was nearly a year ago. I don't want to go now. I would rather stay here."

"Why would you? More of your friends go away than remain. I think a particularly large number of them are going this winter."

"Ha! Ha! Ho! Ho!" laughed Suzanne. "A particularly large number. How you exaggerate, mama, when you want anything. You always amuse me. It's a particularly large number now, just because you want to go," and she laughed again.

Suzanne's defiance irritated her mother. Why should she suddenly take this notion to stay here? It must be this group of girls she was in with, and yet, Suzanne appeared to have so few intimate girl friends. The Almerdings were not going to stay in town all the winter. They were here now because of a fire at their country place, but it would only be for a little while. Neither were the TenEycks. It couldn't be that Suzanne was interested in some man. The only person she cared much about was Eugene Witla, and he was married and only friendly in a brotherly, guardian-like way.

"Now, Suzanne," she said determinedly, "I'm not going to have you talk nonsense. This trip will be a delightful thing for you once you have started. It's useless for you to let a silly notion like not wanting to go stand in your way. You are just at the time when you ought to travel. Now you had better begin to prepare yourself, for we're going."

"Oh, no, I'm not, mama," said Suzanne. "Why, you talk as though I were a very little girl. I don't want to go this fall and I'm not going. You may go if you want to, but I'm not going."

"Why, Suzanne Dale!" exclaimed her mother. "Whatever has come over you? Of course you'll go. Where would you stay if I went? Do you think I would walk off and leave you? Have I ever before?"

"You did when I was at boarding school," interrupted Suzanne.

"That was a different matter. Then you were under proper supervision. Mrs. Hill was answerable to me for your care. Here you would be alone. What do you think I would be doing?"

"There you go, mama, talking as though I was a little girl again. Will you please remember that I am nearly nineteen? I know how to look after myself. Besides, there are plenty of people with whom I might stay if I chose."

"Suzanne Dale, you talk like one possessed. I'll listen to nothing of the sort. You are my daughter, and as such, subject to my guardianship. Of what are you thinking? What have you been reading? There's some silly thing at the bottom of all this. I'll not go away and leave you and you will come with me. I should think that after all these years of devotion on my part, you would take my feelings into consideration. How can you stand there and argue with me in this way?"

"Arguing, mama?" asked Suzanne loftily. "I'm not arguing. I'm just not going. I have my reasons for not wanting to go, and I'm not going, that's all! Now you may go if you want to."

Mrs. Dale looked into Suzanne's eyes and saw for the first time a gleam of real defiance in them. What had brought this about? Why was her daughter so set—of a sudden, so stubborn and hard? Fear, anger, astonishment, mingled equally in her feelings.

"What do you mean by reasons?" asked her mother. "What reasons have you?"

"A very good one," said Suzanne quietly, twisting it to the singular.

"Well, what is it then, pray?"

Suzanne debated swiftly and yet a little vaguely in her own mind. She had hoped for a longer process of philosophic discussion in which to entrap her mother into some moral and intellectual position from which she could not well recede, and by reason of which she would have to grant her the license she desired. From one remark and another dropped in this and the preceding conversation, she realized that her mother had no logical arrangement in her mind whereby she included her in her philosophical calculations at all. She might favor any and every theory and conclusion under the sun, but it would mean nothing in connection with Suzanne. The only thing that remained, therefore, was to defy her, or run away, and Suzanne did not want to do the latter. She was of age. She could adjust her own affairs. She had money. Her mental point of view was as good and sound as her mother's. As a matter of fact, the latter's attitude, in view of Suzanne's recent experience and feelings, seemed weak and futile. What did her mother know of life any more than she? They were both in the world, and Suzanne felt herself to be the stronger—the sounder of the two. Why not tell her now and defy her. She would win. She must. She could dominate her mother, and this was the time to do it.

"Because I want to stay near the man I love," she finally volunteered quietly.

Mrs. Dale's hand, which had been elevated to a position of gesticulation before her, dropped limp, involuntarily, to her side. Her mouth opened the least bit. She stared in a surprised, anguished, semi-foolish way.

"The man you love, Suzanne?" she asked, swept completely from her moorings, and lost upon a boundless sea. "Who is he?"

"Mr. Witla, mama—Eugene. I love him and he loves me. Don't stare, mama. Mrs. Witla knows. She is willing that we should have each other. We love each other. I am going to stay here where I can be near him. He needs me."

"Eugene Witla!" exclaimed her mother, breathless, a look of horror in her eyes, cold fright in her tense hands. "You love Eugene Witla? a married man! He loves you! Are you talking to me? Eugene Witla!! You love him! Why I can't believe this. I'm not in my right mind. Suzanne Dale, don't stand there! Don't look at me like that! Are you telling me, your mother? Tell me it isn't so! Tell me it isn't so before you drive me mad! Oh, great Heavens, what am I coming to? What have I done? Eugene Witla of all men! Oh, God, oh, God, oh, God!"

"Why do you carry on so, mama?" asked Suzanne calmly. She had expected some such scene as this—not quite so intense, so hysterical, but something like it, and was, in a way, prepared for it. A selfish love was her animating, governing impulse—a love also that stilled self, and put aside as nothing all the world and its rules. Suzanne really did not know what she was doing. She was hypnotized by the sense of perfection in her lover, the beauty of their love. Not practical facts but the beauty of the summer, the feel of cool winds, the glory of skies and sunlight and moonlight, were in her mind. Eugene's arms about her, his lips to hers, meant more than all the world beside. "I love him. Of course, I love him. What is there so strange about that?"

"What is strange? Are you in your right mind? Oh, my poor, dear little girl! My Suzanne! Oh, that villain! That scoundrel! To come into my house and make love to you, my darling child! How should you know? How could I expect you to understand? Oh, Suzanne! for my sake, for the love of Heaven, hush! Never breathe it! Never say that terrible thing to me again! Oh, dear! Oh, dear! Oh, dear!!! That I should live to see this! My child! My Suzanne! My lovely, beautiful Suzanne! I shall die unless I can stop this! I shall die! I shall die!"

Suzanne stared at her mother quite astonished at the violent emotion into which she had cast her. Her pretty eyes were open wide, her eyebrows elevated, her lips parted sweetly. She was a picture of intense classic beauty, chiseled, peaceful, self-possessed. Her brow was as smooth as marble, her lips as arched as though they had never known one emotion outside joy. Her look was of a quizzical, slightly amused, but not supercilious character which made her more striking than ever if possible.

"Why, mama! You think I am a child, don't you? All that I say to you is true. I love Eugene. He loves me. I am going to live with him as soon as it can be quietly arranged. I wanted to tell you because I don't want to do anything secretly, but I propose to do it. I wish you wouldn't insist on looking on me as a baby, mama. I know what I am doing. I have thought it all out this long time."

"Thought it all out!" pondered Mrs. Dale. "Going to live with him when it can be arranged! Is she talking of living with a man without a wedding ceremony being performed? With a man already married! Is the child stark mad? Something has turned her brain. Surely something has. This is not my Suzanne—my dear, lovely, entrancing Suzanne."

To Suzanne she exclaimed aloud:

"Are you talking of living with this, with this, oh, I don't dare to name him. I'll die if I don't get this matter straightened out; of living without a marriage ceremony and without his being divorced? I can't believe that I am awake. I can't! I can't!"

"Certainly I am," replied Suzanne. "It is all arranged between us. Mrs. Witla knows. She has given her consent. I expect you to give yours, if you desire me to stay here, mama."

"Give my consent! As God is my witness! Am I alive? Is this my daughter talking to me? Am I in this room here with you? I." She stopped, her mouth wide open. "If it weren't so horribly tragic, I should laugh. I will! I will become hysterical! My brain is whirling like a wheel now. Suzanne Dale, you are insane. You are madly, foolishly insane. If you do not hush and cease this terrible palaver, I will have you locked up. I will have an inquiry made into your sanity. This is the wildest, most horrible, most unimaginable thing ever proposed to a mother. To think that I should have lived with you eighteen long years, carried you in my arms, nursed you at my breast and then have you stand here and tell me that you will go and live unsanctioned with a man who has a good true woman now living as his wife. This is the most astounding thing I have ever heard of. It is unbelievable. You will not do it. You will no more do it than you will fly. I will kill him! I will kill you! I would rather see you dead at my feet this minute than to even think that you could have stood there and proposed such a thing to me. It will never be! It will never be! I will give you poison first. I will do anything, everything, but you shall never see this man again. If he dares to cross this threshold, I will kill him at sight. I love you. I think you are a wonderful girl, but this thing shall never be. And don't you dare to attempt to dissuade me. I will kill you, I tell you. I would rather see you dead a thousand times. To think! To think! To think! Oh, that beast! That villain! that unconscionable cur! To think that he should come into my house after all my courtesy to him and do this thing to me. Wait! He has position, he has distinction. I will drive him out of New York. I will ruin him. I will make it impossible for him to show his face among decent people. Wait and see!"

Her face was white, her hands clenched, her teeth set. She had a keen, savage beauty, much like that of a tigress when it shows its teeth. Her eyes were hard and cruel and flashing. Suzanne had never imagined her mother capable of such a burst of rage as this.

"Why, mama," she said calmly and quite unmoved, "you talk as though you ruled my life completely. You would like to make me feel, I suppose, that I do not dare to do what I choose. I do, mama. My life is my own, not yours. You cannot frighten me. I have made up my mind what I am going to do in this matter, and I am going to do it. You cannot stop me. You might as well not try. If I don't do it now, I will later. I love Eugene. I am going to live with him. If you won't let me I will go away, but I propose to live with him, and you might as well stop now trying to frighten me, for you can't."

"Frighten you! Frighten you! Suzanne Dale, you haven't the faintest, weakest conception of what you are talking about, or of what I mean to do. If a breath of this—the faintest intimation of your intention were to get abroad, you would be socially ostracized. Do you realize that you would not have a friend left in the world—that all the people you now know and are friendly with would go across the street to avoid you? If you didn't have independent means, you couldn't even get a position in an ordinary shop. Going to live with him? You are going to die first, right here in my charge and in my arms. I love you too much not to kill you. I would a thousand times rather die with you myself. You are not going to see that man any more, not once, and if he dares to show his face here, I will kill him. I have said it. I mean it. Now you provoke me to action if you dare."

Suzanne merely smiled. "How you talk, mama. You make me laugh."

Mrs. Dale stared.

"Oh, Suzanne! Suzanne!" she suddenly exclaimed. "Before it is too late, before I learn to hate you, before you break my heart, come to my arms and tell me that you are sorry—that it is all over—that it is all a vile, dark, hateful dream. Oh, my Suzanne! My Suzanne!"

"No, mama, no. Don't come near, don't touch me," said Suzanne, drawing back. "You haven't any idea of what you are talking about, of what I am, or what I mean to do. You don't understand me. You never did, mama. You have always looked down on me in some superior way as though you knew a great deal and I very little. It isn't that way at all. It isn't true. I know what I am about. I know what I am doing. I love Mr. Witla, and I am going to live with him. Mrs. Witla understands. She knows how it is. You will. I don't care anything at all about what people think. I don't care what any society friends do. They are not making my life. They are all just as narrow and selfish as they can be, anyhow. Love is something different from that. You don't understand me. I love Eugene, and he is going to have me, and I am going to have him. If you want to try to wreck my life and his, you may, but it won't make any difference. I will have him, anyhow. We might just as well quit talking about it now."

"Quit talking about it? Quit talking about it? Indeed, I haven't even begun talking yet. I am just trying to collect my wits, that's all. You are raging in insanity. This thing will never be. It will nev-er be. You are just a poor, deluded slip of girl, whom I have failed to watch sufficiently. From now on, I will do my duty by you, if God spares me. You need me. Oh, how you need me. Poor little Suzanne!"

"Oh, hush, mama! Stop the hysteria," interrupted Suzanne.

"I will call up Mr. Colfax. I will call up Mr. Winfield. I will have him discharged. I will expose him in the newspapers. The scoundrel, the villain, the thief! Oh, that I should have lived to see this day. That I should have lived to have seen this day!"

"That's right, mama," said Suzanne, wearily. "Go on. You are just talking, you know, and I know that you are. You cannot change me. Talking cannot. It is silly to rave like this, I think. Why won't you be quiet? We may talk, but needn't scream."

Mrs. Dale put her hands to her temples. Her brain seemed to be whirling.

"Never mind, now," she said. "Never mind. I must have time to think. But this thing you are thinking will never be. It never will be. Oh! Oh!" and she turned sobbing to the window.

Suzanne merely stared. What a peculiar thing emotions were in people—their emotions over morals. Here was her mother, weeping, and she was looking upon the thing her mother was crying about as the most essential and delightful and desirable thing. Certainly life was revealing itself to her rapidly these days. Did she really love Eugene so much? Yes, yes, yes, indeed. A thousand times yes. This was not a tearful emotion for her, but a great, consuming, embracing joy.

CHAPTER XIV

For hours that night, until one, two, and three o'clock in the morning; from five, six and seven on until noon and night of the next day, and the next day after that and the fourth day and the fifth day, the storm continued. It was a terrible, siege, heart burning, heart breaking, brain racking; Mrs. Dale lost weight rapidly. The color left her cheeks, a haggard look settled in her eyes. She was terrified, nonplussed, driven to extremities for means wherewith to overcome Suzanne's opposition and suddenly but terribly developed will. No one would have dreamed that this quiet, sweet-mannered, introspective girl could be so positive, convinced and unbending when in action. She was as a fluid body that has become adamant. She was a creature made of iron, a girl with a heart of stone; nothing moved her—her mother's tears, her threats of social ostracism, of final destruction, of physical and moral destruction for Eugene and herself, her threats of public exposure in the newspapers, of incarceration in an asylum. Suzanne had watched her mother a long time and concluded that she loved to talk imposingly in an easy, philosophic, at times pompous, way, but that really there was very little in what she said. She did not believe that her mother had true courage—that she would risk incarcerating her in an asylum, or exposing Eugene to her own disadvantage, let alone poisoning or killing her. Her mother loved her. She would rage terribly for a time this way, then she would give in. It was Suzanne's plan to wear her down, to stand her ground firmly until her mother wearied and broke under the strain. Then she would begin to say a few words for Eugene, and eventually by much arguing and blustering, her mother would come round. Eugene would be admitted to the family councils again. He and Suzanne would argue it all out together in her mother's presence. They would probably agree to disagree in a secret way, but she would get Eugene and he her. Oh, the wonder of that joyous dénouement. It was so near now, and all for a little courageous fighting. She would fight, fight until her mother broke, and then—Oh, Eugene, Eugene!

Mrs. Dale was not to be so easily overcome as Suzanne imagined. Haggard and worn as she was, she was far from yielding. There was an actual physical conflict between them once when Suzanne, in the height of an argument, decided that she would call up Eugene on the phone and ask him to come down and help her settle the discussion. Mrs. Dale was determined that she should not. The servants were in the house listening, unable to catch at first the drift of the situation, but knowing almost by intuition that there was a desperate discussion going on. Suzanne decided to go down to the library where the phone was. Mrs. Dale put her back to the door and attempted to deter her. Suzanne tried to open it by pulling. Her mother unloosed her hands desperately, but it was very difficult, Suzanne was so strong.

"For shame," she said. "For shame! To make your mother contest with you. Oh, the degradation"—the while she was struggling. Finally, angry, hysteric tears coursed involuntarily down her cheeks and Suzanne was moved at last. It was so obvious that this was real bitter heart-burning on her mother's part. Her hair was shaken loose on one side—her sleeve torn.

"Oh, my goodness! my goodness!" Mrs Dale gasped at last, throwing herself in a chair and sobbing bitterly. "I shall never lift my head again. I shall never lift my head again."

Suzanne looked at her somewhat sorrowfully. "I'm sorry, mama," she said, "but you have brought it all on yourself. I needn't call him now. He will call me and I will answer. It all comes from your trying to rule me in your way. You won't realize that I am a personality also, quite as much as you are. I have my life to live. It is mine to do with as I please. You are not going to prevent me in the long run. You might just as well stop fighting with me now. I don't want to quarrel with you. I don't want to argue, but I am a grown woman, mama. Why don't you listen to reason? Why don't you let me show you how I feel about this? Two people loving each other have a right to be with each other. It isn't anyone else's concern."

"Anyone else's concern! Anyone else's concern!" replied her mother viciously. "What nonsense. What silly, love-sick drivel. If you had any idea of life, of how the world is organized, you would laugh at yourself. Ten years from now, one year even, you will begin to see what a terrible mistake you are trying to make. You will scarcely believe that you could have done or said what you are doing and saying now. Anyone else's concern! Oh, Merciful Heaven! Will nothing put even a suggestion of the wild, foolish, reckless character of the thing you are trying to do in your mind?"

"But I love him, mama," said Suzanne.

"Love! Love! You talk about love," said her mother bitterly and hysterically. "What do you know about it? Do you think he can be loving you when he wants to come here and take you out of a good home and a virtuous social condition and wreck your life, and bring you down into the mire, your life and mine, and that of your sisters and brother for ever and ever? What does he know of love? What do you? Think of Adele and Ninette and Kinroy. Have you no regard for them? Where is your love for me and for them? Oh, I have been so afraid that Kinroy might hear something of this. He would go and kill him. I know he would. I couldn't prevent it. Oh, the shame, the scandal, the wreck, it would involve us all in. Have you no conscience, Suzanne; no heart?"

Suzanne stared before her calmly. The thought of Kinroy moved her a little. He might kill Eugene—she couldn't tell—he was a courageous boy. Still there was no need for any killing, or exposure, or excitement of any kind if her mother would only behave herself. What difference did it make to her, or Kinroy, or anybody anywhere what she did? Why couldn't she if she wanted to? The risk was on her head. She was willing. She couldn't see what harm it would do.

She expressed this thought to her mother once who answered in an impassioned plea for her to look at the facts. "How many evil women of the kind and character you would like to make of yourself, do you know? How many would you like to know? How many do you suppose there are in good society? Look at this situation from Mrs. Witla's point of view. How would you like to be in her place? How would you like to be in mine? Suppose you were Mrs. Witla and Mrs. Witla were the other woman. What then?"

"I would let him go," said Suzanne.

"Yes! Yes! Yes! You would let him go. You might, but how would you feel? How would anyone feel? Can't you see the shame in all this, the disgrace? Have you no comprehension at all? No feeling?"

"Oh, how you talk, mama. How silly you talk. You don't know the facts. Mrs. Witla doesn't love him any more. She told me so. She has written me so. I had the letter and gave it back to Eugene. He doesn't care for her. She knows it. She knows he cares for me. What difference does it make if she doesn't love him. He's entitled to love somebody. Now I love him. I want him. He wants me. Why shouldn't we have each other?"

In spite of all her threats, Mrs. Dale was not without subsidiary thoughts of what any public move on her part would certainly, not probably, but immediately involve. Eugene was well known. To kill him, which was really very far from her thoughts, in any save a very secret way, would create a tremendous sensation and involve no end of examination, discussion, excited publicity. To expose him to either Colfax or Winfield meant in reality exposing Suzanne to them, and possibly to members of her own social set, for these men were of it, and might talk. Eugene's resignation would cause comment. If he left, Suzanne might run away with him—then what? There was the thought on her part that the least discussion or whisper of this to anybody might produce the most disastrous results. What capital the so-called "Yellow" newspapers would make out of a story of this character. How they would gloat over the details. It was a most terrible and dangerous situation, and yet it was plain that something had to be done and that immediately. What?

In this crisis it occurred to her that several things might be done and that without great danger of irremediable consequences if she could only have a little time in which Suzanne would promise to remain quiescent and do so. If she could get her to say that she would do nothing for ten days or five days all might be well for them. She could go to see Angela, Eugene, Mr. Colfax, if necessary. To leave Suzanne in order to go on these various errands, she had to obtain Suzanne's word, which she knew she could respect absolutely, that she would make no move of any kind until the time was up. Under pretense that Suzanne herself needed time to think, or should take it, she pleaded and pleaded until finally the girl, on condition that she be allowed to phone to Eugene and state how things stood, consented. Eugene had called her up on the second day after the quarrel began and had been informed by the butler, at Mrs. Dale's request, that she was out of town. He called the second day, and got the same answer. He wrote to her and Mrs. Dale hid the letter, but on the fourth day, Suzanne called him up and explained. The moment she did so, he was sorry that she had been so hasty in telling her mother, terribly so, but there was nothing to be done now save to stand by his guns. He was ready in a grim way to rise or fall so long as, in doing either, he should obtain his heart's desire.

"Shall I come and help you argue?" he asked.

"No, not for five days. I have given my word."

"Shall I see you?"

"No, not for five days, Eugene."

"Mayn't I even call you up?"

"No, not for five days. After that, yes."

"All right, Flower Face—Divine Fire. I'll obey. I'm yours to command. But, oh, sweet, it's a long time."

"I know, but it will pass."

"And you won't change?"

"No."

"They can't make you?"

"No, you know they can't, dearest. Why do you ask?"

"Oh, I can't help feeling a little fearful, sweet. You are so young, so new to love."

"I won't change. I won't change. I don't need to swear. I won't."

"Very well, then, Myrtle Bloom."

She hung up the receiver, and Mrs. Dale knew now that her greatest struggle was before her.

Her several contemplated moves consisted first, in going to see Mrs. Witla, unknown to Suzanne and Eugene, learning what she knew of how things were and what she would advise.

This really did no good, unless the fact that it fomented anew the rage and grief of Angela, and gave Mrs. Dale additional material wherewith to belabor Eugene, could be said to be of advantage. Angela, who had been arguing and pleading with Eugene all this time, endeavoring by one thought and another to awaken him to a sense of the enormity of the offense he was contemplating, was practically in despair. She had reached the point where she had become rather savage again, and he also. In spite of her condition, in spite of all she could say, he was cold and bitter, so insistent that he was through with the old order that he made her angry. Instead of leaving him, as she might have done, trusting to time to alter his attitude, or to teach her the wisdom of releasing him entirely, she preferred to cling to him, for there was still affection left. She was used to him, he was the father of her coming child, unwelcome as it was. He represented her social position to her, her station in the world. Why should she leave him? Then, too, there was this fear of the outcome, which would come over her like a child. She might die. What would become of the child?

"You know, Mrs. Dale," she said at one point significantly, "I don't hold Suzanne absolutely guiltless. She is old enough to know better. She has been out in society long enough to know that a married man is sacred property to another woman."

"I know, I know," replied Mrs. Dale resentfully, but cautiously, "but Suzanne is so young. You really don't know how much of a child she is. And she has this silly, idealistic, emotional disposition. I suspected something of it, but I did not know it was so strong. I'm sure I don't know where she gets it. Her father was most practical. But she was all right until your husband persuaded her."

"That may be all true," went on Angela, "but she is not guiltless. I know Eugene. He is weak, but he will not follow where he is not led, and no girl need be tempted unless she wants to."

"Suzanne is so young," again pleaded Mrs. Dale.

"Well, I'm sure if she knew Mr. Witla's record accurately," went on Angela foolishly, "she wouldn't want him. I have written her. She ought to know. He isn't honest and he isn't moral as this thing shows. If this were the first time he had fallen in love with another woman, I could forgive him, but it isn't. He did something quite as bad six or seven years ago, and only two years before that there was another woman. He wouldn't be faithful to Suzanne if he had her. It would be a case of blazing affection for a little while, and then he would tire and cast her aside. Why, you can tell what sort of a man he is when he would propose to me, as he did here, that I should let him maintain a separate establishment for Suzanne and say nothing of it. The idea!"

Mrs. Dale clicked her lips significantly. She considered Angela foolish for talking in this way, but it could not be helped now. Possibly Eugene had made a mistake in marrying her. This did not excuse him, however, in her eyes for wanting to take Suzanne under the conditions he proposed. If he were free, it would be an entirely different matter. His standing, his mind, his manners, were not objectionable, though he was not to the manner born.

Mrs. Dale went away toward evening, greatly nonplussed by what she had seen and heard, but convinced that no possible good could come of the situation. Angela would never give him a divorce. Eugene was not a fit man morally for her daughter, anyhow. There was great scandal on the verge of exposure here in which her beloved daughter would be irretrievably smirched. In her desperation, she decided, if she could do no better, she would try to dissuade Eugene from seeing Suzanne until he could obtain a divorce, in which case, to avoid something worse, she would agree to a marriage, but this was only to be a lip promise. The one thing she wanted to do was to get Suzanne to give him up entirely. If Suzanne could be spirited away, or dissuaded from throwing herself away on Eugene, that would be the thing. Still, she proposed to see what a conversation with Eugene would do.

The next morning as he was sitting in his office wondering what the delay of five days portended, and what Suzanne was doing, as well as trying to fix his mind on the multitudinous details which required his constant attention, and were now being rather markedly neglected, the card of Mrs. Emily Dale was laid on his table, and a few moments later, after his secretary had been dismissed, and word given that no one else was to be allowed to enter, Mrs. Dale was shown in.

She was pale and weary, but exquisitely dressed in a greenish blue silk and picture hat of black straw and feathers. She looked quite young and handsome herself, not too old for Eugene, and indeed once she had fancied he might well fall in love with her. What her thoughts were at that time, she was not now willing to recall, for they had involved the probable desertion or divorce, or death of Angela, and Eugene's passionate infatuation for her. All that was over now, of course, and in the excitement and distress, almost completely obliterated. Eugene had not forgotten that he had had similar sensations or imaginations at the time, and that Mrs. Dale had always drawn to him in a sympathetic and friendly way. Here she was, though, this morning coming upon a desperate mission no doubt, and he would have to contend with her as best he could.

The conversation opened by his looking into her set face as she approached and smiling blandly, though it was something of an effort. "Well," he said, in quite a business like way, "what can I do for you?"

"You villain," she exclaimed melodramatically, "my daughter has told me all."

"Yes, Suzanne phoned me that she told you," he replied, in a conciliatory tone.

"Yes," she said in a low, tense voice, "and I ought to kill you where you stand. To think that I should have ever harbored such a monster as you in my home and near my dear, innocent daughter. It seems incredible now. I can't believe it. That you should dare. And you with a dear, sweet wife at home, sick and in the condition she is in. I should think if you had any manhood at all any sense of shame! When I think of that poor, dear little woman, and what you have been doing, or trying to do—if it weren't for the scandal you would never leave this office alive."

"Oh, bother! Don't talk rot, Mrs. Dale," said Eugene quietly, though irritably. He did not care for her melodramatic attitude. "The dear, darling little woman you speak of is not as badly off as you think, and I don't think she needs as much of your sympathy as you are so anxious to give. She is pretty well able to take care of herself, sick as she is. As for killing me, you or anyone else, well that wouldn't be such a bad idea. I'm not so much in love with life. This is not fifty years ago, though, but the nineteenth century, and this is New York City. I love Suzanne. She loves me. We want each other desperately. Now, an arrangement can be made which will not interfere with you in any way, and which will adjust things for us. Suzanne is anxious to make that arrangement. It is as much her proposition as it is mine. Why should you be so vastly disturbed? You know a great deal about life."

"Why should I be disturbed? Why should I? Can you sit in this office, you a man in charge of all this vast public work, and ask me in cold blood why I should be disturbed? And my daughter's very life at stake. Why should I be disturbed and my daughter only out of her short dresses a little while ago and practically innocent of the world. You dare to tell me that she proposed! Oh, you impervious scoundrel! To think I could be so mistaken in any human being. You, with your bland manners and your inconsistent talk of happy family life. I might have understood, though, when I saw you so often without your wife. I should have known. I did, God help me! but I didn't act upon it. I was taken by your bland, gentlemanly attitude. I don't blame poor, dear little Suzanne. I blame you, you utterly deceiving villain and myself for being so silly. I am being justly rewarded, however."

Eugene merely looked at her and drummed with his fingers.

"But I did not come here to bandy words with you," she went on. "I came to say that you must never see my daughter again, or speak of her, or appear where she might chance to be, though she won't be where you may appear, if I have my way, for you won't have a chance to appear anywhere in decent society very much longer. I shall go, unless you agree here and now never to see or communicate with her any more, to Mr. Colfax, whom I know personally, as you are aware, and lay the whole matter before him. I'm sure with what I know now of your record, and what you have attempted to do in connection with my daughter, and the condition of your wife, that he will not require your services very much longer. I shall go to Mr. Winfield, who is also an old friend, and lay the matter before him. Privately you will be drummed out of society and my daughter will be none the worse for it. She is so very young that when the facts are known, you are the only one who will bear the odium of this. Your wife has given me your wretched record only yesterday. You would like to make my Suzanne your fourth or fifth. Well, you will not. I will show you something you have not previously known. You are dealing with a desperate mother. Defy me if you dare. I demand that you write your farewell to Suzanne here and now, and let me take it to her."

Eugene smiled sardonically. Mrs. Dale's reference to Angela made him bitter. She had been there and Angela had talked of him—his past to her. What a mean thing to do. After all, Angela was his wife. Only the morning before, she had been appealing to him on the grounds of love, and she had not told him of Mrs. Dale's visit. Love! Love! What sort of love was this? He had done enough for her to make her generous in a crisis like this, even if she did not want to be.

"Write you a statement of release to Suzanne?" he observed, his lips curling—"how silly. Of course, I won't. And as for your threat to run to Mr. Colfax, I have heard that before from Mrs. Witla. There is the door. His office is twelve flights down. I'll call a boy, if you wish. You tell it to Mr.

Colfax and see how much farther it goes before you are much older. Run to Mr. Winfield also. A lot I care about him or Mr. Colfax. If you want a grand, interesting discussion of this thing, just begin. It will go far and wide, I assure you. I love your daughter. I'm desperate about her. I'm literally crazy about her"—he got up—"she loves me, or I think she does. Anyhow, I'm banking all on that thought. My life from the point of view of affection has been a failure. I have never really been in love before, but I am crazy about Suzanne Dale. I am wild about her. If you had any sympathy for an unhappy, sympathetic, emotional mortal, who has never yet been satisfied in a woman, you would give her to me. I love her. I love her. By God!"— he banged the desk with his fist—"I will do anything for her. If she will come to me, Colfax can have his position, Winfield can have his Blue Sea Corporation. You can have her money, if she wants to give it to you. I can make a living abroad by my art, and I will. Other Americans have done it before me. I love her! I love her! Do you hear me? I love her, and what's more, I'm going to have her! You can't stop me. You haven't the brains; you haven't the strength; you haven't the resources to match that girl. She's brighter than you are. She's stronger, she's finer. She's finer than the whole current day conception of society and life. She loves me and she wants to give herself to me, willingly, freely, joyously. Match that in your petty society circles if you can. Society! You say you will have me drummed out of it, will you? A lot I care about your society. Hacks, mental light weights, money grubbers, gamblers, thieves, leeches—a fine lot! To see you sitting there and talking to me with your grand air makes me laugh. A lot I care for you. I was thinking of another kind of woman when I met you, not a narrow, conventional fool. I thought I saw one in you. I did, didn't I—not? You are like all the rest, a narrow, petty slavish follower after fashion and convention. Well," he snapped his fingers in her face, "go on and do your worst. I will get Suzanne in the long run. She will come to me. She will dominate you. Run to Colfax! Run to Winfield! I will get her just the same. She's mine. She belongs to me. She is big enough for me. The Gods have given her to me, and I will have her if I have to smash you and your home and myself and everyone else connected with me. I'll have her! I'll have her! She is mine! She is mine!" He lifted a tense hand. "Now you run and do anything you want to. Thank God, I've found one woman who knows how to live and love. She's mine!"

Mrs. Dale stared at him in amazement, scarcely believing her ears. Was he crazy? Was he really so much in love? Had Suzanne turned his brain? What an astonishing thing. She had never seen him anything like this— never imagined him capable of anything like it. He was always so quiet, smiling, bland, witty. Here he was dramatic, impassioned, fiery, hungry.

There was a terrible light in his eyes and he was desperate. He must be in love.

"Oh, why will you do this to me?" she whimpered all at once. The terror of his mood conveying itself to her for the moment, and arousing a sympathy which she had not previously felt. "Why will you come into my home and attempt to destroy it? There are lots of women who will love you. There are lots more suited to your years and temperament than Suzanne. She doesn't understand you. She doesn't understand herself. She is just young, and foolish and hypnotized. You have hypnotized her. Oh, why will you do this to me? You are so much older than her, so much more schooled in life. Why not give her up? I don't want to go to Mr. Colfax. I don't want to speak to Mr. Winfield. I will, if I have to, but I don't want to. I have always thought so well of you. I know you are not an ordinary man. Restore my respect for you, my confidence in you. I can forgive, if I can't forget. You may not be happily married. I am sorry for you. I don't want to do anything desperate. I only want to save poor, little Suzanne. Oh, please! please! I love her so. I don't think you understand how I feel. You may be in love, but you ought to be willing to consider others. True love would. I know that she is hard and wilful and desperate now, but she will change if you will help her. Why, if you really love her, if you have any sympathy for me or regard for her future, or your own, you will renounce your schemes and release her. Tell her you made a mistake. Write to her now. Tell her you can't do this and not socially ruin her and me and yourself, and so you won't do it. Tell her that you have decided to wait until time has made you a free man, if that is to be, and then let her have a chance of seeing if she will not be happy in a normal life. You don't want to ruin her at this age, do you? She is so young, so innocent. Oh, if you have any judgment of life at all, any regard, any consideration, anything, I beg of you; I beg as her mother, for I love her. Oh!" Tears came into her eyes again and she cried weakly in her handkerchief.

Eugene stared at her. What was he doing? Where was he going? Was he really as bad as he appeared to be here? Was he possessed? Was he really so hard-hearted? Through her grief and Angela's and the threats concerning Colfax and Winfield, he caught a glimpse of the real heart of the situation. It was as if there had been a great flash of lightning illuminating a black landscape. He saw sympathetically, sorrow, folly, a number of things that were involved, and then the next moment, it was gone. Suzanne's face came back, smooth, classic, chiseled, perfectly modeled, her beauty like a tightened bow; her eyes, her lips, her hair, the gaiety and buoyancy of her motions and her smile. Give her up! Give up Suzanne and that dream of the studio, and of joyous, continuous, delicious companionship? Did Suzanne want him to? What had she said over the phone? No! No! No! Quit now, and her clinging to him. No! No! No! Never!! He would fight first. He would go down fighting. Never! Never! Never!

His brain seethed.

"I can't do it," he said, getting up again, for he had sat down after his previous tirade. "I can't do it. You are asking something that is utterly impossible. It can never be done. God help me, I'm insane, I'm wild over her. Go and do anything you want to, but I must have her and I will. She's mine! She's mine! She's mine!"

His thin, lean hands clenched and he clicked his teeth.

"Mine, mine, mine!" he muttered, and one would have thought him a villain in a cheap melodrama.

Mrs. Dale shook her head.

"God help us both!" she said. "You shall never, never have her. You are not worthy of her. You are not right in your mind. I will fight you with all the means in my power. I am desperate! I am wealthy. I know how to fight. You shall not have her. Now we will see which will win." She rose to go and Eugene followed her.

"Go ahead," he said calmly, "but in the end you lose. Suzanne comes to me. I know it. I feel it. I may lose many other things, but I get her. She's mine."

"Oh," sighed Mrs. Dale wearily, half believing him and moving towards the door. "Is this your last word?"

"It is positively."

"Then I must be going."

"Good-bye," he said solemnly.

"Good-bye," she answered, white faced, her eyes staring.

She went out and Eugene took up the telephone; but he remembered that Suzanne had warned him not to call, but to depend on her. So he put it down again.

CHAPTER XV

The fire and pathos of Mrs. Dale's appeal should have given Eugene pause. He thought once of going after her and making a further appeal, saying that he would try and get a divorce eventually and marry Suzanne, but he remembered that peculiar insistency of Suzanne on the fact that she did not want to get married. Somehow, somewhere, somewhy, she had formulated this peculiar ideal or attitude, which whatever the world might think of it, was possible of execution, providing he and she were tactful enough. It was not such a wild thing for two people to want to come together in this way, if they chose, he thought. Why was it? Heaven could witness there were enough illicit and peculiar relationships in this world to prevent society from becoming excited about one more, particularly when it was to be conducted in so circumspect and subtle a way. He and Suzanne did not intend to blazon their relationship to the world. As a distinguished artist, not active, but acknowledged and accomplished, he was entitled to a studio life. He and Suzanne could meet there. Nothing would be thought of it. Why had she insisted on telling her mother? It could all have been done without that. There was another peculiar ideal of hers, her determination to tell the truth under all circumstances. And yet she had really not told it. She had deceived her mother a long time about him simply by saying nothing. Was this some untoward trick of fate's, merely devised to harm him? Surely not. And yet Suzanne's headstrong determination seemed almost a fatal mistake now. He sat down brooding over it. Was this a terrific blunder? Would he be sorry? All his life was in the balance. Should he turn back?

No! No! No! Never! It was not to be. He must go on. He must! He must! So he brooded.

The next of Mrs. Dale's resources was not quite so unavailing as the others, though it was almost so. She had sent for Dr. Latson Woolley, her family physician—an old school practitioner of great repute, of rigid honor and rather Christian principles himself, but also of a wide intellectual and moral discernment, so far as others were concerned.

"Well, Mrs. Dale," he observed, when he was ushered into her presence in the library on the ground floor, and extending his hand cordially, though wearily, "what can I do for you this morning?"

"Oh, Dr. Woolley," she began directly, "I am in so much trouble. It isn't a case of sickness. I wish it were. It is something so much worse. I have sent for you because I know I can rely on your judgment and sympathy. It concerns my daughter, Suzanne."

"Yes, yes," he grunted, in a rather crusty voice, for his vocal cords were old, and his eyes looked out from under shaggy, gray eyebrows which somehow bespoke a world of silent observation. "What's the matter with her? What has she done now that she ought not to do?"

"Oh, doctor," exclaimed Mrs. Dale nervously, for the experiences of the last few days had almost completely dispelled her normal composure, "I don't know how to tell you, really. I don't know how to begin. Suzanne, my dear precious Suzanne, in whom I have placed so much faith and reliance has, has— —"

"Well, tell me," interrupted Dr. Woolley laconically.

When she had told him the whole story, and answered some of his incisive questions, he said:

"Well, I am thinking you have a good deal to be grateful for. She might have yielded without your knowledge and told you afterwards—or not at all."

"Not at all. Oh, doctor! My Suzanne!"

"Mrs. Dale, I looked after you and your mother before you and Suzanne. I know something about human nature and your family characteristics. Your husband was a very determined man, as you will remember. Suzanne may have some of his traits in her. She is a very young girl, you want to remember, very robust and vigorous. How old is this Witla man?"

"About thirty-eight or nine, doctor."

"Um! I suspected as much. The fatal age. It's a wonder you came through that period as safely as you did. You're nearly forty, aren't you?"

"Yes, doctor, but you're the only one that knows it."

"I know, I know. It's the fatal age. You say he is in charge of the United Magazines Corporation. I have probably heard of him. I know of Mr. Colfax of that company. Is he very emotional in his temperament?"

"I had never thought so before this."

"Well, he probably is. Thirty-eight to thirty-nine and eighteen or nineteen—bad combination. Where is Suzanne?"

"Upstairs in her room, I fancy."

"It might not be a bad thing if I talked to her myself a little, though I don't believe it will do any good."

Mrs. Dale disappeared and was gone for nearly three-quarters of an hour. Suzanne was stubborn, irritable, and to all preliminary entreaties insisted that she would not. Why should her mother call in outsiders, particularly Dr. Woolley, whom she knew and liked. She suspected at once when her mother said Dr. Woolley wanted to see her that it had something to do with her case, and demanded to know why. Finally, after much pleading, she consented to come down, though it was with the intention of showing her mother how ridiculous all her excitement was.

The old doctor who had been meditating upon the inexplicable tangle, chemical and physical, of life—the blowing hither and thither of diseases, affections, emotions and hates of all kinds, looked up quizzically as Suzanne entered.

"Well, Suzanne," he said genially, rising and walking slowly toward her, "I'm glad to see you again. How are you this morning?"

"Pretty well, doctor, how are you?"

"Oh, as you see, as you see, a little older and a little fussier, Suzanne, making other people's troubles my own. Your mother tells me you have fallen in love. That's an interesting thing to do, isn't it?"

"You know, doctor," said Suzanne defiantly, "I told mama that I don't care to discuss this, and I don't think she has any right to try to make me. I don't want to and I won't. I think it is all in rather poor taste."

"Poor taste, Suzanne?" asked Mrs. Dale. "Do you call our discussion of what you want to do poor taste, when the world will think that what you want to do is terrible when you do it?"

"I told you, mama, that I was not coming down here to discuss this thing, and I'm not!" said Suzanne, turning to her mother and ignoring Dr. Woolley. "I'm not going to stay. I don't want to offend Dr. Woolley, but I'm not going to stay and have you argue this all over again."

She turned to go.

"There, there, Mrs. Dale, don't interrupt," observed Dr. Woolley, holding Suzanne by the very tone of his voice. "I think myself that very little is to be gained by argument. Suzanne is convinced that what she is planning to do is to her best interest. It may be. We can't always tell. I think the best thing that could be discussed, if anything at all in this matter can be discussed, is the matter of time. It is my opinion that before doing this thing that Suzanne wants to do, and which may be all right, for all I know, it would be best if she would take a little time. I know nothing of Mr. Witla. He may be a most able and worthy man. Suzanne ought to give herself a little time to think, though. I should say three months, or six months. A great many after effects hang on this decision, as you know," he said, turning to Suzanne. "It may involve responsibilities you are not quite ready to shoulder. You are only eighteen or nineteen, you know. You might have to give up dancing and society, and travel, and a great many things, and devote yourself to being a mother and ministering to your husband's needs. You expect to live with him permanently, don't you?"

"I don't want to discuss this, Dr. Woolley."

"But you do expect that, don't you?"

"Only as long as we love each other."

"Um, well, you might love him for some little time yet. You rather expect to do that, don't you?"

"Why, yes, but what is the good of this, anyhow? My mind is made up." "Just the matter of thinking," said Dr. Woolley, very soothingly and in a voice which disarmed Suzanne and held her. "Just a little time in which to be absolutely sure. Your mother is anxious not to have you do it at all. You, as I understand it, want to do this thing right away. Your mother loves you, and at bottom, in spite of this little difference, I know you love her. It just occurred to me that for the sake of good feeling all around, you might like to strike a balance. You might be willing to take, say six months, or a year and think about it. Mr. Witla would probably not object. You won't be any the less delightful to him at the end of that time, and as for your mother, she would feel a great deal better if she thought that, after all, what you decided to do you had done after mature deliberation."

"Yes," exclaimed Mrs. Dale, impulsively, "do take time to think, Suzanne. A year won't hurt you."

"No," said Suzanne unguardedly. "It is all a matter of whether I want to or not. I don't want to."

"Precisely. Still this is something you might take into consideration. The situation from all outside points of view is serious. I haven't said so, but I feel that you would be making a great mistake. Still, that is only my opinion. You are entitled to yours. I know how you feel about it, but the public is not likely to feel quite the same. The public is a wearisome thing, Suzanne, but we have to take it into consideration."

Suzanne stared stubbornly and wearily at her tormentors. Their logic did not appeal to her at all. She was thinking of Eugene and her plan. It could be worked. What did she care about the world? During all this talk, she drew nearer and nearer the door and finally opened it.

"Well, that is all," said Dr. Woolley, when he saw she was determined to go. "Good morning, Suzanne. I am glad to have seen you again."

"Good morning, Dr. Woolley," she replied.

She went out and Mrs. Dale wrung her hands. "I wish I knew what was to be done," she exclaimed, gazing at her counselor.

Dr. Woolley brooded over the folly of undesired human counsel.

"There is no need for excitement," he observed after a time. "It is obvious to me that if she is handled rightly, she will wait. She is in a state of high strung opposition and emotion for some reason at present. You have driven her too hard. Relax. Let her think this thing out for herself. Counsel for delay, but don't irritate. You cannot control her by driving. She has too stern a will. Tears won't help. Emotion seems a little silly to her. Ask her to think, or better yet, let her think and plead only for delay. If you could get her away for two or three weeks or months, off by herself undisturbed by your pleadings and uninfluenced by his—if she would ask him of her own accord to let her alone for that time, all will be well. I don't think she will ever go to him. She thinks she will, but I have the feeling that she won't. However, be calm. If you can, get her to go away."

"Would it be possible to lock her up in some sanatorium or asylum, doctor, until she has had time to think?"

"All things are possible, but I should say it would be the most inadvisable thing you could do. Force accomplishes nothing in these cases."

"I know, but suppose she won't listen to reason?"

"You really haven't come to that bridge yet. You haven't talked calmly to her yet. You are quarreling with her. There is very little in that. You will simply grow further and further apart."

"How practical you are, doctor," observed Mrs. Dale, in a mollified and complimentary vein.

"Not practical, but intuitional. If I were practical, I would never have taken up medicine."

He walked to the door, his old body sinking in somewhat upon itself. His old, gray eyes twinkled slightly as he turned.

"You were in love once, Mrs. Dale," he said.

"Yes," she replied.

"You remember how you felt then?"

"Yes."

"Be reasonable. Remember your own sensations—your own attitude. You probably weren't crossed in your affair. She is. She has made a mistake. Be patient. Be calm. We want to stop it and no doubt can. Do unto others as you would be done by."

He ambled shufflingly across the piazza and down the wide steps to his car.

"Mama," she said, when after Dr. Woolley had gone her mother came to her room to see if she might not be in a mellower mood, and to plead with her further for delay, "it seems to me you are making a ridiculous mess of all this. Why should you go and tell Dr. Woolley about me! I will never forgive you for that. Mama, you have done something I never thought you would do. I thought you had more pride—more individuality."

One should have seen Suzanne, in her spacious boudoir, her back to her oval mirrored dressing table, her face fronting her mother, to understand her fascination for Eugene. It was a lovely, sunny, many windowed chamber, and Suzanne in a white and blue morning dress was in charming accord with the gay atmosphere of the room.

"Well, Suzanne, you know," she said, rather despondently, "I just couldn't help it. I had to go to someone. I am quite alone apart from you and Kinroy and the children"—she referred to Adele and Ninette as the children when talking to either Suzanne or Kinroy—"and I didn't want to say anything to them. You have been my only confidant up to now, and since you have turned against me——"

"I haven't turned against you, mama."

"Oh, yes you have. Let's not talk about it, Suzanne. You have broken my heart. You are killing me. I just had to go to someone. We have known Dr. Woolley so long. He is so good and kind."

"Oh, I know, mama, but what good will it do? How can anything he might say help matters? He isn't going to change me. You're only telling it to somebody who oughtn't to know anything about it."

"But I thought he might influence you," pleaded Mrs. Dale. "I thought you would listen to him. Oh, dear, oh, dear. I'm so tired of it all. I wish I were dead. I wish I had never lived to see this."

"Now there you go, mama," said Suzanne confidently. "I can't see why you are so distressed about what I am going to do. It is my life that I am planning to arrange, not yours. I have to live my life, mama, not you."

"Oh, yes, but it is just that that distresses me. What will it be after you do this—after you throw it away? Oh, if you could only see what you are contemplating doing—what a wretched thing it will be when it is all over with. You will never live with him—he is too old for you, too fickle, too insincere. He will not care for you after a little while, and then there you will be, unmarried, possibly with a child on your hands, a social outcast! Where will you go?"

"Mama," said Suzanne calmly, her lips parted in a rosy, baby way, "I have thought of all this. I see how it is. But I think you and everybody else make too much ado about these things. You think of everything that could happen, but it doesn't all happen that way. People do these things, I'm sure, and nothing much is thought of it."

"Yes, in books," put in Mrs. Dale. "I know where you get all this from. It's your reading."

"Anyhow, I'm going to. I have made up my mind," added Suzanne. "I have decided that by September fifteenth I will go to Mr. Witla, and you might just as well make up your mind to it now." This was August tenth.

"Suzanne," said her mother, staring at her, "I never imagined you could talk in this way to me. You will do nothing of the kind. How can you be so hard? I did not know that you had such a terrible will in you. Doesn't anything I have said about Adele and Ninette or Kinroy appeal to you? Have you no heart in you? Why don't you wait, as Dr. Woolley suggests, six months or a year? Why do you talk about jumping into this without giving yourself time to think? It is such a wild, rash experiment. You haven't thought anything about it, you haven't had time."

"Oh, yes, I have, mama!" replied Suzanne. "I've thought a great deal about it. I'm fully convinced. I want to do it then because I told Eugene that I would not keep him waiting long; and I won't. I want to go to him. That will make a clear two months since we first talked of this."

Mrs. Dale winced. She had no idea of yielding to her daughter, or letting her do this, but this definite conclusion as to the time brought matters finally to a head. Her daughter was out of her mind, that was all. It gave her not any too much time to turn round in. She must get Suzanne out of the city—out of the country, if possible, or lock her up, and she must do it without antagonizing her too much.

CHAPTER XVI

Mrs. Dale's next step in this struggle was to tell Kinroy, who wanted, of course, in a fit of boyish chivalry, to go immediately and kill Eugene. This was prevented by Mrs. Dale, who had more control over him than she had over Suzanne, pointing out to him what a terrifically destructive scandal would ensue and urging subtlety and patience. Kinroy had a sincere affection for his sisters, particularly Suzanne and Adele, and he wanted to protect all of them. He decided in a pompous, ultra chivalrous spirit that he must help his mother plan, and together they talked of chloroforming her some night, of carrying her thus, as a sick girl, in a private car to Maine or the Adirondacks or somewhere in Canada.

It would be useless to follow all these strategic details in their order. There were, after the five days agreed upon by Suzanne, attempted phone messages by Eugene, which were frustrated by Kinroy, who was now fulfilling the rôle of private detective. Suzanne resolved to have Eugene summoned to the house for a discussion, but to this her mother objected. She felt that additional meetings would simply strengthen their bond of union. Kinroy wrote to Eugene of his own accord that he knew all, and that if he attempted to come near the place he would kill him at sight. Suzanne, finding herself blocked and detained by her mother, wrote Eugene a letter which Elizabeth, her maid, secretly conveyed to the mail for her, telling him how things stood. Her mother had told Dr. Woolley and Kinroy. She had decided that September fifteenth was the time she would leave home, unless their companionship was quietly sanctioned. Kinroy had threatened to kill him to her, but she did not think he had anything to fear. Kinroy was just excited. Her mother wanted her to go to Europe for six months and think it over, but this she would not do. She was not going to leave the city, and he need not fear, if he did not hear anything for a few days at a time, that anything was wrong with her. They must wait until the storm subsided a little. "I shall be here, but perhaps it is best for you not to try to see me just now. When the time comes, I will come to you, and if I get a chance, I will see you before."

Eugene was both pained and surprised at the turn things had taken, but still encouraged to hope for the best by the attitude Suzanne took toward it all. Her courage strengthened him. She was calm, so purposeful! What a treasure she was!

So began a series of daily love notes for a few days, until Suzanne advised him to cease. There were constant arguments between her, her mother and Kinroy. Because she was being so obviously frustrated, she began to grow bitter and hard, and short contradictory phrases passed between her and her mother, principally originating in Suzanne.

"No, no, no!" was her constantly reiterated statement. "I won't do it! What of it? It's silly! Let me alone! I won't talk!" So it went.

Mrs. Dale was planning hourly how to abduct her. Chloroforming and secret removal after the fashion she had in her mind was not so easy of accomplishment. It was such a desperate thing to do to Suzanne. She was afraid she might die under its influence. It could not be administered without a doctor. The servants would think it strange. She fancied there were whispered suspicions already. Finally she thought of pretending to agree with Suzanne, removing all barriers, and asking her to come to Albany to confer with her guardian, or rather the legal representative of the Marquardt Trust Company, which held her share of her father the late Westfield Dale's estate in trust for her, in regard to some property in western New York, which belonged to her. Mrs. Dale decided to pretend to be obliged to go to Albany in order to have Suzanne sign a waiver of right to any share in her mother's private estate, after which, supposedly, she would give Suzanne her freedom, having also disinherited her in her will. Suzanne, according to this scheme, was then to come back to New York and go her way and her mother was not to see her any more.

To make this more effective, Kinroy was sent to tell her of her mother's plan and beg her for her own and her family's sake not to let the final separation come about. Mrs. Dale changed her manner. Kinroy acted his part so effectively that what with her mother's resigned look and indifferent method of address, Suzanne was partly deceived. She imagined her mother had experienced a complete change of heart and might be going to do what Kinroy said.

"No," she replied to Kinroy's pleadings, "I don't care whether she cuts me off. I'll be very glad to sign the papers. If she wants me to go away, I'll go. I think she has acted very foolishly through all this, and so have you."

"I wish you wouldn't let her do that," observed Kinroy, who was rather exulting over the satisfactory manner in which this bait was being swallowed. "Mama is broken hearted. She wants you to stay here, to wait six months or a year before you do anything at all, but if you won't, she's going to ask you to do this. I've tried to persuade her not to. I'd hate like anything to see you go. Won't you change your mind?"

"I told you I wouldn't, Kinroy. Don't ask me."

Kinroy went back to his mother and reported that Suzanne was stubborn as ever, but that the trick would in all probability work. She would go aboard the train thinking she was going to Albany. Once aboard, inside a closed car, she would scarcely suspect until the next morning, and then they would be far in the Adirondack Mountains.

The scheme worked in part. Her mother, as had Kinroy, went through this prearranged scene as well as though she were on the stage. Suzanne fancied she saw her freedom near at hand. Only a travelling bag was packed, and Suzanne went willingly enough into the auto and the train, only stipulating one thing—that she be allowed to call up Eugene and explain. Both Kinroy and her mother objected, but, when finally she refused flatly to go without, they acceded. She called him up at the office—it was four o'clock in the afternoon, and they were leaving at five-thirty—and told him. He fancied at once it was a ruse, and told her so, but she thought not. Mrs. Dale had never lied to her before, neither had her brother. Their words were as bonds.

"Eugene says this is a trap, mama," said Suzanne, turning from the phone to her mother, who was near by. "Is it?"

"You know it isn't," replied her mother, lying unblushingly.

"If it is, it will come to nothing," she replied, and Eugene heard her. He was strengthened into acquiescence by the tone of her voice. Surely she was a wonderful girl—a master of men and women in her way.

"Very well, if you think it's all right," said Eugene; "but I'll be very lonely. I've been so already. I shall be more so, Flower Face, unless I see you soon. Oh, if the time were only up!"

"It will be, Eugene," she replied, "in a very few days now. I'll be back Thursday, and then you can come down and see me."

"Thursday afternoon?"

"Yes. We're to be back Thursday morning."

She finally hung up the receiver and they entered the automobile and an hour later the train.

CHAPTER XVII

It was a Montreal, Ottawa and Quebec express, and it ran without stopping to Albany. By the time it was nearing the latter place Suzanne was going to bed—and because it was a private car—Mrs. Dale explained that the president of the road had lent it to her—no announcement of its arrival, which would have aroused Suzanne, was made by the porter. When it stopped there shortly after ten o'clock it was the last car at the south end of the train, and you could hear voices calling, but just what it was was not possible to say. Suzanne, who had already gone to bed, fancied it might be Poughkeepsie or some wayside station. Her mother's statement was that since they arrived so late, the car would be switched to a siding, and they would stay aboard until morning. Nevertheless, she and Kinroy were alert to prevent any untoward demonstration or decision on Suzanne's part, and so, as the train went on, she slept soundly until Burlington in the far northern part of Vermont was reached the next morning. When she awoke and saw that the train was still speeding on, she wondered vaguely but not clearly what it could mean. There were mountains about, or rather tall, pine-covered hills, mountain streams were passed on high trestles and sections of burned woodlands were passed where forest fires had left lonely, sad charred stretches of tree trunks towering high in the air. Suddenly it occurred to Suzanne that this was peculiar, and she came out of the bath to ask why.

"Where are we, mama?" she asked. Mrs. Dale was leaning back in a comfortable willow chair reading, or pretending to read a book. Kinroy was out on the observation platform for a moment. He came back though shortly, for he was nervous as to what Suzanne would do when she discovered her whereabouts. A hamper of food had been put aboard the night before, unknown to Suzanne, and Mrs. Dale was going shortly to serve breakfast. She had not risked a maid on this journey.

"I don't know," replied her mother indifferently, looking out at a stretch of burnt woods.

"I thought we were to be in Albany a little after midnight?" said Suzanne.

"So we were," replied Mrs. Dale, preparing to confess. Kinroy came back into the car.

"Well, then," said Suzanne, pausing, looking first out of the windows and then fixedly at her mother. It came to her as she saw the unsettled, somewhat nervous expression in her mother's face and eyes and in Kinroy's that this was a trick and that she was being taken somewhere—where?—against her will.

"This is a trick, mama," she said to her mother grandly. "You have lied to me—you and Kinroy. We are not going to Albany at all. Where are we going?"

"I don't want to tell you now, Suzanne," replied Mrs. Dale quietly. "Have your bath and we'll talk about it afterwards. It doesn't matter. We're going up into Canada, if you want to know. We are nearly there now. You'll know fast enough when we get there."

"Mama," replied Suzanne, "this is a despicable trick! You are going to be sorry for this. You have lied to me—you and Kinroy. I see it now. I might have known, but I didn't believe you would lie to me, mama. I can't do anything just now, I see that very plainly. But when the time comes, you are going to be sorry. You can't control me this way. You ought to know better. You yourself are going to take me back to New York." And she fixed her mother with a steady look which betokened a mastership which her mother felt nervously and wearily she might eventually be compelled to acknowledge.

"Now, Suzanne, what's the use of talking that way?" pleaded Kinroy. "Mama is almost crazy, as it is. She couldn't think of any other way or thing to do."

"You hush, Kinroy," replied Suzanne. "I don't care to talk to you. You have lied to me, and that is more than I ever did to you. Mama, I am astonished at you," she returned to her mother. "My mother lying to me! Very well, mama. You have things in your hands today. I will have them in mine later. You have taken just the wrong course. Now you wait and see."

Mrs. Dale winced and quailed. This girl was the most unterrified, determined fighter she had ever known. She wondered where she got her courage—from her late husband, probably. She could actually feel the quietness, grit, lack of fear, which had grown up in her during the last few weeks under the provocation which antagonism had provided. "Please don't talk that way, Suzanne," she pleaded. "I have done it all for your own good. You know I have. Why will you torture me? You know I won't give you up to that man. I won't. I'll move heaven and earth first. I'll die in this struggle, but I won't give you up."

"Then you'll die, mama, for I'm going to do what I said. You can take me to where this car stops, but you can't take me out of it. I'm going back to New York. Now, a lot you have accomplished, haven't you?"

"Suzanne, I am convinced almost that you are out of your mind. You have almost driven me out of mine, but I am still sane enough to see what is right."

"Mama, I don't propose to talk to you any more, or to Kinroy. You can take me back to New York, or you can leave me, but you will not get me out of this car. I am done with listening to nonsense and pretences. You have lied to me once. You will not get a chance to do it again."

"I don't care, Suzanne," replied her mother, as the train sped swiftly along. "You have forced me to do this. It is your own attitude that is causing all the trouble. If you would be reasonable and take some time to think this all over, you would not be where you are now. I won't let you do this thing that you want to do. You can stay in the car if you wish, but you cannot be taken back to New York without money. I will speak to the station agent about that."

Suzanne thought of this. She had no money, no clothes, other than those she had on. She was in a strange country and not so very used to travelling alone. She had really gone to very few places in times past by herself. It took the edge off her determination to resist, but she was not conquered by any means.

"How are you going to get back?" asked her mother, after a time, when Suzanne paid no attention to her. "You have no money. Surely, Suzanne, you are not going to make a scene? I only want you to come up here for a few weeks so that you will have time to think away from that man. I don't want you to go to him on September the fifteenth. I just won't let you do that. Why won't you be reasonable? You can have a pleasant time up here. You like to ride. You are welcome to do that. I will ride with you. You can invite some of your friends up here, if you choose. I will send for your clothes. Only stay here a while and think over what you are going to do."

Suzanne refused to talk. She was thinking what she could do. Eugene was back in New York. He would expect her Thursday.

"Yes, Suzanne," put in Kinroy. "Why not take ma's advice? She's trying to do the best thing by you. This is a terrible thing you are trying to do. Why not listen to common sense and stay up here three or four months?"

"Don't talk like a parrot, Kinroy! I'm hearing all this from mama."

When her mother reproached her, she said: "Oh, hush, mama, I don't care to hear anything more. I won't do anything of the sort. You lied to me. You said you were going to Albany. You brought me out here under a pretence. Now you can take me back. I won't go to any lodge. I won't go anywhere, except to New York. You might just as well not argue with me."

The train rolled on. Breakfast was served. The private car was switched to the tracks of the Canadian Pacific at Montreal. Her mother's pleas continued. Suzanne refused to eat. She sat and looked out of the window, meditating over this strange dénouement. Where was Eugene? What was he doing? What would he think when she did not come back? She was not enraged at her mother. She was merely contemptuous of her. This trick irritated and disgusted her. She was not thinking of Eugene in any wild way, but merely that she would get back to him. She conceived of him much as she did of herself though her conception of her real self was still vague as strong, patient, resourceful, able to live without her a little while if he had to. She was eager to see him, but really more eager that he should see her if he wanted to. What a creature he must take her mother to be!

By noon they had reached Juinata, by two o'clock they were fifty miles west of Quebec. At first, Suzanne thought she would not eat at all to spite her mother. Later she reasoned that that was silly and ate. She made it exceedingly unpleasant for them by her manner, and they realized that by bringing her away from New York they had merely transferred their troubles. Her spirit was not broken as yet. It filled the car with a disturbing vibration.

"Suzanne," questioned her mother at one point, "won't you talk to me? Won't you see I'm trying to do this for your own good? I want to give you time to think. I really don't want to coerce you, but you must see."

Suzanne merely stared out of the window at the green fields speeding by.

"Suzanne! Don't you see this will never do? Can't you see how terrible it all is?"

"Mama, I want you to let me alone. You have done what you thought was the right thing to do. Now let me alone. You lied to me, mama. I don't want to talk to you. I want you to take me back to New York. You have nothing else to do. Don't try to explain. You haven't any explanation."

Mrs. Dale's spirit fairly raged, but it was impotent in the presence of this her daughter. She could do nothing.

Still more hours, and at one small town Suzanne decided to get off, but both Mrs. Dale and Kinroy offered actual physical opposition. They felt intensely silly and ashamed, though, for they could not break the spirit of the girl. She ignored their minds—their mental attitude in the most contemptuous way. Mrs. Dale cried. Then her face hardened. Then she pleaded. Her daughter merely looked loftily away.

At Three Rivers Suzanne stayed in the car and refused to move. Mrs. Dale pleaded, threatened to call aid, stated that she would charge her with insanity. It was all without avail. The car was uncoupled after the conductor had asked Mrs. Dale if she did not intend to leave it. She was beside herself, frantic with rage, shame, baffled opposition.

"I think you are terrible!" she exclaimed to Suzanne. "You are a little demon. We will live in this car, then. We will see."

She knew that this could not be, for the car was only leased for the outward trip and had to be returned the next day.

The car was pushed on to a siding.

"I beg of you, Suzanne. Please don't make a mockery of us. This is terrible. What will people think?"

"I don't care what they think," said Suzanne.

"But you can't stay here."

"Oh, yes, I can!"

"Come, get off, please do. We won't stay up here indefinitely. I'll take you back. Promise me to stay a month and I'll give you my solemn word I'll take you back at the end of that time. I'm getting sick of this. I can't stand it. Do what you like after that. Only stay a month now."

"No, mama," replied Suzanne. "No, you won't. You lied to me. You're lying to me now, just as you did before."

"I swear to you I'm not. I lied that once, but I was frantic. Oh, Suzanne, please, please. Be reasonable. Have some consideration. I will take you back, but wait for some clothes to arrive. We can't go this way."

She sent Kinroy for the station master, to whom was explained the need of a carriage to take them to Mont Cecile and also for a doctor—this was Mrs. Dale's latest thought—to whom she proposed to accuse Suzanne of insanity. Help to remove her was to be called. She told this to Suzanne, who simply glared at her.

"Get the doctor, mama," she said. "We will see if I have to go that way. But you will rue every step of this. You will be thoroughly sorry for every silly step you have taken."

When the carriage arrived, Suzanne refused to get out. The country driver, a French habitant, reported its presence at the car. Kinroy tried to soothe his sister by saying that he would help straighten matters out if she would only go peacefully.

"I'll tell you, Susie, if it isn't all arranged to suit you within a month, and you still want to go back, I'll send you the money. I have to go back tomorrow, or next day for ma, but I'll give you my word. In fact, I'll persuade mother to bring you back in two weeks. You know I never lied to you before. I never will again. Please come. Let's go over there. We can be comfortable, anyhow."

Mrs. Dale had leased the lodge from the Cathcarts by phone. It was all furnished—ready to live in—even wood fires prepared for lighting in the fireplaces. It had hot and cold water controlled by a hot-water furnace system; acetylene gas, a supply of staples in the kitchen. The service to take care of it was to be called together by the caretaker, who could be reached by phone from the depot. Mrs. Dale had already communicated with him by the time the carriage arrived. The roads were so poor that the use of an automobile was impossible. The station agent, seeing a fat fee in sight, was most obliging.

Suzanne listened to Kinroy, but she did not believe him. She did not believe anyone now, save Eugene, and he was nowhere near to advise her. Still, since she was without money and they were threatening to call a doctor, she thought it might be best perhaps to go peacefully. Her mother was most distracted. Her face was white and thin and nervous, and Kinroy was apparently strained to the breaking point.

"Do you promise me faithfully," she asked her mother, who had begun her pleadings anew, corroborating Kinroy in a way, "that you will take me back to New York in two weeks if I promise to stay that long?" This was still within the date in which she had promised to go to Witla, and as long as she got back by that time, she really did not care, provided she could write to her lover. It was a silly arbitrary thing for her mother to have done, but it could be endured. Her mother, seeing no reasonable way to obtain peace, promised. If she could only keep her there two weeks quietly, perhaps that would help. Suzanne could think here under different conditions. New York was so exciting. Out at this lodge all would be still. There was more argument, and, finally, Suzanne agreed to enter the hack, and they drove over toward Mont Cecile and the Cathcarts' Lodge, now vacant and lonely, which was known as "While-a-Way."

CHAPTER XVIII

The Cathcart Lodge, a long, two-story affair, half-way up a fine covered mountain slope, was one of those summer conveniences of the rich, situated just near enough to the primeval wilds to give one a sense of the unexplored and dangerous in raw nature, and yet near enough to the comforts of civilization, as represented by the cities of Quebec and Montreal, to make one feel secure in the possession of those material joys, otherwise so easily interrupted. It was full of great rooms tastefully furnished with simple summery things—willow chairs, box window-seats, structural book shelves, great open fireplaces, surmounted by handsome mantels, outward swinging leaded casements, settees, pillow-strewn rustic couches, great fur rugs and robes and things of that character. The walls were ornamented with trophies of the chase—antlers, raw fox skins, mounted loons and eagles, skins of bears and other animals. This year the Cathcarts were elsewhere, and the lodge was to be had by a woman of Mrs. Dale's standing for the asking.

When they reached While-a-Way, the caretaker, Pierre, an old habitant of musty log-hut origin, who spoke broken English and was dressed in earth-brown khaki over Heaven knows what combination of clothes beneath, had lighted the fires and was bestirring himself about warming the house generally with the furnaces. His wife, a small, broad-skirted, solid-bodied woman, was in the kitchen preparing something to eat. There was plenty of meat to be had from the larder of the habitant himself, to say nothing of flour, butter, and the like. A girl to serve was called from the family of a neighboring trapper. She had worked in the lodge as maid to the Cathcarts. They settled down to make themselves comfortable, but the old discussion continued. There was no cessation to it, and through it all, actually, Suzanne was having her way.

Meanwhile, Eugene back in New York was expecting word from Suzanne on Thursday, and none came. He called up the house only to learn that Mrs. Dale was out of the city and was not expected back soon. Friday came, and no word; and Saturday. He tried a registered letter "for personal delivery only, return signature demanded" but it came back marked "not there." Then he realized that his suspicions were correct and that Suzanne had fallen into a trap. He grew gloomy, fearful, impatient and nervous by turn, and all at the same time. He drummed on his desk at the office, tried almost in vain to fix his mind on the scores of details which were ever before him, wandered aimlessly about the streets at times, thinking. He was asked for his opinion on art plans, and books, and advertising and circulation propositions, but he could not fix his mind closely on what was being said.

"The chief has certainly got something on his mind which is troubling him these days," said Carter Hayes, the advertising man, to the circulation head. "He's not himself. I don't believe he hears what I'm telling him."

"I've noticed that," replied the latter. They were in the reception room outside Eugene's door, and strolled arm in arm down the richly carpeted hall to the elevator. "There's certainly something wrong. He ought to take a rest. He's trying to do too much."

Hayes did not believe Eugene was trying to do too much. In the last four or five months it had been almost impossible to get near him. He came down at ten or ten-thirty in the morning, left frequently at two and three, had lunch engagements which had nothing to do with office work, and at night went into the social world to dinner or elsewhere, where he could not be found. Colfax had sent for him on a number of occasions when he was not present, and on several other occasions, when he had called on his floor and at his office, Eugene was out. It did not strike him as anything to complain of—Eugene had a right to be about—but as inadvisable, in the managing publisher's own interest. He knew that he had a vast number of things to take care of. It would take an exceptionally efficient man to manage them and not give all his time to them. He would not have thought this if Eugene had been a partner with himself, as were other men in other ventures in which he was interested, but not being so, he could not help viewing him as an employee, one who ought to give all his time to his work.

White never asked anything much save the privilege of working, and was always about the place, alert, earnest at his particular duties, not haughty, but calm and absolutely efficient in every way. He was never weary of consulting with Colfax, whereas Eugene was indifferent, not at all desirous of running to him with every little proposition, but preferring to act on his own initiative, and carrying himself constantly with very much of an air.

In other ways there were other things which were and had been militating against him. By degrees it had come to be rumored about the office that Eugene was interested in the Blue Sea or Sea Island Development and Construction Company, of which there was a good deal of talk about the city, particularly in financial and social circles. Colfax had heard of the corporation. He had been interested in the scheme because it promised so much in the way of luxury. Not much of the panoramic whole so beautifully depicted in the colored insets of a thirty-two-page literary prospectus fathered by Eugene was as yet accomplished, but there was enough to indicate that it was going to be a great thing. Already somewhat over a mile and a quarter of the great sea walk and wall were in place. A dining and dancing pavilion had been built, and one of the smaller hotels—all in accordance with the original architectural scheme. There were a number of houses—something like twenty or thirty on plots one hundred and fifty by one hundred and fifty feet, built in the most ornate fashion on ground which had formerly been wet marsh grown high with grass. Three or four islands had been filled in and the club house of a minor yacht club had been constructed, but still the Sea Island Development Company had a long way to go before even a third of its total perfection would be in sight.

Eugene did not know the drift of the company's financial affairs, except in a general way. He had tried to keep out of it so far as public notice of him was concerned, though he was constantly lunching with Winfield, Willebrand, and others, and endeavoring to direct as much attention to the wonders and prospects of the new resort as was possible for him to do. It was an easy thing for him to say to one person and another whom he met that Blue Sea was rapidly becoming the most perfect thing in the way of a summer resort that he had ever seen, and this did good; so did the comments of all the other people who were interested in it, but it did not make it anything of a success as yet. As a matter of fact, the true success of Blue Sea depended on the investment of much more than the original ten millions for which it had been capitalized. It depended on a truly solid growth, which could not be rapid.

The news which came to the United Magazines Corporation and eventually to Colfax and White was that Eugene was heavily interested in this venture, that he was secretary or held some other office in connection with it, and that he was giving a great deal of his time to its development, which might better be employed in furthering the interests of the United Magazines Corporation.

"What do you think of that?" asked Colfax of White, on hearing the news one morning. It had come through the head of the printing department under White, who had mentioned it to Colfax in White's presence by the latter's directions.

"It's just what I've been telling you all along," said the latter blandly. "He isn't interested in this business any more than he is in any other. He's using it as a stepping-stone, and when he's through with it, good-bye. Now that's all right from his point of view. Every man has a right to climb up, but it isn't so good from yours. You'd be better off if you had a man who wanted to stay here. You'd be better off really if you were handling it yourself. You may not want to do that, but with what you know now you can get someone who will work under you quite well. That's the one satisfactory thing about it—you really can get along without him if it comes right down to it now. With a good man in there, it can be handled from your office."

It was about this time that the most ardent phase of Eugene's love affair with Suzanne began. All through the spring and summer Eugene had been busy with thoughts of Suzanne, ways of meeting her, pleasurable rides with her, thinking of things she had done and said. As a rule now, his thoughts were very far from the interests of his position, and in the main it bored him greatly. He began to wish earnestly that his investment in the Sea Island Corporation would show some tangible return in the way of interest, so that he could have means to turn round with. It struck him after Angela's discovery of his intrigue with Suzanne as a most unfortunate thing that he had tied up all his means in this Blue Sea investment. If it had been fated that he was to go on living with Angela, it would have been all right. Then he could have waited in patience and thought nothing of it. Now it simply meant that if he wanted to realize it, it would all be tied up in the courts, or most likely so, for Angela could sue him; and at any rate he would wish to make reasonable provision for her, and that would require legal adjustment. Apart from this investment, he had nothing now save his salary, and that was not accumulating fast enough to do him much good in case Mrs. Dale went to Colfax soon, and the latter broke with him. He wondered if Colfax really would break with him. Would he ask him to give up Suzanne, or simply force him to resign? He had noticed that for some time Colfax had not been as cordial to and as enthusiastic about him as he had formerly been, but this might be due to other things besides opposition. Moreover, it was natural for them to become a little tired of each other. They did not go about so much together, and when they did Colfax was not as high-flown and boyish in his spirits as he had formerly been. Eugene fancied it was White who was caballing against him, but he thought if Colfax was going to change, he was going to change, and there was no help for it. There were no grounds, he fancied, in so far as the affairs of the corporation were concerned. His work was successful.

The storm broke one day out of a clear sky, in so far as the office was concerned, but not until there had been much heartache and misery in various directions—with the Dales, with Angela, and with Eugene himself.

Suzanne's action was the lightning bolt which precipitated the storm. It could only come from that quarter. Eugene was frantic to hear from her, and for the first time in his life began to experience those excruciating and gnawing pangs which are the concomitants of uncertain and distraught love. It manifested itself in an actual pain in his vitals—in the region of the solar plexus, or what is commonly known as the pit of the stomach. He suffered there very much, quite as the Spartan boy may have done who was gnawed by the fox concealed under his belt. He would wonder where Suzanne was, what she was doing, and then, being unable to work, would call his car and ride, or take his hat and walk. It did him no good to ride, for the agony was in sitting still. At night he would go home and sit by one or the other of his studio windows, principally out on the little stone balcony, and watch the changing panorama of the Hudson, yearning and wondering where she was. Would he ever see her again? Would he be able to win this battle if he did? Oh, her beautiful face, her lovely voice, her exquisite lips and eyes, the marvel of her touch and beautiful fancy!

He tried to compose poetry to her, and wrote a series of sonnets to his beloved, which were not at all bad. He worked on his sketch book of pencil portraits of Suzanne seeking a hundred significant and delightful expressions and positions, which could afterwards be elaborated into his gallery of paintings of her, which he proposed to paint at some time. It did not matter to him that Angela was about, though he had the graciousness to conceal these things from her. He was ashamed, in a way, of his treatment of her, and yet the sight of her now was not so much pitiable as objectionable and unsatisfactory. Why had he married her? He kept asking himself that.

They sat in the studio one night. Angela's face was a picture of despair, for the horror of her situation was only by degrees coming to her, and she said, seeing him so moody and despondent:

"Eugene, don't you think you can get over this? You say Suzanne has been spirited away. Why not let her go? Think of your career, Eugene. Think of me. What will become of me? You can get over it, if you try. Surely you won't throw me down after all the years I have been with you. Think how I have tried. I have been a pretty good wife to you, haven't I? I haven't annoyed you so terribly much, have I? Oh, I feel all the time as though we were on the brink of some terrible catastrophe! If only I could do something; if only I could say something! I know I have been hard and irritable at times, but that is all over now. I am a changed woman. I would never be that way any more."

"It can't be done, Angela," he replied calmly. "It can't be done. I don't love you. I've told you that. I don't want to live with you. I can't. I want to get free in some way, either by divorce, or a quiet separation, and go my way. I'm not happy. I never will be as long as I am here. I want my freedom and then I will decide what I want to do."

Angela shook her head and sighed. She could scarcely believe that this was she wandering around in her own apartment wondering what she was going to do in connection with her own husband. Marietta had gone back to Wisconsin before the storm broke. Myrtle was in New York, but she hated to confess to her. She did not dare to write to any member of her own family but Marietta, and she did not want to confess to her. Marietta had fancied while she was here that they were getting along nicely. She had fits of crying, which alternated with fits of anger, but the latter were growing weak. Fear, despondency, and grief were becoming uppermost in her soul again—the fear and despondency that had weighed her down in those lonely days before she married Eugene, the grief that she was now actually and finally to lose the one man whom, in spite of everything, she loved still.

CHAPTER XIX

It was three days later when he was at his office that a telegram came from Mrs. Dale, which read, "I depend on you, on the honor of a gentleman, to ignore any message which may come from my daughter until I see you."

Eugene was puzzled, but fancied that there must be a desperate quarrel on between Suzanne and her mother, wherever they were, and that it was probable that he would hear from her now. It was his first inkling as to her whereabouts, for the telegram was sent off from Three Rivers, in Canada, and he fancied they must be near there somewhere. The place of despatch did him no good from a material point of view, for he could neither write nor pursue Suzanne on the strength of this. He would not know where to find her. He could only wait, conscious that she was having a struggle, perhaps as severe, or possibly more so, than his own. He wandered about with this telegram in his pocket wondering when he should hear—what a day should bring forth, and all those who came in contact with him noticed that there was something wrong.

Colfax saw him, and asked: "What's the matter, old man? You're not looking as chipper as you might." He fancied it might be something in connection with the Blue Sea Corporation. He had heard, after he had learned that Eugene was in it, that it would take much more money than had been invested to date to make it a really successful seaside proposition according to the original outlines, and that it would be years before it could possibly yield an adequate return. If Eugene had put much money in it, he had probably lost it or tied it up in a most unsatisfactory way. Well, it served him right for trifling with things he knew nothing about.

"Oh, nothing," replied Eugene abstractedly. "I'm all right. I'm just a little run down physically. I'll come round."

"You'd better take a month or so off and brace up, if you're not in shape."

"Oh, not at all! Not now, anyhow."

It occurred to Eugene that he might use the time to advantage a little later and that he would claim it.

They proceeded to business, but Colfax noticed that Eugene's eyes were specially hollow and weary and that he was noticeably restless. He wondered whether he might be going to break down physically.

Suzanne had drifted along peacefully enough considering the nature of the feeling between her and her mother at this time. After a few days of desultory discussion, however, along the lines now so familiar, she began to see that her mother had no intention of terminating their stay at the time agreed upon, particularly since their return to New York meant, so far as Suzanne was concerned, her immediate departure to Witla. Mrs. Dale began at first to plead for additional delay, and later that Suzanne should agree not to go to New York but to Lenox for a season. It was cold up here already now, though there were still spells of bright warm summery or autumn weather between ten and four in the day, and sometimes in the evening. The nights usually were cold. Mrs. Dale would gladly have welcomed a compromise, for it was terribly lonely, just herself and Suzanne—after the gaieties of New York. Four days before the time of her proposed departure, Mrs. Dale was still obdurate or parleying in a diplomatic way, and Suzanne, disgusted, made the threat which caused Mrs. Dale to wire distractedly to Eugene. Later, she composed the following, which she gave to Gabrielle:

"DEAR EUGENE—

If you love me, come and get me. I have told mama that
if she did not keep her word to return with me to New
York by the fifteenth, I would write to you and she is
still obstinate. I am at the Cathcart Lodge, While-a-Way,
eighteen miles north of Three Rivers, here in Canada.
Anyone can show you. I will be here when you come. Do
not try to write to me as I am afraid I should not get it. But I
will be at the Lodge.
"With love,

"SUZANNE."

Eugene had never before received a love appeal, nor indeed any such appeal from any woman in his life.

This letter reached him thirty-six hours after the telegram arrived, and set him to planning at once. The hour had struck. He must act. Perhaps this old world was now behind him forever. Could he really get Suzanne, if he went to Canada to find her? How was she surrounded? He thrilled with delight when he realized that it was Suzanne who was calling him and that he was going to find her. "If you love me, come and get me."

Would he?

Watch!

He called for his car, telephoned his valet to pack his bag and bring it to the Grand Central Station, first ascertaining for himself the time of departure, asked to talk to Angela, who had gone to Myrtle's apartment in upper Seventh Avenue, ready at last to confess her woes to Eugene's sister. Her condition did not appeal to Eugene in this situation. The inevitable result, which he thought of frequently, was still far away. He notified Colfax that he was going to take a few days rest, went to the bank where he had over four thousand dollars on deposit, and drew it all. He then went to a ticket office and purchased a one-way ticket, uncertain where his actions would take him once he saw Suzanne. He tried once more to get Angela, intending boldly to tell her that he was going to seek Suzanne, and to tell her not to worry, that he would communicate with her, but she had not returned. Curiously, through all this, he was intensely sorry for her, and wondered how she would take it, if he did not return. How would the child be arranged for? He felt he must go. Angela was heartsick, he knew that, and frightened. Still he could not resist this call. He could not resist anything in connection with this love affair. He was like a man possessed of a devil or wandering in a dream. He knew that his whole career was at stake, but it did not make any difference. He must get her. The whole world could go hang if he could only obtain her,—her the beautiful, the perfect!

At five-thirty the train departed, and then he sat as it rolled northward speculating on what he was to do when he got there. If Three Rivers were much of a place, he could probably hire an automobile. He could leave it some distance from the lodge and then see if he could not approach unobserved and signal Suzanne. If she were about, she would no doubt be on the lookout. At a sign she would run to him. They would hurry to the automobile. The pursuit might quickly follow, but he would arrange it so that his pursuers would not know which railroad station he was going to. Quebec was the nearest big city, he found by studying the map, though he might return to Montreal and New York or Buffalo, if he chose to go west he would see how the train ran.

It is curious what vagaries the human mind is subject to, under conditions of this kind. Up to the time of Eugene's arrival in Three Rivers and after, he had no plan of campaign, or of future conduct beyond that of obtaining Suzanne. He did not know that he would return to New York—he did not know that he would not. If Suzanne wished, and it were best, and they could, they would go to England from Montreal, or France. If necessary, they could go to Portland and sail. Mrs. Dale, on the evidence that he had Suzanne and that of her own free will and volition, might yield and say nothing, in which case he could return to New York and resume his position. This courageous stand on his part if he had only followed it might have solved the whole problem quickly. It might have been the sword that would have cut the Gordian Knot. On the train was a heavy black-bearded man, which was always good luck to him. At Three Rivers, when he dismounted from the train, he found a horseshoe, which was also a lucky sign. He did not stop to think what he would do if he really lost his position and had to live on the sum he had with him. He was really not thinking logically. He was dreaming. He fancied that he would get Suzanne and have his salary, and that somehow things would be much as they were. Of such is the logic of dreams.

When he arrived at Three Rivers, of course the conditions were not what he anticipated. It is true that at times, after a long continued period of dry weather, the roads were passable for automobiles, at least as far as While-a-Way, but the weather had not recently been entirely dry. There had been a short period of cold rain and the roads were practically impassable, save for horses and carryalls. There was a carryall which went as far as St. Jacques, four miles from While-a-Way, where the driver told him he could get a horse, if he wanted one. The owner of this hack line had a stable there.

This was gratifying to him, and he decided to make arrangements for two horses at St. Jacques, which he would take to within a reasonable distance of the lodge and tie in some spot where they would not be seen. Then he could consider the situation and signal Suzanne; if she were there on the lookout. How dramatic the end would be! How happy they would be flying together! Judge then his astonishment on reaching St. Jacques to find Mrs. Dale waiting for him. Word had been telephoned by her faithful representative, the station agent at Three Rivers, that a man of Eugene's description had arrived and departed for While-a-Way. Before this a telegram had come from New York from Kinroy to the effect that Eugene had gone somewhere. His daily habits since Mrs. Dale had gone away had been under observation. Kinroy, on his return, had called at the United Magazines Corporation and asked if Eugene was in the city. Heretofore he had been reported in. When on this day he was reported as having gone, Kinroy called up Angela to inquire. She also stated that he had left the city. He then wired his mother and she, calculating the time of his arrival, and hearing from the station agent of his taking the carryall, had gone down to meet him. She had decided to fight every inch of the way with all the strategy at her command. She did not want to kill him—had not really the courage to do that—but she still hoped to dissuade him. She had not been able to bring herself to resort to guards and detectives as yet. He could not be as hard as he looked and acted. Suzanne was bedeviling him by her support and communications. She had not been able to govern there, she saw. Her only hope was to talk him out of it, or into an additional delay. If necessary, they would all go back to New York together and she would appeal to Colfax and Winfield. She hoped they would persuade him to reason. Anyhow, she would never leave Suzanne for one moment until this thing had been settled in her favor, or brutally against her.

When Eugene appeared she greeted him with her old social smile and called to him affably: "Come, get in."

He looked at her grimly and obeyed, but changed his manner when he saw that she was really kindly in her tone and greeted her sociably.

"How have you been?" he asked.

"Oh, quite well, thank you!"

"And how is Suzanne?"

"All right, I fancy. She isn't here, you know."

"Where is she?" asked Eugene, his face a study in defeat.

"She went with some friends to visit Quebec for ten days. Then she is going from there to New York. I don't expect to see her here any more."

Eugene choked with a sense of repugnance to her airy taradiddles. He did not believe what she was saying—saw at once that she was fencing with him.

"That's a lie," he said roughly, "and it's out of the whole cloth! She's here, and you know it. Anyhow, I am going to see for myself."

"How polite you are!" she laughed diplomatically. "That isn't the way you usually talk. Anyhow, she isn't here. You'll find that out, if you insist. I wouldn't advise you to insist, for I've sent for counsel since I heard you were coming, and you will find detectives as well as guards waiting to receive you. She isn't here, though, even at that, and you might just as well turn round and go back. I will drive you over to Three Rivers, if you wish. Why not be reasonable, now, and avoid a scene? She isn't here. You couldn't have her if she were. The people I have employed will prevent that. If you make trouble, you will simply be arrested and then the newspapers will have it. Why not be reasonable now, Mr. Witla, and go on back? You have everything to lose. There is a train through Three Rivers from Quebec for New York at eleven tonight. We can make it. Don't you want to do that? I will agree, if you come to your senses now, and cause me no trouble here, to bring Suzanne back to New York within a month. I won't let you have her unless you get a divorce and straighten things out with your wife, but if you can do that within six months, or a year, and she still wants you, you can have her. I will promise in writing to withdraw all objection, and see that her full share of her property comes to her uncontested. I will help you and her socially all I can. You know I am not without influence."

"I want to see her first," replied Eugene grimly and disbelievingly.

"I won't say that I will forget everything," went on Mrs. Dale, ignoring his interpolated remark. "I can't—but I will pretend to. You can have the use of my country place at Lenox. I will buy out the lease at Morristown, or the New York House, and you can live in either place. I will set aside a sum of money for your wife, if you wish. That may help you obtain your release. Surely you do not want to take her under the illegal condition which you propose, when you can have her outright in this brilliant manner by waiting a little while. She says she does not want to get married, but that is silly talk, based on nothing except erratic reading. She does, or she will, the moment she comes to think about it seriously. Why not help her? Why not go back now and let me bring her to New York a little later and then we will talk this all over. I shall be very glad to have you in my family. You are a brilliant man. I have always liked you. Why not be reasonable? Come now and let's drive over to Three Rivers and you take the train back to New York, will you?"

While Mrs. Dale had been talking, Eugene had been surveying her calmly. What a clever talker she was! How she could lie! He did not believe her. He did not believe one word that she said. She was fighting to keep him from Suzanne, why he could readily understand. Suzanne was somewhere, here, he fancied, though, as in the case of her recent trip to Albany, she might have been spirited away.

"Absurd!" said Eugene easily, defiantly, indifferently. "I'll not do anything of the sort. In the first place, I don't believe you. If you are so anxious to be nice to me, let me see her, and then you can say all this in front of her. I've come up here to see her, and I'm going to. She's here. I know she is. You needn't lie. You needn't talk. I know she's here. Now I'm going to see her, if I have to stay here a month and search."

Mrs. Dale stirred nervously. She knew that Eugene was desperate. She knew that Suzanne had written to him. Talk might be useless. Strategy might not avail, but she could not help using it.

"Listen to me," she said excitedly. "I tell you Suzanne is not here. She's gone. There are guards up there—lots of them. They know who you are. They have your description. They have orders to kill you, if you try to break in. Kinroy is there. He is desperate. I have been having a struggle to prevent his killing you already. The place is watched. We are watched at this moment. Won't you be reasonable? You can't see her. She's gone. Why make all this fuss? Why take your life in your hands?"

"Don't talk," said Eugene. "You're lying. I can see it in your face. Besides, my life is nothing. I am not afraid. Why talk? She's here. I'm going to see her."

He stared before him and Mrs. Dale ruminated as to what she was to do. There were no guards or detectives, as she said. Kinroy was not there. Suzanne was not away. This was all palaver, as Eugene suspected, for she was too anxious to avoid publicity to give any grounds for it, before she was absolutely driven.

It was a rather halcyon evening after some days of exceeding chill. A bright moon was coming up in the east, already discernible in the twilight, but which later would shine brilliantly. It was not cold but really pleasantly warm, and the rough road along which they were driving was richly odorous. Eugene was not unconscious of its beauty, but depressed by the possibility of Suzanne's absence.

"Oh, do be generous," pleaded Mrs. Dale, who feared that once they saw each other, reason would disappear. Suzanne would demand, as she had been continually demanding, to be taken back to New York. Eugene with or without Suzanne's consent or plea, would ignore her overtures of compromise and there would be immediate departure or defiant union here. She thought she would kill them if need be, but in the face of Eugene's defiant persistence on one side, and Suzanne's on the other, her courage was failing. She was frightened by the daring of this man. "I will keep my word," she observed distractedly. "Honestly she isn't here. She's in Quebec, I tell you. Wait a month. I will bring her back then. We will arrange things together. Why can't you be generous?"

"I could be," said Eugene, who was considering all the brilliant prospects which her proposal involved and being moved by them, "but I can't believe you. You're not telling me the truth. You didn't tell the truth to Suzanne when you took her from New York. That was a trick, and this is another. I know she isn't away. She's right up there in the lodge, wherever it is. You take me to her and then we will talk this thing out together. By the way, where are you going?"

Mrs. Dale had turned into a bypath or half-formed road closely lined with small trees and looking as though it might be a woodchoppers' path.

"To the lodge."

"I don't believe it," replied Eugene, who was intensely suspicious. "This isn't a main road to any such place as that."

"I tell you it is."

Mrs. Dale was nearing the precincts of the lodge and wanted more time to talk and plead.

"Well," said Eugene, "you can go this way if you want to. I'm going to get out and walk. You can't throw me off by driving me around in some general way. I'm going to stay here a week, a month, two months, if necessary, but I'm not going back without seeing Suzanne. She's here, and I know it. I'll go up alone and find her. I'm not afraid of your guards."

He jumped out and Mrs. Dale gave up in despair. "Wait," she pleaded. "It's over two miles yet. I'll take you there. She isn't home tonight, anyhow. She's over at the cottage of the caretaker. Oh, why won't you be reasonable? I'll bring her to New York, I tell you. Are you going to throw aside all those fine prospects and wreck your life and hers and mine? Oh, if Mr. Dale were only alive! If I had a man on whom I could rely! Come, get in, and I'll drive you up there, but promise me you won't ask to see her tonight. She isn't there, anyway. She's over at the caretaker's. Oh, dear, if only something would happen to solve this!"

"I thought you said she was in Quebec?"

"I only said that to gain time. I'm so unstrung. It wasn't true, but she isn't at the lodge, truly. She's away tonight. I can't let you stay there. Let me take you back to St. Jacques and you can stay with old Pierre Gaine. You can come up in the morning. The servants will think it so strange. I promise you you shall see Suzanne. I give you my word."

"Your word. Why, Mrs. Dale, you're going around in a ring! I can't believe anything you say," replied Eugene calmly. He was very much collected and elated now since he knew that Suzanne was here. He was going to see her—he felt it. He had Mrs. Dale badly worsted, and he proposed to drive her until, in the presence of Suzanne, he and his beloved dictated terms.

"I'm going there tonight and you are going to bring her to me. If she isn't there, you know where to find her. She's here, and I'm going to see her tonight. We'll talk of all this you're proposing in front of her. It's silly to twist things around this way. The girl is with me, and you know it. She's mine. You can't control her. Now we two will talk to you together."

He sat back in the light vehicle and began to hum a tune. The moon was getting clearer.

"Promise me just one thing," urged Mrs. Dale despairingly. "Promise me that you will urge Suzanne to accept my proposition. A few months won't hurt. You can see her in New York as usual. Go about getting a divorce. You are the only one who has any influence with her. I admit it. She won't believe me. She won't listen to me. You tell her. Your future is in it. Persuade her to wait. Persuade her to stay up here or at Lenox for a little while and then come down. She will obey you. She will believe anything you say. I have lied. I have lied terribly all through this, but you can't blame me. Put yourself in my place. Think of my position. Please use your influence. I will do all that I say and more."

"Will you bring Suzanne to me tonight?"

"Yes, if you promise."

"Will you bring her to me tonight, promise or no promise? I don't want to say anything to you which I can't say in front of her."

"Won't you promise me that you will accept my proposition and urge her to?"

"I think I will, but I won't say. I want her to hear what you have to say. I think I will."

Mrs. Dale shook her head despondently.

"You might as well acquiesce," went on Eugene. "I'm going to see her anyhow, whether you will or no. She's there, and I'll find her if I have to search the house room by room. She can hear my voice."

He was carrying things with a high hand.

"Well," replied Mrs. Dale, "I suppose I must. Please don't let on to the servants. Pretend you're my guest. Let me take you back to St. Jacques tonight, after you see her. Don't stay with her more than half an hour."

She was absolutely frightened out of her wits at this terrific dénouement.

Eugene sat grimly congratulating himself as they jogged on in the moonlight. He actually squeezed her arm cheerfully and told her not to be so despairing—that all would come out all right. They would talk to Suzanne. He would see what she would have to say.

"You stay here," she said, as they reached a little wooded knoll in a bend of the road—a high spot commanding a vast stretch of territory now lit by a glistening northern moon. "I'll go right inside and get her. I don't know whether she's there, but if she isn't, she's over at the caretaker's, and we'll go over there. I don't want the servants to see you meet her. Please don't be demonstrative. Oh, be careful!"

Eugene smiled. How excited she was! How pointless, after all her threats! So this was victory. What a fight he had made! Here he was outside this beautiful lodge, the lights of which he could see gleaming like yellow gold through the silvery shadows. The air was full of field fragrances. You could smell the dewy earth, soon to be hard and covered deep in snow. There was still a bird's voice here and there and faint stirrings of the wind in the leaves. "On such a night," came back Shakespeare's lines. How fitting that Suzanne should come to him under such conditions! Oh, the wonder of this romance—the beauty of it! From the very beginning it had been set about with perfections of scenery and material environment. Obviously, nature had intended this as the crowning event of his life. Life recognized him as a genius—the fates it was heaping posies in his lap, laying a crown of victory upon his brow.

He waited while Mrs. Dale went to the lodge, and then after a time, true enough, there appeared in the distance the swinging, buoyant, girlish form of Suzanne. She was plump, healthful, vigorous. He could detect her in the shadows under the trees and behind her a little way Mrs. Dale. Suzanne came eagerly on—youthful, buoyant, dancing, determined, beautiful. Her skirts were swinging about her body in ripples as she strode. She looked all Eugene had ever thought her. Hebe—a young Diana, a Venus at nineteen. Her lips were parted in a welcoming smile as she drew near and her eyes were as placid as those dull opals which still burn with a hidden lustre of gold and flame.

She held out her arms to him as she came, running the last few steps.

"Suzanne!" called her mother. "For shame!"

"Hush, mama!" declared Suzanne defiantly. "I don't care. I don't care. It's your fault. You shouldn't have lied to me. He wouldn't have come if I hadn't sent for him. I'm going back to New York. I told you I was."

She did not say, "Oh, Eugene!" as she came close, but gathered his face in her hands and looked eagerly into his eyes. His burned into hers. She stepped back and opened wide her arms only to fold them tightly about him.

"At last! At last!" he said, kissing her feverishly. "Oh, Suzanne! Oh, Flower Face!"

"I knew you would come," she said. "I told her you would. I'll go back with you."

"Yes, yes," said Eugene. "Oh, this wonderful night! This wonderful climax! Oh, to have you in my arms again!"

Mrs. Dale stood by, white, intense. To think a daughter of hers should act like this, confound her so, make her a helpless spectator of her iniquity. What an astounding, terrible, impossible thing!

"Suzanne!" she cried. "Oh, that I should have lived to see this day!"

"I told you, mama, that you would regret bringing me up here," declared Suzanne. "I told you I would write to him. I knew you would come," she said to Eugene, and she squeezed his hand affectionately.

Eugene inhaled a deep breath and stared at her. The night, the stars swung around him in a gorgeous orbit. Thus it was to be victorious. It was too beautiful, too wonderful! To think he should have triumphed in this way! Could any other man anywhere ever have enjoyed such a victory?

"Oh, Suzanne," he said eagerly, "this is like a dream; it's like heaven! I can scarcely believe I am alive."

"Yes, yes," she replied, "it is beautiful, perfect!" And together they strolled away from her mother, hand in hand.

CHAPTER XX

The flaw in this situation was that Eugene, after getting Suzanne in his arms once more, had no particular solution to offer. Instead of at once outlining an open or secret scheme of escape, or taking her by main force and walking off with her, as she more than half expected him to do, here he was repeating to her what her mother had told him, and instead of saying "Come!" he was asking her advice.

"This is what your mother proposed to me just now, Suzanne," he began, and entered upon a full explanation. It was a vision of empire to him.

"I said to her," he said, speaking of her mother, who was near by, "that I would decide nothing. She wanted me to say that I would do this, but I insisted that it must be left to you. If you want to go back to New York, we will go, tonight or tomorrow. If you want to accept this plan of your mother's, it's all right, so far as I am concerned. I would rather have you now, but if I can see you, I am willing to wait."

He was calm now, logical, foolishly speculative. Suzanne wondered at this. She had no advice to offer. She had expected some dramatic climax, but since it had not come about, she had to be content. The truth was that she had been swept along by her desire to be with Eugene. It had seemed to her in the beginning that it was not possible for him to get a divorce. It had seemed also from her reading and youthful philosophizing that it was really not necessary. She did not want to be mean to Angela. She did not want Eugene to mortify her by openly leaving her. She had fancied since Eugene had said that Angela was not satisfactory to him and that there was no real love between them, that Angela really did not care she had practically admitted as much in her letter—that it would not make so much difference if she shared him with her. What was he explaining now—a new theory as to what they were to do? She thought he was coming for her to take her away like a god, whereas here he was presenting a new theory to her in anything but a god-like way. It was confusing. She did not know how it was that Eugene did not want to leave at once.

"Well, I don't know whatever you think," she said. "If you want me to stay here another month— —"

"No, no!" exclaimed Eugene quickly, conscious of a flaw in the arrangement, and anxious to make it seem right. "I didn't mean that. Not that. I want you to come back with me now, if possible, tonight, only I wanted to tell you this. Your mother seems sincere. It seems a shame if we can keep friends with her and still have our way, not to do so. I don't want to do any greater harm than I can help unless you are perfectly willing and——" He hesitated over his own thoughts.

At this moment Suzanne could scarcely have told what she felt. The crux of the situation was being put to her for her decision, and it should not be. She was not strong enough, not experienced enough. Eugene should decide, and whatever he decided would be right.

The truth was that after getting her in his arms again, and that in the presence of her mother, Eugene did not feel that he was quite so much the victor as he had imagined, or that the whole problem of his life was solved. He could not very well ignore, he thought, what Mrs. Dale had to offer, if she was offering it seriously. She had said to him just before he came into the presence of Suzanne that unless he accepted these terms she would go on fighting—that she would telegraph to Colfax and ask him to come up here. Although Eugene had drawn his money and was ready to fly if he could, still the thought of Colfax and the desire to keep his present state of social security and gain all Mrs. Dale had to offer besides were deterrents. He hesitated. Wasn't there some way to smooth everything out?

"I don't want you to decide finally," he said, "but what do you think?"

Suzanne was in a simmering, nebulous state, and could not think. Eugene was here. This was Arcady and the moon was high.

It was beautiful to have him with her again. It was wonderful to feel his caresses. But he was not flying with her. They were not defying the world; they were not doing what she fancied they would be doing, rushing to victory, and that was what she had sent for him for. Mrs. Dale was going to help Eugene get a divorce, so she said. She was going to help subsidize Angela, if necessary. Suzanne was going to get married, and actually settle down after a time. What a curious thought. Why that was not what she had wanted to do. She had wanted to flout convention in some way; to do original things as she had planned, as she had dreamed. It might be disastrous, but she did not think so. Her mother would have yielded. Why was Eugene compromising? It was curious. Such thoughts as these formulated in her mind at this time were the most disastrous things that could happen to their romance. Union should have followed his presence. Flight should have been a portion of it. As it was she was in his arms, but she was turning over vague, nebulous thoughts. Something—a pale mist before an otherwise brilliant moon; a bit of spindrift; a speck of cloud, no bigger than a man's hand that might possibly portend something and might not, had come over the situation. Eugene was as desirable as ever, but he was not flying with her. They were talking about going back to New York afterwards, but they were not going together at once. How was that?

"Do you think mama can really damage you with Mr. Colfax?" she asked curiously at one point, after Eugene had mentioned her mother's threat.

"I don't know," he replied solemnly. "Yes, I think she could. I don't know what he'd do, though. It doesn't matter much one way or the other," he added. Suzanne puzzled.

"Well, if you want to wait, it's all right," she said. "I want to do whatever you think best. I don't want you to lose your position. If you think we ought to wait, we will."

"Not if I'm not to be with you regularly," replied Eugene, who was wavering. He was not your true champion of victory—your administrative leader. Foolishly he was spelling over an arrangement whereby he could eat his cake and have it—see Suzanne, drive with her, dance with her, all but live with her in New York until such time as the actual union could be arranged secretly or openly. Mrs. Dale was promising to receive him as a son, but she was merely plotting for time—time to think, act, permit Suzanne, under argument, to come to her senses. Time would solve everything, she thought, and tonight as she hung about, keeping close and overhearing some of Eugene's remarks, she felt relieved. Either he was coming to his senses and beginning to regret his folly or he was being deluded by her lies. If she could keep him and Suzanne apart one more week, and get to New York herself, she would go to Colfax now, and to Winfield, and see if they could not be induced to use their good offices. Eugene must be broken. He was erratic, insane. Her lies were apparently plausible enough to gain her this delay, and that was all she wanted.

"Well, I don't know. Whatever you think," said Suzanne again, after a time between embraces and kisses, "do you want me to come back with you tomorrow, or——"

"Yes, yes," he replied quickly and vigorously, "tomorrow, only we must try and argue your mother into the right frame of mind. She feels that she has lost now since we are together, and we must keep her in that mind. She talks compromise and that's just what we want. If she is willing to have us make some arrangement, why not? I would be willing to let things rest for a week or so, just to give her a chance if she wishes. If she doesn't change then we can act. You could come as far as Lenox for a week, and then come on."

He talked like one who had won a great victory, whereas he had really suffered a great defeat. He was not taking Suzanne.

Suzanne brooded. It was not what she expected—but— —

"Yes," she said, after a time.

"Will you return with me tomorrow?"

"Yes."

"As far as Lenox or New York?"

"We'll see what mama says. If you can agree with her—anything you want—I am willing."

After a time Eugene and Suzanne parted for the night. It was agreed that they should see each other in the morning, that they should go back as far as Lenox together. Mrs. Dale was to help Eugene get a divorce. It was a delightfully affectionate and satisfactory situation, but somehow Eugene felt that he was not handling it right. He went to bed in one part of the house—Suzanne in another—Mrs. Dale, fearful and watchful, staying near by, but there was no need. He was not desperate. He went to sleep thinking that the near future was going to adjust everything for him nicely, and that he and Suzanne were eventually going to get married.

CHAPTER XXI

The next day, after wavering whether they would not spend a few days here in billing and cooing and listening to Mrs. Dale's veiled pleas as to what the servants might think, or what they might know already or suspect from what the station master at Three Rivers might say, they decided to return, Eugene to New York, Suzanne to Lenox. All the way back to Albany, Eugene and Suzanne sat together in one seat in the Pullman like two children rejoicing in each other's company. Mrs. Dale sat one seat away, turning over her promises and pondering whether, after all, she had not yet better go at once and try to end all by an appeal to Colfax, or whether she had better wait a little while and see if the affair might not die down of its own accord.

At Albany the following morning, Suzanne and Mrs. Dale transferred to the Boston and Albany, Eugene going on to New York. He went to the office feeling much relieved, and later in the day to his apartment. Angela, who had been under a terrific strain, stared at him as if he were a ghost, or one come back to life from the dead. She had not known where he had gone. She had not known whether he would ever come back. There was no use in reproaching him—she had realized that long since. The best she could do was to make an appeal. She waited until after dinner, at which they had discussed the mere commonplaces of life, and then came to his room, where he was unpacking.

"Did you go to find Suzanne?" she asked.

"Yes."

"Is she with you?"

"No."

"Oh, Eugene, do you know where I have spent the last three days?" she asked.

He did not answer.

"On my knees. On my knees," she declared, "asking God to save you from yourself."

"Don't talk rot, Angela," he returned coldly. "You know how I feel about this thing. How much worse am I now than I was before? I tried to get you on the phone to tell you. I went to find her and bring her back, and I did as far as Lenox. I am going to win this fight. I am going to get Suzanne, either legally or otherwise. If you want to give me a divorce, you can. I will provide amply for you. If you don't I'm going to take her, anyhow. That's understood between me and her. Now what's the use of hysterics?"

Angela looked at him tearfully. Could this be the Eugene she had known? In each scene with him, after each plea, or through it, she came to this adamantine wall. Was he really so frantic about this girl? Was he going to do what he said? He outlined to her quite calmly his plans as recently revised, and at one point Angela, speaking of Mrs. Dale, interrupted him—"she will never give her up to you—you will see. You think she will. She says she will. She is only fooling you. She is fighting for time. Think what you are doing. You can't win."

"Oh, yes, I can," said Eugene, "I practically have already. She will come to me."

"She may, she may, but at what a cost. Look at me, Eugene. Am I not enough? I am still good looking. You have declared to me time and again that I have a beautiful form. See, see"—she tore open her dressing gown and the robe de nuit, in which she had come in. She had arranged this scene, especially thought it out, and hoped it would move him. "Am I not enough? Am I not still all that you desire?"

Eugene turned his head away in disgust—wearily—sick of their melodramatic appeals. This was the last rôle Angela should have played. It was the most ineffectual, the least appropriate at the moment. It was dramatic, striking, but totally ineffective under the circumstances.

"It's useless acting in that way to me, Angela," he said. "I'm no longer to be moved in that way by you. All marital affection between us is dead—terribly so. Why plead to me with something that has no appeal. I can't help it. It's dead. Now what are we going to do about it?"

Once more Angela turned wearily. Although she was nerve worn and despairing, she was still fascinated by the tragedy which was being played out under her eyes. Would nothing make him see?

They went their separate ways for the night, and the next day he was at his desk again. Word came from Suzanne that she was still in Lenox, and then that her mother had gone to Boston for a day or two on a visit. The fifth day Colfax stepped into his office, and, hailing him pleasantly, sat down.

"Well, how are things with you, old man?" he asked.

"Oh, about the same," said Eugene. "I can't complain."

"Everything going all right with you?"

"Yes, moderately so."

"People don't usually butt in on you here when I'm here, do they?" he asked curiously.

"I've given orders against anything like that, but I'll make it doubly sure in this case," said Eugene, alert at once. Could Colfax be going to talk to him about anything in connection with his case? He paled a little.

Colfax looked out of the window at the distant panorama of the Hudson. He took out a cigar, and cut the end, but did not light it.

"I asked you about not being interrupted," he began thoughtfully, "because I have a little something I want to talk to you about, which I would rather no one else heard. Mrs. Dale came to me the other day," he said quietly. Eugene started at the mention of her name and paled still more, but gave no other outward sign. "And she told me a long story about something that you were trying to do in connection with her daughter—run away with her, or go and live with her without a license or a divorce, or desert your wife, or something to that effect, which I didn't pay much attention to, but which I have to talk to you about just the same. Now, I never like to meddle with a man's personal affairs. I don't think that they concern me. I don't think they concern this business, except in so far as they may affect it unfavorably, but I would like to know if it is true. Is it?"

"Yes," said Eugene.

"Mrs. Dale is an old friend of mine. I've known her for years. I know Mrs. Witla, of course, but not quite in the same way. I haven't seen as much of her as I have of you. I didn't know that you were unhappily married, but that is neither here nor there. The point is, that she seems to be on the verge of making a great scandal out of this—she seems a little distracted to me—and I thought I'd better come up and have a little talk with you before anything serious really happened. You know it would be a rather damaging thing to this business if any scandal were started in connection with you just at present."

He paused, expecting some protest or explanation, but Eugene merely held his peace. He was tense, pale, harried. So she had gone to Colfax, after all. Instead of going to Boston; instead of keeping her word, she had come down here to New York and gone to Colfax. Had she told him the full story? Very likely Colfax, in spite of all his smooth words, would be inclined to sympathize with her. What must he think of him? He was rather conservative in a social way. Mrs. Dale could be of service to him in her world in one way and another. He had never seen Colfax quite so cool and deliberate as he was now. He seemed to be trying to maintain an exceedingly judicial and impartial tone, which was not characteristic.

"You have always been an interesting study to me, Witla, ever since I first met you," he went on, after a time. "You're a genius, I fancy, if there ever was one, but like all geniuses you are afflicted with tendencies which are erratic. I used to think for a little while that maybe you sat down and planned the things which you have carried through so successfully, but I have since concluded that you don't. You attract some forms of force and order. Also, I think you have various other faculties—it would be hard for me to say just what they are. One is vision. I know you have that. Another is appreciation of ability. I know you have that. I have seen you pick some exceptional people. You plan in a way, but you don't plan logically or deliberately, unless I am greatly mistaken. The matter of this Dale girl now is an interesting case in point, I think."

"Let's not talk of her," said Eugene frigidly and bridling slightly. Suzanne was a sore point with him. A dangerous subject. Colfax saw it. "That's something I can't talk about very well."

"Well, we won't," put in the other calmly, "but the point can be established in other ways. You'll admit, I think, that you haven't been planning very well in connection with this present situation, for if you had been, you would see that in doing what you have been doing you have been riding straight for a fall. If you were going to take the girl, and she was willing, as she appears to be, you should have taken her without her mother's knowledge, old man. She might have been able to adjust things afterward. If not, you would have had her, and I suppose you would have been willing to suffer the consequences, if you had been caught. As it is, you have let Mrs. Dale in on it, and she has powerful friends. You can't ignore her. I can't. She is in a fighting mood, and it looks as though she were going to bring considerable pressure to bear to make you let go."

He paused again, waiting to see if Eugene would say something, but the latter made no comment.

"I want to ask one question, and I don't want you to take any offense at it, for I don't mean anything by it, but it will help to clear this matter up in my own mind, and probably in yours later, if you will. Have you had anything to do in a compromising way with Miss——?"

"No," said Eugene before he could finish.

"How long has this fight been going on?"

"Oh, about four weeks, or a little less."

Colfax bit at the end of his cigar.

"You have powerful enemies here, you know, Witla. Your rule hasn't been very lenient. One of the things I have noticed about you is your utter inability to play politics. You have picked men who would be very glad to have your shoes, if they could. If they could get the details of this predicament, your situation wouldn't be tenable more than fifteen minutes. You know that, of course. In spite of anything I might do you would have to resign. You couldn't maintain yourself here. I couldn't let you. You haven't thought of that in this connection, I suppose. No man in love does. I know just how you feel. From having seen Mrs. Witla, I can tell in a way just what the trouble is. You have been reined in too close. You haven't been master in your own home. It's irritated you. Life has appeared to be a failure. You have lost your chance, or thought you had on this matrimonial game, and it's made you restless. I know this girl. She's beautiful. But just as I say, old man, you haven't counted the cost—you haven't calculated right—you haven't planned. If anything could prove to me what I have always faintly suspected about you, it is this: You don't plan carefully enough——" and he looked out of the window.

Eugene sat staring at the floor. He couldn't make out just what it was that Colfax intended to do about it. He was calmer in his thinking than he had ever seen him before—less dramatic. As a rule, Colfax yelled things—demonstrated, performed—made excited motions. This morning, he was slow, thoughtful, possibly emotional.

"In spite of the fact that I like you personally, Witla—and every man owes a little something to friendship—it can't be worked out in business, though—I have been slowly coming to the conclusion that perhaps, after all, you aren't just the ideal man for this place. You're too emotional, I fancy—too erratic. White has been trying to tell me that for a long time, but I wouldn't believe it. I'm not taking his judgment now. I don't know that I would ever have acted on that feeling or idea, if this thing hadn't come up. I don't know that I am going to do so finally, but it strikes me that you are in a very ticklish position—one rather dangerous to this house, and you know that this house could never brook a scandal. Why the newspapers would never get over it. It would do us infinite harm. I think, viewing it all in all, that you had better take a year off and see if you can't straighten this out quietly. I don't think you had better try to take this girl unless you can get a divorce and marry her, and I don't think you had better try to get a divorce unless you can do it quietly. I mean so far as your position here is concerned only. Apart from that, you can do what you please. But remember! a scandal would affect your usefulness here. If things can be patched up, well and good. If not, well then they can't. If this thing gets talked about much, you know that there will be no hope of your coming back here. I don't suppose you would be willing to give her up?"

"No," said Eugene.

"I thought as much. I know just how you take a thing of this kind. It hits your type hard. Can you get a divorce from Mrs. Witla?"

"I'm not so sure," said Eugene. "I haven't any suitable grounds. We simply don't agree, that's all—my life has been a hollow shell."

"Well," said Colfax, "it's a bad mix up all around. I know how you feel about the girl. She's very beautiful. She's just the sort to bring about a situation of this kind. I don't want to tell you what to do. You are your own best judge, but if you will take my advice, you won't try to live with her without first marrying her. A man in your position can't afford to do it. You're too much in the public eye. You know you have become fairly conspicuous in New York during the last few years, don't you?"

"Yes," said Eugene. "I thought I had arranged that matter with Mrs. Dale."

"It appears not. She tells me that you are trying to persuade her daughter to live with you; that you have no means of obtaining a divorce within a reasonable time; that your wife is in a—pardon me, and that you insist on associating with her daughter, meanwhile, which isn't possible, according to her. I'm inclined to think she's right. It's hard, but it can't be helped. She says that you say that if you are not allowed to do that, you will take her and live with her."

He paused again. "Will you?"

"Yes," said Eugene.

Colfax twisted slowly in his chair and looked out of the window. What a man! What a curious thing love was! "When is it," he asked finally, "that you think you might do this?"

"Oh, I don't know. I'm all tangled up now. I'll have to think."

Colfax meditated.

"It's a peculiar business. Few people would understand this as well as I do. Few people would understand you, Witla, as I do. You haven't calculated right, old man, and you'll have to pay the price. We all do. I can't let you stay here. I wish I could, but I can't. You'll have to take a year off and think this thing out. If nothing happens—if no scandal arises—well, I won't say what I'll do. I might make a berth for you here somewhere—not exactly in the same position, perhaps, but somewhere. I'll have to think about that. Meanwhile"—he stopped and thought again.

Eugene was seeing clearly how it was with him. All this talk about coming back meant nothing. The thing that was apparent in Colfax's mind was that he would have to go, and the reason that he would have to go was not Mrs. Dale or Suzanne, or the moral issue involved, but the fact that he had lost Colfax's confidence in him. Somehow, through White, through Mrs. Dale, through his own actions day in and day out, Colfax had come to the conclusion that he was erratic, uncertain, and, for that reason, nothing else, he was being dispensed with now. It was Suzanne—it was fate, his own unfortunate temperament. He brooded pathetically, and then he said: "When do you want this to happen?"

"Oh, any time, the quicker, the better, if a public scandal is to grow out of it. If you want you can take your time, three weeks, a month, six weeks. You had better make it a matter of health and resign for your own good.—I mean the looks of the thing. That won't make any difference in my subsequent conclusions. This place is arranged so well now, that it can run nicely for a year without much trouble. We might fix this up again—it depends——"

Eugene wished he had not added the last hypocritical phrase.

He shook hands and went to the door and Eugene strolled to the window. Here was all the solid foundation knocked from under him at one fell stroke, as if by a cannon. He had lost this truly magnificent position, $25,000 a year. Where would he get another like it? Who else—what other company could pay any such salary? How could he maintain the Riverside Drive apartment now, unless he married Suzanne? How could he have his automobile—his valet? Colfax said nothing about continuing his income— why should he? He really owed him nothing. He had been exceedingly well paid—better paid than he would have been anywhere else.

He regretted his fanciful dreams about Blue Sea—his silly enthusiasm in tying up all his money in that. Would Mrs. Dale go to Winfield? Would her talk do him any real harm there? Winfield had always been a good friend to him, had manifested a high regard. This charge, this talk of abduction. What a pity it all was. It might change Winfield's attitude, and still why should it? He had women; no wife, however. He hadn't, as Colfax said, planned this thing quite right. That was plain now. His shimmering world of dreams was beginning to fade like an evening sky. It might be that he had been chasing a will-o'-the-wisp, after all. Could this really be possible? Could it be?

CHAPTER XXII

One would have thought that this terrific blow would have given Eugene pause in a way, and it did. It frightened him. Mrs. Dale had gone to Colfax in order to persuade him to use his influence to make Eugene behave himself, and, having done so much, she was actually prepared to go further. She was considering some scheme whereby she could blacken Eugene, have his true character become known without in any way involving Suzanne. Having been relentlessly pursued and harried by Eugene, she was now as relentless in her own attitude. She wanted him to let go now, entirely, if she could, not to see Suzanne any more and she went, first to Winfield, and then back to Lenox with the hope of preventing any further communication, or at least action on Suzanne's part, or Eugene's possible presence there.

In so far as her visit to Winfield was concerned, it did not amount to so much morally or emotionally in that quarter, for Winfield did not feel that he was called upon to act in the matter. He was not Eugene's guardian, nor yet a public censor of morals. He waived the whole question grandly to one side, though in a way he was glad to know of it, for it gave him an advantage over Eugene. He was sorry for him a little—what man would not be? Nevertheless, in his thoughts of reorganizing the Blue Sea Corporation, he did not feel so bad over what might become of Eugene's interests. When the latter approached him, as he did some time afterward, with the idea that he might be able to dispose of his holdings, he saw no way to do it. The company was really not in good shape. More money would have to be put in. All the treasury stock would have to be quickly disposed of, or a reorganization would have to be effected. The best that could be promised under these circumstances was that Eugene's holdings might be exchanged for a fraction of their value in a new issue by a new group of directors. So Eugene saw the end of his dreams in that direction looming up quite clearly.

When he saw what Mrs. Dale had done, he saw also that it was necessary to communicate the situation clearly to Suzanne. The whole thing pulled him up short, and he began to wonder what was to become of him. With his twenty-five thousand a year in salary cut off, his prospect of an independent fortune in Blue Sea annihilated, the old life closed to him for want of cash, for who can go about in society without money? he saw that he was in danger of complete social and commercial extinction. If by any chance a discussion of the moral relation between him and Suzanne arose, his unconscionable attitude toward Angela, if White heard of it for instance, what would become of him? The latter would spread the fact far and wide. It would be the talk of the town, in the publishing world at least. It would close every publishing house in the city to him. He did not believe Colfax would talk. He fancied that Mrs. Dale had not, after all, spoken to Winfield, but if she had, how much further would it go? Would White hear of it through Colfax? Would he keep it a secret if he knew? Never! The folly of what he had been doing began to dawn upon him dimly. What was it that he had been doing? He felt like a man who had been cast into a deep sleep by a powerful opiate and was now slowly waking to a dim wondering sense of where he was. He was in New York. He had no position. He had little ready money—perhaps five or six thousand all told. He had the love of Suzanne, but her mother was still fighting him, and he had Angela on his hands, undivorced. How was he to arrange things now? How could he think of going back to her? Never!

He sat down and composed the following letter to Suzanne, which he thought would make clear to her just how things stood and give her an opportunity to retract if she wished, for he thought he owed that much to her now:

"Flower Face:

I had a talk with Mr. Colfax this morning and what I feared might happen has happened. Your mother, instead of going to Boston as you thought, came to New York and saw him and, I fancy, my friend Winfield, too. She cannot do me any harm in that direction, for my relationship with that company does not depend on a salary, or a fixed income of any kind, but she has done me infinite harm here. Frankly, I have lost my position. I do not believe that would have come about except for other pressure with which she had nothing to do, but her charges and complaints, coming on top of opposition here on the part of someone else, has done what she couldn't have done alone. Flower Face, do you know what that means? I told you once that I had tied up all my spare cash in Blue Sea, which I hoped would come to so much. It may, but the cutting off my salary here means great changes for me there, unless I can make some other business engagement immediately. I shall probably have to give up my apartment in Riverside Drive and my automobile, and in other ways trim my sails to meet the bad weather. It means that if you come to me, we should have to live on what I can earn as an artist unless I should decide and be able to find something else. When I came to Canada for you, I had some such idea in mind, but since this thing has actually happened, you may think differently. If nothing happens to my Blue Sea investment, there may be an independent fortune some day in that. I can't tell, but that is a long way off, and meanwhile, there is only this, and I don't know what else your mother may do to my reputation. She appears to be in a very savage frame of mind. You heard what she said at While-a-Way. She has evidently gone back on that completely.

"Flower Face, I lay this all before you so that you may see how things are. If you come to me it may be in the face of a faded reputation. You must realize that there is a great difference between Eugene Witla, Managing Publisher of the United Magazines Corporation, and Eugene Witla, Artist. I have been very reckless and defiant in my love for you. Because you are so lovely—the most perfect thing that I have ever known, I have laid all on the altar of my affection. I would do it again, gladly—a thousand times. Before you came, my life was a gloomy thing. I thought I was living, but I knew in my heart that it was all a dusty shell—a lie. Then you came, and oh, how I have lived! The nights, the days of beautiful fancy. Shall I ever forget White Wood, or Blue Sea, or Briarcliff, or that wonderful first day at South Beach? Little girl, our ways have been the ways of perfectness and peace. This has been an intensely desperate thing to do, but for my sake, I am not sorry. I have been dreaming a wonderfully sweet and perfect dream. It may be when you know all and see how things stand, and stop and think, as I now ask you to do, you may be sorry and want to change your mind. Don't hesitate to do so if you feel that way. You know I told you to think calmly long ago before you told your mother. This is a bold, original thing we have been planning. It is not to be expected that the world would see it as we have. It is quite to be expected that trouble would follow in the wake of it, but it seemed possible to me, and still seems so. If you want to come to me, say so. If you want me to come to you, speak the word. We will go to England or Italy, and I will try my hand at painting again. I can do that I am sure. Or, we can stay here, and I can see if some engagement cannot be had.

"You want to remember, though, that your mother may not have finished fighting. She may go to much greater lengths than she has gone. You thought you might control her, but it seems not. I thought we had won in Canada, but it appears not. If she attempts to restrain you from using your share of your father's estate, she may be able to cause you trouble there. If she attempts to incarcerate you, she might be successful. I wish I could talk to you. Can't I see you at Lenox? Are you coming home next week? We ought to think and plan and act now if at all. Don't let any consideration for me stand in your way, though, if you are doubtful. Remember that conditions are different now. Your whole future hangs on your decision. I should have talked this way long ago, perhaps, but I did not think your mother could do what she has succeeded in doing. I did not think my financial standing would play any part in it.

"Flower Face, this is the day of real trial for me. I am unhappy, but only at the possible prospect of losing you. Nothing of all these other things really matters. With you, everything would be perfect, whatever my condition might be. Without you, it will be as dark as night. The decision is in your hands and you must act. Whatever you decide, that I will do. Don't, as I say, let consideration for me stand in the way. You are young. You have a social career before you. After all, I am twice your age. I talk thus sanely because if you come to me now, I want you to understand clearly how you come.

"Oh, I wonder sometimes if you really understand. I wonder if I have been dreaming a dream. You are so beautiful. You have been such an inspiration to me. Has this been a lure—a will-o'-the wisp? I wonder. I wonder. And yet I love you, love you, love you. A thousand kisses, Divine Fire, and I wait for your word.
"Eugene."

Suzanne read this letter at Lenox, and for the first time in her life she began to think and ponder seriously. What had she been doing? What was Eugene doing? This dénouement frightened her. Her mother was more purposeful than she imagined. To think of her going to Colfax—of her lying and turning so in her moods. She had not thought this possible of her mother. Had not thought it possible that Eugene could lose his position. He had always seemed so powerful to her; so much a law unto himself. Once when they were out in an automobile together, he had asked her why she loved him, and she said, "because you are a genius and can do anything you please."

"Oh, no," he answered, "nothing like that. I can't really do very much of anything. You just have an exaggerated notion of me."

"Oh, no, I haven't," she replied. "You can paint, and you can write" — she was judging by some of the booklets about Blue Sea and verses about herself and clippings of articles done in his old Chicago newspaper days, which he showed her once in a scrapbook in his apartment—"and you can run that office, and you were an advertising manager and an art director."

She lifted up her face and looked into his eyes admiringly.

"My, what a list of accomplishments!" he replied. "Well whom the gods would destroy they first make mad." He kissed her.

"And you love so beautifully," she added by way of climax.

Since then, she had thought of this often, but now, somehow, it received a severe setback. He was not quite so powerful. He could not prevent her mother from doing this, and could she really conquer her mother? Whatever Suzanne might think of her deceit, she was moving Heaven and earth to prevent this. Was she wholly wrong? After that climacteric night at St. Jacques, when somehow the expected did not happen, Suzanne had been thinking. Did she really want to leave home, and go with Eugene? Did she want to fight her mother in regard to her estate? She might have to do that. Her original idea had been that she and Eugene would meet in some lovely studio, and that she would keep her own home, and he would have his. It was something very different, this talk of poverty, and not having an automobile, and being far away from home. Still she loved him. Maybe she could force her mother to terms yet.

There were more struggles in the two or three succeeding days, in which the guardian of the estate—Mr. Herbert Pitcairn, of the Marquardt Trust Company, and, once more, Dr. Woolley, were called in to argue with her. Suzanne, unable to make up her mind, listened to her mother's insidious plea, that if she would wait a year, and then say she really wanted him, she could have him; listened to Mr. Pitcairn tell her mother that he believed any court would on application adjudge her incompetent and tie up her estate; heard Dr. Woolley say in her presence to her mother that he did not deem a commission in lunacy advisable, but if her mother insisted, no doubt a judge would adjudge her insane, if no more than to prevent this unhallowed consummation. Suzanne became frightened. Her iron nerve, after Eugene's letter, was weakening. She was terribly incensed against her mother, but she began now for the first time to think what her friends would think. Supposing her mother did lock her up. Where would they think she was? All these days and weeks of strain, which had worn her mother threadbare had told something on her own strength, or rather nerve. It was too intense, and she began to wonder whether they had not better do as Eugene suggested, and wait a little while. He had agreed up at St. Jacques to wait, if she were willing. Only the provision was that they were to see each other. Now her mother had changed front again, pleading danger, undue influence, that she ought to have at least a year of her old kind of life undisturbed to see whether she really cared.

"How can you tell?" she insisted to Suzanne, in spite of the girl's desire not to talk. "You have been swept into this, and you haven't given yourself time to think. A year won't hurt. What harm will it do you or him?"

"But, mama," asked Suzanne over and over at different times, and in different places, "why did you go and tell Mr. Colfax? What a mean, cruel thing that was to do!"

"Because I think he needs something like that to make him pause and think. He isn't going to starve. He is a man of talent. He needs something like that to bring him to his senses. Mr. Colfax hasn't discharged him. He told me he wouldn't. He said he would make him take a year off and think about it, and that's just what he has done. It won't hurt him. I don't care if it does. Look at the way he has made me suffer."

She felt exceedingly bitter toward Eugene, and was rejoicing that at last she was beginning to have her innings.

"Mama," said Suzanne, "I am never going to forgive you for this. You are acting horribly—I will wait, but it will come to the same thing in the end. I am going to have him."

"I don't care what you do after a year," said Mrs. Dale cheerfully and subtly. "If you will just wait that long and give yourself time to think and still want to marry him, you can do so. He can probably get a divorce in that time, anyhow." She did not mean what she was saying, but any argument was good for the situation, if it delayed matters.

"But I don't know that I want to marry him," insisted Suzanne, doggedly, harking back to her original idea. "That isn't my theory of it."

"Oh, well," replied Mrs. Dale complaisantly, "you will know better what to think of that after a year. I don't want to coerce you, but I'm not going to have our home and happiness broken up in this way without turning a hand, and without your stopping to think about it. You owe it to me—to all these years I have cared for you, to show me some consideration. A year won't hurt you. It won't hurt him. You will find out then whether he really loves you or not. This may just be a passing fancy. He has had other women before you. He may have others after you. He may go back to Mrs. Witla. It doesn't make any difference what he tells you. You ought to test him before you break up his home and mine. If he really loves you, he will agree readily enough. Do this for me, Suzanne, and I will never cross your path any more. If you will wait a year you can do anything you choose. I can only hope you won't go to him without going as his wife, but if you insist, I will hush the matter up as best I can. Write to him and tell him that you have decided that you both ought to wait a year. You don't need to see him any more. It will just stir things all up afresh. If you don't see him, but just write, it will be better for him, too. He won't feel so badly as he will if you see him again and go all over the ground once more."

Mrs. Dale was terribly afraid of Eugene's influence, but she could not accomplish this.

"I won't do that," said Suzanne, "I won't do it. I'm going back to New York, that's all there is about it!" Mrs. Dale finally yielded that much. She had to.

There was a letter from Suzanne after three days, saying that she couldn't answer his letter in full, but that she was coming back to New York and would see him, and subsequently a meeting between Suzanne and Eugene at Daleview in her mother's presence—Dr. Woolley and Mr. Pitcairn were in another part of the house at the time—in which the proposals were gone over anew.

Eugene had motored down after Mrs. Dale's demands had been put before him in the gloomiest and yet more feverish frame of mind in which he had ever been,—gloomy because of heavy forebodings of evil and his own dark financial condition—while inspirited at other moments by thoughts of some splendid, eager revolt on the part of Suzanne, of her rushing to him, defying all, declaring herself violently and convincingly, and so coming off a victor with him. His faith in her love was still so great.

The night was one of those cold October ones with a steely sky and a sickle moon, harbinger of frost, newly seen in the west, and pointed stars thickening overhead. As he sat in his car on the Staten Island ferry boat, he could see a long line of southward bound ducks, homing to those reedy marshes which Bryant had in mind when he wrote "To a Waterfowl." They were honking as they went, their faint "quacks" coming back on the thin air and making him feel desperately lonely and bereft. When he reached

Daleview, speeding past October trees, and entered the great drawing-room where a fire was blazing and where once in spring he had danced with Suzanne, his heart leaped up, for he was to see her, and the mere sight of her was as a tonic to his fevered body—a cool drink to a thirsting man.

Mrs. Dale stared at Eugene defiantly when he came, but Suzanne welcomed him to her embrace. "Oh!" she exclaimed, holding him close for a few moments and breathing feverishly. There was complete silence for a time.

"Mama insists, Eugene," she said after a time, "that we ought to wait a year, and I think since there is such a fuss about it, that perhaps it might be just as well. We may have been just a little hasty, don't you think? I have told mama what I think about her action in going to Mr. Colfax, but she doesn't seem to care. She is threatening now to have me adjudged insane. A year won't make any real difference since I am coming to you, anyhow, will it? But I thought I ought to tell you this in person, to ask you about it"—she paused, looking into his eyes.

"I thought we settled all this up in St. Jacques?" said Eugene, turning to Mrs. Dale, but experiencing a sinking sensation of fear.

"We did, all except the matter of not seeing her. I think it is highly inadvisable that you two should be together. It isn't possible the way things stand. People will talk. Your wife's condition has to be adjusted. You can't be running around with her and a child coming to you. I want Suzanne to go away for a year where she can be calm and think it all out, and I want you to let her. If she still insists that she wants you after that, and will not listen to the logic of the situation in regard to marriage, then I propose to wash my hands of the whole thing. She may have her inheritance. She may have you if she wants you. If you have come to your senses by that time, as I hope you will have, you will get a divorce, or go back to Mrs. Witla, or do whatever you do in a sensible way."

She did not want to incense Eugene here, but she was very bitter.

Eugene merely frowned.

"Is this your decision, Suzanne, too?" he asked wearily.

"I think mama is terrible, Eugene," replied Suzanne evasively, or perhaps as a reply to her mother. "You and I have planned our lives, and we will work them out. We have been a little selfish, now that I think of it. I think a year won't do any harm, perhaps, if it will stop all this fussing. I can wait, if you can."

An inexpressible sense of despair fell upon Eugene at the sound of this, a sadness so deep that he could scarcely speak. He could not believe that it was really Suzanne who was saying that to him. Willing to wait a year! She who had declared so defiantly that she would not. It would do no harm? To think that life, fate, her mother were triumphing over him in this fashion, after all. What then was the significance of the black-bearded men he had seen so often of late? Why had he been finding horseshoes? Was fate such a liar? Did life in its dark, subtle chambers lay lures and traps for men? His position gone, his Blue Sea venture involved in an indefinite delay out of which might come nothing, Suzanne going for a whole year, perhaps for ever, most likely so, for what could not her mother do with her in a whole year, having her alone? Angela alienated—a child approaching. What a climax!

"Is this really your decision, Suzanne?" he asked, sadly, a mist of woe clouding his whole being.

"I think it ought to be, perhaps, Eugene," she replied, still evasively. "It's very trying. I will be faithful to you, though. I promise you that I will not change. Don't you think we can wait a year? We can, can't we?"

"A whole year without seeing you, Suzanne?"

"Yes, it will pass, Eugene."

"A whole year?"

"Yes, Eugene."

"I have nothing more to say, Mrs. Dale," he said, turning to her mother solemnly, a sombre, gloomy light in his eye, his heart hardening towards Suzanne for the moment. To think she should treat him so—throw him down, as he phrased it. Well, such was life. "You win," he added. "It has been a terrible experience for me. A terrible passion. I love this girl. I love her with my whole heart. Sometimes I have vaguely suspected that she might not know."

He turned to Suzanne, and for the first time he thought that he did not see there that true understanding which he had fancied had been there all the time. Could fate have been lying to him also in this? Was he mistaken in this, and had he been following a phantom lure of beauty? Was Suzanne but another trap to drag him down to his old nothingness? God! The prediction of the Astrologer of a second period of defeat after seven or eight years came back.

"Oh, Suzanne!" he said, simply and unconsciously dramatic. "Do you really love me?"

"Yes, Eugene," she replied.

"Really?"

"Yes."

He held out his arms and she came, but for the life of him he could not dispel this terrible doubt. It took the joy out of his kiss—as if he had been dreaming a dream of something perfect in his arms and had awaked to find it nothing—as if life had sent him a Judas in the shape of a girl to betray him.

"Do let us end this, Mr. Witla," said Mrs. Dale coldly, "there is nothing to be gained by delaying. Let us end it for a year, and then talk."

"Oh, Suzanne," he continued, as mournful as a passing bell, "come to the door with me."

"No, the servants are there," put in Mrs. Dale. "Please make your farewells here."

"Mama," said Suzanne angrily and defiantly, moved by the pity of it, "I won't have you talk this way. Leave the room, or I shall go to the door with him and further. Leave us, please."

Mrs. Dale went out.

"Oh, Flower Face," said Eugene pathetically, "I can't believe it. I can't. I can't! This has been managed wrong. I should have taken you long ago. So it is to end this way. A year, a whole year, and how much longer?"

"Only a year," she insisted. "Only a year, believe me, can't you? I won't change, I won't!"

He shook his head, and Suzanne as before took his face in her hands. She kissed his cheeks, his lips, his hair.

"Believe me, Eugene. I seem cold. You don't know what I have gone through. It is nothing but trouble everywhere. Let us wait a year. I promise you I will come to you. I swear. One year. Can't we wait one year?"

"A year," he said. "A year. I can't believe it. Where will we all be in a year? Oh, Flower Face, Myrtle Bloom, Divine Fire. I can't stand this. I can't. It's too much. I'm the one who is paying now. Yes, I pay."

He took her face and looked at it, all its soft, enticing features, her eyes, her lips, her cheeks, her hair.

"I thought, I thought," he murmured.

Suzanne only stroked the back of his head with her hands.

"Well, if I must, I must," he said.

He turned away, turned back to embrace her, turned again and then, without looking back, walked out into the hall. Mrs. Dale was there waiting.

"Good night, Mrs. Dale," he said gloomily.

"Good night, Mr. Witla," she replied frigidly, but with a sense of something tragic in her victory at that.

He took his hat and walked out.

Outside the bright October stars were in evidence by millions. The Bay and Harbor of New York were as wonderfully lit as on that night when Suzanne came to him after the evening at Fort Wadsworth on her own porch. He recalled the spring odours, the wonderful feel of youth and love—the hope that was springing then. Now, it was five or six months later, and all that romance was gone. Suzanne, sweet voice, accomplished shape, light whisper, delicate touch. Gone. All gone—

"Faded the flower and all its budded charms,
Faded the sight of beauty from my eyes,
Faded the shape of beauty from my arms,
Faded the voice, warmth, whiteness, paradise."

Gone were those bright days in which they had ridden together, dined together, walked in sylvan places beside their car. A little way from here he first played tennis with her. A little way from here he had come so often to meet her clandestinely. Now she was gone—gone.

He had come in his car, but he really did not want it. Life was accursed. His own was a failure. To think that all his fine dreams should crumble this way. Shortly he would have no car, no home on Riverside Drive, no position, no anything.

"God, I can't stand this!" he exclaimed, and a little later—"By God, I can't! I can't!"

He dismissed his car at the Battery, telling his chauffeur to take it to the garage, and walking gloomily through all the tall dark streets of lower New York. Here was Broadway where he had often been with Colfax and Winfield. Here was this great world of finance around Wall Street in which he had vaguely hoped to shine. Now these buildings were high and silent— receding from him in a way. Overhead were the clear bright stars, cool and refreshing, but without meaning to him now. How was he to settle it? How adjust it? A year! She would never come back—never! It was all gone. A bright cloud faded. A mirage dissolved into its native nothingness. Position, distinction, love, home—where were they? Yet a little while and all these things would be as though they had never been. Hell! Damn! Curse the brooding fates that could thus plot to destroy him!

Back in her room in Daleview Suzanne had locked herself in. She was not without a growing sense of the tragedy of it. She stared at the floor, recalled his face.

"Oh, oh," she said, and for the first time in her life felt as though she could cry from a great heartache—but she could not.

And in Riverside Drive was another woman brooding, lonely, despondently, desperately, over the nature of the tragedy that was upon her. How were things to be adjusted? How was she to be saved? Oh! oh! her life, her child! If Eugene could be made to understand! If he could only be made to see!

CHAPTER XXIII

During the weeks which followed Colfax's talk with him, and Suzanne's decision, which amounted practically to a dismissal, Eugene tried to wind up his affairs at the United Magazines Corporation, as well as straighten out his relationship with Angela. It was no easy task. Colfax helped him considerably by suggesting that he should say he was going abroad for the company, for the time being, and should make it appear imperative that he go at once. Eugene called in his department heads, and told them what Colfax suggested, but added that his own interests elsewhere, of which they knew, or suspected, were now so involved that he might possibly not return, or only for a little while at best. He put forward an air of great sufficiency and self-satisfaction, considering the difficulties he was encountering, and the thing passed off as a great wonder, but with no suspicion of any immediate misfortune attaching to him. As a matter of fact, it was assumed that he was destined to a much higher estate—the control of his private interests.

In his talk with Angela he made it perfectly plain that he was going to leave her. He would not make any pretence about this. She ought to know. He had lost his position; he was not going to Suzanne soon; he wanted her to leave him, or he would leave her. She should go to Wisconsin or Europe or anywhere, for the time being, and leave him to fight this thing out alone. He was not indispensable to her in her condition. There were nurses she could hire—maternity hospitals where she could stay. He would be willing to pay for that. He would never live with her any more, if he could help it—he did not want to. The sight of her in the face of his longing for Suzanne would be a wretched commentary—a reproach and a sore shame. No, he would leave her and perhaps, possibly, sometime when she obtained more real fighting courage, Suzanne might come to him. She ought to. Angela might die. Yes, brutal as it may seem, he thought this. She might die, and then—and then—— No thought of the child that might possibly live, even if she died, held him. He could not understand that, could not grasp it as yet. It was a mere abstraction.

Eugene took a room in an apartment house in Kingsbridge, where he was not known for the time being, and where he was not likely to be seen. Then there was witnessed that dreary spectacle of a man whose life has apparently come down in a heap, whose notions, emotions, tendencies and feelings are confused and disappointed by some untoward result. If Eugene had been ten or fifteen years older, the result might have been suicide. A shade of difference in temperament might have resulted in death, murder, anything. As it was, he sat blankly at times among the ruins of his dreams speculating on what Suzanne was doing, on what Angela was doing, on what people were saying and thinking, on how he could gather up the broken pieces of his life and make anything out of them at all.

The one saving element in it all was his natural desire to work, which, although it did not manifest itself at first, by degrees later on began to come back. He must do something, if it was not anything more than to try to paint again. He could not be running around looking for a position. There was nothing for him in connection with Blue Sea. He had to work to support Angela, of whom he was now free, if he did not want to be mean; and as he viewed it all in the light of what had happened, he realized that he had been bad enough. She had not been temperamentally suited to him, but she had tried to be. Fundamentally it was not her fault. How was he to work and live and be anything at all from now on?

There were long arguments over this situation between him and Angela—pleas, tears, a crashing downward of everything which was worth while in life to Angela, and then, in spite of her pathetic situation, separation. Because it was November and the landlord had heard of Eugene's financial straits, or rather reverse of fortune, it was possible to relinquish the lease, which had several years to run, and the apartment was given up. Angela, distraught, scarcely knew which way to turn. It was one of those pitiless, scandalous situations in life which sicken us of humanity. She ran helplessly to Eugene's sister, Myrtle, who first tried to conceal the scandal and tragedy from her husband, but afterward confessed and deliberated as to what should be done. Frank Bangs, who was a practical man, as well as firm believer in Christian Science because of his wife's to him miraculous healing from a tumor several years before, endeavored to apply his understanding of the divine science—the omnipresence of good to this situation.

"There is no use worrying about it, Myrtle," he said to his wife, who, in spite of her faith, was temporarily shaken and frightened by the calamities which seemingly had overtaken her brother. "It's another evidence of the workings of mortal mind. It is real enough in its idea of itself, but nothing in God's grace. It will come out all right, if we think right. Angela can go to a maternity hospital for the time being, or whenever she's ready. We may be able to persuade Eugene to do the right thing."

Angela was persuaded to consult a Christian Science practitioner, and Myrtle went to the woman who had cured her and begged her to use her influence, or rather her knowledge of science to effect a rehabilitation for her brother. She was told that this could not be done without his wish, but that she would pray for him. If he could be persuaded to come of his own accord, seeking spiritual guidance or divine aid, it would be a different matter. In spite of his errors, and to her they seemed palpable and terrible enough at present, her faith would not allow her to reproach him, and besides she loved him. He was a strong man, she said, always strange. He and Angela might not have been well mated. But all could be righted in *Science*. There was a dreary period of packing and storing for Angela, in which she stood about amid the ruins of her previous comfort and distinction and cried over the things that had seemed so lovely to her. Here were all Eugene's things, his paintings, his canes, his pipes, his clothes. She cried over a handsome silk dressing gown in which he had been wont to lounge about—it smacked so much, curiously, of older and happier days. There were hard, cold and determined conferences also in which some of Angela's old fighting, ruling spirit would come back, but not for long. She was beaten now, and she knew it—wrecked. The roar of a cold and threatening sea was in her ears.

It should be said here that at one time Suzanne truly imagined she loved Eugene. It must be remembered, however, that she was moved to affection for him by the wonder of a personality that was hypnotic to her. There was something about the personality of Eugene that was subversive of conventionality. He approached, apparently a lamb of conventional feelings and appearances; whereas, inwardly, he was a ravening wolf of indifference to convention. All the organized modes and methods of life were a joke to him. He saw through to something that was not material life at all, but spiritual, or say immaterial, of which all material things were a shadow. What did the great forces of life care whether this system which was maintained here with so much show and fuss was really maintained at all or not? How could they care? He once stood in a morgue and saw human bodies apparently dissolving into a kind of chemical mush and he had said to himself then how ridiculous it was to assume that life meant anything much to the forces which were doing these things. Great chemical and physical forces were at work, which permitted, accidentally, perhaps, some little shadow-play, which would soon pass. But, oh, its presence— how sweet it was!

Naturally Suzanne was cast down for the time being, for she was capable of suffering just as Eugene was. But having given her word to wait, she decided to stick to that, although she had not stuck to her other. She was between nineteen and twenty now—Eugene was nearing forty. Life could still soothe her in spite of herself. In Eugene's case it could only hurt the more. Mrs. Dale went abroad with Suzanne and the other children, visiting with people who could not possibly have heard, or ever would except in a vague, uncertain way for that matter. If it became evident, as she thought it might, that there was to be a scandal, Mrs. Dale proposed to say that Eugene had attempted to establish an insidious hold on her child in defiance of reason and honor, and that she had promptly broken it up, shielding Suzanne, almost without the latter's knowledge. It was plausible enough.

What was he to do now? how live? was his constant thought. Go into a wee, small apartment in some back street with Angela, where he and she, if he decided to stay with her, could find a pretty outlook for a little money and live? Never. Admit that he had lost Suzanne for a year at least, if not permanently, in this suddenly brusque way? Impossible. Go and confess that he had made a mistake, which he still did not feel to be true? or that he was sorry and would like to patch things up as before? Never. He was not sorry. He did not propose to live with Angela in the old way any more. He was sick of her, or rather of that atmosphere of repression and convention in which he had spent so many years. He was sick of the idea of having a child thrust on him against his will. He would not do it. She had no business to put herself in this position. He would die first. His insurance was paid up to date. He had carried during the last five years a policy for something over eighteen thousand in her favor, and if he died she would get that. He wished he might. It would be some atonement for the hard knocks which fate had recently given her, but he did not wish to live with her any more. Never, never, child or no child. Go back to the apartment after this night— how could he? If he did, he must pretend that nothing had happened—at least, nothing untoward between him and Suzanne. She might come back. Might! Might! Ah, the mockery of it—to leave him in this way when she really could have come to him—should have—oh, the bitterness of this thrust of fate!

There was a day when the furniture was sent away and Angela went to live with Myrtle for the time being. There was another tearful hour when she left New York to visit her sister Marietta at Racine, where they now were, intending to tell her before she came away, as a profound secret, the terrible tragedy which had overtaken her. Eugene went to the train with her, but with no desire to be there. Angela's one thought, in all this, was that somehow time would effect a reconciliation. If she could just wait long enough; if she could keep her peace and live and not die, and not give him a divorce, he might eventually recover his sanity and come to think of her as at least worth living with. The child might do it, its coming would be something that would affect him surely. He was bound to see her through it. She told herself she was willing and delighted to go through this ordeal, if only it brought him back to her. This child—what a reception it was to receive, unwanted, dishonored before its arrival, ignored; if by any chance she should die, what would he do about it? Surely he would not desert it. Already in her nervous, melancholy way, she was yearning toward it.

"Tell me," she said to Eugene one day, when they were alternately quarreling and planning, "if the baby comes, and I—and I—die, you won't absolutely desert it? You'll take it, won't you?"

"I'll take it," he replied. "Don't worry. I'm not an absolute dog. I didn't want it. It's a trick on your part, but I'll take it. I don't want you to die. You know that."

Angela thought if she lived that she would be willing to go through a period of poverty and depression with him again, if only she could live to see him sane and moral and even semi-successful. The baby might do it. He had never had a child. And much as he disliked the idea now, still, when it was here, he might change his mind. If only she could get through that ordeal. She was so old—her muscles so set. Meanwhile she consulted a lawyer, a doctor, a fortune teller, an astrologer and the Christian Science practitioner to whom Myrtle had recommended her. It was an aimless, ridiculous combination, but she was badly torn up, and any port seemed worth while in this storm.

The doctor told her that her muscles were rather set, but with the regimen he prescribed, he was satisfied she would be all right. The astrologer told her that she and Eugene were fated for this storm by the stars—Eugene, particularly, and that he might recover, in which case, he would be successful again in a measure. As for herself, he shook his head. Yes, she would be all right. He was lying. The fortune teller laid the cards to see if Eugene would ever marry Suzanne, and Angela was momentarily gratified to learn that she would never enter his life—this from a semi-cadaverous, but richly dressed and bejeweled lady whose ante-room was filled with women whose troubles were of the heart, the loss of money, the enmity of rivals, or the dangers of childbirth. The Christian Science practitioner declared all to be divine mind—omnipotent, omnipresent, omniscient good, and that evil could not exist in it—only the illusion of it. "It is real enough to those who give it their faith and believe," said the counselor, "but without substance or meaning to those who know themselves to be a perfect, indestructible reflection of an idea in God. God is a principle. When the nature of that principle is realized and yourself as a part of it, evil falls away as the troublesome dream that it is. It has no reality." She assured her that no evil could befall her in the true understanding of Science. God is love.

The lawyer told her, after listening to a heated story of Eugene's misconduct, that under the laws of the State of New York, in which these misdeeds were committed, she was not entitled to anything more than a very small fraction of her husband's estate, if he had any. Two years was the shortest time in which a divorce could be secured. He would advise her to sue if she could establish a suitable condition of affluence on Eugene's part, not otherwise. Then he charged her twenty-five dollars for this advice.

CHAPTER XXIV

To those who have followed a routine or system of living in this world—who have, by slow degrees and persistent effort, built up a series of habits, tastes, refinements, emotions and methods of conduct, and have, in addition, achieved a certain distinction and position, so that they have said to one "Go!" and he goes, and to another "Come!" and he comes, who have enjoyed without stint or reserve, let or hindrance, those joys of perfect freedom of action, and that ease and deliberation which comes with the presence of comparative wealth, social position, and comforts, the narrowing that comes with the lack of means, the fear of public opinion, or the shame of public disclosure, is one of the most pathetic, discouraging and terrifying things that can be imagined. These are the hours that try men's souls. The man who sits in a seat of the mighty and observes a world that is ruled by a superior power, a superior force of which he by some miraculous generosity of fate has been chosen apparently as a glittering instrument, has no conception of the feelings of the man who, cast out of his dignities and emoluments, sits in the dark places of the world among the ashes of his splendor and meditates upon the glory of his bygone days. There is a pathos here which passes the conception of the average man. The prophets of the Old Testament discerned it clearly enough, for they were forever pronouncing the fate of those whose follies were in opposition to the course of righteousness and who were made examples of by a beneficent and yet awful power. "Thus saith the Lord: Because thou hast lifted thyself up against the God of Heaven, and they have brought the vessels of His house before thee, and thou and thy Lords, thy wives and concubines, have drank wine in them, and thou hast praised the gods of silver and gold, of brass, iron, wood, and stone...God hath numbered thy Kingdom and finished it. Thou art weighed in the balance and found wanting; thy Kingdom is divided and given to the Medes and the Persians."

Eugene was in a minor way an exemplification of this seeming course of righteousness. His Kingdom, small as it was, was truly at an end. Our social life is so organized, so closely knit upon a warp of instinct, that we almost always instinctively flee that which does not accord with custom, usage, preconceived notions and tendencies—those various things which we in our littleness of vision conceive to be dominant. Who does not run from the man who may because of his deeds be condemned of that portion of the public which we chance to respect? Walk he ever so proudly, carry himself with what circumspectness he may, at the first breath of suspicion all are off—friends, relations, business acquaintances, the whole social fabric in toto. "Unclean!" is the cry. "Unclean! Unclean!" And it does not matter how inwardly shabby we may be, what whited sepulchres shining to the sun, we run quickly. It seems a tribute to that providence which shapes our ends, which continues perfect in tendency however vilely we may overlay its brightness with the rust of our mortal corruption, however imitative we may be.

Angela had gone home by now to see her father, who was now quite old and feeble, and also down to Alexandria to see Eugene's mother, who was also badly deteriorated in health.

"I keep hoping against hope that your attitude will change toward me," wrote Angela. "Let me hear from you if you will from time to time. It can't make any difference in your course. A word won't hurt, and I am so lonely. Oh, Eugene, if I could only die—if I only could!" No word as to the true state of things was given at either place. Angela pretended that Eugene had long been sick of his commercial career and was, owing to untoward conditions in the Colfax Company, glad to return to his art for a period. He might come home, but he was very busy. So she lied. But she wrote Myrtle fully of her hopes and, more particularly, her fears.

There were a number of conferences between Eugene and Myrtle, for the latter, because of their early companionship, was very fond of him. His traits, the innocent ones, were as sweet to her as when they were boy and girl together. She sought him out in his lovely room at Kingsbridge.

"Why don't you come and stay with us, Eugene?" she pleaded. "We have a comfortable apartment. You can have that big room next to ours. It has a nice view. Frank likes you. We have listened to Angela, and I think you are wrong, but you are my brother, and I want you to come. Everything is coming out right. God will straighten it out. Frank and I are praying for you. There is no evil, you know, according to the way we think. Now"—and she smiled her old-time girlish smile—"don't stay up here alone. Wouldn't you rather be with me?"

"Oh, I'd like to be there well enough, Myrtle, but I can't do it now. I don't want to. I have to think. I want to be alone. I haven't settled what I want to do. I think I will try my hand at some pictures. I have a little money and all the time I want now. I see there are some nice houses over there on the hill that might have a room with a north window that would serve as a studio. I want to think this thing out first. I don't know what I'll do."

He had now that new pain in his groin, which had come to him first when her mother first carried Suzanne off to Canada and he was afraid that he should never see her any more. It was a real pain, sharp, physical, like a cut with a knife. He wondered how it was that it could be physical and down there. His eyes hurt him and his finger tips. Wasn't that queer, too?

"Why don't you go and see a Christian Science practitioner?" asked Myrtle. "It won't do you any harm. You don't need to believe. Let me get you the book and you can read it. See if you don't think there is something in it. There you go smiling sarcastically, but, Eugene, I can't tell you what it hasn't done for us. It's done everything—that's just all. I'm a different person from what I was five years ago, and so is Frank. You know how sick I was?"

"Yes, I know."

"Why don't you go and see Mrs. Johns? You needn't tell her anything unless you want to. She has performed some perfectly wonderful cures."

"What can Mrs. Johns do for me?" asked Eugene bitterly, his lip set in an ironic mould. "Cure me of gloom? Make my heart cease to ache? What's the use of talking? I ought to quit the whole thing." He stared at the floor.

"She can't, but God can. Oh, Eugene, I know how you feel! Please go. It can't do you any harm. I'll bring you the book tomorrow. Will you read it if I bring it to you?"

"No."

"Oh, Eugene, please for my sake."

"What good will it do? I don't believe in it. I can't. I'm too intelligent to take any stock in that rot."

"Eugene, how you talk! You'll change your mind some time. I know how you think. But read it anyhow. Will you please? Promise me you will. I shouldn't ask. It isn't the way, but I want you to look into it. Go and see Mrs. Johns."

Eugene refused. Of asinine things this seemed the silliest. Christian Science! Christian rot! He knew what to do. His conscience was dictating that he give up Suzanne and return to Angela in her hour of need—to his coming child, for the time being anyhow, but this awful lure of beauty, of personality, of love—how it tugged at his soul! Oh, those days with Suzanne in the pretty watering and dining places about New York, those hours of bliss when she looked so beautiful! How could he get over that? How give up the memory? She was so sweet. Her beauty so rare. Every thought of her hurt. It hurt so badly that most of the time he dared not think—must, perforce, walk or work or stir restlessly about agonized for fear he should think too much. Oh, life; oh, hell!

The intrusion of Christian Science into his purview just now was due, of course, to the belief in and enthusiasm for that religious idea on the part of Myrtle and her husband. As at Lourdes and St. Anne de Beau Pré and other miracle-working centres, where hope and desire and religious enthusiasm for the efficacious intervention of a superior and non-malicious force intervenes, there had occurred in her case an actual cure from a very difficult and complicated physical ailment. She had been suffering from a tumor, nervous insomnia, indigestion, constipation and a host of allied ills, which had apparently refused to yield to ordinary medical treatment. She was in a very bad way mentally and physically at the time the Christian Science textbook, "Science and Health, with Key to the Scriptures," by Mrs. Eddy, was put into her hands. While attempting to read it in a hopeless, helpless spirit, she was instantly cured — that is, the idea that she was well took possession of her, and not long after she really was so. She threw all her medicines, of which there was quite a store, into the garbage pail, eschewed doctors, began to read the Christian Science literature, and attend the Christian Science church nearest her apartment, and was soon involved in its subtle metaphysical interpretation of mortal life. Into this faith, her husband, who loved her very much, had followed, for what was good enough for her and would cure her was good enough for him. He soon seized on its spiritual significance with great vigor and became, if anything, a better exponent and interpreter of the significant thought than was she herself.

Those who know anything of Christian Science know that its main tenet is that God is a principle, not a personality understandable or conceivable from the mortal or sensory side of life (which latter is an illusion), and that man (spiritually speaking) in His image and likeness. Man is not God or any part of Him. He is an idea in God, and, as such, as perfect and indestructible and undisturbably harmonious as an idea in God or principle must be. To those not metaphysically inclined, this is usually dark and without significance, but to those spiritually or metaphysically minded it comes as a great light. Matter becomes a built-up set or combination of illusions, which may have evolved or not as one chooses, but which unquestionably have been built up from nothing or an invisible, intangible idea, and have no significance beyond the faith or credence, which those who are at base spiritual give them. Deny them — know them to be what they are — and they are gone.

To Eugene, who at this time was in a great state of mental doldrums—blue, dispirited, disheartened, inclined to see only evil and destructive forces—this might well come with peculiar significance, if it came at all. He was one of those men who from their birth are metaphysically inclined. All his life he had been speculating on the subtleties of mortal existence, reading Spencer, Kant, Spinoza, at odd moments, and particularly such men as Darwin, Huxley, Tyndall, Lord Avebury, Alfred Russel Wallace, and latterly Sir Oliver Lodge and Sir William Crookes, trying to find out by the inductive, naturalistic method just what life was. He had secured inklings at times, he thought, by reading such things as Emerson's "Oversoul," "The Meditations of Marcus Aurelius," and Plato. God was a spirit, he thought, as Christ had said to the woman at the well in Samaria, but whether this spirit concerned itself with mortal affairs, where was so much suffering and contention, was another matter. Personally he had never believed so—or been at all sure. He had always been moved by the Sermon on the Mount; the beauty of Christ's attitude toward the troubles of the world, the wonder of the faith of the old prophets in insisting that God is God, that there are no other Gods before him, and that he would repay iniquity with disfavor. Whether he did or not was an open question with him. This question of sin had always puzzled him—original sin. Were there laws which ante-dated human experience, which were in God—The Word—before it was made flesh? If so, what were these laws? Did they concern matrimony—some spiritual union which was older than life itself? Did they concern stealing? What was stealing outside of life? Where was it before man began? Or did it only begin with man? Ridiculous! It must relate to something in chemistry and physics, which had worked out in life. A sociologist—a great professor in one of the colleges had once told him that he did not believe in success or failure, sin, or a sense of self-righteousness except as they were related to built-up instincts in the race—instincts related solely to the self-preservation and the evolution of the race. Beyond that was nothing. Spiritual morality? Bah! He knew nothing about it.

Such rank agnosticism could not but have had its weight with Eugene. He was a doubter ever. All life, as I have said before, went to pieces under his scalpel, and he could not put it together again logically, once he had it cut up. People talked about the sanctity of marriage, but, heavens, marriage was an evolution! He knew that. Someone had written a two-volume treatise on it—"The History of Human Marriage," or something like that and in it animals were shown to have mated only for so long as it took to rear the young, to get them to the point at which they could take care of themselves. And wasn't this really what was at the basis of modern marriage? He had read in this history, if he recalled aright, that the only reason marriage had come to be looked upon as sacred, and for life, was the length of time it took to rear the human young. It took so long that the parents were old, safely so, before the children were launched into the world. Then why separate?

But it was the duty of everybody to raise children.

Ah! there had been the trouble. He had been bothered by that. The home centered around that. Children! Race reproduction! Pulling this wagon of evolution! Was every man who did not inevitably damned? Was the race spirit against him? Look at the men and women who didn't—who couldn't. Thousands and thousands. And those who did always thought those who didn't were wrong. The whole American spirit he had always felt to be intensely set in this direction—the idea of having children and rearing them, a conservative work-a-day spirit. Look at his father. And yet other men were so shrewd that they preyed on this spirit, moving factories to where this race spirit was the most active, so that they could hire the children cheaply, and nothing happened to them, or did something happen?

However, Myrtle continued to plead with him to look into this new interpretation of the Scriptures, claiming that it was true, that it would bring him into an understanding of spirit which would drive away all these mortal ills, that it was above all mortal conception—spiritual over all, and so he thought about that. She told him that if it was right that he should cease to live with Angela, it would come to pass, and that if it was not, it would not; but anyhow and in any event in this truth there would be peace and happiness to him. He should do what was right ("seek ye first the Kingdom of God"), and then all these things would be added unto him.

And it seemed terribly silly at first to Eugene for him to be listening at all to any such talk, but later it was not so much so. There were long arguments and appeals, breakfast and dinner, or Sunday dinners at Myrtle's apartment, arguments with Bangs and Myrtle concerning every phase of the Science teaching, some visits to the Wednesday experience and testimony meetings of their church, at which Eugene heard statements concerning marvelous cures which he could scarcely believe, and so on. So long as the testimonies confined themselves to complaints which might be due to nervous imagination, he was satisfied that their cures were possibly due to religious enthusiasm, which dispelled their belief in something which they did not have, but when they were cured of cancer, consumption, locomotor-ataxia, goitres, shortened limbs, hernia—he did not wish to say they were liars, they seemed too sincere to do that, but he fancied they were simply mistaken. How could they, or this belief, or whatever it was, cure cancer? Good Lord! He went on disbelieving in this way, and refusing also to read the book until one Wednesday evening when he happened to be at the

Fourth Church of Christ Scientist in New York that a man stood up beside him in his own pew and said:

"I wish to testify to the love and mercy of God in my case, for I was hopelessly afflicted not so very long ago and one of the vilest men I think it is possible to be. I was raised in a family where the Bible was read night and morning—my father was a hidebound Presbyterian—and I was so sickened by the manner in which it was forced down my throat and the inconsistencies which I thought I saw existing between Christian principle and practice, even in my own home, that I said to myself I would conform as long as I was in my father's house and eating his bread, but when I got out I would do as I pleased. I was in my father's house after that a number of years, until I was seventeen, and then I went to a large city, Cincinnati, but the moment I was away and free I threw aside all my so-called religious training and set out to do what I thought was the most pleasant and gratifying thing for me to do. I wanted to drink, and I did, though I was really never a very successful drinker." Eugene smiled. "I wanted to gamble, and I did, but I was never a very clever gambler. Still I did gamble a bit. My great weakness was women, and here I hope none will be offended, I know they will not be, for there may be others who need my testimony badly. I pursued women as I would any other lure. They were really all that I desired—their bodies. My lust was terrible. It was such a dominant thought with me that I could not look at any good-looking woman except, as the Bible says, to lust after her. I was vile. I became diseased. I was carried into the First Church of Christ Scientist in Chicago, after I had spent all my money and five years of my time on physicians and specialists, suffering from locomotor ataxia, dropsy and kidney disease. I had previously been healed of some other things by ordinary medicine.

"If there is anyone within the sound of my voice who is afflicted as I was, I want him to listen to me.

"I want to say to you tonight that I am a well man—not well physically only, but well mentally, and, what is better yet, in so far as I can see the truth, spiritually. I was healed after six months' treatment by a Christian Science practitioner in Chicago, who took my case on my appealing to her, and I stand before you absolutely sound and whole. God is good."

He sat down.

While he had been talking Eugene had been studying him closely, observing every line of his features. He was tall, lean, sandy-haired and sandy-bearded. He was not bad-looking, with long straight nose, clear blue eyes, a light pinkish color to his complexion, and a sense of vigor and health about him. The thing that Eugene noted most was that he was calm, cool, serene, vital. He said exactly what he wanted to say, and he said it vigorously. His voice was clear and with good carrying power. His clothes were shapely, new, well made. He was no beggar or tramp, but a man of some profession—an engineer, very likely. Eugene wished that he might talk to him, and yet he felt ashamed. Somehow this man's case paralleled his own; not exactly, but closely. He personally was never diseased, but how often he had looked after a perfectly charming woman to lust after her! Was the thing that this man was saying really true? Could he be lying? How ridiculous! Could he be mistaken? *This man?* Impossible! He was too strong, too keen, too sincere, too earnest, to be either of these things. Still—But this testimony might have been given for his benefit, some strange helpful power—that kindly fate that had always pursued him might be trying to reach him here. Could it be? He felt a little strange about it, as he had when he saw the black-bearded man entering the train that took him to Three Rivers, the time he went at the call of Suzanne, as he did when horseshoes were laid before him by supernatural forces to warn him of coming prosperity. He went home thinking, and that night he seriously tried to read "Science and Health" for the first time.

CHAPTER XXV

Those who have ever tried to read that very peculiar and, to many, very significant document know what an apparent jumble of contradictions and metaphysical balderdash it appears to be. The statement concerning the rapid multiplication and increased violence of diseases since the flood, which appears in the introduction is enough to shock any believer in definite, material, established natural science, and when Eugene came upon this in the outset, it irritated him, of course, greatly. Why should anybody make such a silly statement as this? Everybody knew that there had never been a flood. Why quote a myth as a fact? It irritated and from a critical point of view amused him. Then he came upon what he deemed to be a jumble of confusion in regard to matter and spirit. The author talked of the evidences of the five physical senses as being worthless, and yet was constantly referring to and using similes based upon those evidences to illustrate her spiritual meanings. He threw the book down a number of times, for the Biblical references irritated him. He did not believe in the Bible. The very word Christianity was a sickening jest, as sickening as it had been to the man in the church. To say that the miracles of Christ could be repeated today could not be serious. Still the man had testified. Wasn't that so? A certain vein of sincerity running through it all—that profound evidence of faith and sympathy which are the characteristics of all sincere reformers—appealed to him. Some little thoughts here and there—a profound acceptance of the spiritual understanding of Jesus, which he himself accepted, stayed with him. One sentence or paragraph somehow stuck in his mind, because he himself was of a metaphysical turn— —

"Become conscious for a single moment that life and intelligence are purely spiritual, neither in nor of matter, and the body will then utter no complaints. If suffering from a belief in sickness, you will find yourself suddenly well. Sorrow is turned into joy when the body is controlled by spiritual life and love."

"God is a spirit," he recalled Jesus as saying. "They that worship Him must worship in spirit and in truth."

"You will find yourself suddenly well," thought Eugene. "Sorrow is turned into joy."

"Sorrow. What kind of sorrow? Love sorrow? This probably meant the end of earthly love; that that too was mortal."

He read on, discovering that Scientists believed in the immaculate conception of the Virgin Mary, which struck him as silly; also that they believed in the ultimate abolition of marriage as representing a mortal illusion of self-creation and perpetuation, and of course the having of children through the agency of the sexes, also the dematerialization of the body—its chemicalization into its native spirituality, wherein there can be neither sin, sickness, disease, decay nor death, were a part of their belief or understanding. It seemed to him to be a wild claim, and yet at the time, because of his natural metaphysical turn, it accorded with his sense of the mystery of life.

It should be remembered as a factor in this reading that Eugene was particularly fitted by temperament—introspective, imaginative, psychical— and by a momentarily despairing attitude, in which any straw was worth grasping at which promised relief from sorrow, despair and defeat, to make a study of this apparently radical theory of human existence. He had heard a great deal of Christian Science, seeing its churches built, its adherents multiplying, particularly in New York, and enthusiastically claiming freedom from every human ill. Idle, without entertainment or diversion and intensely introspective, it was natural that these curious statements should arrest him.

He was not unaware, also, from past reading and scientific speculation, that Carlyle had once said that "matter itself—the outer world of matter, was either nothing, or else a product due to man's mind" (Carlyle's Journal, from Froude's Life of Carlyle), and that Kant had held the whole universe to be something in the eye or mind—neither more nor less than a thought. Marcus Aurelius, he recalled, had said somewhere in his meditations that the soul of the universe was kind and merciful; that it had no evil in it, and was not harmed by evil. This latter thought stuck in his mind as peculiar because it was so diametrically opposed to his own feelings that the universe, the spirit of it that is, was subtle, cruel, crafty, and malicious. He wondered how a man who could come to be Emperor of Rome could have thought otherwise. Christ's Sermon on the Mount had always appealed to him as the lovely speculations of an idealist who had no real knowledge of life. Yet he had always wondered why "Lay not up for yourselves treasures upon earth, where moth and rust doth corrupt, and where thieves break through and steal" had thrilled him as something so beautiful that it must be true "For where your treasure is there will your heart be also." Keats had said "beauty is truth—truth beauty," and still another "truth is what is."

"And what is?" he had asked himself in answer to that.

"Beauty," was his reply to himself, for life at bottom, in spite of all its teeming terrors, was beautiful.

Only those of a metaphysical or natural religious turn of mind would care to follow the slow process of attempted alteration, which took place during the series of months which followed Angela's departure for Racine, her return to New York at Myrtle's solicitation, the time she spent in the maternity hospital, whither she was escorted on her arrival by Eugene and after. These are the deeps of being which only the more able intellectually essay, but Eugene wandered in them far and wide. There were long talks with Myrtle and Bangs—arguments upon all phases of mortal thought, real and unreal, with which Angela's situation had nothing to do. Eugene frankly confessed that he did not love her—that he did not want to live with her. He insisted that he could scarcely live without Suzanne. There was the taking up and reading or re-reading of odd philosophic and religious volumes, for he had nothing else to do. He did not care at first to go and sit with Angela, sorry as he was for her. He read or re-read Kent's "History of the Hebrews"; Weiniger's "Sex and Character"; Carl Snyder's "The World Machine"; Muzzey's "Spiritual Heroes"; Johnston's translation of "Bhagavad Ghita"; Emerson's essay on the Oversoul, and Huxley's "Science and Hebrew Tradition" and "Science and Christian Tradition." He learned from these things some curious facts which relate to religion, which he had either not known before or forgotten, i.e., that the Jews were almost the only race or nation which developed a consecutive line of religious thinkers or prophets; that their ideal was first and last a single God or Divinity, tribal at first, but later on universal, whose scope and significance were widened until He embraced the whole universe—was, in fact, the Universe—a governing principle—one God, however, belief in whom, His power to heal, to build up and overthrow had never been relinquished.

The Old Testament was full of that. Was that. The old prophets, he learned to his astonishment, were little more than whirling dervishes when they are first encountered historically, working themselves up into wild transports and frenzies, lying on the ground and writhing, cutting themselves as the Persian zealots do to this day in their feast of the tenth month and resorting to the most curious devices for nurturing their fanatic spirit, but always setting forth something that was astonishingly spiritual and great. They usually frequented the holy places and were to be distinguished by their wild looks and queer clothing. Isaiah eschewed clothing for three years (Is. 22, 21); Jeremiah appeared in the streets of the capital (according to Muzzey) with a wooden yoke on his neck, saying, "Thus shalt Juda's neck be bent under bondage to the Babylonian" (Jer. 27; 2 ff); Zedekiah came to King Ahab, wearing horns of iron like a steer, and saying, "Thus shalt thou push the Syrians" (1 Kings 22, 11). The prophet was called mad because he acted like a madman. Elisha dashed in on the gruff captain, Jehu, in his camp and broke a vial of oil on his head, saying, "Thus saith the Lord God of Israel, I have made thee king over the people of the Lord"; then he opened the door and fled. Somehow, though these things seemed wild, yet they accorded with Eugene's sense of prophecy. They were not cheap but great— wildly dramatic, like the word of a Lord God might be. Another thing that fascinated him was to find that the evolutionary hypothesis did not after all shut out a conception of a ruling, ordaining Divinity, as he had supposed, for he came across several things in the papers which, now that he was thinking about this so keenly, held him spellbound. One was quoted from a biological work by a man named George M. Gould, and read:

"Life reaches control of physical forces by the cell-mechanism, and, so far as we know, by it solely." From reading Mrs. Eddy and arguing with Bangs, Eugene was not prepared to admit this, but he was fascinated to see how it led ultimately to an acknowledgment of an active Divinity which shapes our ends. "No organic molecule shows any evidence of intellect, design or purpose. It is the product solely of mathematically determinate and invariable physical forces. Life becomes conscious of itself through specialized cellular activity, and human personality, therefore, can only be a unity of greater differentiations of function, a higher and fuller incarnation than the single cell incarnation. Life, or God, is in the cell.... (And everywhere outside of it, quite as active and more so, perhaps, Eugene reserved mentally.) The cell's intelligence is His. (From reading Mrs. Eddy, Eugene could not quite agree with this. According to her, it was an illusion.) The human personality is also at last Himself and only Himself.... If you wish to say 'Biologos' or God instead of Life, I heartily agree, and we are face to face with the sublime fact of biology. The cell is God's instrument and mediator in materiality; it is the mechanism of incarnation, the word made flesh and dwelling among us."

The other was a quotation in a Sunday newspaper from some man who appeared to be a working physicist of the time—Edgar Lucien Larkin:

"With the discovery and recent perfection of the new ultra-violet light microscope and the companion apparatus, the microphotographic camera, with rapidly moving, sensitive films, it seems that the extreme limit of vision of the human eye has been reached. Inorganic and organic particles have been seen, and these so minute that (the smallest) objects visible in the most powerful old-style instruments are as huge chunks in comparison. An active microscopic universe as wonderful as the sidereal universe, the stellar structure, has been revealed. This complexity actually exists; but exploration has scarcely commenced. Within a hundred years, devoted to this research, the micro-universe may be partially understood. Laws of micro-movements may be detected and published in textbooks like those of the gigantic universe suns and their concentric planets and moons. I cannot look into these minute moving and living deeps without instantly believing that they are mental—every motion is controlled by mind. The longer I look at the amazing things, the deeper is this conviction. This micro-universe is rooted and grounded in a mental base. Positively and without hope of overthrow, this assertion is made—the flying particles know where to go. Coarse particles, those visible in old-time microscopes, when suspended in liquids, were observed to be in rapid motion, darting to all geometrical directions with high speed. But the ultra-violet microscope reveals moving trillions of far smaller bodies, and these rush on geometric lines and cutout angles with the most incredible speed, specific for each kind and type."

What were the angles? Eugene asked himself. Who made them? Who or what arranged the geometric lines? The "Divine Mind" of Mrs. Eddy? Had this woman really found the truth? He pondered this, reading on, and then one day in a paper he came upon this reflection in regard to the universe and its government by Alfred Russel Wallace, which interested him as a proof that there might be, as Jesus said and as Mrs. Eddy contended, a Divine Mind or central thought in which there was no evil intent, but only good. The quotation was: "Life is that power which, from air and water and the substances dissolved therein, builds up organized and highly complex structures possessing definite forms and functions; these are presented in a continuous state of decay and repair by internal circulation of fluids and gases; they reproduce their like, go through various phases of youth, maturity and age, die and quickly decompose into their constituent elements. They thus form continuous series of similar individuals and so long as external conditions render their existence possible seem to possess a potential immortality.

"It is very necessary to presuppose some vast intelligence, some pervading spirit, to explain the guidance of the lower forces in accordance with the preordained system of evolution we see prevailing. Nothing less will do....

"If, however, we go as far as this, we must go further.... We have a perfect right, on logical and scientific grounds, to see in all the infinitely varied products of the animal and vegetable kingdoms, which we alone can make use of, a preparation for ourselves, to assist in our mental development, and to fit us for a progressively higher state of existence as spiritual beings.

"...It seems only logical to assume that the vast, the infinite chasm between ourselves and the Deity, is to some extent occupied by an almost infinite series of grades of beings, each successive grade having higher and higher powers in regard to the origination, the development and the control of the universe.

"...There may have been a vast system of co-operation of such grades of beings, from a very high grade of power and intelligence down to those unconscious or almost unconscious cell souls posited by Haeckel....

"I can imagine the ... Infinite Being, foreseeing and determining the broad outlines of a universe....

"He might, for instance, impress a sufficient number of his highest angels to create by their will power the primal universe of ether, with all those inherent properties and forces necessary for what was to follow. Using this as a vehicle, the next subordinate association of angels would so act upon the ether as to develop from it, in suitable masses and at suitable distances, the various elements of matter, which, under the influence of such laws and forces as gravitation, heat, and electricity, would thenceforth begin to form those vast systems of nebulæ and suns which constitute our stellar universe.

"Then we may imagine these hosts of angels, to whom a thousand years are as one day, watching the development of this vast system of suns and planets until some one or more of them combined in itself all those conditions of size, of elementary constitution, of atmosphere, of mass of water and requisite distance from its source of heat as to insure a stability of constitution and uniformity of temperature for a given minimum of millions of years, or of ages, as would be required for the full development of a life world from amœba to man, with a surplus of a few hundreds of millions for his adequate development.

"We are led, therefore, to postulate a body of what we may term organizing spirits, who would be charged with the duty of so influencing the myriads of cell souls as to carry out their part of the work with accuracy and certainty....

"At successive stages of the development of the life world, more and perhaps higher intelligences might be required to direct the main lines of variation in definite directions, in accordance with the general design to be worked out, and to guard against a break in the particular line, which alone could lead ultimately to the production of the human form.

"This speculative suggestion, I venture to hope, will appeal to some of my readers as the very best approximation we are now able to formulate as to the deeper, the most fundamental causes of matter and force of life and consciousness, and of man himself, at his best, already a little lower than the angels, and, like them, destined to a permanent progressive existence in a world of spirit."

This very peculiar and apparently progressive statement in regard to the conclusion which naturalistic science had revealed in regard to the universe struck Eugene as pretty fair confirmation of Mrs. Eddy's contention that all was mind and its infinite variety and that the only difference between her and the British scientific naturalists was that they contended for an ordered hierarchy which could only rule and manifest itself according to its own ordered or self-imposed laws, which they could perceive or detect, whereas, she contended for a governing spirit which was everywhere and would act through ordered laws and powers of its own arrangement. God was a principle like a rule in mathematics—two times two is four, for instance— and was as manifest daily and hourly and momentarily in a hall bedroom as in the circling motions of suns and systems. God was a principle. He grasped that now. A principle could be and was of course anywhere and everywhere at one and the same time. One could not imagine a place for instance where two times two would not be four, or where that rule would not be. So, likewise with the omnipotent, omniscient, omnipresent mind of God.

CHAPTER XXVI

The most dangerous thing to possess a man to the extent of dominating him is an idea. It can and does ride him to destruction. Eugene's idea of the perfection of eighteen was one of the most dangerous things in his nature. In a way, combined with the inability of Angela to command his interest and loyalty, it had been his undoing up to this date. A religious idea followed in a narrow sense would have diverted this other, but it also might have destroyed him, if he had been able to follow it. Fortunately the theory he was now interesting himself in was not a narrow dogmatic one in any sense, but religion in its large aspects, a comprehensive resumé and spiritual co-ordination of the metaphysical speculation of the time, which was worthy of anyone's intelligent inquiry. Christian Science as a cult or religion was shunned by current religions and religionists as something outré, impossible, uncanny—as necromancy, imagination, hypnotism, mesmerism, spiritism—everything, in short, that it was not, and little, if anything, that it really was. Mrs. Eddy had formulated or rather restated a fact that was to be found in the sacred writings of India; in the Hebrew testaments, old and new; in Socrates, Marcus Aurelius, St. Augustine, Emerson, and Carlyle. The one variation notable between her and the moderns was that her *ruling unity* was not malicious, as Eugene and many others fancied, but helpful. Her *unity* was a *unity* of love. God was everything but the father of evil, which according to her was an illusion—neither fact nor substance—sound and fury, signifying nothing.

It must be remembered that during all the time Eugene was doing this painful and religious speculation he was living in the extreme northern portion of the city, working desultorily at some paintings which he thought he might sell, visiting Angela occasionally, safely hidden away in the maternity hospital at One Hundred and Tenth Street, thinking hourly and momentarily of Suzanne, and wondering if, by any chance, he should ever see her any more. His mind had been so inflamed by the beauty and the disposition of this girl that he was really not normal any longer. He needed some shock, some catastrophe greater than any he had previously experienced to bring him to his senses. The loss of his position had done something. The loss of Suzanne had only heightened his affection for her. The condition of Angela had given him pause, for it was an interesting question what would become of her. "If she would only die!" he said to himself, for we have the happy faculty of hating most joyously on this earth the thing we have wronged the most. He could scarcely go and see her, so obsessed was he with the idea that she was a handicap to his career. The idea of her introducing a child into his life only made him savage. Now, if she should die, he would have the child to care for and Suzanne, because of it, might never come to him.

His one idea at this time was not to be observed too much, or rather not at all, for he considered himself to be in great disfavor, and only likely to do himself injury by a public appearance—a fact which was more in his own mind than anywhere else. If he had not believed it, it would not have been true. For this reason he had selected this quiet neighborhood where the line of current city traffic was as nothing, for here he could brood in peace. The family that he lived with knew nothing about him. Winter was setting in. Because of the cold and snow and high winds, he was not likely to see many people hereabouts—particularly those celebrities who had known him in the past. There was a great deal of correspondence that followed him from his old address, for his name had been used on many committees, he was in "Who's Who," and he had many friends less distinguished than those whose companionship would have required the expenditure of much money who would have been glad to look him up. He ignored all invitations, however; refused to indicate by return mail where he was for the present; walked largely at night; read, painted, or sat and brooded during the day. He was thinking all the time of Suzanne and how disastrously fate had trapped him apparently through her. He was thinking that she might come back, that she ought. Lovely, hurtful pictures came to him of re-encounters with her in which she would rush into his arms, never to part, from him any more. Angela, in her room at the hospital, received little thought from him. She was there. She was receiving expert medical attention. He was paying all the bills. Her serious time had not yet really come. Myrtle was seeing her. He caught glimpses of himself at times as a cruel, hard intellect driving the most serviceable thing his life had known from him with blows, but somehow it seemed justifiable. Angela was not suited to him. Why could she not live away from him? Christian Science set aside marriage entirely as a human illusion, conflicting with the indestructible unity of the individual with God. Why shouldn't she let him go?

He wrote poems to Suzanne, and read much poetry that he found in an old trunkful of books in the house where he was living. He would read again and again the sonnet beginning, "When in disgrace with fortune and men's eyes"—that cry out of a darkness that seemed to be like his own. He bought a book of verse by Yeats, and seemed to hear his own voice saying of Suzanne,

"Why should I blame her that she filled my days
With misery ...

He was not quite as bad as he was when he had broken down eight years before, but he was very bad. His mind was once more riveted upon the uncertainty of life, its changes, its follies. He was studying those things only which deal with the abstrusities of nature, and this began to breed again a morbid fear of life itself. Myrtle was greatly distressed about him. She worried lest he might lose his mind.

"Why don't you go to see a practitioner, Eugene?" she begged of him one day. "You will get help—really you will. You think you won't, but you will. There is something about them—I don't know what. They are spiritually at rest. You will feel better. Do go."

"Oh, why do you bother me, Myrtle? Please don't. I don't want to go. I think there is something in the idea metaphysically speaking, but why should I go to a practitioner? God is as near me as He is anyone, if there is a God."

Myrtle wrung her hands, and because she felt so badly more than anything else, he finally decided to go. There might be something hypnotic or physically contagious about these people—some old alchemy of the mortal body, which could reach and soothe him. He believed in hypnotism, hypnotic suggestion, etc. He finally called up one practitioner, an old lady highly recommended by Myrtle and others, who lived farther south on Broadway, somewhere in the neighborhood of Myrtle's home. Mrs. Althea Johns was her name—a woman who had performed wonderful cures. Why should he, Eugene Witla, he asked himself as he took up the receiver, why should he, Eugene Witla, ex-managing publisher of the United Magazines Corporation, ex-artist (in a way, he felt that he was no longer an artist in the best sense) be going to a woman in Christian Science to be healed of what? Gloom? Yes. Failure? Yes. Heartache? Yes. His evil tendencies in regard to women, such as the stranger who had sat beside him had testified to? Yes. How strange! And yet he was curious. It interested him a little to speculate as to whether this could really be done. Could he be healed of failure? Could this pain of longing be made to cease? Did he want it to cease? No; certainly not! He wanted Suzanne. Myrtle's idea, he knew, was that somehow this treatment would reunite him and Angela and make him forget Suzanne, but he knew that could not be. He was going, but he was going because he was unhappy and idle and aimless. He was going because he really did not know what else to do.

The apartment of Mrs. Johns—Mrs. Althea Johns—was in an apartment house of conventional design, of which there were in New York hundreds upon hundreds at the time. There was a spacious areaway between two wings of cream-colored pressed brick leading back to an entrance way which was protected by a handsome wrought-iron door on either side of which was placed an electric lamp support of handsome design, holding lovely cream-colored globes, shedding a soft lustre. Inside was the usual lobby, elevator, uniformed negro elevator man, indifferent and impertinent, and the telephone switchboard. The building was seven storeys high. Eugene went one snowy, blustery January night. The great wet flakes were spinning in huge whirls and the streets were covered with a soft, slushy carpet of snow. He was interested, as usual, in spite of his gloom, in the picture of beauty the world presented—the city wrapped in a handsome mantle of white. Here were cars rumbling, people hunched in great coats facing the driving wind. He liked the snow, the flakes, this wonder of material living. It eased his mind of his misery and made him think of painting again. Mrs. Johns was on the seventh floor. Eugene knocked and was admitted by a maid. He was shown to a waiting room, for he was a little ahead of his time, and there were others—healthy-looking men and women, who did not appear to have an ache or pain—ahead of him. Was not this a sign, he thought as he sat down, that this was something which dealt with imaginary ills? Then why had the man he had heard in the church beside him testified so forcibly and sincerely to his healing? Well, he would wait and see. He did not see what it could do for him now. He had to work. He sat there in one corner, his hands folded and braced under his chin, thinking. The room was not artistic but rather nondescript, the furniture cheap or rather tasteless in design. Didn't Divine Mind know any better than to present its representatives in such a guise as this? Could a person called to assist in representing the majesty of God on earth be left so unintelligent artistically as to live in a house like this? Surely this was a poor manifestation of Divinity, but— —

Mrs. Johns came—a short, stout, homely woman, gray, wrinkled, dowdy in her clothing, a small wen on one side of her mouth, a nose slightly too big to be pleasing—all mortal deficiencies as to appearance highly emphasized, and looking like an old print of Mrs. Micawber that he had seen somewhere. She had on a black skirt good as to material, but shapeless, commonplace, and a dark blue-gray waist. Her eye was clear and gray though, he noticed, and she had a pleasing smile.

"This is Mr. Witla, I believe," she said, coming across the room to him, for he had got into a corner near the window, and speaking with an accent which sounded a little Scotch. "I'm so glad to see you. Won't you come in?" she said, giving him precedence over some others because of his appointment, and re-crossed the room preceding him down the hall to her practice room. She stood to one side to take his hand as he passed.

He touched it gingerly.

So this was Mrs. Johns, he thought, as he entered, looking about him. Bangs and Myrtle had insisted that she had performed wonderful cures—or rather that Divine Mind had, through her. Her hands were wrinkled, her face old. Why didn't she make herself young if she could perform these wonderful cures? Why was this room so mussy? It was actually stuffy with chromos and etchings of the Christ and Bible scenes on the walls, a cheap red carpet or rug on the floor, inartistic leather-covered chairs, a table or desk too full of books, a pale picture of Mrs. Eddy and silly mottoes of which he was sick and tired hung here and there. People were such hacks when it came to the art of living. How could they pretend to a sense of Divinity who knew nothing of life? He was weary and the room here offended him. Mrs. Johns did. Besides, her voice was slightly falsetto. Could *she* cure cancer? and consumption? and all other horrible human ills, as Myrtle insisted she had? He didn't believe it.

He sat down wearily and yet contentiously in the chair she pointed out to him and stared at her while she quietly seated herself opposite him looking at him with kindly, smiling eyes.

"And now," she said easily, "what does God's child think is the matter with him?"

Eugene stirred irritably.

"God's child," he thought; "what cant!" What right had he to claim to be a child of God? What was the use of beginning that way? It was silly, so asinine. Why not ask plainly what was the matter with him? Still he answered:

"Oh, a number of things. So many that I am pretty sure they can never be remedied."

"As bad as that? Surely not. It is good to know, anyhow, that nothing is impossible to God. We can believe that, anyhow, can't we?" she replied, smiling. "You believe in God, or a ruling power, don't you?"

"I don't know whether I do or not. In the main, I guess I do. I'm sure I ought to. Yes, I guess I do."

"Is He a malicious God to you?"

"I have always thought so," he replied, thinking of Angela.

"Mortal mind! Mortal mind!" she asseverated to herself. "What delusions will it not harbor!"

And then to him:

"One has to be cured almost against one's will to know that God is a God of love. So you believe you are sinful, do you, and that He is malicious? It is not necessary that you should tell me how. We are all alike in the mortal state. I would like to call your attention to Isaiah's words, 'Though your sins be as scarlet, they shall be as white as snow; though they be red like crimson, they shall be as wool.'"

Eugene had not heard this quotation for years. It was only a dim thing in his memory. It flashed out simply now and appealed, as had all these Hebraic bursts of prophetic imagery in the past. Mrs. Johns, for all her wen and her big nose and dowdy clothes, was a little better for having been able to quote this so aptly. It raised her in his estimation. It showed a vigorous mind, at least a tactful mind.

"Can you cure sorrow?" he asked grimly and with a touch of sarcasm in his voice. "Can you cure heartache or fear?"

"I can do nothing of myself," she said, perceiving his mood. "All things are possible to God, however. If you believe in a Supreme Intelligence, He will cure you. St. Paul says 'I can do all things through Christ which strengtheneth me.' Have you read Mrs. Eddy's book?"

"Most of it. I'm still reading it."

"Do you understand it?"

"No, not quite. It seems a bundle of contradictions to me."

"To those who are first coming into Science it nearly always seems so. But don't let that worry you. You would like to be cured of your troubles. St. Paul says, 'For the wisdom of this world is foolishness with God.' 'The Lord knoweth the thoughts of the wise—that they are vain.' Do not think of me as a woman, or as having had anything to do with this. I would rather have you think of me as St. Paul describes anyone who works for truth—'Now then we are ambassadors for Christ, as though God did beseech you by us, we pray you in Christ's stead, be ye reconciled to God.'"

"You know your Bible, don't you?" said Eugene.

"It is the only knowledge I have," she replied.

There followed one of those peculiar religious demonstrations so common in Christian Science—so peculiar to the uninitiated—in which she asked Eugene to fix his mind in meditation on the Lord's prayer. "Never mind if it seems pointless to you now. You have come here seeking aid. You are God's perfect image and likeness. He will not send you away empty-handed. Let me read you first, though, this one psalm, which I think is always so helpful to the beginner." She opened her Bible, which was on the table near her, and began:

"He that dwelleth in the secret place of the most high shall abide under the shadow of the Almighty.

"I will say of the Lord, He is my refuge and my fortress; my God; in him will I trust.

"Surely he shall deliver thee from the snare of the fowler, and from the noisome pestilence.

"He shall cover thee with his feathers, and under his wings shalt thou trust: his truth shall be thy shield and thy buckler.

"Thou shalt not be afraid for the terror by night, nor for the arrow that flieth by day. Nor for the pestilence that walketh in the darkness; nor for destruction that wasteth at noonday.

"A thousand shall fall at thy side, and ten thousand at thy right hand; but it shall not come nigh thee.

"Only with thine eyes shalt thou behold and see the reward of the wicked.

"Because thou hast made the Lord, which is my refuge, even the most High, thy habitation; There shall no evil befall thee, neither shall any plague come nigh thy dwelling.

"For he shall give his angels charge over thee, to keep thee in all thy ways.

"They shall bear thee up in their hands, lest thou dash thy foot against a stone.

"Thou shalt tread upon the lion and the adder, the young lion and the dragon shalt thou trample under foot.

"Because he hath set his love upon me, therefore will I deliver him. I will set him on high, because he hath known my name.

"He shall call upon me, and I will answer him: I will be with him in trouble. I will deliver him and honor him.

"With long life will I satisfy him, and show him my salvation."

During this most exquisite pronunciamento of Divine favor Eugene was sitting with his eyes closed, his thoughts wandering over all his recent ills. For the first time in years, he was trying to fix his mind upon an all-wise, omnipresent, omnipotent generosity. It was hard and he could not reconcile the beauty of this expression of Divine favor with the nature of the world as he knew it. What was the use of saying, "They shall bear thee up in their hands lest thou dash thy foot against a stone," when he had seen Angela and himself suffering so much recently? Wasn't he dwelling in the secret place of the Most High when he was alive? How could one get out of it? Still — — "Because he hath set his love on me — therefore will I deliver him." Was that the answer? Was Angela's love set on him? Was his own? Might not all their woes have sprung from that?

"He shall call upon me and I shall answer. I will deliver him in trouble. I will deliver him and honor him."

Had he ever really called on *Him*? Had Angela? Hadn't they been left in the slough of their own despond? Still Angela was not suited to him. Why did not God straighten that out? He didn't want to live with her.

He wandered through this philosophically, critically, until Mrs. Johns stopped. What, he asked himself, if, in spite of all his doubts, this seeming clamor and reality and pain and care were an illusion? Angela was suffering. So were many other people. How could this thing be true? Did not these facts exclude the possibility of illusion? Could they possibly be a part of it?

"Now we are going to try to realize that we are God's perfect children," she said, stopping and looking at him. "We think we are so big and strong and real. We are real enough, but only as a thought in God — that is all. No harm can happen to us there — no evil can come nigh us. For God is infinite, all power, all life. Truth, Love, over all, and all."

She closed her eyes and began, as she said, to try to realize for him the perfectness of his spirit in God. Eugene sat there trying to think of the Lord's prayer, but in reality thinking of the room, the cheap prints, the homely furniture, her ugliness, the curiousness of his being there. He, Eugene Witla, being prayed for! What would Angela think? Why was this woman old, if spirit could do all these other things? Why didn't she make herself beautiful? What was it she was doing now? Was this hypnotism, mesmerism, she was practicing? He remembered where Mrs. Eddy had especially said that these were not to be practiced — could not be in Science. No, she was no doubt sincere. She looked it — talked it. She believed in this beneficent spirit. Would it aid as the psalm said? Would it heal this ache? Would it make him not want Suzanne ever any more? Perhaps that was evil? Yes, no doubt it was. Still — — Perhaps he had better fix his mind on the Lord's Prayer. Divinity could aid him if it would. Certainly it could. No doubt of it. There was nothing impossible to this vast force ruling the universe. Look at the telephone, wireless telegraphy. How about the stars and sun? "He shall give his angels charge over thee."

"Now," said Mrs. Johns, after some fifteen minutes of silent meditation had passed and she opened her eyes smilingly—"we are going to see whether we are not going to be better. We are going to feel better, because we are going to do better, and because we are going to realize that nothing can hurt an idea in God. All the rest is illusions. It cannot hold us, for it is not real. Think good—God—and you are good. Think evil and you are evil, but it has no reality outside your own thought. Remember that." She talked to him as though he was a little child.

He went out into the snowy night where the wind was whirling the snow in picturesque whirls, buttoning his coat about him. The cars were running up Broadway as usual. Taxicabs were scuttling by. There were people forging their way through the snow, that ever-present company of a great city. There were arc lights burning clearly blue through the flying flakes. He wondered as he walked whether this would do him any good. Mrs. Eddy insisted that all these were unreal, he thought—that mortal mind had evolved something which was not in accord with spirit—mortal mind "a liar and the father of it," he recalled that quotation. Could it be so? Was evil unreal? Was misery only a belief? Could he come out of his sense of fear and shame and once more face the world? He boarded a car to go north. At Kingsbridge he made his way thoughtfully to his room. How could life ever be restored to him as it had been? He was really forty years of age. He sat down in his chair near his lamp and took up his book, "Science and Health," and opened it aimlessly. Then he thought for curiosity's sake he would see where he had opened it—what the particular page or paragraph his eye fell on had to say to him. He was still intensely superstitious. He looked, and here was this paragraph growing under his eyes:

"When mortal man blends his thoughts of existence with the spiritual, and works only as God works, he will no longer grope in the dark and cling to earth because he has not tasted heaven. Carnal beliefs defraud us. They make man an involuntary hypocrite—producing evil when he would create good, forming deformity when he would outline grace and beauty, injuring those whom he would bless. He becomes a general mis-creator, who believes he is a semi-God. His touch turns hope to dust, the dust we all have trod. He might say in Bible language, 'The good that I would, I do not, but evil, which I would not, I do.'"

He closed the book and meditated. He wished he might realize this thing if this were so. Still he did not want to become a religionist—a religious enthusiast. How silly they were. He picked up his daily paper—

the *Evening Post*—and there on an inside page quoted in an obscure corner was a passage from a poem by the late Francis Thompson, entitled "The Hound of Heaven." It began:

> "I fled Him, down the nights and down the days;
> I fled Him, down the arches of the years ...

The ending moved him strangely:

> Still with unhurrying chase,
> And unperturbèd face
> Deliberate speed, majestic instancy
> Came on the following Feet,
> And a voice above their beat—
> "Naught shelters thee, who wilt not shelter Me."

Did this man really believe this? Was it so?

He turned back to his book and read on, and by degrees he came half to believe that sin and evil and sickness might possibly be illusions—that they could be cured by aligning one's self intellectually and spiritually with this Divine Principle. He wasn't sure. This terrible sense of wrong. Could he give up Suzanne? Did he want to? No!

He got up and went to the window and looked out. The snow was still blowing.

"Give her up! Give her up!" And Angela in such a precarious condition. What a devil of a hole he was in, anyway! Well, he would go and see her in the morning. He would at least be kind. He would see her through this thing. He lay down and tried to sleep, but somehow sleep never came to him right any more. He was too wearied, too distressed, too wrought up. Still he slept a little, and that was all he could hope for in these days.

CHAPTER XXVII

It was while he was in this state, some two months later, that the great event, so far as Angela was concerned, came about, and in it, of necessity, he was compelled to take part. Angela was in her room, cosily and hygienically furnished, overlooking the cathedral grounds at Morningside Heights, and speculating hourly what her fate was to be. She had never wholly recovered from the severe attack of rheumatism which she had endured the preceding summer and, because of her worries since, in her present condition was pale and weak though she was not ill. The head visiting obstetrical surgeon, Dr. Lambert, a lean, gray man of sixty-five years of age, with grizzled cheeks, whose curly gray hair, wide, humped nose and keen gray eyes told of the energy and insight and ability that had placed him where he was, took a slight passing fancy to her, for she seemed to him one of those plain, patient little women whose lives are laid in sacrificial lines. He liked her brisk, practical, cheery disposition in the face of her condition, which was serious, and which was so noticeable to strangers. Angela had naturally a bright, cheery face, when she was not depressed or quarrelsome. It was the outward sign of her ability to say witty and clever things, and she had never lost the desire to have things done efficiently and intelligently about her wherever she was. The nurse, Miss De Sale, a solid, phlegmatic person of thirty-five, admired her spunk and courage and took a great fancy to her also because she was lightsome, buoyant and hopeful in the face of what was really a very serious situation. The general impression of the head operating surgeon, the house surgeon and the nurse was that her heart was weak and that her kidneys might be affected by her condition. Angela had somehow concluded after talks with Myrtle that Christian Science, as demonstrated by its practitioners, might help her through this crisis, though she had no real faith in it. Eugene would come round, she thought, also, for Myrtle was having him treated absently, and he was trying to read the book, she said. There would be a reconciliation between them when the baby came — because — because — — Well, because children were so winning! Eugene was really not hard-hearted — he was just infatuated. He had been ensnared by a siren. He would get over it.

Miss De Sale let her hair down in braids, Gretchen style, and fastened great pink bows of ribbon in them. As her condition became more involved, only the lightest morning gowns were given her—soft, comfortable things in which she sat about speculating practically about the future. She had changed from a lean shapeliness to a swollen, somewhat uncomely object, but she made the best of a bad situation. Eugene saw her and felt sorry. It was the end of winter now, with snow blowing gaily or fiercely about the windows, and the park grounds opposite were snow-white. She could see the leafless line of sentinel poplars that bordered the upper edges of Morningside. She was calm, patient, hopeful, while the old obstetrician shook his head gravely to the house surgeon.

"We shall have to be very careful. I shall take charge of the actual birth myself. See if you can't build up her strength. We can only hope that the head is small."

Angela's littleness and courage appealed to him. For once in a great many cases he really felt sorry.

The house surgeon did as directed. Angela was given specially prepared food and drink. She was fed frequently. She was made to keep perfectly quiet.

"Her heart," the house surgeon reported to his superior, "I don't like that. It's weak and irregular. I think there's a slight lesion."

"We can only hope for the best," said the other solemnly. "We'll try and do without ether."

Eugene in his peculiar mental state was not capable of realizing the pathos of all this. He was alienated temperamentally and emotionally. Thinking that he cared for his wife dearly, the nurse and the house surgeon were for not warning him. They did not want to frighten him. He asked several times whether he could be present during the delivery, but they stated that it would be dangerous and trying. The nurse asked Angela if she had not better advise him to stay away. Angela did, but Eugene felt that in spite of his alienation, she needed him. Besides, he was curious. He thought Angela would stand it better if he were near, and now that the ordeal was drawing nigh, he was beginning to understand how desperate it might be and to think it was only fair that he should assist her. Some of the old pathetic charm of her littleness was coming back to him. She might not live. She would have to suffer much. She had meant no real evil to him— only to hold him. Oh, the bitterness and the pathos of this welter of earthly emotions. Why should they be so tangled?

The time drew very near, and Angela was beginning to suffer severe pains. Those wonderful processes of the all-mother, which bind the coming life in a cradle of muscles and ligaments were practically completed and were now relaxing their tendencies in one direction to enforce them in another. Angela suffered at times severely from straining ligaments. Her hands were clenched desperately, her face would become deathly pale. She would cry. Eugene was with her on a number of these occasions and it drove home to his consciousness the subtlety and terror of this great scheme of reproduction, which took all women to the door of the grave, in order that this mortal scheme of things might be continued. He began to think that there might be something in the assertion of the Christian Science leaders that it was a lie and an illusion, a terrible fitful fever outside the rational consciousness of God. He went to the library one day and got down a book on obstetrics, which covered the principles and practice of surgical delivery. He saw there scores of pictures drawn very carefully of the child in various positions in the womb—all the strange, peculiar, flower-like positions it could take, folded in upon itself like a little half-formed petal. The pictures were attractive, some of them beautiful, practical as they were. They appealed to his fancy. They showed the coming baby perfect, but so small, its head now in one position, now in another, its little arms twisted about in odd places, but always delightfully, suggestively appealing. From reading here and there in the volume, he learned that the great difficulty was the head—the delivery of that. It appeared that no other difficulty really confronted the obstetrician. How was that to be got out? If the head were large, the mother old, the walls of the peritoneal cavity tight or hard, a natural delivery might be impossible. There were whole chapters on Craniotomy, Cephalotripsy, which in plain English means crushing the head with an instrument....

One chapter was devoted to the Cæsarian operation, with a description of its tremendous difficulties and a long disquisition on the ethics of killing the child to save the mother, or the mother to save the child with their relative values to society indicated. Think of it—a surgeon sitting in the seat of judge and executioner at the critical moment! Ah, life with its petty laws did not extend here. Here we came back to the conscience of man which Mrs. Eddy maintained was a reflection of immanent mind. If God were good, He would speak through that—He was speaking through it. This surgeon referred to that inmost consciousness of supreme moral law, which alone could guide the practitioner in this dreadful hour.

Then he told of what implements were necessary, how many assistants (two), how many nurses (four), the kinds of bandages, needles, silk and catgut thread, knives, clamp dilators, rubber gloves. He showed how the cut was to be made—when, where. Eugene closed the book, frightened. He got up and walked out in the air, a desire to hurry up to Angela impelling him. She was weak, he knew that. She had complained of her heart. Her muscles were probably set. Supposing these problems, any one of them, should come in connection with her. He did not wish her to die.

He had said he had—yes, but he did not want to be a murderer. No, no! Angela had been good to him. She had worked for him. Why, God damn it, she had actually suffered for him in times past. He had treated her badly, very badly, and now in her pathetic little way she had put herself in this terrific position. It was her fault, to be sure it was. She had been trying as she always had to hold him against his will, but then could he really blame her? It wasn't a crime for her to want him to love her. They were just mis-mated. He had tried to be kind in marrying her, and he hadn't been kind at all. It had merely produced unrest, dissatisfaction, unhappiness for him and for her, and now this—this danger of death through pain, a weak heart, defective kidneys, a Cæsarian operation. Why, she couldn't stand anything like that. There was no use talking about it. She wasn't strong enough—she was too old.

He thought of Christian Science practitioners, of how they might save her—of some eminent surgeon who would know how without the knife. How? How? If these Christian Scientists could only *think* her through a thing like this—he wouldn't be sorry. He would be glad, for her sake, if not his own. He might give up Suzanne—he might—he might. Oh, why should that thought intrude on him now?

When he reached the hospital it was three o'clock in the afternoon, and he had been there for a little while in the morning when she was comparatively all right. She was much worse. The straining pains in her side which she had complained of were worse and her face was alternately flushed and pale, sometimes convulsed a little. Myrtle was there talking with her, and Eugene stood about nervously, wondering what he should do—what he could do. Angela saw his worry. In spite of her own condition she was sorry for him. She knew that this would cause him pain, for he was not hard-hearted, and it was his first sign of relenting. She smiled at him, thinking that maybe he would come round and change his attitude entirely. Myrtle kept reassuring her that all would be well with her. The nurse said to her and to the house doctor who came in, a young man of twenty-eight, with keen, quizzical eyes, whose sandy hair and ruddy complexion bespoke a fighting disposition, that she was doing nicely.

"No bearing down pains?" he asked, smiling at Angela, his even white teeth showing in two gleaming rows.

"I don't know what kind they are, doctor," she replied. "I've had all kinds."

"You'll know them fast enough," he replied, mock cheerfully. "They're not like any other kind."

He went away and Eugene followed him.

"How is she doing?" he asked, when they were out in the hall.

"Well enough, considering. She's not very strong, you know. I have an idea she is going to be all right. Dr. Lambert will be here in a little while. You had better talk to him."

The house surgeon did not want to lie. He thought Eugene ought to be told. Dr. Lambert was of the same opinion, but he wanted to wait until the last, until he could judge approximately correctly.

He came at five, when it was already dark outside, and looked at Angela with his grave, kindly eyes. He felt her pulse, listened to her heart with his stethoscope.

"Do you think I shall be all right, doctor?" asked Angela faintly.

"To be sure, to be sure," he replied softly. "Little woman, big courage." He smoothed her hand.

He walked out and Eugene followed him.

"Well, doctor," he said. For the first time for months Eugene was thinking of something besides his lost fortune and Suzanne.

"I think it advisable to tell you, Mr. Witla," said the old surgeon, "that your wife is in a serious condition. I don't want to alarm you unnecessarily — it may all come out very satisfactorily. I have no positive reason to be sure that it will not. She is pretty old to have a child. Her muscles are set. The principal thing we have to fear in her case is some untoward complication with her kidneys. There is always difficulty in the delivery of the head in women of her age. It may be necessary to sacrifice the child. I can't be sure. The Cæsarian operation is something I never care to think about. It is rarely used, and it isn't always successful. Every care that can be taken will be taken. I should like to have you understand the conditions. Your consent will be asked before any serious steps are taken. Your decision will have to be quick, however, when the time comes."

"I can tell you now, doctor, what my decision will be," said Eugene realizing fully the gravity of the situation. For the time being, his old force and dignity were restored. "Save her life if you can by any means that you can. I have no other wish."

"Thanks," said the surgeon. "We will do the best we can."

There were hours after that when Eugene, sitting by Angela, saw her endure pain which he never dreamed it was possible for any human being to endure. He saw her draw herself up rigid time and again, the color leaving her face, the perspiration breaking out on her forehead only to relax and flush and groan without really crying out. He saw, strange to relate, that she was no baby like himself, whimpering over every little ill, but a representative of some great creative force which gave her power at once to suffer greatly and to endure greatly. She could not smile any more. That was not possible. She was in a welter of suffering, unbroken, astonishing. Myrtle had gone home to her dinner, but promised to return later. Miss De Sale came, bringing another nurse, and while Eugene was out of the room, Angela was prepared for the final ordeal. She was arrayed in the usual open back hospital slip and white linen leggings. Under Doctor Lambert's orders an operating table was got ready in the operating room on the top floor and a wheel table stationed outside the door, ready to remove her if necessary. He had left word that at the first evidence of the genuine childbearing pain, which the nurse understood so well, he was to be called. The house surgeon was to be in immediate charge of the case.

Eugene wondered in this final hour at the mechanical, practical, business-like manner in which all these tragedies—the hospital was full of women—were taken. Miss De Sale went about her duties calm, smiling, changing the pillows occasionally for Angela, straightening the disordered bedclothes, adjusting the window curtains, fixing her own lace cap or apron before the mirror which was attached to the dresser, or before the one that was set in the closet door, and doing other little things without number. She took no interest in Eugene's tense attitude, or Myrtle's when she was there, but went in and out, talking, jesting with other nurses, doing whatever she had to do quite undisturbed.

"Isn't there anything that can be done to relieve her of this pain?" Eugene asked wearily at one point. His own nerves were torn. "She can't stand anything like that. She hasn't the strength."

She shook her head placidly. "There isn't a thing that anyone can do. We can't give her an opiate. It stops the process. She just has to bear it. All women do."

"All women," thought Eugene. Good God! Did all women go through a siege like this every time a child was born? There were two billion people on the earth now. Had there been two billion such scenes? Had he come this way?—Angela? every child? What a terrible mistake she had made—so unnecessary, so foolish. It was too late now, though, to speculate concerning this. She was suffering. She was agonizing.

The house surgeon came back after a time to look at her condition, but was not at all alarmed apparently. He nodded his head rather reassuringly to Miss De Sale, who stood beside him. "I think she's doing all right," he said.

"I think so, too," she replied.

Eugene wondered how they could say this. She was suffering horribly.

"I'm going into Ward A for an hour," said the doctor. "If any change comes you can get me there."

"What change could come," asked Eugene of himself, "any worse than had already appeared?" He was thinking of the drawings, though, he had seen in the book—wondering if Angela would have to be assisted in some of the grim, mechanical ways indicated there. They illustrated to him the deadly possibilities of what might follow.

About midnight the expected change, which Eugene in agonized sympathy was awaiting, arrived. Myrtle had not returned. She had been waiting to hear from Eugene. Although Angela had been groaning before, pulling herself tense at times, twisting in an aimless, unhappy fashion, now she seemed to spring up and fall as though she had fainted. A shriek accompanied the movement, and then another and another. He rushed to the door, but the nurse was there to meet him.

"It's here," she said quietly. She went to a phone outside and called for Dr. Willets. A second nurse from some other room came in and stood beside her. In spite of the knotted cords on Angela's face, the swollen veins, the purple hue, they were calm. Eugene could scarcely believe it, but he made an intense effort to appear calm himself. So this was childbirth!

In a few moments Dr. Willets came in. He also was calm, business like, energetic. He was dressed in a black suit and white linen jacket, but took that off, leaving the room as he did so, and returned with his sleeves rolled up and his body incased in a long white apron, such as Eugene had seen butchers wear. He went over to Angela and began working with her, saying something to the nurse beside him which Eugene did not hear. He could not look—he dared not at first.

At the fourth or fifth convulsive shriek, a second doctor came in, a young man of Willets' age, and dressed as he was, who also took his place beside him. Eugene had never seen him before. "Is it a case of forceps?" he asked.

"I can't tell," said the other. "Dr. Lambert is handling this personally. He ought to be here by now."

There was a step in the hall and the senior physician or obstetrician had entered. In the lower hall he had removed his great coat and fur gloves. He was dressed in his street clothes, but after looking at Angela, feeling her heart and temples, he went out and changed his coat for an apron, like the others. His sleeves were rolled up, but he did not immediately do anything but watch the house surgeon, whose hands were bloody.

"Can't they give her chloroform?" asked Eugene, to whom no one was paying any attention, of Miss De Sale.

She scarcely heard, but shook her head. She was busy dancing attendance on her very far removed superiors, the physicians.

"I would advise you to leave the room," said Dr. Lambert to Eugene, coming over near him. "You can do nothing here. You will be of no assistance whatsoever. You may be in the way."

Eugene left, but it was only to pace agonizedly up and down the hall. He thought of all the things that had passed between him and Angela—the years—the struggles. All at once he thought of Myrtle, and decided to call her up—she wanted to be there. Then he decided for the moment he would not. She could do nothing. Then he thought of the Christian Science practitioner. Myrtle could get her to give Angela absent treatment. Anything, anything— it was a shame that she should suffer so.

"Myrtle," he said nervously over the phone, when he reached her, "this is Eugene. Angela is suffering terribly. The birth is on. Can't you get Mrs. Johns to help her? It's terrible!"

"Certainly, Eugene. I'll come right down. Don't worry."

He hung up the receiver and walked up and down the hall again. He could hear mumbled voices—he could hear muffled screams. A nurse, not Miss De Sale, came out and wheeled in the operating table.

"Are they going to operate?" he asked feverishly. "I'm Mr. Witla."

"I don't think so. I don't know. Dr. Lambert wants her to be taken to the operating room in case it is necessary."

They wheeled her out after a few moments and on to the elevator which led to the floor above. Her face was slightly covered while she was being so transferred, and those who were around prevented him from seeing just how it was with her, but because of her stillness, he wondered, and the nurse said that a very slight temporary opiate had been administered—not enough to affect the operation, if it were found necessary. Eugene stood by dumbly, terrified. He stood in the hall, outside the operating room, half afraid to enter. The head surgeon's warning came back to him, and, anyhow, what good could he do? He walked far down the dim-lit length of the hall before him, wondering, and looked out on a space where was nothing but snow. In the distance a long lighted train was winding about a high trestle like a golden serpent. There were automobiles honking and pedestrians laboring along in the snow. What a tangle life was, he thought. What a pity. Here a little while ago, he wanted Angela to die, and now,—God Almighty, that was her voice groaning! He would be punished for his evil thoughts— yes, he would. His sins, all these terrible deeds would be coming home to him. They were coming home to him now. What a tragedy his career was! What a failure! Hot tears welled up into his eyes, his lower lip trembled, not for himself, but for Angela. He was so sorry all at once. He shut it all back. No, by God, he wouldn't cry! What good were tears? It was for Angela his pain was, and tears would not help her now.

Thoughts of Suzanne came to him—Mrs. Dale, Colfax, but he shut them out. If they could see him now! Then another muffled scream and he walked quickly back. He couldn't stand this.

He didn't go in, however. Instead he listened intently, hearing something which sounded like gurgling, choking breathing. Was that Angela?

"The low forceps"—it was Dr. Lambert's voice.

"The high forceps." It was his voice again. Something clinked like metal in a bowl.

"It can't be done this way, I'm afraid," it was Dr. Lambert's voice again. "We'll have to operate. I hate to do it, too."

A nurse came out to see if Eugene were near. "You had better go down into the waiting room, Mr. Witla," she cautioned. "They'll be bringing her out pretty soon. It won't be long now."

"No," he said all at once, "I want to see for myself." He walked into the room where Angela was now lying on the operating table in the centre of the room. A six-globed electrolier blazed close overhead. At her head was Dr. Willets, administering the anæsthetic. On the right side was Dr. Lambert, his hands encased in rubber gloves, bloody, totally unconscious of Eugene, holding a scalpel. One of the two nurses was near Angela's feet, officiating at a little table of knives, bowls, water, sponges, bandages. On the left of the table was Miss De Sale. Her hands were arranging some cloths at the side of Angela's body. At her side, opposite Dr. Lambert, was another surgeon whom Eugene did not know. Angela was breathing stertorously.

She appeared to be unconscious. Her face was covered with cloths and a rubber mouth piece or cone. Eugene cut his palms with his nails.

So they have to operate, after all, he thought. She is as bad as that. The Cæsarian operation. Then they couldn't even get the child from her by killing it. Seventy-five per cent. of the cases recorded were successful, so the book said, but how many cases were not recorded. Was Dr. Lambert a great surgeon? Could Angela stand ether—with her weak heart?

He stood there looking at this wonderful picture while Dr. Lambert quickly washed his hands. He saw him take a small gleaming steel knife— bright as polished silver. The old man's hands were encased in rubber gloves, which looked bluish white under the light. Angela's exposed flesh was the color of a candle. He bent over her.

"Keep her breathing normal if you can," he said to the young doctor. "If she wakes give her ether. Doctor, you'd better look after the arteries."

He cut softly a little cut just below the centre of the abdomen apparently, and Eugene saw little trickling streams of blood spring where his blade touched. It did not seem a great cut. A nurse was sponging away the blood as fast as it flowed. As he cut again, the membrane that underlies the muscles of the abdomen and protects the intestines seemed to spring into view.

"I don't want to cut too much," said the surgeon calmly—almost as though he were talking to himself. "These intestines are apt to become unmanageable. If you just lift up the ends, doctor. That's right. The sponge, Miss Wood. Now, if we can just cut here enough"—he was cutting again like an honest carpenter or cabinet worker.

He dropped the knife he held into Miss Wood's bowl of water. He reached into the bleeding, wound, constantly sponged by the nurse, exposing something. What was that? Eugene's heart jerked. He was reaching down now in there with his middle finger—his fore and middle fingers afterwards, and saying, "I don't find the leg. Let's see. Ah, yes. Here we have it!"

"Can I move the head a little for you, doctor?" It was the young doctor at his left talking.

"Careful! Careful! It's bent under in the region of the coccyx. I have it now, though. Slowly, doctor, look out for the placenta."

Something was coming up out of this horrible cavity, which was trickling with blood from the cut. It was queer a little foot, a leg, a body, a head.

"As God is my judge," said Eugene to himself, his eyes brimming again.

"The placenta, doctor. Look after the peritoneum, Miss Wood. It's alive, all right. How is her pulse, Miss De Sale?"

"A little weak, doctor."

"Use less ether. There, now we have it! We'll put that back. Sponge. We'll have to sew this afterwards, Willets. I won't trust this to heal alone. Some surgeons think it will, but I mistrust her recuperative power. Three or four stitches, anyhow."

They were working like carpenters, cabinet workers, electricians. Angela might have been a lay figure for all they seemed to care. And yet there was a tenseness here, a great hurry through slow sure motion. "The less haste, the more speed," popped into Eugene's mind—the old saw. He stared as if this were all a dream—a nightmare. It might have been a great picture like Rembrandt's "The Night Watch." One young doctor, the one he did not know, was holding aloft a purple object by the foot. It might have been a skinned rabbit, but Eugene's horrified eyes realized that it was his child—Angela's child—the thing all this horrible struggle and suffering was about. It was discolored, impossible, a myth, a monster. He could scarcely believe his eyes, and yet the doctor was striking it on the back with his hand, looking at it curiously. At the same moment came a faint cry—not a cry, either—only a faint, queer sound.

"She's awfully little, but I guess she'll make out." It was Dr. Willets talking of the baby. Angela's baby. Now the nurse had it. That was Angela's flesh they had been cutting. That was Angela's wound they were sewing. This wasn't life. It was a nightmare. He was insane and being bedeviled by spirits.

"Now, doctor, I guess that will keep. The blankets, Miss De Sale. You can take her away."

They were doing lots of things to Angela, fastening bandages about her, removing the cone from her mouth, changing her position back to one of lying flat, preparing to bathe her, moving her to the rolling table, wheeling her out while she moaned unconscious under ether.

Eugene could scarcely stand the sickening, stertorous breathing. It was such a strange sound to come from her—as if her unconscious soul were crying. And the child was crying, too, healthily.

"Oh, God, what a life, what a life!" he thought. To think that things should have to come this way. Death, incisions! unconsciousness! pain! Could she live? Would she? And now he was a father.

He turned and there was the nurse holding this littlest girl on a white gauze blanket or cushion. She was doing something to it—rubbing oil on it. It was a pink child now, like any other baby.

"That isn't so bad, is it?" she asked consolingly. She wanted to restore Eugene to a sense of the commonplace. He was so distracted looking.

Eugene stared at it. A strange feeling came over him. Something went up and down his body from head to toe, doing something to him. It was a nervous, titillating, pinching feeling. He touched the child. He looked at its hands, its face. It looked like Angela. Yes, it did. It was his child. It was hers. Would she live? Would he do better? Oh, God, to have this thrust at him now, and yet it was his child. How could he? Poor little thing. If Angela died—if Angela died, he would have this and nothing else, this little girl out of all her long, dramatic struggle. If she died, came this. To do what to him? To guide? To strengthen? To change? He could not say. Only, somehow, in spite of himself, it was beginning to appeal to him. It was the child of a storm. And Angela, so near him now—would she ever live to see it? There she was unconscious, numb, horribly cut. Dr. Lambert was taking a last look at her before leaving.

"Do you think she will live, doctor?" he asked the great surgeon feverishly. The latter looked grave.

"I can't say. I can't say. Her strength isn't all that it ought to be. Her heart and kidneys make a bad combination. However, it was a last chance. We had to take it. I'm sorry. I'm glad we were able to save the child. The nurse will give her the best of care."

He went out into his practical world as a laborer leaves his work. So may we all. Eugene went over and stood by Angela. He was tremendously sorry for the long years of mistrust that had brought this about. He was ashamed of himself, of life—of its strange tangles. She was so little, so pale, so worn. Yes, he had done this. He had brought her here by his lying, his instability, his uncertain temperament. It was fairly murder from one point of view, and up to this last hour he had scarcely relented. But life had done things to him, too. Now, now—— Oh, hell, Oh, God damn! If she would only recover, he would try and do better. Yes, he would. It sounded so silly coming from him, but he would try. Love wasn't worth the agony it cost. Let it go. Let it go. He could live. Truly there were hierarchies and powers, as Alfred Russel Wallace pointed out. There was a God somewhere. He was on His throne. These large, dark, immutable forces, they were not for nothing. If she would only not die, he would try—he would behave. He would! he would!

He gazed at her, but she looked so weak, so pale now he did not think she could come round.

"Don't you want to come home with me, Eugene?" said Myrtle, who had come back some time before, at his elbow. "We can't do anything here now! The nurse says she may not become conscious for several hours. The baby is all right in their care."

The baby! the baby! He had forgotten it, forgotten Myrtle. He was thinking of the long dark tragedy of his life—the miasma of it.

"Yes," he said wearily. It was nearly morning. He went out and got into a taxi and went to his sister's home, but in spite of his weariness, he could scarcely sleep. He rolled feverishly.

In the morning he was up again, early, anxious to go back and see how Angela was—and the child.

CHAPTER XXVIII

The trouble with Angela's system, in addition to a weak heart, was that it was complicated at the time of her delivery by that peculiar manifestation of nervous distortion or convulsions known as eclampsia. Once in every five hundred cases (or at least such was the statistical calculation at the time), some such malady occurred to reduce the number of the newborn. In every two such terminations one mother also died, no matter what the anticipatory preparations were on the part of the most skilled surgeons. Though not caused by, it was diagnosed by, certain kidney changes. What Eugene had been spared while he was out in the hall was the sight of Angela staring, her mouth pulled to one side in a horrible grimace, her body bent back, canoe shape, the arms flexed, the fingers and thumbs bending over each other to and fro, in and out, slowly, not unlike a mechanical figure that is running down. Stupor and unconsciousness had immediately followed, and unless the child had been immediately brought into the world and the womb emptied, she and it would have died a horrible death. As it was she had no real strength to fight her way back to life and health. A Christian Science practitioner was trying to "realize her identity with good" for her, but she had no faith before and no consciousness now. She came to long enough to vomit terribly, and then sank into a fever. In it she talked of Eugene. She was in Blackwood, evidently, and wanted him to come back to her. He held her hand and cried, for he knew that there was never any recompense for that pain. What a dog he had been! He bit his lip and stared out of the window.

Once he said: "Oh, I'm no damned good! I should have died!"

That whole day passed without consciousness, and most of the night. At two in the morning Angela woke and asked to see the baby. The nurse brought it. Eugene held her hand. It was put down beside her, and she cried for joy, but it was a weak, soundless cry. Eugene cried also.

"It's a girl, isn't it?" she asked.

"Yes," said Eugene, and then, after a pause, "Angela, I want to tell you something. I'm so sorry, I'm ashamed. I want you to get well. I'll do better. Really I will." At the same time he was wondering, almost subconsciously, whether he would or no. Wouldn't it be all the same if she were really well—or worse?

She caressed his hand. "Don't cry," she said, "I'll be all right. I'm going to get well. We'll both do better. It's as much my fault as yours. I've been too hard." She worked at his fingers, but he only choked. His vocal cords hurt him.

"I'm so sorry. I'm so sorry," he finally managed to say.

The child was taken away after a little while and Angela was feverish again. She grew very weak, so weak that although she was conscious later, she could not speak. She tried to make some signs. Eugene, the nurse, Myrtle, understood. The baby. It was brought and held up before her. She smiled a weak, yearning smile and looked at Eugene. "I'll take care of her," he said, bending over her. He swore a great oath to himself. He would be decent— he would be clean henceforth and for ever. The child was put beside her for a little while, but she could not move. She sank steadily and died.

Eugene sat by the bed holding his head in his hands. So, he had his wish. She was really dead. Now he had been taught what it was to fly in the face of conscience, instinct, immutable law. He sat there an hour while Myrtle begged him to come away.

"Please, Eugene!" she said. "Please!"

"No, no," he replied. "Where shall I go? I am well enough here."

After a time he did go, however, wondering how he would adjust his life from now on. Who would take care of of— —

"Angela" came the name to his mind. Yes, he would call her "Angela." He had heard someone say she was going to have pale yellow hair.

The rest of this story is a record of philosophic doubt and speculation and a gradual return to normality, his kind of normality—the artistic normality of which he was capable. He would—he thought—never again be the maundering sentimentalist and enthusiast, imagining perfection in every beautiful woman that he saw. Yet there was a period when, had Suzanne returned suddenly, all would have been as before between them, and even more so, despite his tremulousness of spirit, his speculative interest in Christian Science as a way out possibly, his sense of brutality, almost murder, in the case of Angela—for, the old attraction still gnawed at his vitals. Although he had Angela, junior, now to look after, and in a way to divert him,—a child whom he came speedily to delight in—his fortune to restore, and a sense of responsibility to that abstract thing, society or public opinion as represented by those he knew or who knew him, still there was this ache and this non-controllable sense of adventure which freedom to contract a new matrimonial alliance or build his life on the plan he schemed with Suzanne gave him. Suzanne! Suzanne!—how her face, her gestures, her voice, haunted him. Not Angela, for all the pathos of her tragic ending, but Suzanne. He thought of Angela often—those last hours in the hospital, her last commanding look which meant "please look after our child," and whenever he did so his vocal cords tightened as under the grip of a hand and his eyes threatened to overflow, but even so, and even then, that undertow, that mystic cord that seemed to pull from his solar plexus outward, was to Suzanne and to her only. Suzanne! Suzanne! Around her hair, the thought of her smile, her indescribable presence, was built all that substance of romance which he had hoped to enjoy and which now, in absence and probably final separation, glowed with a radiance which no doubt the reality could never have had.

"We are such stuff as dreams are made on and our little life is rounded with a sleep." We are such stuff as dreams are made on, and only of dreams are our keen, stinging realities compounded. Nothing else is so moving, so vital, so painful as a dream.

For a time that first spring and summer, while Myrtle looked after little Angela and Eugene went to live with her and her husband, he visited his old Christian Science practitioner, Mrs. Johns. He had not been much impressed with the result in Angela's case, but Myrtle explained the difficulty of the situation in a plausible way. He was in a terrific state of depression, and it was while he was so that Myrtle persuaded him to go again. She insisted that Mrs. Johns would overcome his morbid gloom, anyhow, and make him feel better. "You want to come out of this, Eugene," she pleaded. "You will never do anything until you do. You are a big man. Life isn't over. It's just begun. You're going to get well and strong again. Don't worry. Everything that is is for the best."

He went once, quarreling with himself for doing so, for in spite of his great shocks, or rather because of them, he had no faith in religious conclusions of any kind. Angela had not been saved. Why should he?

Still the metaphysical urge was something—it was so hard to suffer spiritually and not believe there was some way out. At times he hated Suzanne for her indifference. If ever she came back he would show her. There would be no feeble urgings and pleadings the next time. She had led him into this trap, knowing well what she was doing—for she was wise enough—and then had lightly deserted him. Was that the action of a large spirit? he asked himself. Would the wonderful something he thought he saw there be capable of that? Ah, those hours at Daleview—that one stinging encounter in Canada!—the night she danced with him so wonderfully!

During a period of nearly three years all the vagaries and alterations which can possibly afflict a groping and morbid mind were his. He went from what might be described as *almost* a belief in Christian Science to almost a belief that a devil ruled the world, a Gargantuan Brobdingnagian Mountebank, who plotted tragedy for all ideals and rejoiced in swine and dullards and a grunting, sweating, beefy immorality. By degrees his God, if he could have been said to have had one in his consciousness, sank back into a dual personality or a compound of good and evil—the most ideal and ascetic good, as well as the most fantastic and swinish evil. His God, for a time at least, was a God of storms and horrors as well as of serenities and perfections. He then reached a state not of abnegation, but of philosophic open-mindedness or agnosticism. He came to know that he did not know what to believe. All apparently was permitted, nothing fixed. Perhaps life loved only change, equation, drama, laughter. When in moments of private speculation or social argument he was prone to condemn it loudest, he realized that at worst and at best it was beautiful, artistic, gay, that, however, he might age, groan, complain, withdraw, wither, still, in spite of him, this large thing which he at once loved and detested was sparkling on. He might quarrel, but it did not care; he might fail or die, but it could not. He was negligible—but, oh, the sting and delight of its inner shrines and favorable illusions.

And curiously, for a time, even while he was changing in this way, he went back to see Mrs. Johns, principally because he liked her. She seemed to be a motherly soul to him, contributing some of the old atmosphere he had enjoyed in his own home in Alexandria. This woman, from working constantly in the esoteric depths, which Mrs. Eddy's book suggests, demonstrating for herself, as she thought, through her belief in or understanding of, the oneness of the universe (its non-malicious, affectionate control, the non-existence of fear, pain, disease, and death itself), had become so grounded in her faith that evil positively did not exist save in the belief of mortals, that at times she almost convinced Eugene that it was so. He speculated long and deeply along these lines with her. He had come to lean on her in his misery quite as a boy might on his mother.

The universe to her was, as Mrs. Eddy said, spiritual, not material, and no wretched condition, however seemingly powerful, could hold against the truth—could gainsay divine harmony. God was good. All that is, is God. Hence all that is, is good or it is an illusion. It could not be otherwise. She looked at Eugene's case, as she had at many a similar one, being sure, in her earnest way, that she, by realizing his ultimate fundamental spirituality, could bring him out of his illusions, and make him see the real spirituality of things, in which the world of flesh and desire had no part.

"Beloved," she loved to quote to him, "now are we the sons of God, and it doth not yet appear what we shall be, but we know that when he shall appear"—(and she explained that *he* was this universal spirit of perfection of which we are a part)—"we shall be like him; for we shall see him as He is."

"And every man that has this hope in him purifieth himself even as He is pure."

She once explained to him that this did not mean that the man must purify himself by some hopeless moral struggle, or emaciating abstinance, but rather that the fact that he had this hope of something better in him, would fortify him in spite of himself.

"You laugh at me," she said to him one day, "but I tell you you are a child of God. There is a divine spark in you. It must come out. I know it will. All this other thing will fall away as a bad dream. It has no reality."

She even went so far in a sweet motherly way as to sing hymns to him, and now, strange to relate, her thin voice was no longer irritating to him, and her spirit made her seemingly beautiful in his eyes. He did not try to adjust the curiosities and anomalies of material defects in so far as she was concerned. The fact that her rooms were anything but artistically perfect; that her body was shapeless, or comparatively so, when contrasted with that standard of which he had always been so conscious; the fact that whales were accounted by her in some weird way as spiritual, and bugs and torturesome insects of all kinds as emanations of mortal mind, did not trouble him at all. There was something in this thought of a spiritual universe—of a kindly universe, if you sought to make it so, which pleased him. The five senses certainly could not indicate the totality of things; beyond them must lie depths upon depths of wonder and power. Why might not this act? Why might it not be good? That book that he had once read—"The World Machine"—had indicated this planetary life as being infinitesimally small; that from the point of view of infinity it was not even thinkable—and yet here it appeared to be so large. Why might it not be, as Carlyle had said, a state of mind, and as such, so easily dissolvable. These thoughts grew by degrees, in force, in power.

At the same time he was beginning to go out again a little. A chance meeting with M. Charles, who grasped his hand warmly and wanted to know where he was and what he was doing, revived his old art fever. M. Charles suggested, with an air of extreme interest, that he should get up another exhibition along whatever line he chose.

"You!" he said, with a touch of heartening sympathy, and yet with a glow of fine corrective scorn, for he considered Eugene as an artist only, and a very great one at that. "You,—Eugene Witla—an editor—a publisher! Pah! You—who could have all the art lovers of the world at your feet in a few years if you chose—you who could do more for American art in your life time than anyone I know, wasting your time art directing, art editing—publishing! Pouf! Aren't you really ashamed of yourself? But it isn't too late. Come now—a fine exhibition! What do you say to an exhibition of some kind next January or February, in the full swing of the season? Everybody's interested then. I will give you our largest gallery. How is that? What do you say?" he glowed in a peculiarly Frenchy way,—half commanding, half inspiring or exhorting.

"If I can," said Eugene quietly, with a deprecating wave of the hand, and a faint line of self-scorn about the corners of his mouth. "It may be too late."

"'Too late! Too late!' What nonsense! Do you say that to me? If you can! If you can! Well, I give you up! You with your velvet textures and sure lines. It is too much. It is unbelievable!"

He raised his hands, eyes, and eye-brows in Gallic despair. He shrugged his shoulders, waiting to see a change of expression in Eugene.

"Very good!" said Eugene, when he heard this. "Only I can't promise anything. We will see." And he wrote out his address.

This started him once more. The Frenchman, who had often heard him spoken of and had sold all his earlier pictures, was convinced that there was money in him—if not here then abroad—money and some repute for himself as his sponsor. Some American artists must be encouraged—some *must* rise. Why not Eugene? Here was one who really deserved it.

So Eugene worked, painting swiftly, feverishly, brilliantly—with a feeling half the time that his old art force had deserted him for ever—everything that came into his mind. Taking a north lighted room near Myrtle he essayed portraits of her and her husband, of her and baby Angela, making arrangements which were classically simple. Then he chose models from the streets,—laborers, washerwomen, drunkards—characters all, destroying canvases frequently, but, on the whole, making steady progress. He had a strange fever for painting life as he saw it, for indicating it with exact portraits of itself, strange, grim presentations of its vagaries, futilities, commonplaces, drolleries, brutalities. The mental, fuzzy-wuzzy maunderings and meanderings of the mob fascinated him. The paradox of a decaying drunkard placed against the vivid persistence of life gripped his fancy. Somehow it suggested himself hanging on, fighting on, accusing nature, and it gave him great courage to do it. This picture eventually sold for eighteen thousand dollars, a record price.

In the meantime his lost dream in the shape of Suzanne was traveling abroad with her mother—in England, Scotland, France, Egypt, Italy, Greece. Aroused by the astonishing storm which her sudden and uncertain fascination had brought on, she was now so shaken and troubled by the disasters which had seemed to flow to Eugene in her wake, that she really did not know what to do or think. She was still too young, too nebulous. She was strong enough in body and mind, but very uncertain philosophically and morally—a dreamer and opportunist. Her mother, fearful of some headstrong, destructive outburst in which her shrewdest calculations would prove of no avail, was most anxious to be civil, loving, courteous, politic anything to avoid a disturbing re-encounter with the facts of the past, or a sudden departure on the part of Suzanne, which she hourly feared. What was she to do? Anything Suzanne wanted—her least whim, her moods in dress, pleasure, travel, friendship, were most assiduously catered to. Would she like to go here? would she like to see that? would this amuse her? would that be pleasant? And Suzanne, seeing always what her mother's motives were, and troubled by the pain and disgrace she had brought on Eugene, was uncertain now as to whether her conduct had been right or not. She puzzled over it continually.

More terrifying, however, was the thought which came to her occasionally as to whether she had really loved Eugene at all or not. Was this not a passing fancy? Had there not been some chemistry of the blood, causing her to make a fool of herself, without having any real basis in intellectual rapprochement. Was Eugene truly the one man with whom she could have been happy? Was he not too adoring, too headstrong, too foolish and mistaken in his calculations? Was he the able person she had really fancied him to be? Would she not have come to dislike him—to hate him even—in a short space of time? Could they have been truly, permanently happy? Would she not be more interested in one who was sharp, defiant, indifferent—one whom she could be compelled to adore and fight for rather than one who was constantly adoring her and needing her sympathy? A strong, solid, courageous man—was not such a one her ideal, after all? And could Eugene be said to be that? These and other questions tormented her constantly.

It is strange, but life is constantly presenting these pathetic paradoxes— these astounding blunders which temperament and blood moods bring about and reason and circumstance and convention condemn. The dreams of man are one thing—his capacity to realize them another. At either pole are the accidents of supreme failure and supreme success—the supreme failure of an Abélard for instance, the supreme success of a Napoleon, enthroned at Paris. But, oh, the endless failures for one success.

But in this instance it cannot be said that Suzanne had definitely concluded that she did not love him. Far from it. Although the cleverest devices were resorted to by Mrs. Dale to bring her into contact with younger and to her—now—more interesting personalities, Suzanne—very much of an introspective dreamer and quiet spectator herself, was not to be swiftly deluded by love again—if she had been deluded. She had half decided to study men from now on, and use them, if need be, waiting for the time when some act, of Eugene's, perhaps, or some other personality, might decide for her. The strange, destructive spell of her beauty began to interest her, for now she knew that she really was beautiful. She looked in her mirror very frequently now—at the artistry of a curl, the curve of her chin, her cheek, her arm. If ever she went back to Eugene how well she would repay him for his agony. But would she? Could she? Would he have not recovered his sanity and be able to snap his fingers in her face and smile superciliously? For, after all, no doubt he was a wonderful man and would shine as something somewhere soon again. And when he did—what would he think of her— her silence, her desertion, her moral cowardice?

"After all, I am not of much account," she said to herself. "But what he thought of me!—that wild fever—that was wonderful! Really he was wonderful!"

CHAPTER XXIX

The dénouement of all this, as much as ever could be, was still two years off. By that time Suzanne was considerably more sobered, somewhat more intellectually cultivated, a little cooler—not colder exactly—and somewhat more critical. Men, when it came to her type of beauty, were a little too suggestive of their amorousness. After Eugene their proffers of passion, adoration, undying love, were not so significant.

But one day in New York on Fifth Avenue, there was a re-encounter. She was shopping with her mother, but their ways, for a moment, were divided. By now Eugene was once more in complete possession of his faculties. The old ache had subsided to a dim but colorful mirage of beauty that was always in his eye. Often he had thought what he would do if he saw Suzanne again—what say, if anything. Would he smile, bow—and if there were an answering light in her eye, begin his old courtship all over, or would he find her changed, cold, indifferent? Would he be indifferent, sneering? It would be hard on him, perhaps, afterwards, but it would pay her out and serve her right. If she really cared, she ought to be made to suffer for being a waxy fool and tool in the hands of her mother. He did not know that she had heard of his wife's death—the birth of his child—and that she had composed and destroyed five different letters, being afraid of reprisal, indifference, scorn.

She had heard of his rise to fame as an artist once more, for the exhibition had finally come about, and with it great praise, generous acknowledgments of his ability—artists admired him most of all. They thought him strange, eccentric, but great. M. Charles had suggested to a great bank director that his new bank in the financial district be decorated by Eugene alone, which was eventually done—nine great panels in which he expressed deeply some of his feeling for life. At Washington, in two of the great public buildings and in three state capitols were tall, glowing panels also of his energetic dreaming,—a brooding suggestion of beauty that never was on land or sea. Here and there in them you might have been struck by a face—an arm, a cheek, an eye. If you had ever known Suzanne as she was you would have known the basis—the fugitive spirit at the bottom of all these things.

But in spite of that he now hated her—or told himself that he did. Under the heel of his intellectuality was the face, the beauty that he adored. He despised and yet loved it. Life had played him a vile trick—love—thus to frenzy his reason and then to turn him out as mad. Now, never again, should love affect him, and yet the beauty of woman was still his great lure—only he was the master.

And then one day Suzanne appeared.

He scarcely recognized her, so sudden it was and so quickly ended. She was crossing Fifth Avenue at Forty-second Street. He was coming out of a jeweler's, with a birthday ring for little Angela. Then the eyes of this girl, a pale look—a flash of something wonderful that he remembered and then — —

He stared curiously—not quite sure.

"He does not even recognize me," thought Suzanne, "or he hates me now. Oh!—all in five years!"

"It is she, I believe," he said to himself, "though I am not quite sure. Well, if it is she can go to the devil!" His mouth hardened. "I will cut her as she deserves to be cut," he thought. "She shall never know that I care."

And so they passed,—never to meet in this world—each always wishing, each defying, each folding a wraith of beauty to the heart.

L'ENVOI

There appears to be in metaphysics a basis, or no basis, according as the temperament and the experience of each shall incline him, for ethical or spiritual ease or peace. Life sinks into the unknowable at every turn and only the temporary or historical scene remains as a guide,—and that passes also. It may seem rather beside the mark that Eugene in his moral and physical depression should have inclined to various religious abstrusities for a time, but life does such things in a storm. They constituted a refuge from himself, from his doubts and despairs as religious thought always does.

If I were personally to define religion I would say that it is a bandage that man has invented to protect a soul made bloody by circumstance; an envelope to pocket him from the unescapable and unstable illimitable. We seek to think of things as permanent and see them so. Religion gives life a habitation and a name apparently—though it is an illusion. So we are brought back to time and space and illimitable mind—as what? And we shall always stand before them attributing to them all those things which we cannot know.

Yet the need for religion is impermanent, like all else in life. As the soul regains its health, it becomes prone to the old illusions. Again women entered his life—never believe otherwise—drawn, perhaps, by a certain wistfulness and loneliness in Eugene, who though quieted by tragedy for a little while was once more moving in the world. He saw their approach with more skepticism, and yet not unmoved—women who came through the drawing rooms to which he was invited, wives and daughters who sought to interest him in themselves and would scarcely take no for an answer; women of the stage—women artists, poetasters, "varietists," critics, dreamers. From the many approaches, letters and meetings, some few relationships resulted, ending as others had ended. Was he not changed, then? Not much—no. Only hardened intellectually and emotionally—tempered for life and work. There were scenes, too, violent ones, tears, separations, renouncements, cold meetings—with little Angela always to one side in Myrtle's care as a stay and consolation.

In Eugene one saw an artist who, pagan to the core, enjoyed reading the Bible for its artistry of expression, and Schopenhauer, Nietzsche, Spinoza and James for the mystery of things which they suggested. In his child he found a charming personality and a study as well—one whom he could brood over with affectionate interest at times, seeing already something of himself and something of Angela, and wondering at the outcome. What would she be like? Would art have any interest for her? She was so daring, gay, self-willed, he thought.

"You've a Tartar on your hands," Myrtle once said to him, and he smiled as he replied:

"Just the same I'll see if I can't keep up with her."

One of his occasional thoughts was that if he and Angela, junior, came to understand each other thoroughly, and she did not marry too soon, he could build a charming home around her. Perhaps her husband might not object to living with them.

The last scene of all may be taken from his studio in Montclair, where with Myrtle and her husband as resident housekeepers and Angela as his diversion he was living and working. He was sitting in front of his fireplace one night reading, when a thought in some history recalled to his mind a paragraph somewhere in Spencer's astonishing chapters on "the unknowable" in his "Facts and Comments," and he arose to see if he could find it. Rummaging around in his books he extracted the volume and reread it, with a kind of smack of intellectual agreement, for it suited his mood in regard to life and his own mental state in particular. Because it was so peculiarly related to his own viewpoint I quote it:

"Beyond the reach of our intelligence as are the mysteries of the objects known by our senses, those presented in this universal matrix are, if we may say so, still further beyond the reach of our intelligence, for whereas, those of the one kind may be, and are, thought of by many as explicable on the hypothesis of creation, and by the rest on the hypothesis of evolution, those of the other kind cannot by either be regarded as thus explicable. Theist and Agnostic must agree in recognizing the properties of Space as inherent, eternal, uncreated—as anteceding all creation, if creation has taken place.

Hence, could we penetrate the mysteries of existence, there would still remain more transcendent mysteries. That which can be thought of as neither made nor evolved presents us with facts the origin of which is even more remote from conceivability than is the origin of the facts presented by visible and tangible things.... The thought of this blank form of existence which, explored in all directions as far as eye can reach, has, beyond that, an unexplored region compared with which the part imagination has traversed is but infinitesimal—the thought of a space, compared with which our immeasurable sidereal system dwindles to a point, is a thought too overwhelming to be dwelt upon. Of late years the consciousness that without origin or cause, infinite space has ever existed and must ever exist produces in me a feeling from which I shrink."

"Well," said Eugene, turning as he thought he heard a slight noise, "that is certainly the sanest interpretation of the limitations of human thought I have ever read"—and then seeing the tiny Angela enter, clad in a baggy little sleeping suit which was not unrelated to a Harlequin costume, he smiled, for he knew her wheedling, shifty moods and tricks.

"Now what are you coming in here for?" he asked, with mock severity. "You know you oughn't to be up so late. If Auntie Myrtle catches you!"

"But I can't sleep, Daddy," she replied trickily, anxious to be with him a little while longer before the fire, and tripping coaxingly across the floor. "Won't you take me?"

"Yes, I know all about your not being able to sleep, you scamp. You're coming in here to be cuddled. You beat it!"

"Oh, no, Daddy!"

"All right, then, come here." And he gathered her up in his arms and reseated himself by the fire. "Now you go to sleep or back you go to bed."

She snuggled down, her yellow head in his crook'd elbow while he looked at her cheek, recalling the storm in which she had arrived.

"Little flower girl," he said. "Sweet little kiddie."

His offspring made no reply. Presently he carried her asleep to her couch, tucked her in, and, coming back, went out on the brown lawn, where a late November wind rustled in the still clinging brown leaves. Overhead were the star—Orion's majestic belt and those mystic constellations that make Dippers, Bears, and that remote cloudy formation known as the Milky Way.

"Where in all this—in substance," he thought, rubbing his hand through his hair, "is Angela? Where in substance will be that which is me? What a sweet welter life is—how rich, how tender, how grim, how like a colorful symphony."

Great art dreams welled up into his soul as he viewed the sparkling deeps of space.

"The sound of the wind—how fine it is tonight," he thought.

Then he went quietly in and closed the door.